ALASKA BECKONS

All Things Work Together

PATRICIA FRIEND

WESTBOW
PRESS
A DIVISION OF THOMAS NELSON

The Cover Photo is of the Matanuska River near Palmer, Alaska and was taken by the author's daughter, Holly Friend.

WestBow Press books may be ordered through booksellers or by contacting:

WestBow Press
A Division of Thomas Nelson
1663 Liberty Drive
Bloomington, IN 47403
www.westbowpress.com
1-(866) 928-1240

ISBN: 978-1-4497-7596-4 (sc)
Library of Congress Control Number: 2012921471

Scripture taken from the New King James Version. Copyright 1979, 1980, 1982 by Thomas Nelson, inc. Used by permission. All rights reserved.

Scripture taken from the King James Version of the Bible.

Printed in the United States of America

WestBow Press rev. date: 1/23/2013

To Louis, my lifelong friend.
To our daughters, Heather, Heidi, and Holly--
Who grew up in a Preacher's Home.
To my Parents, Olin & Elsie Race who are loving examples of Christ
Thank you to the Team at West Bow Press for walking me through
publishing this first book. Thank you to Julie Gray whose friendship
and advice always comes in a timely manner. Thank you to friends
and family for indulging my whim and passion for writing.
Psalm 143:8

CONTENTS

PROLOGUE

THERE ARE PLACES THAT BECKON SOME of us to visit while we daydream. Then there are places that clearly summon some of us to come and live out those daydreams as residents, neighbors, and friends. In 1935, two hundred and three families from the North Central United States were selected to pioneer a federal farm colony in South Central Alaska. One of the purposes of this farm colony project was to help open up Alaska's great wilderness and provide opportunities to families desiring a new beginning during the Depression Era. With the help of the Alaska Railroad, people and supplies were transported from the port of Anchorage to the rich farm valley referred to as the Matanuska Valley. Their new home eventually became the town of Palmer. These colonists were preceded by others who homesteaded in the area prior to World War I. Only a few of those early farmers remained due to the war, rugged climate, and a frustrated ability to market their farm products. Before them, Russian traders came as fur trappers but not settlers. Athabascan Indians were the first inhabitants of this beautiful and productive valley.

As in all pioneering endeavors, there has to be a beginning, a continuing, and a remaining until, at last, the vision is realized some years later in the descendants. Of the two hundred-three families that made the journey, forty percent became residents, neighbors, and friends throughout the progressing years of Palmer's continuing history.

While Palmer grew and changed through the years and seasons, so two young people changed and grew while finding there is a purpose and a time to everything. They didn't fully understand that God brings all things together at just the right time or that He cares even though they were indifferent to Him. One would make the journey to the land of the Northern Lights at the invitation of the other and the burgeoning city of Palmer would host their view to this spectacular display in the star-bright heavens.

Chapter 1

Good Luck!

"Who are you going to find to ride the second horse?" The crow's feet around Weston's brilliant blue eyes deepened in merriment as the second foal struggled to his feet beside his mother and gangly sister. Both foals wobbled unsteadily on spindly legs as observers noted the marks of their excellent heritage with raised eyebrows. Thad Tucker had paid his old friend and former boss, John Weston, handsomely to breed Phantom to a fine mare named Bonny Bright. To everyone's surprise, Bonny Bright birthed twins.

"Someone who loves horses as much as I do, I guess," Thad replied easy enough. He didn't miss the subtle hint about his bachelor status because Weston never missed an opportunity to remind him. Thad didn't mind his old friend's teasing because lately he'd been thinking on the subject, too. As he continued to watch the fledgling antics of the two marvelous animals before him, Weston's question provided further motivation to find a rider for the second horse.

"Good luck, Thad. You'll need it!" Weston joked benignly and slapped Thad on the back amiably.

"Luck!" He mumbled, "It's going to take more than luck," Thad pushed away from the hard wood wall of the stable to change viewing position.

Weston laughed and crossed his arms over his chest like a genie from a magic lamp.

"You seem to be miracle-favored right now, Thad," he suggested easily, but Thad shook his head in doubt as he turned to stroke Bonny Bright with pride before replying.

"Miracles?" Thad's voice was suddenly cool and distant. "I'd rather give credit to Phantom and to scientific fact than rely on luck or miracles." The comment revealed a logical man whose thinking was based upon facts and not some mysterious faith.

Weston slowly breathed out, "Who is God to you, Thad?" he went on, "Why can't there be miracles for you, too?"

Thad turned from Phantom and regarded Weston with a smile. "My mother taught me about God," his smile faded somewhat. "Miracles are for people who believe that God exists." The topic was supposed to be closed.

Weston smiled. "And you don't believe He exists?"

Thad laughed when Weston pressed for more parleys on religion. His eyebrows raised in consideration of the answer he would articulate and hoped it would end the chat.

"I believe God could exist, but I choose to look for the evidence in visual proof. I don't see it. So then, there can be no miracles for me because if I can't see God, He doesn't exist," he finished. Weston's eyes squinted as he pursed his lips together.

"Thad, God is spirit and no man can see Him. We know He exists as a result of a purposeful creation and the reading of the Bible which tells us about His Son, Jesus Christ." Weston saw Thad's chin set in rigid lines and tried another direction. "You know? Sometimes God works through circumstances in our lives to bring us to faith. One of many favorite verses is Romans 8:28, "And we know that all things work together for good to them that love God, to them who are the called according to His purpose." Thad looked over at Weston in consideration. As a boy, Thad's mother had repeated this verse to him numerous times. Weston took Thad's attention as a good sign.

"What would you have God do on your behalf to show Himself real to you, Thad? I'll pray and we'll see what God will do."

Thad blinked in surprise at the audacity of Weston's simple faith. He checked the sarcasm that threatened an unholy response. Instead he chose another answer.

"A wife!" he purposed and couldn't stop the faithless chuckle that escaped. "A wife to ride the other horse." He spoke out loud and wondered if doing so would make his request a self-fulfilled prophecy.

"Done!" Weston did not laugh. His expression was as serious as his faith.

Thad smiled in friendship at the one man whom he held in high regard.

"Done," he repeated quietly and then forgot all about it in his further attentions to Sunrise and Sunset.

⋊═o

One sunny Sunday afternoon in mid-May Thad rode the Arabian horse named Sunset to green mountain foothills. Below the horse and rider a ridge of black spruce and white birch trees spread to encircle the farm valley of Palmer, Alaska. At thirty-four years of age and six foot three inches in height, Thad had a strong built frame that evidenced the work hardened experience of a ranch hand. His hair was dark brown with only a slight wave if he let it go too long without being cut. Hazel eyes squinted in the bright sunshine as he surveyed the rugged landscape in efforts to take in every detail of the noble mountain beauty from his perch near the Lazy Mountain trail. A smile appeared on his short bearded face as he watched the antics of white Dall sheep on the side of a steep ledge. Beyond the playful sheep, the distant snow capped Pioneer Peak captured his further attention. His confident profile masked searching eyes that roamed the unspoiled earth for something special and unique in the practice of life. For several minutes he studied the high places of this dominant peak and noted its breadth across the horizon.

When the grazing horse lifted its head and snorted at a small varmint, Thad bent forward to stroke the copper colored Sunset and smooth the flexing muscles that shimmered in the sunlight. The fine horse was a twin to another horse named Sunrise. Thad had recently moved them from the Weston Ranch in Arizona to a newly constructed stable just below his cabin on Lazy Mountain.

The Talkeetna Mountain Range spread across the horizon from east to west when Thad turned Sunset for a view. Rays of sunshine fell across high mountain meadows turning shadowed grasses into distant carpets of green velvet. A reminder of Weston's promised prayer passed through Thad's thoughts before he pulled an envelope from his jacket pocket and opened it carefully. A varmint or two skittered in and out of twisted bushes nearby making the proud horse snort its displeasure at remaining still. Thad spoke comfort to Sunset and returned his full attention once again to the penned words of the letter that softly whispered, 'miracle!'

CHAPTER 2

ESCAPE ARTISTS

WHEN HER DAD SAID, "AMEN", LEAH Grant glanced around the church auditorium for a quick escape from Mrs. Glick and her thirty-four year old bachelor son. Russell Glick tried her patience at every opportunity by cornering her to talk about spiritual things. His pious discussions always ended up with a request for a date she was quick to refuse with any excuse she could think of at the moment. Just as she reached for the door handle to make a clean get away, Russell's ingratiating voice spoke her name.

"Leah!"

She cringed and was about to proceed out the door anyway until her mother's voice called her back into the abyss of match making. Forcing a smile to her lips, she turned to greet Mrs. Glick and Russell graciously. His cocky grin showed he was pleased her escape had failed, which only charged her resistance.

Rusty tells me there's a Gospel Life Concert this coming Friday at the Highland Hotel in Greensburg, Leah," Mrs. Grant initiated the conversation. "It sounds like something you'd be interested to attend. Royce Thornhill is playing the piano, too. You like to hear him play, I know you do. You even have some of his CDs and sheet music."

Yes, I do have some of his music." Leah made the polite effort to sound interested and Russell jumped in to the conversation. His eyes constantly traced her figure from head to foot. The censure spurred her irritation.

"How about it, Leah?" With her mother's approval, he was sure of their acceptance.

"Sorry, Russ, I can't make it." There was no hint of regret in her voice and no apology in her honey brown eyes.

Mrs. Grant blinked in surprise at Leah's brassy refusal.

"Why can't you make it?" she challenged.

"I already have plans for Friday night, Mom," Leah said with more civility than she felt.

"But, surely, you could cancel those plans," Russell pressed. "I already have the tickets for the concert and reservations for dinner afterwards." Leah saw the irritation in his eyes though he kept his tone of voice docile enough to encourage a change of heart from her. But he saw even these tantalizing details did nothing to coax Leah's acceptance.

"Sorry, Russ, they're set in stone." She shrugged and brushed a long strand of curly brown hair behind her ear while stifling a yawn.

"What plans?" Mrs. Grant wanted to know, eyes sparking confrontation.

"My plans. Please excuse me," Leah smiled at Mrs. Glick, turned, and headed directly for the door, eager to escape. Once outside she took a deep breath and released it slowly before mumbling her thoughts aloud.

"Tickets and dinner," she snorted at the idea. "If he was the last man on earth, I'd build a space ship and go where no man has ever gone before." Leah raised a pointer finger skyward, "Where no **woman** has gone before!"

True to her plans, Leah spent Friday evening writing a long letter to Denise and enjoying every moment of it. As she reflected on thoughts to Denise, she realized most of her best memories were of college days. Leah looked up from the floral stationary pad and stared out the bedroom window to the autumn foliage covering the rolling hills of Pennsylvania. For a while, daydreams claimed first place over letter writing.

In the total of their college experiences, Leah and Denise had contributed a great deal of negative information to personal files in the Dean's office as opposed to being on the Dean's famous "List". As roommates from their freshman year, they'd enjoyed a lasting friendship despite their differences and the folly often present when away from home for the first time. Their sisterhood drew from the fellowship of being kindred spirits in so many ways though Leah came from Irish-American family ancestry and Denise, African-American.

After a first meeting revealed their father's professions, both quickly decided not to mention to perspective suitors that Denise's Dad was a policeman and Leah's Dad was a preacher. A policeman dad scared perspective dates away while a preacher dad encouraged ministry minded guys too much. Both daughters had determined to overcome these familial hindrances and had done well since they were fast approaching thirty and were still single!

Leah was the school-teacher-type whose only antics were the mishaps suffered by those who endured her absent-minded activities. Denise was vivacious, energetic, and daring. She had beautiful ebony skin, the flawless figure of a model, and she was often the life of the party. Leah didn't mind her best friend's flair for the spotlight either. As least not until Denise needed her help to pull off a crazy scheme. Then she was a reluctant best friend.

For the past month they had been planning to get together for a visit over the Thanksgiving Holiday. Both looked forward to more of the fun and frolic marking their friendship when Leah would travel to Denise's hometown, Chicago.

On the Friday after Thanksgiving Day, Denise decided it was time to show Leah the sights of the big city. It had been several years since Leah had worked in Chicago while in college so she welcomed this grand tour of the Chicago skyline. They left Park Ridge early in the morning and drove south to the Chicago Loop. Traffic was a steady 35 miles per hour in some places and a maniacal 55 to 60 in other spots on this first day of Christmas shopping. The maddening traffic tested Leah's peace of mind. She gripped the armrest with one hand and held on to the bucket seat with the other. The old candy-apple-red Mustang roared and shook as they rattled along. Denise looked over at the anxious Leah and Laughed.

"What's wrong? This is nothing. You ought to try the Dan Ryan Expressway. That's nuts!"

Leah looked petrified and Denise snickered at her friend as the Mustang accelerated. The engine roared louder making the little car shake as they passed other vehicles. Denise checked her mirrors then crossed two lanes of traffic and breezed onto an exit ramp. She pressed the brake-peddle firmly sending both driver and passenger forward until the car came to a halt before a red light.

"Dee-Dee," Leah stammered nervously. "Do you have a death wish I don't know about?"

"Nah. I just wish I had a Corvette. Oh! I love Corvettes. Not that I don't love my 'Stang, but there just isn't anything like a 'Vette." She sighed dreamily.

"I'm glad you don't have a 'Vette!" Leah declared seriously. "I don't remember you driving like this while we were in college."

"That's because I didn't have a car when we were in college." Denise stated dryly and gave Leah a long look. She drove at a moderate speed for a few city blocks then slowed to turn onto a parking ramp.

"Now we know why." Leah side cracked. Denise pulled a ticket from the machine and headed for a parking spot.

"Someday I will have my 'Vette. Jack will buy me one after we're married. He's got the money," she said confidently.

"You seem pretty sure about it," Leah stated soberly.

"He lets me have my own way and I let him know he's supposed to!" Denise proclaimed. Leah shook her head doubtfully.

"Are you sure you really want it this way?" Leah frowned. Denise was thoughtful.

"I haven't met anyone who could convince me otherwise. Anyway, Jack is the best man I've met so far. We seem to get along okay together."

"When you get your own way?"

Denise laughed, "Always!"

"Do you love him?" Leah asked frankly as Denise parked the car and turned the engine off. She was quiet. Leah began to wonder if she had asked something too personal.

"Love?" Denise scoffed, then more mild, "Honestly, Leah, I'm still working on loving Jack. I'm 28 and it feels like the romance thing passed me by. Sure, guys like having me around for the show. They love the outside of me, but not the inside of me, who I am. Jack accepts me and likes having me around. I like being around him. Besides, I have to think about the possibilities of living at home the rest of my life or living alone. It's not something I ever imagined or wanted for myself. I've always wanted to be married. I've dreamed about it almost as much as owning a Corvette."

"Denise, love isn't like owning a Corvette. You can trade a Corvette every four years, but you can't trade a husband," Leah chuckled then added piously, "at least the Bible says you can't."

"Well, thank you for that little sermon, Leah!" Denise was suddenly miffed. "When did you begin to care anything about what the Bible says?" Leah cringed knowing she'd deserved the biting rebuke.

"I'm just afraid you're marrying for all the wrong reasons. I'd hate to ever see you regretful and unhappy." Leah was serious, though the sting of Denise's words still tugged at her conscience. Why did she always feel guilty?

"Leah, I'm always happy. See my smile? I've prayed about Jack and me and if God doesn't want us to marry, He'll show me somehow," she said rather flippantly wanting to be done with this line of conversation.

"Denise, that's a lark!" Leah said a little too sharply. Denise looked at her as if to retort, but Leah waved her hand. "I'm sorry." Her tone softened. "Sometimes Christians use this line of thinking to make something right when all the evidence they can see themselves reveals it as a wrong move. They spiritualize their own wills, go ahead with their own plans, and when everything goes wrong, they blame God or whimper and whine. God just sits up there, where ever, and lets it happen."

Denise chuckled at the preachy Leah.

"You know, Leah? I think you just stuck up for God."

Yah, right," Leah sighed dully. "Picture that."

Denise considered her best friend's soulful comment.

"Leah," Denise's voice was gentle and kind, "you're right. We pretty much do what we want to do. Human nature battles God's nature all the time. You're mistaken about God. It's not God who falls short by just letting things happen. When Christians fall short, and we often do, it's our own fault, not His. Don't blame God for hypocrites. I don't honestly know if Jack is the right one for me or not, but I have to step out in faith and see what God wants. I'm not going to be afraid to try and fail. I'm just going to believe God is directing my steps and I'm going to trust Him with my wandering heart. God loves me and He loves you right where we are now. " Denise smiled broadly. "Come on! We've got lots to see and do."

Leah didn't say anything as they left the car and took an elevator to the street some five levels below. It was a brisk three-block walk to catch a tour bus to Buckingham Fountain. Denise explained that the illuminated fountain was a spectacular sight at night from a tour boat on Lake Michigan.

By the time they were seated on the tour bus, Leah was smiling again. "If it's such a beautiful view at night, why didn't you bring me to see it then?"

"Okay!" Denise offered enthusiastically.

"No thanks." Leah hastened to decline. "I'll take your word for it. One nail-biting ride into this city is enough for me!"

"I'd call you a coward, but I remember what happened the last time I did."

"When it comes to places like this, I'll readily admit to being a coward!" said Leah. "We may have worked here in Chicago for four years, but I never got used to the big city." Denise shook her head and grinned at Leah.

"You wouldn't know what to do in the city and I wouldn't know what to do in the country." Denise was thoughtful. They walked around for a while, then took another bus and toured the skyline of Chicago until at last they arrived back at Michigan Avenue. After checking the time, they chose to walk to NBC Towers and browse around the Chicago Maritime Museum on Ogden Slip.

As they approached the TV station and tower, they talked about how exciting it would be to see a live program and sit in a real audience.

"Wow!" Leah exclaimed. "I'd love to see a show."

"Let's go see if we can," Denise headed through the revolving doors toward an information desk. A short, husky man smiled a greeting to them. When he spoke it was with a Spanish accent.

"Ola', can I help you?" he asked pleasantly.

"Yes, we were wondering if we could be audience participants in one of the shows," Denise inquired.

"Yes. You many check the bulletin board over there," he pointed.

"Gracias," Denise smiled and Leah followed her to a large bulletin board where show times were posted.

"Look, Leah! There's a show we can get into right now! It's called the George Endicott Show."

Leah's eyes followed Denise's finger as she pointed to the listing of programs scheduled on the program board.

"Oh Leah! Here's a good one. Maybe you could find a husband for yourself. They're going to interview single men from Alaska. These bachelors are looking for brides! We really ought to go to that one." Denise raised her eyebrows at Leah several times.

"Hah!" Leah exclaimed. "I may be from the country, but homemaking in an igloo? I don't think so!"

"Leah, they don't all live in igloos. They live in little log-type houses with snow piled around them to keep the drafts out." Denise informed but it didn't sound any better to Leah.

"I'm chilled just thinking about it." Leah laughed and shivered. "Besides, how do you know so much about houses in Alaska?"

"I watched a John Wayne movie called *North to Alaska* and I didn't see even one igloo in the whole movie."

"John Wayne?" Leah cocked her head off to the side. "Really, Denise. You're joking, right?"

"Awe, come on, girlfriend," Denise begged, "we'll sit way in the back so you're not tempted."

"Tempted?" Leah bulked. "It sounds to me like you're the one who has to worry about temptation. You seem more interested in this than I am."

"Maybe." Denise admitted with a spark of excitement in her eyes.

"Denise Cox! You're engaged. You're getting married next July!" Leah waved her hand in front of her best friend's face. "Hello! Is anyone home?" Denise brushed her hand away.

"A lot can happen between now and then," Denise remarked with raised eyebrows as Leah groaned at the inevitable.

"Denise, maybe we better not." Leah turned to walk out the entrance, but Denise grabbed her arm and pulled her along.

"We're going! Let's get tickets!"

The show was about to begin as they handed their tickets to the usher.

"You're just in time, ladies. It's a packed audience and we were about to close the doors. You ladies can take seats down there." He pointed down to the front. Leah pursed her lips tightly together to protest when Denise agreed to take the specified seats in the front row. Leah's mouth dropped open.

"What! No! Denise!" Leah whispered urgently. "Not the front row!"

"Leah, knock it off! The chairs are behind the camera. That's why nobody is sitting there. We'll just peek around the camera."

"Oh, all right," she moaned. "Let's go before it starts and we're caught on another camera."

"It's going to be fun, Leah. Just relax and enjoy this opportunity."

Down they went and took their seats behind a large TV camera which sufficiently hid them from plain sight.

"I wonder why they're not using this camera?" Denise asked as she struggled to see around it. At that moment the audience was queued to clap as George Endicott walked on stage and greeted the audience. The vacated camera was quickly whisked away by a woman who looked like she knew what to do with it.

Suddenly, Leah and Denise were smack dab in the middle of the front row. Their front and center seats gave them a panoramic view of the entire show. At the same time it gave everyone else in TV land a panoramic view of them! Denise was ecstatic. Leah's eyes were wide with perfect shock at first then they sparked with exasperation. The bachelors from Alaska walked out onto stage and sat down on what looked like square, low-backed doctor's office chairs.

The audience went wild with feminine frenzy! Leah's face went hot. She couldn't decide if she was more embarrassed for the bachelors or for herself. The loud whistling, wild cheering, and applauding continued as Endicott called for order. The Alaska bachelors looked amused if not a little wary.

Denise sat wide-eyed with her hands covering her gaping mouth. Leah nudged her.

"Close your mouth, DeeDee. You're scaring me!"

"Wow, there's black bachelors up there, too!" Denise exclaimed.

"Well, why wouldn't there be?"

"I just thought there were Eskimos and Russians up there. That's all I've ever noticed in the pictures of Alaska."

"You forget John Wayne and Fabian," Leah piped up. "I just remembered watching that movie with my Dad when I was…" Leah words drifted away when she noticed one of the bachelors wink at her and smile. She averted her eyes as heat colored her face again.

As women from the audience asked the bachelors questions, Leah and Denise jabbered back and forth. Some of the questions sounded downright suggestive to two church-going best friends. Both noted several of the Alaska men remained quiet. Only one or two did the talking most of the time. It wasn't long before they could tell which bachelors might be nice enough to date and which ones they probably wouldn't trust as far as they could spit.

George Endicott did his best to excite the female audience and exploit the bachelors. This rather irritated Leah, especially when a ditzy redhead acted totally obnoxious to one of the nicer guys.

"Oh please!" Leah groaned. "She makes us all look bad!"

"I know, Sis'. Most of those men look like they really would like a nice bride." Denise frowned. She was suddenly disenchanted with the direction of the show.

"Endicott is treating them like they're sides of beef for sale. What a creep!" Leah protested a little louder and Denise gave her a look of warning. Leah was good at soap-boxing.

"Well, don't be too hard on Endicott because the one bachelor with the long wavy hair is just as bad as some of those women are."

Denise noticed one rather quiet bachelor looking Leah's way.

"Hay, Leah! That one keeps looking your way," she whispered close to Leah's ear while privately pointing him out. "And, he's a handsome one, too!"

"Oh, no!" Leah cringed. She'd noticed him watching her a few times. "I'm trying not to look his direction. I don't want to encourage him. So don't you keep looking at him." Leah sunk down in her seat hoping she would somehow become invisible.

"He's still looking at you."

"And I suppose you've managed to catch the eye of a bachelor yourself, right?" Leah asked frankly.

"Maybe," Denise admitted with a smile and raised eyebrows. At once, Leah sat up straight and turned to face Denise.

"How can you be considering such an idea!" She was amazed.

"Oh, Leah!" Denise retorted aggravated. "I'm not married, yet. Like I told you, July is a long way off. I just like to look."

"Denise, why don't you just let Jack go?" Leah rolled her eyes and sighed. Suddenly Denise laughed outright.

"You sound like Moses!"

Leah couldn't resist a giggle as they turned to see what was happening on stage.

"Let my people go!" Denise laughed again as she repeated the Biblical phrase with emphasis then spoke hastily, "He's still looking."

"Quiet!" Leah whispered loudly as Denise continued to chuckle at her friend. Endicott came up into the audience.

"Do we have any ladies who would like to pick an Alaskan bachelor out today?" He asked enthusiastically. He was on the other side of the stage and Leah was relieved he didn't walk in their direction.

As each woman picked out the man of her choice, they came up onto the stage and sat on a bachelor's knee. Some of them put their arms around the men's neck. Denise and Leah sat perfectly still. Their dubious expressions revealed concern about what their fathers would think if they knew where their daughters were at this moment. Though they might be almost thirty, ingrained training from childhood remained intact in their concept of propriety and dignity.

"We shouldn't have come in here," Denise finally acknowledged slowly. "My Mama told me never to sit on any strange man's lap!"

"Mine told me never to wink back at them." Leah said with penance. Her ire was raised at Denise for this present predicament.

"Finally, you get the picture on the wall straight then it's too late because the wall sags to the left!"

Denise cringed at another one of Leah's odd analogies. It was those strange Pennsylvania Dutch sayings that kept her guessing if Leah was in her right mind.

"I won't be able to take communion this Sunday after being here. It's the mourner's bench for this sinner," Denise said in a low tone. Now it was Leah's turn to be determined.

"During the next commercial break, we're out of here!" Leah declared and started pulling her coat from behind her chair as Mr. Endicott told the bachelors who didn't have someone on their laps to go out into the audience and pick a lovely lady to sit with them.

Denise saw him coming first. Leah was still untangling her coat. The women behind them had been such a wild bunch that they had stomped Leah's long coat into a dust ball in their frenzy.

"Oh, boy!" Denise moaned hopelessly. "Leah, you've got company."

"Huh?" She looked up at Denise while she yanked her coat almost free of one hefty woman's foot. The woman nearly fell backwards and started swearing at Leah. Uttering a sincere apology to the irate woman, Leah yanked again. This time the coat was freed so quickly Leah flew backwards, arms outstretched and coat flying like a super hero. A hard landing was stopped by someone's hands steadying her shoulders and helping her to stand upright. Grateful for the save, Leah turned to thank the person for saving her from a bad fall and was astonished to find a pair of brilliant blue eyes smiling down at her. He was much taller than her and was built like the "Rock of Gibraltar." His hair was blond and there was a Norwegian appearance of health about him Leah could not help but admire.

"Thank you," she managed politely and smiled her admiration.

"You're welcome," he replied cheerfully. "May I ask you to accompany me back to my seat, please?"

"Huh?" Leah was dumbfounded.

"I promise I won't bite," he assured her with some amusement when he saw the confusion in her large brown eyes. Leah looked quickly at Denise who simply shrugged and did not say a word. Endicott came over.

"Well, well. I see one of our handsome Alaska bachelors has made his choice but I think this pretty little lady is a bit hesitant," he mocked and it raised Leah's ire. She considered the man standing before her who seemed to be just as uncomfortable as she was and addressed him graciously.

"I'd be glad to accompany you."

Although he seemed relieved, Leah was not. Even as she said the words, a thought of a doomed reputation flashed through her mind as he took her hand and led her over to the narrow chair.

"I hope nobody I know is watching right now, or I'm dead."

"What?" the fellow said as he sat down and patted his knee. Leah swallowed with difficulty. There wasn't anything else to do but sit on his offered knee. With consideration to this present state of affairs, she sat as ladylike as was possible.

"Are you comfortable?" he asked kindly. Leah looked at him dubiously.

"Yes. No. Yes." She shook her head as he regarded her with a smile of amusement.

"You're more nervous than I am."

"You're right about that!" She managed a side grin. "If my Dad is watching this show, I'm going to have to stay in Chicago."

"Are you safe at home?" he asked serious. Leah stifled a smile.

"Yes, I'm safe at home, except that my Dad's a preacher," she said lamely.

"Aw, I see." He keenly regarded her with one eyebrow raised.

Leah wondered what exactly he did see. She glanced over to where Denise sat stock-still. She looked miserable enough to make Leah feel sorry her best friend was not enjoying similar company.

"What's your name?" her escort wanted to know.

"Leah."

"Ah," he said again, "that's a Bible name."

"Yes, it is," Leah was surprised. "What's yours?"

"My Bible name is Andrew."

"Ah." Leah imitated and drew a smile from Andrew.

"Andrew was a fisherman," Leah continued.

"So am I." Leah smiled at him and Andrew basked in the sunshine of her admiration.

The black bachelor who sat beside Andrew leaned over to Leah and introduced himself.

"I'm J.C. Is that lady over there your friend?" A multitude of ideas went through Leah's mind before she responded.

"Yes. She's my best friend. Her name is Denise."

"I'd like to meet her."

"I'm sure she'd like to meet you, too, J.C."

"Good." He seemed encouraged. The woman he'd chosen decided to go for another guy who was from New York City's group of suburban bachelors Endicott had brought on stage to stir up some competition.

Leah looked over at Denise, who sat suddenly quiet. She smiled Cheshire-cat style at the remorseful Denise while pointing to J.C. Denise's eyes grew large and she pointed to herself in disbelief.

Leah nodded affirmative. J.C. watched the unspoken conversation pass quickly between the two of them and chuckled.

Denise looked from side to side as if she were going to cross a busy road. J.C. looked hopeful. Thankfully, Endicott went to the last commercial break before the end of the show. J.C. got up and walked over to Denise.

"Hello! I'm J.C. Would you like to come up there with me and keep your best friend company?" It came out sounding like a poem and he laughed at himself. Denise couldn't help but laugh with him.

"You're a poet and don't know it!" She bantered in return and basked in the sense of humor that sparkled in his eyes.

"Let's go." She stood resolutely. "I'd better come with you or Leah will never come visit me again. I put her up to this," Denise admitted.

"Some friend you are," J.C. teased her good natured as they sat down and Leah greeted Denise ever so pleasantly.

"Well, Denise, nice to have you along," Leah teased solicitously as they faced each other. Both men watched the two with interest. J.C. thought Denise was a keeper…until she raised her left hand to point at Leah.

"I felt I had to. Anyway--," she giggled. "I like J.C." She flirted, but J.C. didn't smile back which made Denise frown.

"Is that an engagement ring?" he asked with mild amusement. Denise faltered, feeling offended by the tell-tale ring that felt suddenly like a noose around her neck.

"Yes." When she saw his head tilt off to the side, she hurried to assure him, "Oh! Jack won't mind too much, J.C." He gave her a look of doubt. She was a beautiful woman up close as well as far away. J.C. looked directly into her eyes and spoke frankly.

"If he doesn't mind, you ought to break off the engagement, now. If you were my fiancé, I'd mind very much!" Denise regarded him thoughtfully.

"I keep telling her to break it off," Leah insisted and Denise gave her a long look of disapproval.

"Are you engaged as well, Leah?" Andrew asked frankly.

"No," Leah answered. Denise spoke up.

"She's had three proposals, though." Andrew's eyebrows rose. "And she turned them all down, too," Denise added. Leah responded by shrugging indifferently.

"They just weren't…" Leah paused, "something." She couldn't find a word to describe what former proposers weren't.

"They just weren't from Alaska," Andrew tried. Leah and Denise looked at each other and then at J.C. and Andrew, respectively.

"You just might be right." Leah said thoughtfully. Denise's eyes widened at Leah's contemplation. Endicott was closing the show and still the four of them carried on their own conversation as the audience clapped the show into commercials. The audience began to clear out so the studio could be set up for another TV taping. Denise and J.C. were carrying on a conversation about life in Alaska.

"Well," Andrew smiled as they all stood to leave, "I don't think I'm your man, Leah, but you ladies are fine examples of what we 'Alaska Bachelors' might just be looking for," he looked at Leah thoughtfully.

"You know, Leah, I think you'd make a perfect bride for a friend of mine up in Palmer, Alaska." Leah was surprised at his candidness.

"I even tried to get him to come along with us to this show, but he refused. He's kind of shy around women in general and he's shy about marriage, too, I think. Of course, he works all the time."

"Oh." Leah replied with polite disinterest.

"I don't know why he is, though. His business is taking people on hunting and fishing excursions." Andrew shrugged and smiled. "Wolfe Tucker isn't afraid of grizzly bears, just women."

"WOLFE Tucker?" Leah questioned totally put off by the name. His name seemed audacious enough to squelch any interest she might have ventured.

"Yup! Great guy. A little dull." Andrew warranted, "But a nice guy, anyway."

"Well, after what I've seen today, I'd be a little leery of women if I were you guys." Leah assured.

"Nah. It doesn't bother us much. When we signed up to come on this show, we kind of figured it would be this way. It's been fun. If I hadn't come, I'd be out on a fishing skiff instead of here enjoying your company."

Leah smiled. She couldn't remember the last genuine compliment she'd received from any man in years.

They walked with the others who prepared to leave. J.C. was talking to Denise in earnest.

"Here's my number." He handed her his company's business card with his name and job title of chief engineer. "In case your plans change, Denise." He smiled and wondered if she'd take it. Denise did accept it and J.C. North was almost more puzzled than pleased.

He sensed something was not quite right with Denise's relationship to her perspective husband. He wondered if it was because she wasn't faithful or maybe the guy couldn't handle her. In their short conversation, he hadn't sensed she would be the unfaithful type. She seemed decent and had a sense of propriety. However, he'd also sensed she was a handful as he'd watched her throughout the program. She had been just as wild with enthusiasm as the audience at first. That's what had grabbed his attention from the start of the show. While Denise was carrying on, he'd noticed her friend sitting quietly and looking very chagrined and out of place. Andrew had commented that the quiet one was cute, but that Denise looked like a cover girl model. Indeed, J.C. was hoping even now that she would call him.

J.C. and Andrew introduced Leah and Denise to the other bachelors. They talked for a little while longer before the best friends left the studio chattering all the way back to the parking garage.

"Boy!" J.C. sighed deeply, "I think my heart just walked out that door." Then he chuckled, "I wish I had a picture of her to show Tyrone Johnson. I'd show him what he missed by not coming with us!"

"Get a tape of the show." Andrew suggested. "I'm going to get one."

"I think I will, too. I'll just show ole Thad and Tyrone what they missed." J.C. decided.

"Yah, that little Leah would have sparked up Thad Tucker's dull life." Andrew commented and he glanced again and again at the stage exit door. Someone was getting his undivided attention.

"She wasn't for you, Andy?"

"Nope! I need a tall wife." He was watching a tall blonde near the exit door who was holding a coat over her arm. She had glanced at him a number of times since the end of the show, but seemed to be waiting for someone else at the moment.

"Like that one," Andrew pointed her out to J.C.

"Not that one, Andy," J.C. discouraged, teasing. "She's Mr. Endicott's daughter."

Andrew smiled with interest as he made his way over to introduce himself to Jennifer Endicott. Some six months to the day, Jennifer Endicott became Mrs. Andrew Vanderhoof! It's the one show George Endicott would remember in infamy.

Chapter 3

Buttons and Bios

THAD TUCKER LOOKED AT THE EARLY December sky that threatened another snowstorm on top of the six inches of crystalline flakes accumulated overnight. Everything was covered in a soft blanket of white. Even the mountains could not fight the covering of snow that hid their rough rock faces. But he didn't really see the beauty of it because he was thinking of what Andrew and J.C. had told him about their experiences at the George Endicott show in Chicago.

"Alaska bachelors." He sighed at the oddity of the two words repeated over and over again on the tape of the show he'd seen. Andrew had lent him the taped copy of the show and told him there was a nice girl whom he'd met that Thad should see. Naturally, Thad balked at the idea and teased Andrew about letting her get away.

"She wasn't my type," Andrew had replied as he pulled a picture of Jennifer Endicott out of his wallet.

"Well, if she wasn't your type, what makes you think she would be mine?" Thad remarked doubtfully as Andrew showed Thad the picture of Jennifer.

"She looks like a nice girl for you, Andy." Thad said sincerely.

"She is and I'm going to marry her." He was confident. "Now, about the one I picked for you, Wolfe. She was cute."

Thad frowned, confused. "Who was cute?" He'd lost the focus of the conversation when Andrew changed it to show him the picture of Jennifer. Andrew chuckled.

"You need to get out more, friend! I was talking about the girl in the video who sat on my knee. She's the one I'd pick for you. She had brown eyes and curly brown hair...and she was cute."

"Cute?" Thad cocked his head to the side and frowned. "She sat on YOUR knee? What makes you think I'd want your rejects?"

"You're a tough one, old man! Here, just watch the tape." Andrew handed the tape to Thad and laughed at Thad's sardonic expression.

"Her name was Linda, I think." By now, Andrew could only guess the name. "Or maybe it was Lisa. Some name like that." He shrugged then added quickly, "It was a Bible name, but I can't think what it was."

"A Bible name, huh." The cynical quality in his voice prevented any further consideration of "cute."

"Just watch the tape."

Thad took the tape and tossed it on the front seat of the pick-up. It would be a while before he'd get to it.

However, another blinding snowstorm prevented a trip into Anchorage for supplies and Thad was stuck at the cabin waiting for the storm to pass. So, he decided to watch the tape at Andrew's insistence. When he viewed the part where the obnoxious redhead had come onto the scene, he'd pushed the "stop" button without ever looking for Miss Cute—the one who had sat on Andy's lap. When he returned it to Andrew before Christmas, Andrew had asked what Thad thought about the "cute one".

"Oh, I didn't make it all the way through the tape, Andy. I did see you, though; but I guess I didn't get far enough in the tape to notice the one that sat on your knee." Thad's tone carried a bit of good-natured tease. Andrew shook his head in resignation; but encouraged Thad to go to the dating service there in Anchorage and fill out a Bio anyway.

"I don't think so, Andy," Thad declined.

"Why not? At least you ought to give it a try. I met Jennifer at the show even if I did fill out a Bio. But, at least I did something about it instead of wishing for a wife. Wishing doesn't do any good, Wolfe

Tucker." Although Thad couldn't disagree with Andrew's little lecture, he caught the implication of the use of his renowned nickname.

"Maybe I'll take up howling and see what happens," he laughed out loud, "or maybe just put an advertisement in the paper, WIFE WANTED, DIAL 1-4 WOLFE."

"Thad, you'd better check out the dating service" Andrew replied serious. "At least you'd have some choice as to what comes to your howl."

This thought sobered Thad considerably.

"Well, that's true enough. I'll think about it. See you around, Andy." Thad left the marina's repair shop in Anchorage and headed back to Palmer after he picked up some hunting items for Thunder's Trading Post.

The forty mile trip back to Palmer was a long one. Snow had fallen heavily and the driving was slow and treacherous as he drove over several inches of tire-packed snow. Although Thad turned on the radio, he realized he'd much rather enjoy the company of someone "cute". Then, he wondered what his mother would think of "cute" for him? She was always asking him when the grandchildren would be visiting. He smiled remembering her last phone call a few weeks ago. She'd returned to Arizona almost eight years earlier to care for her aging brother, Peter and his sickly wife, Anna.

"Thad," she'd counseled, "I'm still praying for those grandkids to show up. You've just got to get out more and look for a wife. At least see what's out there."

"I know Mom. I'm out there and I'm looking—when I have any time."

"Why don't you come for a visit? Take some time off. There are lots of nice girls at the church where Peter and I attend. They have singles parties every so often and you might meet someone nice."

"I'd love to come for a visit, but the business keeps Tyrone and me pretty busy. Besides, Mom," Thad emphasized, "I'm not one for church socials."

"I know," Louise Tucker acknowledged with a sigh, "I'm just trying to help. You know how mothers get."

Thad chuckled. "You keep praying for me. God answers your prayers. Maybe there's a miracle he could spare on my behalf." He finished and his Mom understood she was to go on to another subject.

Thoughts of the phone call floated back into his sub-conscience as he checked the Hay Flats for sightings of moose. About a half dozen of the large lumbering animals were grouped together on the flat, open landscape. They chewed on thin tree bark and twigs protruding through the snow. A few moose dumbly watched cars zip by on the four-lane highway. Though the moose seemed docile enough in this setting, Thad well knew mood changes in these animals could trigger aggressive behavior with disastrous results. He observed their lazy movements as he drove.

When he finally reached Palmer, Thad stopped to take the hunting items into the trading post for Taima, (TAY-mah) a longtime friend. Taima and his sister, Alma, were of Athabascan ancestry. In his mid fifties, Taima was a bachelor, and the owner of Thunder's Trading Post on the outskirts of Palmer. He sold just about everything a hunter or fisherman could need as well as sports equipment and a few food staples and household supplies. Both Taima and Alma lived at Thad's cabin a few miles from central Palmer on Lazy Mountain.

As Thad brought in the box of requested hunting items, a shirt button caught on the bottom edge of the box and popped off.

"Aw-w-w!" Thad groaned as he set the box down on the counter. "Another button." Taima looked up at him from the paperwork he was reviewing.

"You're a wreck, Thad. How many buttons does that make?"

"Well, I'm missing two on this shirt already." He replied dryly. "Alma's good about putting them back on, but I forget to tell her they're missing."

"You need a wife to sew your buttons back on your shirts, Thad Tucker."

"Prospective brides seem to be in short supply up here."

"Maybe you'll just have to go find one." Taima commented. Thad shrugged as he looked around the floor for the missing button and found it beside the footboard of the cash register. He tossed it into the air, caught it, and dropped it into a shirt pocket.

"Andy told me to go to the dating service and fill out a Bio."

"So do it!" Taima declared. Thad looked up at the tone of command.

"Okay, I will."

A week later he was in Anchorage to pick up four clients for a three-day seminar he and Tyrone gave on tracking wildlife in Alaska. It was also part of a university study. Before picking them up, he stopped at the dating service and gave them his personal information. Included in his Bio was the request for a wife to sew buttons back on his shirts!

The week of Christmas, Thad started to get responses from the dating service. They sent the Bios and pictures of several inquiries to his postal address. After stopping by the Palmer Post Office to check the box for business mail and thinking there was a lot more "junk mail" than usual, he dropped the bundle on the seat in the old Chevy pickup.

Later that day he stopped in at the trading post for a few minutes to see if Taima had any calls for him on the repairs to a boat motor that had seized up during a fishing excursion the end of September. The repair shop in Anchorage was backlogged with other work on boat engines and skiffs for local commercial fisherman who had priority over his small excursion boat motor. He didn't mind because he still had time for the repairs to be made before the thaw.

When he finally broke the bundle of envelopes with strange names from unfamiliar places, it was in front of Taima whose eyebrows rose at the evidence of Thad's efforts to find a wife.

"Well, there they are. Now what do I do?"

"Let's look them over." Taima put his glasses on and began to examine the pictures while Thad looked over the basic information of these prospective brides.

"Too skinny," Taima announced. "Too much makeup. Trouble!" He commented on each picture. "Too old. Too ugly. You'd have better luck dealing with a bear!"

"These comments leave a lot to be desired, too," Thad muttered as he read one his own mother would have balked at because of the suggestive comments. He frowned, "Here's one. 'I'm the adventurous type and I think I'd really like to try living in an igloo. I've lived in a grass hut in Africa, a cave in Australia, and a tent in Afghanistan. An igloo in Alaska would round it off for me." Thad looked at Taima with skepticism.

"Is this real?" he asked. Taima laughed.

"They think we all live in igloos," he replied.

"I've been here almost all of my life and I have yet to see a real igloo."

"I guess she's been around." Thad dismissed that prospect with a toss of the bio and drummed his fingers on the countertop twice before pulling at another loose button on his shirt pocket. It came off easily and he blinked in surprise.

"Still going around, I'd say."

"That was a waste of time and money." He sighed and dropped the second button into the shirt pocket with the other one. "I'll contact the dating service tomorrow and tell them not to bother with any more bios."

"Don't be so hasty." Taima counseled as he noticed another button missing from the pocket flap. "There were a few that weren't too bad. Give it a while. Maybe the dating service gives all the new people a quick response to keep up the interest and let you know they're working on it for you. Give it a couple of months at least. See what happens."

"I did pay for three months, anyway." Thad amended and patted the shirt pocket which held the sorry buttons.

For the next several weeks, Thad continued to receive bios, and, each time he did, he and Taima looked them over carefully, but with the same results. None seemed to be just what he'd hoped.

By Valentine's Day, Thad Tucker was disenchanted with the whole idea. Somehow, his phone number had been given out even though he had specifically insisted it not be made know to any of the inquiries. He began getting phone calls all hours of the day and night from women who had no idea of the time differences between the East Coast and Alaska's Pacific Time Zone.

The morning after Valentine's Day, Thad left for Anchorage to take two homebound clients to the airport to catch their flights. On his way back, he stopped at the dating service to submit a complaint. However, just as he was about to speak, the receptionist greeted him with an envelope.

"Mr. Tucker, I just received this bio for you by FAX. It's a hot one directly from the Pittsburgh, Pennsylvania branch of our dating service. Usually it takes a couple of days to get the information to us. This one was actually filled out yesterday afternoon and sent last night. They're either pretty efficient down there, or else there's a very good reason for this coming directly to our office so fast. And here you are to pick it up!"

"Well, thank you." He accepted the envelope and tucked it under his arm to leave. "This is the last one I'll be receiving. Please take my name and information off your lists and return any further inquiries. I'm no longer available." The woman smiled broadly.

"Maybe you won't need any more inquiries, Mr. Tucker." She'd seen Leah's picture briefly as it came through the FAX machine with her bio. This Miss Grant just seemed to look like his type. Thad gave her the satisfaction of a small grin of courtesy.

"Thank you." He offered then headed directly for the truck. The wind was a chilling eighteen degrees below zero and he longed to get back home to some of Alma's hot caribou stew. The truck started hard and by the time he'd let it run for a few minutes to warm the cab up, the windows were frosted over from his breath. He turned the defogger on and welcomed the smallest amount of heat as the windows slowly began to clear. Glancing down at the envelope, he decided to open it and see what "hot" new bio this might be from Pittsburgh! A smirk formed on his lips as he thought about what he'd come to expect. Yet, he had to admit there had been bios from women who seemed to be good prospects, but they just hadn't moved him to any response.

He pulled the bio out first and wondered where the picture was before noticing it was on another sheet of FAX paper. The portrait looked like it had been enlarged to make up for the small size of the photo or something. His eyebrows rose.

"Hum. Not bad for Pittsburgh." He spoke aloud as the steam rolled from his mouth in the still cold cab of the truck. Leah's smile and friendly eyes seemed to say, "Hello!" to him right away. The FAX copy was not a very good one, but Thad liked what he saw even if it was rough. His interest was captured and he began reading her information.

"Leah Annette Grant." He repeated her name as he read it off her bio sheet. It sounded feminine, soft, and it matched her pretty face perfectly.

"Twenty-seven," he read and mused about the fact that he was almost seven years older than she was. The cab was starting to get warm as the windows defrosted to reveal long violet shadows against the Chugach Mountain ranch.

"School teacher." He nodded positively then read the reason why she chose to inquire about him. It got his undivided attention.

"I've inquired about Mr. Tucker because I'd be happy to sew his buttons back on his shirts, just to help him out." Thad smiled at the simple offer of sincere help and the connection it immediately made between them.

She seemed to be like-minded and to be answering his request directly and in a sincere way. He laid the bio on the seat beside him with her picture so he could glance at it as he drove. Smiling, he wondered what Taima would think about this particular bio.

The ride back to Palmer was just as miserable as it had been in early December, but not nearly as lonely. Thad had someone interesting to think and wonder about.

When he arrived at the trading post, Taima was getting ready to leave for the cabin to get some lunch. After he closed up the shop, they headed for the cabin. The countryside was pure white and glistened in the emerging noon sunshine making both drivers squint until each could retrieve sunglasses for relief. As Taima followed Thad's truck with the Suburban, he recalled the smile of greeting he'd received just moments ago from Thad. He wondered about it as he checked his rear view mirror before turning on his left signal to enter the long gravel drive up to the cabin. The black spruce trees on either side bowed low under several inches of snow frosted winter green branches.

The warm cabin smelled of hot caribou stew, coffee, and fresh baked bread. Alma was setting the food on the table in the kitchen as they entered the large front hallway. At forty-four years of age, she was a single woman with shoulder-length black hair that curled under and was tucked neatly behind her ears. The energy of her personhood was noticeable in her homemaking and crafting activities. Alma was speech and hearing impaired and had been since a disease in early childhood. She greeted both men in sign language.

"It's ready."

"Hey, Alma, it smells good. I'm starved!" Thad exclaimed. Both men returned a signed greeting, then sat down to eat just as basket of steaming biscuits and a bowl of homemade strawberry jam were placed on the round oak table.

"You're always starved, Thad," she signed with a knowing smile sitting down to eat as well.

Thad laid the envelope down on the table. It was a plain manila envelope, so nobody asked about it and Thad didn't say a word until after they'd all finished lunch. When he took the information out of the envelope, he sat for a few moments studying the picture of Leah again until Taima asked him what he was looking at so intently.

"I picked this up today while I was at the dating service. Here," he stretched the photo toward Taima, "take a look at this face and see what you think." Thad kept as serious a face as he could manage.

Taima took the picture as Alma came in back of him to look at it also. He regarded the portrait without so much as batting an eye. Alma waited for Taima's comment. She already knew what she thought.

"Kinda' plain." He tested Thad's opinion of her.

"You don't have your glasses on, Taima. Besides, the FAX is rough. You have to see beyond the poor copy of her photo." Thad defended Pittsburgh.

Taima smiled slyly at him as he restated his comment.

"She has a pleasant face and her eyes look like she has a kind heart." He summed up his opinion and handed the picture to Alma for her close inspection.

"She's cute!" Taima appended as Thad watched Alma's lack of reaction with easy patience until he registered Taima's "cute"

"Cute?" Thad repeated curiously and wondered where he'd heard that before. Taima then shrugged indifferently and said no more.

Alma handed the picture back to Thad with a grin and winked.

"This one has possibilities," she signed and did not say any more either, but got up and started clearing the table. When she returned from putting the dishes in the sink, there was the tiniest smile on her face.

"Between the two of you losing your buttons and all the other mending, I think this Leah would be a welcome relief for me. I might finally have some time to do some crafting for once or go shopping in Anchorage or visit some friends…"

Thad was a little surprised that Alma had already included Leah in the scheme of things. Taima didn't miss it either and chuckled to himself. Life was going to change in a big way over the next few months.

Later that afternoon, Thad sat at his desk just off the great room and wrote a short letter of introduction to Leah. He mailed it and began the wait for a reply with a little more attention to the mail than his usual toss of it into the mail basket.

CHAPTER 4

THE AFTERMATH

IF LEAH AND DENISE THOUGHT NOBODY had watched the George Endicott Show on TV that particular Friday, they were sadly mistaken. It seemed everyone had seen them sitting on those handsome Alaska bachelors' laps! They graciously endured the teasing and the disapproving comments, hoping it would all go away soon. Thankfully, Christmas came and for a while all else was forgotten during the celebrations of this joyous season.

Jack Diamond and Denise Cox had a rousting fight over the whole thing and broke off their engagement for the second time. But, Denise didn't call J.C. North--so miffed was she with men in general!

With the coming new year of 1997, old things passed away in efforts to make all things new. When Denise came to visit Leah during New Year's, she brought with her a newspaper clipping. It was an advertisement concerning several more Alaska bachelors who were looking for prospective brides. Inquiries were to be made in person at a national dating service.

"Just ask for information on the Alaska Bachelors," Leah read aloud.

"I thought you might like this clipping as a memento of our trip to the TV station," Denise suggested. "Despite all the teasing we've endured, it was still worth the fun of that experience, I think."

"Yes, in a way it was." Leah agreed. "Can you ever imagine the two of us going to Alaska and marrying two total strangers?" It seemed unthinkable.

"Why not, Leah?" Denise asked straightaway. "You're twenty-seven and there are no eligible bachelors around this little place that are worth considering unless you've suddenly developed a liking for Rusty." Leah threw a couch pillow at Denise making her shift quickly to escape the soft hit.

"Guess not!" Denise laughed.

"What's the latest with you and Jack?" Leah asked.

"Oh, Jack and I will be back together eventually. I think we're really going to be able to build a good, lasting relationship. We've already talked over the phone about meeting." Denise said without joy.

"Denise, not Jack again."

"Leah!" Denise sounded hurt, "can't you be happy for me and encourage me even a little bit? I really do care about Jack."

"Okay. I'll quit being a spoilsport. I wish you happiness. You deserve the best, DeeDee."

"Thanks, I think." She said quietly. Leah regarded her friend with interest and changed the subject.

"Denise, would you be interested in teaching at the academy in the fall? Mrs. Falosa is retiring in June and another supervisor is needed to take her place."

"What grade level?"

"Well, it's not really any one grade level as much as its multi-grade levels. The students are deaf and you'd have ten students from grades two to six. I will be taking the high school deaf students this next year. Sign language shouldn't be a problem for you, Denise. That's about the only class in college we really excelled at." Denise Chuckled.

"What great conversations we had during Quiet Hours!"

Leah chuckled. "I think we should have studied more."

"I should have studied more, you always managed to pass with flying colors."

"That's what I mean. I was responsible for keeping you from your studies." They both laughed.

"Oh, Leah! We had so much fun in college. Why do things have to change?"

"We're not having fun anymore?" Leah pointed to the Alaska advertisement on her mirror dresser.

"Only when we went to that TV show," Denise retorted with a nod.

"Do you still remember those guys?" Leah ventured.

"No, not really, although now you mention it, I should give J.C. a call. I'm available again." Denise smiled in remembrance. "Why do you ask about them?"

"Oh, I was just thinking I might check the dating service out in Pittsburgh after all."

"Leah Grant! Don't you even think about it, girlfriend." It was a command. "You have to be very careful these days. Not all those bachelors were as nice as the two we met."

"I know. Maybe it isn't a good idea anyway." Leah admitted though not totally dissuaded. Denise looked at her suspiciously.

"You're not really this desperate, are you?" Denise inquired with concern.

"No, not really. Right now I feel like it's time for me to move on to something new and different." Leah didn't say anything more, but Denise understood.

"Are you being pressured to date Rusty again?"

"Always," Leah chuckled. "But that's not the reason. I feel restless and in need of a change." She signed the boredom she felt.

"Be careful, Leah. It's easy to do stupid things when a person's restless."

Leah gave Denise a side glance and could have given her the same advice.

By the time Denise left to return to Chicago, she'd let Pastor Grant know she would be interested in the teaching position for next fall. Leah and Denise had already decided to get an apartment together since Denise wasn't sure if she and Jack would be back together.

A month later, Denise was engaged to Jack for a third time, even though she'd persuaded him to postpone the wedding for yet another year in view of her plans to teach in Pennsylvania. This puzzled Leah when she had a few moments during the academy day to think about the whole situation.

On the afternoon of the fourteenth of February, Leah gazed beyond the red hearts that were taped to the windows of her classroom and peered outside into the arctic-like landscape. The snowdrifts and blowing snow made beautiful ripples across the open fields and along the rolling hills. Her thoughts wandered from Denise and Jack to her own restless state of mind. While the students were busy with their lessons and workbooks, she took a few moments to contemplate the loneliness of this time of year as a single woman with no prospects of a valentine to speak of, either now or in the future. Over the last week, Leah had taken the newspaper advertisement regarding the Alaska bachelors from her wallet and read it until she'd all but memorized the information. She toyed with the idea of going to the dating service in Pittsburgh several times, but couldn't seem to muster the courage when she thought about others reaction. Today, however, the red hearts in the window seemed to jump out at her and encourage her to make the journey as did the many Valentine cards and wishes from her students. By the time she left school at three-thirty, she was headed to the advertised dating service in downtown Pittsburgh on Forbes Avenue. A call home to let family know she wouldn't be home until later in the evening was made so there wouldn't be cause for concern or questions. It took her about an hour to drive into the city and another twenty minutes to locate the office complex and find a parking space. The snow was pushed to the curb in gray piles so that she had to carefully climb over the top of them to put change in the parking meter. At the moment, it was flurrying. Leah knew if it continued to snow, these grungy snow piles would be covered with white flakes in no time. She hoped it didn't take long to fill out her information and select a bachelor from Alaska—if she picked one! For a moment the idea of what she was doing nearly made her turn and leave. But, she figured it to be a waste of gas for a joy ride on a night that promised foul weather and a long, tedious drive home.

Leah plodded along slowly over the snow-covered sidewalks. The center of the city was not only dressed in red hearts and cupids, it still looked as clean and polished as it always did to Leah. The red brick and the tan stone buildings gave the city of Pittsburgh a pristine look. The rolling mountains surrounding the city and the three rivers running through its middle distinguished it as the city of tunnels and bridges. The ornate stone columns of Carnegie Mellon University's buildings always gave Leah the sense of old world wisdom after the kind reflected in the Parthenon in Athens.

When Leah entered the dating service, a receptionist greeted her. The woman looked as though she was preparing to leave for the day. She had been applying red lipstick to her lips that matched red finger-nail polish. Her red dress was fitted snugly to her midlife figure. The sight of the woman made Leah check the misgivings threatening to send her in an opposite direction. However, the woman's friendly greeting encouraged Leah to accept her assistance

"Can I help you?" she asked expectantly.

Leah hesitated briefly, "I'd like to inquire about the bachelors from Alaska, please."

The women instantly looked Leah up and down as if evaluating her. Leah wondered what she was looking for until she remembered she still wore the navy and white teacher's uniform that showed under the unzipped school jacket. The jacket had the Christian Academy's name on the left shoulder along with her name. Leah smiled to herself as she realized how very peculiar she must look to this woman right about now.

"How old are you?" she asked curiously. Leah blinked at the unexpected question.

"I'm twenty-seven," she replied with a frown. The woman shrugged and stood up then walked over to a computer as Leah warily followed.

"You don't look that old, Leah." The woman had read Leah's name off her jacket. "Boy! Do I wish I had your complexion." She chuckled and Leah relaxed a little.

"Please key in your personal information and follow the directions given in the boxes. Do you have a picture of yourself with you or will you need to have one taken here?"

"I have one with me." Leah began to search her purse for the wallet-sized photo.

"Alaska bachelors, so you ask." The woman stated more than questioned. "We had a lot of interest a few months ago, but that eventually dwindled." Her strong perfume made Leah blink away tearing eyes. "That George Endicott Show really helped us bring in a bunch of new names and faces for a while. But its February and somehow the snow outside doesn't promise much for Alaska bachelors this time of year."

Leah gave no hint that she had been on the live show as she smiled and handed her school staff picture to the receptionist. The woman continued to study the photo while regarding Leah closely again. A doubtful frown crossed the woman's face.

"I'm a teacher." Leah laughed. "You think I'm a student, don't you?"

She smiled affirmation. Leah reached for her driver's license. "I'm always asked to show my driver's license."

After a quick glance at the card and a nod, the woman had another question. "Why would you ever want to inquire about bachelors in Alaska? I know a lot of nice fellows around here."

"I've seen what's around here." Leah shrugged indifference. The woman laughed and shook her head in agreement.

"I guess I can understand that, too. Here, write your name on the reverse and a phone number where just the dating service can reach you if necessary." She then left to get the paperwork started and make a copy of Leah's picture. There hadn't been too many requests lately for bachelors from Alaska. Since it was Valentine's Day, she decided that Leah's request would be on its way to Anchorage, Alaska via FAX before she left!

When Leah's personal information was keyed in, Leah followed the woman, who by now had introduced herself as Peggy. Peggy led her to a small room where Leah could sit privately and review the information on each of the bachelors' Bios. Some had a studio picture taken by the dating services in either Anchorage or Fairbanks while others had snap shot pictures from family cameras.

"When you've picked a Bio, please see me at the information desk before you leave. We're supposed to close at five-thirty tonight, but take your time, Leah. I can't leave until my escort arrives."

For several minutes, Leah looked at the information and pictures until she was somewhat discouraged. Her eyes fell to the bottom of the Bio page to the statements made by the bachelors in regards to why they were looking for "that special someone."

She found she could put aside several from the group right away as she read them. Soon, she was to the final five remaining Bios and checked the time on her wrist watch. It was almost 5:45 and she was tempted to quit. However, not one to quit, Leah quickly read these last ones without looking at the pictures.

"Wouldn't you know!" she said softly as she re-read the last Bio of a bachelor from someplace called Palmer, Alaska. She didn't even look at the name or the picture but read the simple statement again.

"Wife wanted! I need a wife to sew buttons on my shirts for me." That's all it said. Leah smiled at its simplicity and then looked at his picture. He looked studious and businesslike, was clean-cut, and his hair was the same dark brown color as Leah's. He looked good to Leah. There was a quiet security about him that drew Leah. She checked his age to be thirty-four. Seven years older than she. Scanning to the top of his Bio for his name, Leah pondered his information.

"Thaddeus Wayne Tucker," she said aloud and liked the rhythm of it. She looked at his picture and repeated his name slowly. He was the Alaska bachelor for her! A last glance over the Bio and Leah wondered if he would respond to her inquiry. It would be nice to have a pen pal. Leah figured distance would hinder her from ever being considered as a possible wife anyway.

"No worry there!" She sighed easily. "He can send me his buttons and shirts via UPS and I'll send them back mended."

One week later, Leah received a response from Thad Tucker! It was the most exciting day she'd had since…her first horse ride on Sunset. She read and reread his letter.

Dear Miss Leah Grant;

I am writing in response to your inquiry received from the dating service here in Anchorage. I would be interested in writing to you in hopes of forming a friendship.

There is such a great distance between us, as I am sure you realize, letter writing will have to suffice at present. Maybe email in the future if you have an email address and access. May I ask you about your sewing skills and any hobbies you may have to start us along. I look forward to hearing from you if you still wish to correspond.

Sincerely,

Thad Tucker

Leah smiled again as she read the short letter another time. In fact, she smiled all day—even after a snowball she threw shattered a classroom window during a snowball fight with her students at recess. Her deaf students could only shrug their shoulders in wonder at their supervisor's unusually sunny disposition.

As soon as the last students left the room for bus rides home, Leah shut the door, took pen in hand, and began her first letter to Thad Tucker. She dropped it in the mailbox two hours later and hoped it wasn't too corny.

Due to the terrible weather and the flooding in the Mid-West that winter, it took two weeks for an exchange of letters between Alaska and Pennsylvania when it should have only taken three days. Both wondered about the other as they peered out windows and watched the howling winds blow snow across the winter wonderlands in their respective home states.

On the eighth of March, Thad checked the mail at the Palmer Post Office. It was almost five o'clock in the evening and the postmistress was getting ready to lock the main entrance when Thad hailed her and asked if he could get his mail.

"You've been keeping your box clean recently, Thad. Even Tyrone mentioned you're beating him to the mailbox," she teased.

Mary was sixty-three and a grandmother nineteen times over. Her husband was a retired engineer from the Alaska Railroad and together, they had raised seven children in Alaska. She was a jovial woman who set a pleasant and positive mood in her workplace. Those who worked under her supervision affectionately and respectfully called her "Grandma Mary." She did not tolerate griping and complaining. "It's a waste of life and breath!" she always said. Her post office had one of the best records of mail service anywhere.

"You must be expecting something important." She ventured expectantly as her blue eyes twinkled. She smoothed a loose strand of gray hair behind her ear and patted it into place with practiced ease.

"New Year's resolution, Mary," he dodged. "Got to' keep the box empty. It helps you out."

"Yah!" she snickered as he retrieved mail from a wall of post boxes.

"Thanks, Mary."

"Sure. I hope she's a nice girl, Thad. You deserve one." Mary remarked, wise to these ways. Thad chuckled at her attempt for more information, but gave none mostly because he didn't have any to give, yet.

"Mary, if I ever have a nice girl to talk about, I'll let you know right away, so you won't have to lie awake all night wondering."

Thad braced for the cold, sharp air that engulfed and clung to him until he was inside the running and warm Suburban. He turned on the dome light and flipped through the mail, tossing each piece in a pile on the seat beside him. He stopped suddenly when he saw first, his name and address written in neat script across the envelope and then the return address in the left corner.

"Leah Grant." He read aloud as he picked it up and threw the other mail on top of the pile without even looking to see if it landed or scattered. Removing his gloves, he opened the envelope. It smelled faintly like roses when he pulled the pink stationary from its paper cloak. He smiled at the pleasure of opening the message and read it with eagerness.

Dear Thad Tucker;

I was happy to receive your letter and I welcome your friendship in correspondence. You asked about hobbies. At present, I am enjoying bird watching from inside my classroom due to the rainy spring weather outside. All the snow has melted and there is a whole field of noisy black crows and swallows fighting it out, or something—probably over bugs and such. The field is almost black with these birds and at random moments a multitude of black birds will suddenly rise together to form a tidal wave of flapping wings to the tree tops. Instead of leaves, the trees are filled with birds. When I open the window, the noise of their squawking is almost deafening. I guess you could say this activity is for the birds!

Thad's eyes widened at the corny humor. He continued to read with a grin.

I also would like to know if you have hobbies or handyman skills. I am asking about your handyman skills because I have managed, once again, to break another heel off my shoe. Our academy is in an old building that still has steel-grated heat vents in the floor. Occasionally, I forget they're there and I manage to snap the heels off. I have three pairs of shoes with one broken heel each. I'm running out of matching shoes!

Thad laughed outright and marveled at the sound of his own outburst in the silence of the vehicle cabin. Letters did indeed reveal a lot about a person. It continued:

On to more serious things. You asked about my sewing skills. I noticed you mentioned in your bio that you need some buttons sewn on your shirts. I am a competent seamstress and enjoy sewing both as a hobby and for its usefulness in making clothes for my mother, sisters, nieces, and myself. I'm not real sure how we'd manage it, but I'd be glad to take care of sewing some buttons on your shirts. I have a machine that will attach some types of buttons to fabric in a very short time. It's great!

As a teacher in the Christian Academy, I guess my work is also my hobby. I have sixteen deaf students from second grade to sixth grade. They are all great kids and excellent students. We use a self-teaching educational program with materials appropriate to their individual scholastic level and ability. I am a supervising teacher. In my spare time, I teach music classes and occasionally an art class.

My family and I live in the country, in a small place called the Village of Limestone. We tell people who come to visit us that if they blink, they've missed the place. It's nestled in between two Pennsylvania sized mountains and it is known for its three RV camping grounds. One of the campgrounds is host to the annual caravan of Airstream campers that visit in the fall of the year. One year, my sisters and I counted a caravan of some thirty-six Airstream trailers. That was a big event in our neck of the woods!

I found Palmer, Alaska in the travel atlas my Dad keeps in the car. At least now I have a clue where you live. I just have to ask how much snow you have up there. Last week we had white-out conditions and sub-zero temperatures. Today, its fifty degrees and looks like Spring is on its way. It's such a drastic change that most of us don't know whether to be hot or cold yet. I must admit, I was beginning to wonder if Spring would ever come!

Sincerely,
Leah

Thad was still smiling when he finished reading the letter.

"I was wondering if Spring would ever come, too," he agreed. "I know it has," he smiled relief that she'd replied.

Her letter had a warm, friendly ease to it that was like talking to a neighbor over the fence. It was free of underlying meaning and suggestive improprieties. He did wish he could somehow manage for her to sew his buttons on his shirts. The thought struck him how easily Leah Grant could fit into his life. He knew something was in the works because she needed shoes fixed and he needed mending done.

He was startled from his musings by a tapping on the window. Pushing the button on the armrest, the window hummed down. Mary was standing there all bundled up and making an effort to keep warm.

"Thad, my car won't start again. Could you give me a lift home? I'll call the garage and have the guys swing by and jump the battery with the tow truck later."

"Sure! Hop in." he encouraged cheerfully. Mary moved gingerly around the Suburban and got into the warmed vehicle. She shivered and rubbed her hands together.

"This is what I get for being the last one out tonight," she joked. "I'm glad you were still here, Thad. It may be cold and blustery out, but it's March and there's hope for spring when it's March in Alaska, even if there's still two feet of snow on the ground." Mary sniffed as her nose warmed up.

"Smells like roses in here." She wrinkled her nose. "Is that a new air freshener you're using for your client's pleasure on their hunting expeditions?" She grinned mischievously making Thad laugh at that ridiculous idea.

"No, Mary. It's not air freshener." He grinned but didn't offer anymore information. There was a little smirk on his face as he waited for Mary to ask him about the letter. He didn't have long to wait.

"Thad, I just can't stand it! Are you gonna' tell me about your letter?"

Thad smiled. "Well, Mary, you were right about my rather persistent efforts to pick up my mail lately. I'm just beginning to correspond with a young woman named, Leah." Mary brightened.

"I knew it!"

"Actually, I just received her first rose-scented letter. I'm glad you let me in to pick up my mail, Mary."

"So am I, Thad. Well, I can tell by the smile on your face you're already a happy man. But still, I hope everything works out for you and this Leah." Thad turned into Mary's driveway.

"You know, Thad. This is going to be all over Palmer by noon tomorrow," she assured. Thad nodded.

"Well, you can tell everyone you heard it directly from this Alaskan bachelor himself."

Mary laughed happily and winked at him.

"Thanks for the ride, Thad." And she was out of the vehicle and into the house in a few moments. She waved from a window inside her home before Thad shifted into reverse and backed out of the drive.

He thought about the fact that he was already committing himself to a relationship with this Leah woman. He had no idea where Limestone, Pennsylvania was or if it was big enough to warrant an ink spot on a road map. But he'd commit to getting a map out and hunting for her hometown if it would bring her closer to Alaska. Strangely enough, he already sensed he knew her well enough to associate with her. He wondered if she would ever think the same. The rose-scented letter was tucked safely away in his shirt pocket underneath the warm parka.

When Leah received Thad's second letter some four days later, she was sitting at her desk during a teacher break. Mrs. Falosa had handed the letter addressed to Leah with the school's address instead of her home address. She felt some odd bumps protruding from the inside of the envelope. As she took his letter from the envelope, two green buttons fell from its pages to her navy plaid skirt. Leah's eyes widened in surprise!

CHAPTER 5

PALMER BECKONS

TAIMA AND ALMA READ THAD'S FIRST letter from Leah, too. Alma looked at Thad with raised eyebrows and smiled.

"She knows sign language. We can talk," she signed. There was a happy expression across her face.

Taima piped up with a serious tone of voice.

"Maybe she's deaf or speech impaired, Thad." Alma and Thad looked at each other.

"Her Bio said nothing about being deaf." Thad frowned thoughtful.

"Does it even ask if she has impairments?" Taima wondered.

"I don't remember if mine asked about handicaps," he answered.

Alma signed, "Does it matter?" She wasn't being defensive; just concerned an opportunity for friendship would not be influenced if impairment existed.

"No, it doesn't matter." Thad affirmed. "I still want to correspond with Leah. Maybe try to meet her if things progress that way."

"You could call her." Taima suggested. He seemed eager to get the proverbial ball rolling on the whole idea.

"No. Not yet. This is only the first letter. I just want to wait a while. Time will tell lots of things."

During the rest of March and all the month of April, Thad and Leah kept a steady flow of letters coming and going. Always, Leah's stationery smelled of some type of flower. And always, Mary was quick to notice them with a knowing wink at Thad.

By May, letters were going in both directions almost daily. Thad wrote his letters to her wherever he could find a decent place to put a piece of paper. Leah never left her classroom in the afternoon until she'd written her own thoughts to Thad about the day's events and her interests in his affairs and ideas. Thad suggested email, but Leah seemed hesitant about it for some reason she didn't disclose, so they continued sending letters. Every button that fell off Thad's shirts he sent to Leah until she had quite a collection of colors and sizes. In one letter, she'd asked what she was supposed to do with all the buttons. His most recent letter suggested that if she were to sew the buttons on his shirts, she'd have to come to Palmer! Leah thought Thad was joking. She had laughed at the idea and dismissed it. Later, as she thought about it, she wondered why he would tease about something of such consequence. His letters were always more of a serious nature. Could Thaddeus Wayne Tucker really be serious…?

When the first week of June passed, Thad decided it was time to call Leah. He still had no idea if she was hearing impaired, speech-impaired, both, or neither. She'd never mentioned anything more about it in all of her letters which, by now, had amassed in quite a fragrant stack on his armoire.

He figured it was noon her time and she had written that today was the last day of school at the academy. He hoped she'd still be there. With the operator's help, he was given the phone number of the academy. Thad took a deep breath before picking up the phone and dialing through. It rang and rang again. On the third ring, he heard the receiver click as it was picked up.

"Hello! Liberty Christian Academy. Leah Grant speaking." She seemed a little out of breath if not harried.

Thad had not anticipated Leah would answer the phone. He'd expected to get the school secretary and leave a message for her to call him collect at her convenience. It caught him off guard for a brief second.

"Hello." He started, a little taken aback. Thad had naturally come to accept the idea Leah was both hearing and speech impaired. Obviously, this wasn't true.

"Hello? May I help you?" she asked. Her voice was clearly feminine, with the precise enunciation of a school teacher and a professional.

"Hello, Leah. This is Thad Tucker from Palmer, Alaska," he finally managed and the phone went silent until he heard a barrage of things crashing in the background.

"Leah?" he asked with concern. "Is everything okay?" Leah giggled nervously.

"Hello, Thad." She spoke quickly. "It will be in a couple of minutes. I just knocked a box of pencils over and they're scattered across the floor in all directions." She giggled again as Thad smiled at the sound of her voice. Leah, however, made a goofy face on her end of the receiver.

"I hope I haven't surprised you too much."

"No. Well, yes. But your call is a nice surprise, Thad. My mind is just six ways to Georgia right now." She heard Thad laugh at the strange phrase. Boy! Was she distracted! Yellow number two pencils lay scattered across the floor. Leah hoped no one would come into the learning center or it would be like a logger's roll in a lumber jack contest.

"Today was the last day of school for us. I just dismissed my students for summer break and things are still a little crazy around here. I was walking back to the classroom to write you a letter before leaving to go home."

"Well, I thought I'd give you a call and save you a stamp." He offered in a practical voice. A lump formed in Leah's throat as she tried to swallow his statement.

"Oh," she said slowly as her stomach knotted. "Does this mean you don't want to correspond any longer?" Her voice almost cracked as she prepared for his rejection.

"Huh?" Thad's eyes widened at the wrong way she'd taken his well-intentioned statement. "No, Leah, I meant instead of writing a letter today, we could talk over the phone for a change." He wondered how this little misunderstanding had taken place so fast. He rubbed his forehead anxiously.

"Oh!" Leah exclaimed and laughed. "I'm so relieved. I'm sorry I took it the wrong way, Thad. Your call is a big surprise, although I was hoping that somehow we'd be able to talk to each other soon. I must admit I'm really excited to hear your voice, too. I wondered what you would sound like." She revealed more to Thad than she'd thought she would. He was grinning.

"Well—"

"Oh! Thad, someone is coming and I need to warn them about the pencils on the floor," Leah interrupted quickly with a short laugh. Thad smiled and waited as she covered the phone to speak to someone. He could hear her muffled talking in the background.

"Okay, Thad, I'm back. Mrs. Falosa came through the learning center door and I didn't want her to fall."

"How many pencils are on the floor?" he asked curious.

"Oh, about a hundred colored and number-two pencils or so."

"I guess I really surprised you! You won't be going home anytime soon, will you?"

"Not if I keep knocking pencils all over the floor." A few more fell off the desk and clattered to the floor. Leah just let them fall.

"Well, you certainly surprised me when you answered the phone. I couldn't think of a thing to say for a moment." Thad admitted. "I was expecting to get the school secretary, first. It took me a few moments to collect my thoughts when you answered. I might add, I was surprised for another reason which I am somewhat embarrassed to admit."

"Tell me."

"For the last three months, I have obviously been under the wrong impression that you might be hearing and speech impaired." He hastened to say, "My friend suggested you might be because you were teaching deaf children. But whether you were or not didn't change the fact that I'd already decided to write to you, Leah." Leah pursed her lips together at the pleasure of his ready acceptance.

"Thad, that's the nicest thing anyone's said to me in a long time." Leah's voice was soft and timid. Thad was both relieved and stirred by her grateful response.

"I've enjoyed your letters," he continued.

"Same here, Thad. You've told me so many things about Alaska and I've enjoyed learning about your state. I think I'd like to visit sometime," Leah said. Thad jumped on this opportunity trying to keep too much eagerness out of his voice.

"You're welcome to come up and visit anytime. I'd be glad to show you around." Leah hadn't expected her remark about a visit to Alaska to be returned in the form of an invitation. She'd thought about what it would be like to go there and see the beauty of the land Thad described in glowing terms, but she was unaware of how it could ever happen.

"I-I'd love to visit," Leah stammered. Her eyes widened as she found herself wanting to accept his invitation.

"What are your plans for the summer, if I may ask?" Thad ventured. Leah's forehead wrinkled as her heart pounded.

"Well, I'm scheduled to be at our Christian Camp as a counselor from July 6th to August 5th, so that's five weeks right there. These next two weeks our church has Vacation Bible School and I teach a fourth grade class. I guess if I was to visit, it wouldn't be until the middle of August, Thad." Leah couldn't believe she was talking about taking such a trip. It seemed like the whole idea was taking off on its own. She didn't know if she could or would stop it either.

"August is good, as-a-matter-of-fact, the Alaska State Fair is the last week of August and the first week of September here in Palmer. That would be a very good time for you to come, Leah." Thad wondered if she was willing to take him up on his invitation.

"I'll have to check plane fares and I don't know what else." She ran her fingers through her hair as if it would help her to organize her thoughts and give her answers to the unbelievable idea she was almost surely beginning to contemplate.

"Let me know what you find out," he pressed onward. Leah scratched her head as she found herself saying the words that formed an initial commitment.

"Okay. I'll do that." She managed with an astonished nod at her own words. Thad moved ahead some more.

"Let's see, you'd be coming up August 13th or 14th. I'll pencil it in." Leah's mouth dropped open, but she managed not to gasp. This whole idea was moving ahead faster than an unexpected skid across the top of the scattered pencils on the floor. She'd gone from thinking about a visit at some very far off time in the future to setting a date only some ten weeks away!

"Thad," she hesitated, not sure what to say because she really wanted to meet him and see him face to face. However, she'd figured he would be the first to visit her at some future time. But it wasn't working out that way at all!

Thad heard the tremor in her voice as she said his name. He smiled and moved on yet again.

"Leah, see what you can find out about a plane ticket for those dates and let me know. I might be able to get a better plane fare for you." At that moment, Leah knew she was going to Alaska the middle of August. With the decision made, Leah plunged forward enthusiastically.

"I'll call the airlines as soon as we're finished chatting!" It was settled in her heart and mind. Now it was Thad's turn to be amazed.

"Great!" He could hardly believe it himself. "I'll give you my number and you can call me when you get the information." He gave Leah his cell phone number and his business phone number.

"I'll talk to you later, then?"

"Yes. I'll call you, Thad," she guaranteed. "I'm glad you called. It's nice to hear the voice that goes with the letters."

"And you have a fine teacher's voice, too." It sounded corny but Thad wanted to linger. "By the way, may I ask for a picture of you, Leah? The FAX picture wasn't real clear."

"Sure. What size?"

"What sizes can I pick from?"

"Oh, let's see. Five by seven inches, eight by ten, wallets—"

"Okay." Thad replied simply. Leah frowned.

"Okay? Which one?" she asked. There was no response. "You want all of them?" She laughed suddenly.

"All you'll send me."

"All right then. I'll send a selection of this year's school pictures. It will red-up my desk drawer a little bit."

"Red up?" Thad had never heard the phrase.

"It's a PA colloquialism which means to straighten up or clean up something," Leah explained. "We have a lot of those sayings in this area." A curious question came to mind.

"Thad, do you speak Alaskan?" Leah wondered and Thad stifled the urge to laugh outright.

"Fluently."

"Oh, good! Maybe you can teach me how to speak some Alaskan when I visit." Leah was serious. Thad was valiantly trying to contain his laughter. He swallowed, cleared his throat, and spoke matter-of-factly.

"I'm sure you'll catch on fast, Leah," he assured then changed the subject. "I'll begin checking plane fares here while you check in your area. I'm sure we can get a good price between the two of us."

Shortly thereafter, the conversation ended with unseen smiles for each other. Both Thad and Leah remained where they were as they contemplated the results of the phone conversation and the direction it had taken. The possibilities were awesome. A few minutes later, Thad reached for a phone index as Leah reached for the phone book. Both called travel agencies.

It was late Sunday evening in Phoenix, Arizona when Thad's mother, Louise Tucker, returned home from Sunday evening church services. She greeted her older brother, Peter, as she stepped onto the front porch of the modest stucco home. She walked into the air conditioned living room to check on Anna, her elderly brother's ailing wife. Anna was first to greet Louise cheerfully.

"Oh, Louise, how was the service tonight? I wish I felt up to going."

"It was great, my dear!" Louise patted Anna's arm affectionately as she passed by. "The missionary speaker was pretty good for a young guy fresh out of Bible college. " She chuckled easily. "All the single girls crowded around him after the service. He was new blood!" Louise said tongue-in-cheek. "The young man is going to some Polynesian Island in the Pacific. Of course, that may have had a little to do with all the feminine interest as well." She continued to chuckle as she set her Bible down on a lamp stand, kicked her sandals off, then picked them up and put them in her bedroom close by. Anna enjoyed the irony as well, smiling broadly.

"We should get my handsome nephew down here for a while. Maybe he could find a nice girl in the singles group at church who would be willing to live in Alaska." Anna ventured.

"That's a fabulous idea, Anna! Unfortunately, Thad wouldn't be interested in any girl who goes to church." Louise spoke frankly. Her somber tone reflected the disappointment. "Thad has no interest in church or God and most girls from Arizona prefer warm sunny winters to dark, sub-zero arctic ones."

"I know, Louise. I'm still praying. I remember all those summers he spent with us while you were in nursing school in Anchorage. Peter and I offered as much spiritual advice as he could politely tolerate. Even John Weston tried." Louise nodded her agreement.

"I know you did. I tried often enough, myself, but Thad hated my preaching. I'll always remember the day he left for the University of Alaska Fairbanks. I tried to speak of Salvation and faith in Christ, but he left the apartment in anger. I cried my good-byes after the door slammed." As usual, Louise had to blink the tears away. She did not continue to speak because these thoughts brought to light the fact that Thad had refused to answer her letters or take her phone calls for three months after he'd left for college. She said reflectively, "That's been almost sixteen years ago. Imagine that!"

"Thank goodness, he's changed quite a bit since then." Anna offered positively.

"He was so much like his father then." Louise said softly. Anna tried to encourage another more cheerful topic of conversation. "Age is mellowing Thaddeus Wayne Tucker."

"Didn't he mention he was corresponding with a young woman when you spoke with him just a few hours ago?" Anna asked.

"Yes, dear, but that was a mere slip of his tongue, I'm sure. I asked him who she was and he closed up tighter than a clam at a clam bake. Thad said she was a distant friend." She chuckled and Anna sighed thoughtfully."

"I talked to our old friends, Arnie and Else, in Wasilla just before you came in from church."

"Oh?" Louise was interested.

"They saw Thad at the Pioneer Days equestrian competition with Sunrise and Sunset. I guess they teased him about needing another rider for the second horse. Else told me he smiled and said he might just have the second rider if things worked out." Anna offered with excitement.

"Everybody knows but his own mother!" Louise said with chagrin.

"Do you miss Palmer, Louise?" Anna suddenly asked changing the subject. Louise moved over beside Anna and gently patted her soft wrinkled hand affectionately.

"I miss the homestead as much as you and Peter do, Sweetie. I miss our people and all the friends we have there who still keep in touch with us and miss us as much as ever. You and Peter both remember those early days when the farm colony was just beginning, don't you?" Louise encouraged and Anna smiled fond remembrance.

"Peter and I were only five years old when our families left Minnesota to homestead in Alaska." Her eyes brightened as she reminisced. "Peter and I first met in the infirmary on the big boat..."

"The St. Mihiel," Louise prompted. She knew Anna loved to talk about this special time in her life.

"Yes. The St. Mihiel. We both were sick from the rocking of that huge tub of a boat." She chuckled. "Our mother's weren't doing any better. They talked about their sick stomachs while Peter and I just stared at each other shyly and groaned."

"And from what you've always told me, you and Peter stared at each other for a number of years until he got up the nerve to ask you on a date. After that, it was still another couple of years before there was a proposal of marriage." Louise laughed with Anna.

"It was worth all the waiting and all his nerve." Anna quipped, happiness evident in her bright eyes.

"Oh! I had the nerve." Peter entered the room smiling. "I just didn't have the time to ask her. My family was kept so busy working from dawn to dusk on the colony farm that when social events came up, I was always too tired to enjoy her company." He teased and winked at Anna. "But, I finally got around to it."

"You sure did." Anna bobbed her white head of downy soft hair and pretended shyness. "You fell asleep on the hay wagon during a Harvest Hayride and I pushed you off that wagon to wake you up!" She paused to enjoy a twittered laugh of mischief.

"I was so startled by such a rude awakening," Peter shared, "and the laughter of the others, that I could only lay in the middle of the road with my mouth open in bewilderment! I didn't know Anna had pushed me off until I saw the disgusted look on her face. I really thought I had fallen off the wagon." Peter reasoned as Anna took up their courtship story.

"I was so mad at him. Every time he came to my house to see me, he would just lean back into the cushions of that old green couch and fall fast asleep after only a few minutes of conversation."

Peter nodded affirmative.

"After the hayride, she refused to ever see me again and, boy, did that ever wake me up!" Louise watched the two reminisce about their romance. She reflected silently that every couple who has ever fallen in love and stayed together in love has greater treasure than anything the world can offer. She rejoiced for their lifelong love journey. Her hasty marriage had ended in failure shortly after Thad had been born. Louise quickly broke that train of thought and focused on Peter's account.

"I was so shook up, I couldn't do my farm chores right. Dad was mad at me for forgetting to put the cows out to pasture and Mom was madder than a wet hen when I killed the wrong chicken for supper. That chicken was her prize layer and I knew that, but I couldn't think at all, except that Anna would never be my gal again. Finally, Dad got so upset with me that he told me to go for a long walk. 'Don't come back until you have a return of your senses, son!' he yelled after me."

"Naturally, he headed for my home." Anna put in. "He was in pitiful shape."

"And, when I got there, Anna met me at the front door with none too happy an expression on her lovely face. Then she burst into tears. I was baffled. Why was she crying?" Peter shrugged and leaned forward hinting for Anna to take over.

"Peter Jorgensen, 'I said', you always fall asleep when you're near me." Anna playfully shook her finger at Peter.

"Well," Peter continued, "I told Anna that I felt real comfortable around her and I told her I was thinking about asking her to marry me, but if she couldn't accept the fact that I was comfortable enough to fall asleep in her presence then we'd just have to forget about getting married because I couldn't help it!" It was perhaps a senseless thing to say, but youthful thinking tended to folly until age and experience taught a little bit of wisdom.

"I told him I felt real comfortable around him, too, but I always made the effort to stay awake during our dates. Then I had an idea." Anna raised her pointer finger and winked. "I asked him if he stayed awake during his farm chores."

"I told her indeed I did!" Peter answered and Anna reminisced.

"Are you awake at breakfast?"

"Yes."

"Are you awake at lunch?"

"Yes."

"Are you awake at supper?"

"Barely."

"Well, if we get married, I'll be around you during the day when you're awake." Anna finished and Peter returned them to the present.

"I thought it was the best idea I'd ever heard so I asked her to marry me right then. Two weeks later we were married in the Thousand Log church in Palmer."

"And I got to be with him when he was asleep and awake!" Anna smiled brightly.

"Well, Anna, it's been fifty-two years and I still feel real comfortable around you, Sweetheart." Peter bent down to kiss his wife. Soft pillows helped her remain upright and comfortable on the overstuffed sofa.

"I wish we could go back to Palmer, Peter," she admitted sincerely, "but this old arthritis won't let me. I know it! I ask the Lord for grace to bear the disappointment." She was resigned to the crippling effects of the elderly disease, but not depressed. Not one to linger on troubles, Anna brightened. "The Colony Days Celebration is coming up in June. This year is going to be real special, too. The St. Mihiel's bell is to be brought back to Palmer for the 65th Anniversary celebration. Oh, how I'd love to hear the beautiful ring of that ship's bell again! It would bring back so many wonderful memories for us, wouldn't it, Peter, darling?"

"Yes, it would, Anna. It's amazing that after all these years the bell was found and was still ringing out the hour at the University of Richmond. Now it will go home to Palmer and ring out for memory's sake. God sure knows how to work all things together at the right time and with just the right people connections."

"He sure does," Louise echoed. "I just hope and pray this new friend of Thad's is worth his notice and all his hard work. It's difficult to find a young woman that appreciates effort and sacrifice."

"You sound like a future mother-in-law," Peter teased.

"We'll see." Louise Tucker needed more information!

CHAPTER 6

A HOUSE DIVIDED

ONE WEEK LATER, LEAH RECEIVED HER travel itinerary in the mail from a travel agency in Palmer. Thad had made the arrangements for her airfare and she had wired the money from her savings directly to him. However, he'd returned the money. Rather than his chivalry encouraging her visit, it so overwhelmed Leah she nearly canceled the trip. She was determined to pay her own way. Thad spent a few tense moments assuring Leah the invitation to come to Alaska had been his idea in the first place. Earning her trust as a result of his chivalry was another factor he'd not considered. He sensed that somewhere along the line his pen-pal's trust in people in general had been tested and all but lost.

Over the next seven weeks, Thad called Leah whenever she gave him phone numbers and times to call. At first it was tedious. Leah never gave Thad her home number nor did she call him from her home. He wondered why and asked Leah.

"I haven't told my family we've been corresponding, yet, Thad. Things are a little different in my home," Leah answered truthfully. "I don't know how to explain it to you. It's not you, it's me. I have to deal with it myself. Just keep calling me, please." Leah's voice had faltered and Thad had sensed she was struggling. He wished he could help, but wisdom willed him to wait and see how things progressed, so Thad continued to call her as she designated the times and places. He could not help but wonder why a twenty-eight year old woman would hesitate to tell her parents about her plans. Then again, Alaska was the end of the world for most people from the Lower 48. He wondered if Leah was strong enough in her person for Alaska. The sooner they both found out, the better because Thad's heart was losing the battle to safeguard his bachelorhood.

During the five weeks at summer camp, Thad began to learn more about Leah Grant. Their conversations lasted longer and Leah was relaxed and vibrant. She was funny and quite a tease along with the fact she was opening up to him a little more each time they talked.

He continued to send buttons and she continued sending pictures of camp activities. It was also during these lighthearted weeks that Leah was beginning to wonder more about the love of God as she realized something similar growing in her heart for Thad. It was a new experience for someone who'd heard about God's love all her life, but pushed it away at the same time.

The week before Leah was to leave for Alaska, she was totally dependent upon the encouragement of Thad's calls. His voice cheered her, consoled her, and gave her courage to make the journey to Alaska. At times during their conversations, Thad could tell Leah was trying to remain upbeat. He encouraged her as best he could by writing a long letter in which he all but proposed.

The letter had been a balm to the heavy-hearted Leah as she faced her baptism by fire. Her major concern had been finding the right time to speak to her family about Thad and her visit to Alaska. She had spent a good deal of time thinking about how she would broach the news, but for lack of knowing how to pull it off, she had put it off. Finally, on the last weekend before she was to leave for Alaska, Leah was compelled to make her plans known to her family.

Rachel, Leah's oldest sister, had dropped in for a visit with her pastor husband, Clive, and their two children. They had occupied Leah's bedroom which was in a state of chaos from church camping gear. Sarah, Leah's next older sister, and her daughter, Angie, occupied a very small bedroom barely large enough for them. Debbie and Danny slept on the living room floor while Leah slept on the couch. On top of this, Denise had stopped by to sign a contract to teach for the next year. It had been a sore spot for Leah, because she had not renewed her own teaching contract as a result of undisclosed plans for Alaska. This little tidbit caused a ruckus all by itself and had pressed Leah to procrastinate telling about her trip to Alaska to visit a single man who was seven years older than she.

When she confided everything to Denise during lunch at Short Stop Cafe, an astonished best friend worked hard to stifle an outburst.

"Leah!" she whispered loudly, then glanced around for listeners from other tables, "are you out of your mind? You don't know this, this man from Adam. And you're going up to that frozen no-man's land to meet him? That's almost ten thousand miles away!" Denise leaned in toward Leah to study her unaffected countenance.

"It's less than 5,000 miles away, Denise." Leah corrected calmly as she observed another customer wearing a soft yellow summer dress with honey-eyed interest.

"But, but," Denise stammered, "are you sure he's a gentleman and not some rough, ill-mannered—

"Yes, I'm sure Thad is a gentleman, Denise." Leah interrupted. "Look, I have a letter here for you to read if you will. You'll see." Leah was confident as she handed Denise the recent letter from Thad. Denise frowned as she accepted it and read in silence. Leah smiled as she watched the expression change several times on Denise's face from interest to surprise and finally wide-eyed wonder.

Dear Leah,

In just a few days, letters and phone calls will be a thing of the past. Not that I haven't enjoyed both; however, I know that I especially look forward to talking with you and seeing you face to face. Somehow I have the idea that you are very animated and expressive when you converse. Maybe it's because you sound like that. There is a lot about you that causes me to think about you much of the time. I become more anxious to see you as the time for your visit approaches. I also have come to understand you are very much a part of my life and I want it this way. It is a hard thing

for me to admit, because I have been self-sufficient most of my life. Then,
too, if a close friend of mine had not kept after me to find a wife to sew
popped buttons back on my shirts, I wouldn't have stuck with the dating
service idea. And, if he hadn't encouraged me to continue to write to you
when we waded through several misunderstandings in those first letters,
I'd have spent the rest of my life wondering if somehow we were meant to
be together. You've taught me that friendship is the wonder of two hearts
learning to beat as one. Our differences have enhanced this instead of
divided it. I can see this now and am glad for it.

I sensed from our phone conversation this past Monday evening
that you are struggling with your trip to visit me. Although I don't fully
understand your situation, I have an idea this was a very difficult decision
for you to make. Perhaps there are and will be many consequences as
a result of your decision. I only know I want you to come to Alaska. It
would be an honor to show you my home and my state with the hopes of
it becoming our home and our state.

I'll see you in Alaska, Leah.

Thad

"Wow!" Denise's voice was filled with awe. She saw Leah's quiet exuberance and understood the reason for all the commotion surrounding her friend's refusal to renew her teaching contract.

Leah smiled and put the letter back into her purse as though it was a priceless treasure. Denise suddenly stood and reached for her jacket.

"Come on! We've got shopping to do for your trip to Alaska. Let's get to it! Wow," she whispered in amazement. "I'm beginning to wish I was you, girlfriend."

"I'm so glad I am." Leah grinned happily. Denise's positive reaction to Thad's letter bolstered both Leah's spirits and her courage so much so that the two best friends really enjoyed their shopping spree.

It was Saturday afternoon when Leah's plans for Alaska became known before she could speak to her family about them. Rachel found Thad's letters to Leah in her top dresser drawer. Amazed and then indignant with Leah for her secrecy, Rachel headed to their parents with the evidence in hand. She didn't give Leah any opportunity to explain when they met in the hallway.

"Leah! What are these letters about?" Rachel demanded. "Who is this Thad guy and what are you up to? Does Mom and Dad know about him?" She fired questions at a stunned Leah who became angered by the invasion of privacy. Before Leah could answer, Rachel rushed on.

"He says he'll see you in Alaska next week! I'd like to know how? Where would you ever get the money for such a trip unless he's paying your way. What else is he paying for?" This last dig cut Leah to the heart. The insult to Thad's character was more then she would tolerate from a self-righteous older sister.

"You had no business going through my things, Rachel! Please give me my letters. I don't have to explain anything to you." Rachel took the affront as a trumpet blast and headed to Mom Grant with the crimson letters.

Leah tried to remain calm. The thought of Thad's letters in the hands of someone who could destroy both them and her hopes filled her with caution and a steely resolve to retrieve them gingerly. Sarah, Leah's next older sister, met her in the hall with a hushed warning that "war had just broken out." Though Sarah had never read any of the letters or knew of Leah's friendship with Thad, little hints had her guessing about Leah's unaffected cheerfulness over the last couple of months.

Sarah quickly hugged Leah, "So that's why you've been so cheerful lately! I wondered," she smiled then counseled, "I love you, Sis. If you want this, you'll have to fight for it."

"I know. I just wish…" Leah paused.

"You just wish you'd had the chance to talk to Dad, first?" Sarah finished.

"Right! Now, there's no way he can support me and it's my own fault." The weight of what she would do without her Dad's blessing made her heart heavy.

"At the moment I'd say its Rachel's fault!" Sarah teased and Leah smiled at the conspiracy. As girls, they'd always stuck up for each other over their bossy oldest sister. Animated voices could be heard below.

"I have to leave, Sarah. I just have to." Leah's eyes stung with tears but she blinked them away.

"I know, Leah. I'm praying for you." Sarah promised eternal loyalty.

"I'll need it."

Taking a deep breath, she turned and headed in the direction of the kitchen. Voices she'd heard all her life in good and bad times as family sounded more like foes. A week from now, these voices would be distant memories.

"God, I don't honestly know You..." She started a prayer, but old heartaches stopped it cold as she braced for the onslaught coming directly toward her upon entering the kitchen.

"Leah!" Mrs. Grant's voice accused, "What are these letters all about? Who is this man you're writing to and why haven't you mentioned anything about it to your Dad and me? Rachel found them in your drawer and it's a good thing. Were you just planning to leave without saying a word?"

Rachel glanced over at Leah, but she dropped her eyes and turned leaving the room. Leah guessed she was going to find their Dad. There was no hope of telling them anything in a reasonable manner now. Mrs. Grant thrust the letters at her with a look of disgust. Leah slowly took the letters from her mother's hand and held them tightly.

"How long has this been going on?" The questions continued one after the other with no chance to answer. It made her feel little and childish under the thumb of a domineering parent. There was a pattern to the diatribe that Leah and her sisters knew well. She hoped her Dad would appear, soon. The barrage continued.

"This was deceitful of you, Leah. I thought we raised you better than this. But it seems we have two daughters who think nothing of going off and doing as they please." The sarcasm was thick in her voice and Leah saw an old bitterness rise upon remembrance.

"First, Sarah goes off to work in a mission in Chicago and then comes home pregnant with some stupid story about being married. Yet she has no ring, no license, and no husband to show for her condition." Leah's jaw clinched tightly as she fought the desire to defend Sarah.

"If Sarah said she was married, then I believe her," Leah defended quietly thought she shook inside. It was out before she could stop it and immediately saw that her Mom was incensed with anger. Strange that this didn't have anything to do with her going to Alaska, but standing up for Sarah seemed to bolster her courage and help her forge ahead into womanhood. It was no longer childish defiance but a declaration of independence long in the making.

"So, you justify babies born out of wedlock?" Mrs. Grant tried to break her. But Leah did not break down into tears as she always did under emotional pressure from belittling.

"No. I just believe Sarah, Mom. She would never lie about something like that." Leah's voice was low and mild. Doris Grant saw the transformation of a little girl into a woman who was becoming an equal and she felt the intimidation and loss of control keenly. Picking up a glass vase of daffodils, she threw it across the kitchen. Leah moved aside as it flew past her face and shattered into pieces on a countertop. The yellow flowers scattered limply in all directions. For years her daughters had feared her, but it had not earned their confidential trust and respect in times when they'd needed their mother's understanding and advice the most.

"So, you're going off to Alaska to shack up with some man like a common tramp!"

"That's not true! I wouldn't do that, Mom."

"You don't know what you'd do because you've never been in a serious relationship with a man. All you know how to do is run the opposite direction otherwise you'd have been married by now. Rusty has been so patient with you."

At the mention of Rusty's name, the molten lava of raw courage erupted within Leah spewing truth from a long held secret.

"Rusty has been dating a seventeen year old girl he met at Joe's Bar and Grill in Clarion for almost a year now. The only reason he kept showing interest in me was to cover his jail bait trail." There! Leah had finally told it like it was. The only reason she knew this tidbit of information was because one of her deaf students was this seventeen year old's little sister. That seventeen year old's family members were considered pillars of the church. It was definitely a case for "what the deaf man heard."

"What!" Mrs. Grant was caught off guard. Her ire dropped like a cooling candy thermometer as Leah's comment registered.

"How long have you known this, Leah?"

"Since the rehearsal for the Spring Program in April," Leah nodded affirmative. Mrs. Grant was thunderstruck then the color of anger rose upon her face once again.

"Why am I the last one to know anything in this house!" she stormed and stepped toward her daughter. "You could have told me instead of letting me make a fool of myself encouraging him to date you!"

"Doris!" Cole Grant intervened in a firm tone. "Let's all calm down."

Doris pinched her lips together, her eyes sparked her fight to submit and let the anger go. She moved to a chair and sat down beside her husband. Rachel stood at the doorway to the kitchen.

"Rachel, your Mom, Leah and I have something to talk about. Please leave us for a while." He smiled then motioned Leah to sit down at the table as well.

"I believe you have something to tell your mother and me."

Doris opened her mouth to speak, but her husband raised his hand for silence. "We need to hear what Leah has to say."

"I have been corresponding with a man by the name of Thad Tucker since the first of March." Leah began sincerely glad to set things straight. "We met through a dating service. He's from Alaska and I believe his desire from the start of our correspondence has been to find a wife. He's a good and honest man as his letters will confirm if you want to read them, Dad." She offered sincerely. "I told him I'd like to come up for a visit sometime and he invited me to come as a guest. I've already made arrangements to stay with a missionary family for the entire month's stay. I have no intention or desire to put myself or him in any compromising situation. If our relationship continues, I will marry him just like you have taught us girls. I'm to leave the fourteenth of August and fly to Anchorage to meet him."

"Can't he come and visit you here, Leah?" Dad Grant reasoned.

"No. His business keeps him far too busy to take time off in mid-summer, Dad. If I'm going to marry him, I have to know if I can live in Alaska, first."

"Do you think his intentions truly are to marry you, Leah?" He asked directly. Leah swallowed.

"Although he has not asked me to marry him yet, I can honestly say his plans seem headed in that direction, Dad."

"Is Thad Tucker a Christian man?" Leah's Dad asked knowing the spiritual lack in Leah and saw her lips tighten in response.

"No, he's not." He answered for her. With a heavy heart and voice he continued. "You understand how dangerous this is for you, Leah? You have no idea what you're walking into or what could happen to you. Do you know if he smokes, drinks alcohol, or has been with other women?" His eyes reddened as tears filled them. "We'd be too far away, sweetheart, if you needed us." Doris took up the offense.

"You'd willingly break your father's heart to do this, wouldn't you, Leah? Say nothing of our family's ministry reputation. I can't sit here any longer and listen to this...this foolishness. You're being foolish, Leah!" With this last remark, Leah's Mom stood and left the kitchen. Dad Grant sat quietly regarding his youngest daughter. Memories of her love of horses and all things wild and wacky caused him to review their adventures together. With all his heart he didn't want to see her go so far away, but there was nothing here for her adventurous, often reckless spirit.

"Leah, the success or failure of our ministry isn't dependent upon your actions, past or present. Yes, it will be disappointing and certain people will enjoy our family's little catastrophe for a while, but God knows all things. You celebrated your twenty-eighth birthday in May. You're old enough to make your own decisions. I wish you had the Lord Jesus to help you, but I have faith you will come to know Him as Savior and Lord of your life. You know I will be praying for you and for this man's salvation as well." He paused to reach for a Bible the family kept at the table for family devotions when there was opportunity to gather.

"I want to give you some words of wisdom from the scriptures if I may." Leah nodded her encouragement. Her pastor dad opened to Genesis chapter twenty-four and read the entire sixty-seven verses aloud to Leah. It was the account of Abraham sending his servant to find a worthy bride for his son, Isaac. After reading this portion, Pastor Grant smiled at Leah timorously.

"Right about now I feel like Rebekah's dad, Bethual. Some stranger from a faraway place needs a worthy wife and you are apparently the one who will be leaving your home to go to him. I'd say he will make you his bride by the looks of things. I've never met him so I don't know anything about him other than the fact that you mother had the same look on her face as you do on yours when I asked her to marry me. I can see by your determination that you're going to meet your Isaac, because, like Rebekah, you're not wasting any time about it." He directed with raised eyebrows. Leah's mouth curved upward in agreement.

"Are these some of his letters to you?" he pointed.

"Yes. Would you like to read some of them?"

"Yes. I'd like to read a few of them and the one that caused all the commotion about you leaving for Alaska." Leah handed several letters over and her dad spent several minutes reading them. There was a thoughtful expression on his face as he looked up at Leah.

"He makes a statement to the affect his mother is apparently a Christian and faithfully attends a Bible Church in Phoenix."

"Yes. I told him about our church and asked him if there were any similar churches I could attend in Palmer."

Dad Grant folded the letter and replaced it in the envelope.

"I can see by this letter Thad Tucker is looking forward to your coming as much, if not more, than you are looking forward to going to see him." He could not help but smile as he remembered how it had been with him and Doris.

"Let me read the last few verses to you again."

"And Isaac went out to meditate in the field at the eventide, and, behold the camels were coming. And Rebekah lifted up her eyes, and when she saw Isaac, she lighted off the camel. For she had said unto the servant, 'What man is this that walks in the field to meet us?' And the servant had said, 'It is my master,' therefore she took a veil, and covered herself. And the servant told Isaac all things that he had done. And Isaac brought her into his mother Sarah's tent, and took Rebecca and she became his wife: and he loved her: and Isaac was comforted after his mother's death.

"As with Rebecca, you too, have a veil to wear until you are declared husband and wife. If he is an honorable man, he will respect your chastity. It will secure the love, devotion, and respect you have for each other long after your wedding day." He was earnest. "This will be the test for both you and Thad, Leah. You'll have to be as responsible as Rebekah was when she covered her face. By doing this, she was saying two things. One, she was saying to Isaac that she was a woman of worth and purity and, second, she was betrothed to Isaac and not available for consideration by any other man." He squinted and frowned. "What is expected of a woman is also expected of a man. If Thad does not respect the standards you have kept throughout your life or if he has wandering eyes for other women, he doesn't deserve what God has fearfully and wonderfully made-namely, you!"

Leah regarded her dad's words long after he'd said them. She understood what her dad was saying. Although she felt she could trust Thad, she didn't exactly know how their situation would seal this trust in a marriage commitment. She wondered how God would fit into the scheme of things. It surprised her that her dad believed she would come to faith.

"Dad, can you give me a blessing as I go?"

"Yes, but not in going because I don't agree with the method you used to leave your home, your family, and the faith you have been taught since childhood. However, the blessing I will speak over you as my daughter is from Ephesians 1:15-23. May God grant you and Thad the blessings of faith, love, and peace in the knowledge of His Son, Jesus Christ. Christ's saving faith is life's greatest blessing. It is the blessing of eternal Salvation. I hope in time you and Thad will receive this blessing for Christ's sake, not man's approval."

There was so much to consider all of a sudden. The dreaded confrontation had turned out much better than she dared hope. Leah longed for someplace to go where she would be free to find such blessings without the watchful eyes and condemning mouths. That it was to be Alaska and possibly a small log cabin in the middle of another world make it all the more inviting.

CHAPTER 7

I'LL FLY AWAY

MONDAY ARRIVED FOR LEAH'S TRIP TO Alaska. The stress of the past week nearly exhausted her courage but hope fueled her enthusiasm. Denise helped her repack a carryon with last minute items such as a toothbrush and toothpaste; the last items of her hygiene routine after dressing. Leah was a flurry of activity to the point that Denise had to remind her to breathe!

"Oh, Denise, how will I have the courage to walk out the front door?"

"Leah, you just put one foot in front of the other and keep the rhythm going." Denise encouraged with a quick hug. "If you need me, just give me a call and I'll come right away. I have a little money of my own stashed away for such an occasion. Actually, I wish I could go, too. I wonder if that J.C. is still single?"

"Call him," Leah suggested.

"Nah. I'm trying to make it work this time with Jack. Three strikes and I'll be out! Jack as much as said so. That stinker even hinted to there being other fish in the sea."

"You sound a little subdued." Leah noticed with concern.

"I'm rethinking a lot of things lately, especially in light of your situation. Thad seems like a really nice guy and it's obvious you think so.

Whenever you speak of him, it's with respect and admiration. You seem more secure in your friendship than Jack and I have ever been."

"There's no Corvette in your future if you decided to end your relationship." It was meant as a tease, but Denise didn't seem to care.

"Corvette. What's a Corvette when there's little love to go with it? I'm beginning to see that what you and Thad have is more meaningful. I'd rather live in a shack with lots of love than a mansion full of loneliness."

"Well, I'm going to be living in a little cabin. Thad's never said much about the place where he lives other than that it is indeed a cabin he shares with a friend of his called Taima and his sister, Alma. So, I've kind of pictured the *Little House on the Prairie* type homestead in my mind." Leah offered with unseen acceptance. She felt like a pioneer woman--but hoped for indoor plumbing.

"Like I said, if you need me, just call me." Denise urged and finished shutting the suitcase as Leah rechecked her duffel bag for all the letters Thad had sent her. She wanted them handy to reread as she made the journey to Alaska.

There were a few tense moments as good-byes were said. Leah's Mom wasn't there to see her youngest daughter off to Alaska, but her Dad gave her a hug while encouraging her to read the Bible he had given her. It was the one from which he'd studied and preached for many years. This precious gift Leah packed carefully with Thad's letters. Sarah and little Angie were there to hug Leah and wish her a safe trip and happy visit though Sarah understood Leah probably wouldn't return for a long time. There were tears all around the little group as Denise picked up Leah's travel bags and began to move toward the door.

"We need to go, Leah."

"I'll call you if I need anything." Leah assured with a lingering look of sincerity and meaning at her Dad. He managed a tight lipped smile but could not speak.

"Good-bye, everyone!" Leah attempted to be cheerful as she left through the front door and followed Denise. The click of her heels on the concrete sidewalk sounded like a rhythm and, as Denise had told her, Leah kept that rhythm going as she walked to Denise's red Mustang.

When Denise dropped her off at the main doors of the Delta Air terminal at the Pittsburgh airport, they said quick good-byes. Both sensed this trip would change their friendship somehow. Each would be traveling in opposite directions with thousands of miles between visits.

"Take care, girlfriend. If you need me…"

"I'll call you!" Leah smiled. Her heart was gradually growing lighter. She was on her way to see Thad. "I'll be fine, Denise. Thanks!" Leah waved and stepped away from the curb to pick up luggage then turn to enter the busy airport. Moving to a place where she could retrieve her ticket information from her purse, she glanced at the clock on the wall then hurried to the check-in counter. Her luggage disappeared behind leather flaps as the ticket agent handed her the boarding passes and gave directions to the correct terminal and gate. The long walk to the gate was a pleasant one. Leah had never flown before and noting the Jetson décor of the modern airport made this new experience feel VIP. Outside the continental United States, a flight to distant Alaska could make one feel like a world traveler. By the time Leah reached Gate B36, the plane was in the final stages of boarding. She must have looked a little dubious, because a ticket agent looked her way with a smile and pointed to a line of passengers waiting to embark. She passed through a metal detector then handed her boarding pass to a uniformed attendant. A black marker strike was made on her pass and Leah walked through the doorway and down a long narrow tunnel to the plane's gangway. A smiling stewardess greeted her and directed her to a window seat as indicated on the boarding pass.

After putting the duffel bag in the compartment above the seat and tucking her purse under a forward seat, Leah settled back and looked out the window of the plane at all the activity below. First-experience excitement filled her as suitcases of every size and color were being thrown onto a conveyer belt moving up into the plane's underbelly. Twenty minutes later, the plane accelerated down the runway with a powerful force that gently pushed Leah back into her seat as it lifted off and climbed steadily into the blue morning sky. There were a few slight rattles here and there along with the whoosh of wind against the sides of the plane. The plane banked to the right then climbed again for a few seconds until it gradually leveled off above the clouds. Leah turned to look at the view of the retreating airport as it appeared smaller and distant before clouds blocked her sight. She smiled broadly at the feeling of being so far above the earth. The sun showered rays of golden sunshine over the top of pudgy clouds. They looked like cotton balls all snagged together to make a pillow cushion to catch the plane if it fell. Leah entertained this thought for a brief moment and quickly decided to reach for a travel magazine instead.

The pilot introduced the crew to the passengers before giving the status of the flight and the designated time of arrival in Atlanta, Georgia. Leah would change planes in Atlanta and fly directly to Anchorage. It was time to sit back, relax, and collect her harried thoughts. The last week had been an emotional roller coaster and, at the moment, she wasn't sure whether to laugh or cry. It had taken a good deal of fortitude to withstand the constant onslaughts of her mother's disapproval. But with each barbed comment, Leah's resolve to visit Thad had grown. Wednesday had been an emotional nightmare on which she chose not to dwell. She couldn't have stayed even if she'd backed down and canceled the trip. It had been time to leave over a year ago, but with no plans or place to go, Leah had remained and waited for some kind of direction. Never would she have guessed that a bachelor in Alaska would provide such a change of direction.

His letters she reviewed randomly, remembering the significance in each of those reread about his hunting and fishing trips with clients. Alaska was clearly Thad's favorite place on the globe. All the buttons he'd sent were in a zip-lock bag in one of her suitcases. She smiled at the thought of going to Palmer to sew buttons on Thad's shirts.

As she thought on their several months of letters and phone calls, a wonder filled her at how everything seemed to come together. For a moment, she considered God and what He was doing. She did not sense His punishment, but a purpose rather than a demand for her faith in Him. When the clouds thinned and released the plane into the clear, blue skies once again, the green fields and meandering paths below curried a desire to find and follow God. Leah was amazed to see the checkerboard patterns of farm crops. The roads looked like brown and gray knitting yarn scattered in all directions. A feeling of great relief came to Leah as the plane flew over the earth. It was as if she had left troubles far behind and was moving towards a northern light beckoning rebirth. This was right and, for once, she recognized the hand of God moving her towards a Savior to whom she'd sung Christmas Carols since childhood. She was considering God for Himself without comparing Him to those whom she viewed as pretenders.

Thad surveyed the sky then the river. It was a cloudless azure blue August sky that was reflected over the waters beneath the fishing boat. He looked at his watch and figured Leah was in the air in route to Anchorage by now. She'd hopefully left Pittsburgh at 6:30 a.m. At around 10:30 she'd have been in Atlanta changing planes for the six hour flight to Anchorage. It was now about 1:30 in the afternoon--his time--and he figured given the two hour layover in Atlanta, Leah should arrive at about 7:30, Anchorage time. A smile ran across his face. Leah would be in Palmer tonight. So far, everything was going fine. Tyrone was along to take over his post as fishing guide after lunch. Their two executive clients also knew about Leah's arrival and had enjoyed reminding him of the time every so often. Thad would barely have enough time to shower, shave, and change into fresh clothes before driving to the airport to meet his pen pal bride to be. He usually didn't look at his watch or even wear one, but today was different. Tyrone noticed and smiled.

"Maybe Leah knows of a real nice single lady for me."

"Could be. I know she has a best friend named Denise who lives in Chicago. Apparently, Denise's Dad is one of Chicago's finest."

"I'll have to ask Leah about her." Tyrone said aloud.

They chatted on until noon when the four men stopped to cook their fish over an open fire on the shore. At 2:30 they headed back upstream towards the two Chevy Suburbans parked a distance of fifteen miles upstream. It was not all that far until the boat motor decided to spit and sputter then smoke. Thad moved quickly to check the problem as it sparked. He shut it off and heard the awful sound of a crackling, smoldering engine. The odor of burnt engine oil assaulted his nose. He surveyed the area and realized they were only about halfway back to the vehicles.

Gurgling water and a sea crane screeching joyously above them were the only other sounds heard. Nobody said a word for several moments while they evaluated this new development.

"Scre-e-e-ech, schre-e-e-ech!" The huge white bird cried.

"If I only had a gun handy," Tyrone muttered, "I'd shoot that bird!"

"Well, we'd better get the boat over to the bank. It's already drifting back downstream." Thad said as he shook his head in resignation.

"I've got to get back to the Sub to phone Taima and let him know what's up. There's no way I can call from here. The cell phone is dead in this area." So saying, all four men set to work. Two rowed against the strong current of the Talkeetna River until they were able to bump the boat beside the steep bank. One steered and the other bailed water. With effort they unhooked the burnt motor and set it aside. Thad and Tyrone would have to come back and get it with a four-wheeler and small utility trailer later. The boat was a simple twelve foot skimmer and was made of lightweight fiberglass. At least it was lightweight until it had to be carried over seven miles of rough terrain.

"Thad, you go on ahead." Tyrone directed. "Don and Richard will help me carry this. You get to the Sub and call Taima or Alma, then come back and help us."

"Go ahead," the two clients encouraged. Thad moved on ahead.

He reached the Sub by 4:30 and called Taima at the Trading Post from the cell phone. The phone kept cutting out the whole time Thad attempted to talk with Taima.

"She called---Atlanta---10:30." Taima shouted. Thad didn't know whether she had arrived or left Atlanta.

"Taima, I'm stuck. I can't make it to pick up Leah!" he returned at the same volume.

"What?" Taima yelled.

"I'm stuck. I can't---Leah!"

"I'll tell her---cab---trading post." Taima shouted and hung up.

"Taima!" Thad shouted hoping to ask Taima to pick Leah up at the airport for him. But he heard the word "cab" and his heart sank as he replaced the mobile phone on the console and sat for a few moments to think. He mumbled aloud.

"Why today?" He looked up and heard the screech of a bird above. "It can't be the same bird!" Leaving the Sub behind, he started back to assist the other men.

Right at 7:30 p.m. Leah's plane landed at Anchorage International Airport. Thad and Tyrone were just finishing cinching the straps around the skimmer they'd loaded onto the boat trailer. It would take them a half hour to drive to Palmer from their present location. Thad could have left the skimmer at the boat dock there, but a mishap on the trail had necessitated repairs to the skimmer as well. What a day this had turned out to be and it wasn't over, yet! These last four hours had been passed within the realm of "Alaska Time." Thad didn't know what to think other than to hope that somehow Taima would either pick Leah up or get word to her that he couldn't meet her at the airport. But, it wasn't like Taima had Alma to cover the Trading Post for him today. She had several errands to run getting supplies for the cabin and Leah's visit.

Thad couldn't do a thing but hope Leah would understand.

When Leah landed in Anchorage, her stomach was in knots at the prospect of seeing Thad. She had done just fine until taking off from Atlanta. Then she'd realized that in a few short hours she'd be meeting Thad for the first time face to face. A glance at a clock in the terminal showed it was 7:45 p.m. while her wristwatch showed 3:45 Eastern Time. The sun was as bright as noon day. Thad had written that Alaska was the "Land of the Midnight Sun". Leah felt like it had been a very long day already. Now she looked around for Thad and didn't see him.

"I wonder where he could be?" she mumbled aloud. "Maybe he was delayed." She sat down nervously, then thought to go pick up her luggage. After retrieving her suitcases and setting them all together near a waiting area, she moved to a phone booth to call Thad's cell phone, but couldn't get through. The second call was to the cabin, but there was no answer there, either. Leah swallowed and thought for a moment. A number for the Trading Post was obtained from an operator and Taima's voice brought instant relief.

"Taima, this is Leah Grant. Boy! Am I glad to hear your voice! I'm at the airport here in Anchorage. Is Thad on his way?"

"No. He can't make it. You'll need to get a cab to Palmer and come to the Trading Post." Taima couldn't detect an irritation in Leah's voice when she replied.

"Oh! Okay. I'll see you at the Trading Post then!"

"Okay." He hung up. Taima grinned slightly. Miss Grant was glad to hear his voice. It must have been a long journey.

The receiver clicked off before Leah could say "good-bye". She was happy to speak to anyone who might know Thad at this point. His not being there to pick her up made her a little bit wary. Having decided she would stay in Alaska and find a teaching position if things didn't work out with Thad, Leah walked over to a Delta information cube and canceled the return plane ticket. Though she believed everything would work out just fine, Denise's history and her Dad's counsel had encouraged her to have a backup plan ready. An Internet inquiry revealed there were several public and private schools in the area to which she could apply for a teaching or aid position if necessary. With these thoughts in mind, Leah carefully considered the path she had chosen and wondered how Thad's presence would affect her life and their relationship. She also realized that careful thought and chaos were sometimes stirred together in the same cup of life.

The cab ride to Palmer started as a quiet one. Anchorage was a mix of native Alaskan influence and international culture blended with American contribution and independence. Leah studied the people of this arctic state as they stood at intersections waiting for bus rides or crosswalk signals. The diversity of culture could clearly be seen as Chinese, Russian, Eskimo, Scandinavian, African America, and Polynesian waited together for a few moments in time. Though newly arrived, Leah was now a part of them as she passed by them. To others, diversity might be disconcerting, but to Leah who'd felt singled out as a preacher's daughter, this diversity of people meant that Alaska had room for her if she chose to take up space here. In the moment, Alaska welcomed her home.

Mountain chains rose to her left as the taxi picked up speed on the six-lane Glenn Highway. The height of the mountains rose above thin filmy clouds to hold her gaze and cause her heart to be glad she had made the long journey. Signs with unfamiliar names like Eagle River and Eklutna passed amid tall stands of thin scrub pine and dwarfed evergreen trees. Birch trees with bright yellow leaves blended into the rugged northwestern landscape and added layers of glory along the base of rocky heights. It was autumn already. Leah had gone from summer to early autumn in less than twenty-four hours!

When the mile sign for Palmer came into view, Leah checked the distance given as eighteen miles on the Old Glenn Highway and fourteen miles on the present four-lane highway. She asked the cab driver about the four-mile difference and his easy reply was, "This way will cost you less to get to Palmer."

"I'll bet the more expensive route will take longer, too," Leah figured and the driver laughed.

"Is this your first visit to Alaska?"

"Yes."

"If you look over to your left, you'll see a mountain called Susitna or the Sleeping Lady. If you look closely you can see what looks like the form of a sleeping woman. Legend has it an Indian maiden loved a warrior who went off to battle. To make the time pass, she laid down to sleep. He was to awaken her when he returned. Obviously, he hasn't returned, yet, although we've had a few earthquakes that have stirred the Sleeping Lady."

"That's so sad," Leah was mortified because at the moment she knew exactly how this Indian maiden felt!

"Are you visiting family in Palmer?"

"No. I'm visiting a friend," she answered simply not wanting to divulge information to a stranger. She guessed the cab driver must be in his mid-fifties by the salt and pepper gray of his hair and mustache.

"My name is John and my family and I live in Palmer," he went on. "My wife has taught fourth-grade at Sherrod Elementary for nine years. Our children are grown and both our son and daughter live in the Sutton area with their families. That's about fourteen miles further northeast of Palmer. We've lived here for almost fifteen years and love it. I was stationed in Alaska at Elmendorf Air Force Base when our kids were young. When I retired from the military eleven years ago, we promised ourselves we'd settle here and we've never regretted it."

"I hope to live here, too," Leah offered feeling comfortable with sharing now she was in the company of someone who had a fellow teacher in the family.

"If you don't mind my asking, is your friend a fellow?" he inquired upbeat.

"Yes. We've corresponded for several months. I decided to come up and sew the buttons back on his shirts for him." Leah added lighthearted.

"It sounds like he needs help."

"Well, I'm hoping so." Leah smiled bashfully. Railroad tracks ran beside the four-lane highway off to her right. Could this be the Old West with Indians chasing trains? Of course this thought was absurd but for an easterner who was viewing the western frontier for the first time, those images seemed to fit the scenery!

"We've got a lot of Alaska bachelors up here." John laughed, "It reminds me of that crazy George Endicott Show last fall. My wife and I watched it and got quite a hoot out of it!"

Leah shot a glance at the cab driver and looked down hoping he didn't recognize her, too! 'Did absolutely everyone watch that stupid show?' she thought with amazement!

"Well, good luck, Leah, and welcome to the city of Palmer."

"We're in Palmer?" Leah couldn't believe it. There were no tall buildings or crowds of people. She reasoned that "city" here wasn't the same as "city" back home.

"This is the outskirts of Palmer. Several farms surround Palmer. There's quite a history of agriculture centered here. Off to your right are the Alaska State Fairgrounds. There's lots of activity all over the fairgrounds this week in preparation for its start. It's quite a nice little fair for this district." John said with unmistakable pride.

"I hope we'll have the opportunity to go to the fair."

"Who's your fellow, if I may ask?"

"Thad Tucker. He and his partner, Tyrone Johnson, are hunting and fishing guides."

"Oh, Thad!" John burst out. "I know Thad real well. I've taken several of his clients to and from the airport." He checked the rear-view mirror for a good look at Leah and smiled. He could see she was surprised.

"It's a small world," she reckoned.

"It is, indeed! We are a rather small community of family and friends." John winked as he pulled into the parking area in front of Thunder's Trading Post.

Chapter 8

Wolfe Tucker's Bride Arrives

Leah's first impression of Thunder's Trading Post was surreal. It was as if they'd entered the Old West via a time warp someplace between Palmer and the trading post. Hitching posts lined the front of the long log cabin and Leah expected to see horses tied to them instead of cars parked in front. The building was not fancy by East Coast standards, but it looked in good repair and the porch, which was clean swept, ran the full length of the rustic cabin.

The pricy fare from Anchorage to Palmer reminded her that this wasn't the Old West after all. It took some effort to keep the shock from registering on her face as she paid the steep taxi fare while managing a gracious smile. John saw the surprise and smiled with understanding.

"Alaska is an expensive place to live for sure; but the scenery and frontier opportunities make up for the cost in the long run. At least my wife and I think so. Still, it takes a little getting used to when a person first comes to Alaska. Don't worry, you'll adjust in time," he said with confidence as he moved from the vehicle to unload the suitcases. Leah pondered the fact she would be staying in Alaska for a long time. Taking a deep breath of the fresh cool air made her feel a little heady for a brief moment. Thad had mentioned this sensation might occur until the body adjusted to the higher levels of oxygen.

"I wonder if, indeed, I'll be staying in Palmer?" She spoke the thought out loud. John glanced at her as he lifted the last suitcase from the trunk and set it on the gravel beside the others.

"We Alaskans figure there are visitors who come to Alaska we hope will not stay long. Then, there are those who come to visit that we hope will make their home here with us. Leah, I'm hoping you're coming home today. Good luck!"

"Thank you, John. I'll hope to see you again, then." John nodded and a few moments later the taxi turned back onto the Glenn Highway and headed south leaving Leah to stand in front of the trading post feeling suddenly awkward and unsure of her next step.

Denise's words echoed in her head and Leah realized the only way into the trading post to meet Thad was to take the first step forward and "keep the rhythm going." Mustering all her courage and a great deal of physical strength, Leah drew the duffel bag straps over her left shoulder and put a small travel case under one arm. Next, her purse strap was pulled over the other arm before she picked up one large suitcase and laid a clothes bag over that arm. The other large suitcase was hoisted with her free hand. Leah counted three steps to the porch and judged the distance to the door while hoping not to drop the luggage in the process. Slowly, she lifted one foot then the other until both feet were solidly planted on the porch.

How she managed to get the door open was not as amazing as it was curious to Taima who watched her every move from his vantage point behind the counter to the left of the front door. He offered no help and no welcome. Why? Maybe he didn't because it was just interesting to watch her efforts.

A smile escaped his lips when Leah dropped one suitcase to open the door then shoved it through with her foot while balancing to keep the door open with her elbow. The second suitcase was next to slide through the narrow opening. She managed to keep the heavy clothes bag from falling, but only for a few seconds. When her purse strap caught the door handle, Leah was pulled backwards and the clothes bag slipped to the plank floor. Taima stifled laughter when he heard her muttering.

"I wonder where the help is around here…"

A small travel case was pushed through the door and bumped the large suitcases. By now, Leah was inside the door but the luggage prevented her from going any further. Indeed, she had gone as far as she could go! At this point a sigh escaped the damsel in distress and Taima figured it was time to come to the rescue to prevent further peril. She looked up to see a man coming towards her whom she hoped was Taima.

He looked at the woman before him and saw a pleasant smile of greeting accompanied by sparkling chocolate-brown eyes. He had not been prepared for the fact that the FAX picture had done her a grave injustice. Thad hadn't shown him the recent school pictures she'd sent in June either. All Taima could think was, 'Not bad for Pittsburgh!'

"Hello! You must be Taima. I'm Leah Grant. Is Thad Tucker here?"

Leah offered her hand and Taima shook it awkwardly. He hated to admit it, but Thad's prospective bride had charmed him instantly and he could not have been more annoyed nor could he stop the gruff retort that escaped from his lips.

"Thad Tucker?" he barked. "We call him Wolfe Tucker around here, Miss Grant!" At once he saw the anxiety in Leah's face.

"Wolfe Tucker?" Leah asked softly as vivid images course rapidly through her tired mind. Thad had never told her about any such nickname. And yet, she vaguely remembered hearing that name somewhere before, but couldn't figure out why it sounded familiar.

"Wolfe," she repeated with squinted eyes.

"Yah!" Taima huffed with a crocked grin. He realized he was behaving badly, but he couldn't help having a little fun with the new arrival. He motioned Leah to follow as he picked up two of the suitcases blocking the stores entrance. Leah followed him to the rear of the store where he placed her suitcases next to a chair. A potbellied stove had a small fire burning in it and crackled a warm welcome to Leah. There were several other chairs of various shapes and sizes around the stove giving the impression that the trading post was a meeting place for news and gossip.

"Wolfe and Tyrone should be back any time now, so you won't have too long to wait."

He regarded her for a moment as she put her other bags on another chair, and wondered if Thad had any idea of what he would find waiting by the stove. Taima might even wish he had someone waiting for him. But he was an old man with a story of his own. At one time he'd wondered if this Leah would appreciate Thad. Now he wondered if Thad could comprehend what just flew in from Pittsburgh!

He offered Leah some coffee that was scalding hot and very strong. She felt the indigestion rise to her throat instantly and knew an antacid tablet would be a necessity, maybe even two of those soothing tablets! After a few sips, Leah gingerly cleared her throat and asked to use the phone. Taima showed her to his office and she attempted to call the missionary family to let them know she was in town and would be over to meet them that evening. But, there was no answer at their residence either.

"There doesn't seem to be anyone at home in Palmer right now." Leah replaced the phone, puzzled.

"If those people aren't able to accommodate you, Wolfe will see that you have a place to stay at the cabin," Taima assured Leah. She swallowed with some difficulty not totally due to the strong coffee and changed the subject not knowing what she would do if the missionary family couldn't provide housing for the month. The arrangements would be tenuous either way.

"Why is he called Wolfe?" she asked curious. Taima wasn't going to answer that one. "That is something you can ask him sometime."

The door opened and a customer entered to Taima's relief. He excused himself and left Leah to explore her new surroundings before sitting down on a wooden chair near her luggage. On a table in one corner was an Espresso coffee machine and a Cappuccino coffee maker that looked to be relatively new and used a good deal. These two items seemed to be the only modern conveniences in the store. The trading post smelled of leather, burnt coffee grounds, spices, and wood smoke. Leah had never seen so much hunting and fishing equipment in her life. She looked for something familiar and recognized a wall display of cowboy hats that always reminded her of horses. In this strange new place, old memories stirred that had been safely stored away from frequent recall.

Leah fingered the beadwork on her leather purse as if this would pull her thoughts from the past to the present. But even the beads spoke of finer moments in her life and prompted the memory of a special horse she'd loved to ride. It was as if the trading post, with all its smells and hunting regalia urged a person to share daydreams and stories with friends and listening log walls.

Taima's voice drifted back to her secluded spot but Leah didn't catch too much of the conversation. She studied the cowboy hats on display and wondered if Thad wore one while riding a horse. Some of his letters had been about experiences with horses on a ranch in Arizona, but he never mentioned anything about riding. One letter Leah had written to Thad was about a beloved horse she'd groomed and ridden during high school years. But she hadn't gone into too much detail. In the solitude of these moments as Leah waited for the future to take shape, the memory of a horse named Sunrise pulled her back to a frigid day in February years ago when her world had fallen apart. For a while the trading post faded into yesterday as Leah sat mesmerized by the fire dance in the potbellied stove.

The year of 1984 had been one of the coldest winters on record in western Pennsylvania. The church academy was closed because the ancient furnace exploded with the overwhelming effort to heat the old buildings. As a result the water pipes burst in the sub-zero temperatures and left two inches of solid ice over the tiled floors. A sixteen year old Leah and her two sisters ice-skated in the church basement until space heaters thawed the floor enough for mops and buckets. However, a greater catastrophe occurred when Leah's twenty-five year old Arabian trail horse named Sunrise, contracted pneumonia.

Six years prior, Dad Grant had taken Leah to Bailey's Horse Ranch for riding lessons on Christmas day when she was ten. The present of a horse had been her only request and he made the arrangements for her to be around the horses she loved so well. When she saw Sunrise looking over the fence and wagging his long tail gaily, she took to him immediately and they had been inseparable. Between school, piano lessons, and Sunrise, there had been no time for anything but church services and home chores.

"It's pneumonia." Doctor Wagner confirmed regretfully. "I'm sorry, Mr. Bailey." He addressed the horse's owner and then attempted to reason with Leah. "I'm sorry, Leah." Sadness filled his haggard voice. "I can't offer you any hope. I've done all I can to help Sunrise get better." His voice trailed off as he noted the unbelief and accusation in Leah's brown eyes. He could see she'd expected him to do the miraculous.

Leah turned away from Dr. Wagner, bent down and knelt by the suffering Sunrise. Tears of disappointment and anger gathered then spilled down her cheeks. She didn't want others to see her pain and anger.

"Leah," her Dad moved toward her, "Sunrise is very sick. Dr. Wagner thinks it would be best to—"

"No!" Leah shouted. "I'll stay with Sunrise. I'm not going to give up on him, Dad!"

The determination in her voice and eyes dared anyone to challenge her resolve. He stepped back to consider her defiant response and checked his own reaction, first. At sixteen years of age and a senior in the academy, his youngest daughter still looked far too young to be giving the valedictorian's speech at graduation in four months and going off to college at the end of the summer. Leah's Dad saw a child in the process of embracing womanhood, yet reluctant to cater to its natural demands. Her eyes pleaded for lenience. He was grieved by her disrespect for the doctor and himself, but returned mercy.

"I'll get some blankets for you, Leah." Tight lipped, Dad Grant turned from his daughter, but not before he saw the gratefulness flash across her relieved face.

"Thanks, Dad," she replied quietly and turned to attend to Sunrise with soothing strokes and words of friendship and comfort.

"I'll be handy if you need me, Lady Leah," he used the affectionate nickname. Leah didn't look up, just nodded.

"There now, Sunrise. We'll get through this just like all the other times when we've had our adventures." Leah paused to think for a moment before continuing to talk to her horse. A smile formed on her lips.

"Do you remember the first time I rode you, boy? Sure you do," she answered for him and patted the side of his cheek tenderly. Sunrise snorted in response.

"I was scared to death of you the first time I stood next to you. I had wanted a horse so badly and even dreamed of having a horse so much that when I finally got one, I didn't know what to do. You must have known that, too." Leah had laughed.

"All the other kids knew how to ride their horses and then there was me. You were saddled and ready to go, but I wasn't. The other kids took off and I commanded you to 'giddy-up!' But you didn't move an inch. And it was a good thing because if you had taken off, I wouldn't have stayed in the saddle very long."

Leah's giggle was light and girlish. Even Sunrise moved his head at the familiar sound of her joy.

"So, we just sat there. You didn't move an inch and I didn't encourage you either. You know, Sunrise, we must have sat there in the same spot for over an hour, so we did." Her ponytail had bobbed up and down.

"When the other student riders returned, I sat tall in the saddle looking very confident and in control. They asked me how I'd gotten back to the gate before any of them. Well, I had no intention of telling them we hadn't moved one inch from the place where we stood. That would have looked bad for both of us, you know." Leah patted Sunrise proudly. "So, when they insisted, I just smiled and said, 'Fast horse!' Sunrise snorted and twitched his ears as Leah laughed merrily.

"Well, I think they got wise to both of us when I tried to dismount and required Mr. Bailey's help untangling the reigns and stirrup from around my ankle." A shiver coursed through Sunrise and Leah gently stroked the suffering horse. His intense suffering startled her, made her short of breath as though her heart had been squeezed as his life was being pulled out of hers. She felt incredible loss. Leah knew Sunrise would not stand again: but still she breathed for him, willing life to return in full.

Through that blustery cold night, Leah spoke quietly of their adventure together until she could no longer stay awake. Sleep overcame her as the snow blanketed the land beyond the stable. The sound of Sunrise's staggered breathing grew faint as Leah's breathing became sweet and steady. When she awoke, Sunrise was gone. Tears fell from Leah's eyes as acceptance formed hardness in her heart.

She wept over the horse until her Dad pulled her gently away and moved her from the stable. Mr. Bailey patted her arm as she moved past him.

"Sunrise has lived a longer happier life because of you, Leah. I know this for sure." His raspy voice was filled with emotion.

"Thank you, Mr. Bailey." Leah mumbled cold and numb from sorrow.

"Come on, Lady Leah," her Dad coaxed with sympathy. "God will care for His creatures just as He directs every sunrise and sunset." It was meant to comfort her with the knowledge of God's sustaining presence in all places and times, but Leah didn't see it that way.

"If this is how God takes care of His creation, I don't want Him taking care of me?" she cried in grief. "Sunrise was my happiness." Leah stormed. "He took my happiness away. What did I do wrong? I don't want to be bothered with Him!" Leah ran ahead of her Dad to the old station wagon, climbed in and slammed the door with finality.

Dad Grant regarded his daughter thoughtfully before walking to the car and climbing into the driver's seat. They drove in silence sometime before he spoke.

"Leah, please don't shut God out. Sometimes it's hard to understand that any good can come out of shocking pain and senseless loss except that suffering can draw us to a loving Creator Who will make all the wrongs we have ever suffered, right. I can't tell you when that will happen, but I know that God works all things together for good to those who commit to loving Him, even in times of unspeakable sorrow. The only way I know this is that Jesus healed all that came to Him whether they came during his earthly ministry or received saving grace in faith after He suffered, died then came back to life, triumphing over death. Jesus heals the soul. It's the most affected by sin and sorrow…" he stopped short. He glanced over at his daughter and noted her granite-like silhouette. Her hurt and resistance to spiritual things was deeper than he had figured.

"I love you, Leah. Always have and always will, daughter." He finished, yielding his love as a parent to a Higher Power.

Leah made no reply. He did not press further. Sunrise had been Leah's only friend. Most of her conversations started and ended with Sunrise. Without him, she had no one with whom she could speak the secrets of her heart in confidence. Not even God.

Unbeknown to Leah, Pastor Grant began a prayer vigil for her that cold February day. When she'd walked out the door to leave for Alaska just hours ago, he'd relived the death of Sunset all over again as a Dad.

"It looks like they're here!" Taima announced and Leah jumped back to the present. She shot a glance at the front door of the store and saw two dark-green Chevy suburbans pass by the large display window. One was pulling a boat trailer and the second followed the first.

Leah felt her stomach knot in anxious anticipation. She tried to steady nerves by taking a deep breath and releasing it slowly. There was a small bathroom off to her left and she headed there to check hair and makeup. Uncertainty filled her in this new place as she mentally waved away the cobwebs of distant memories. Then the name "Wolfe" came to mind and Leah moaned, "What have I done now?"

CHAPTER 9

THE WELCOME WAGON

THAD GLANCED AT THE DIGITAL CLOCK on the dash display while driving back toward Palmer. Tyrone followed in the second SUV with the two clients, Don and Richard, who slept peacefully after their laborious boat hike. Thad phoned back to Tyrone.

"Tyrone, I'm going to drive directly to the trading post. Leah should be there by now."

"That sounds good." He agreed.

"We'll have to trade vehicles there. You can take the boat up to the cabin after you drop Don and Richard off at the Homesteader's Inn. I'm not sure how things are going to work out at this point. I had planned to take Leah to a fancy restaurant in Anchorage, but I canceled the reservations and asked Alma to have something fixed for us." Conversation resumed after they pulled into the trading post and parked.

"She's had a long day." Tyrone commented at the same time Thad thought it.

"I know. I'd take her to a nice place to eat here in Palmer, but I'm not cleaned up at all and she'll need to check in with the family she's supposed to be staying with tonight."

"Thad, I don't think they're even in the area."

"They hardly ever are."

"Last time I knew anything about them, they were headed out into the bush villages for Bible Studies again." Tyrone offered.

"Well, I'm hoping so. I'd rather Leah stayed with us at the cabin." Thad replied with candidness as he turned into the parking lot of the trading post and went around the back with the boat and trailer in tow.

Tyrone awakened his "sleeping beauties" as he parked the suburban in front of a hitching post. They awoke with groans and moans of stiff and sore muscles. By the time Thad joined them, they were already stepping down onto the gravel and joking.

"Boy! You should have seen the one that got away!" Don Ishioti, a short man of Japanese descent teased as he stretched and yawned.

"How big was she?" Richard O'Brien joined his partner in the fun. A medium built man with short curly red hair, he had blue-green eyes and a handle bar mustache. Tyrone began shaking his head. These two guys never stopped with the joking around.

"She must have been about five feet long. What a catch she would have been!" They started up the steps. Thad figured this was for his benefit somehow.

"What color were her eyes?" Richard asked to further the fun.

"They were the color of golden marbles." Ishioti sang. His Japanese accent heightened the animated description.

"Golden marbles?" Richard enunciated.

"Yes." He replied dreamily, a smile of delight on his face.

"Well, why did you let her get away?" Richard asked incredulously.

"I saw her long whiskers and she reminded me of an old-maid school teacher I once had." Ishioti blurted and laughed loudly. Richard joined him. Neither man knew that Thad's lady friend was indeed a school teacher. Tyrone and Thad just looked at each other and smiled as they shook their heads. Once inside the store, the fishing party was greeted by Joe and Taima.

"What's the joke?" Taima inquired.

Thad shrugged as Tyrone raised both hands and said, "I'm not touching that one."

"Hey, Wolfe! How was the fishing?" Taima asked and this sent roars of laughter up from Richard and Don once again.

"That depends on which fish got away," Thad yawned, stretched, and grinned slyly then looked at Taima for direction on Leah's location.

"Yah! Only the ones that remind you of old-maid school teachers." Ishioti shrieked with laughter.

Taima nodded at Thad and pointed to the back of the store. He knew Leah was somewhere near and wondered what she might be thinking. Tyrone dismissed himself to get the suburban and boat while telling Don and Richard he'd be around front to pick them up in a few minutes. Thad quickly nodded agreement to Tyrone and looked back at Taima who simply pointed once again to the rear of the store. Thad's eyebrows rose as he looked in that general direction. He'd just turned to start back the aisle when Leah walked toward the front of the store. He blinked and swallowed in amazement.

From the small bathroom in the rear of the store, Leah had quickly brushed her hair out and was about to put the banana comb back in place when she heard a familiar voice from the front of the store. Suddenly, an attack of nervous jitters tested her calm and patience. It was now impossible to get the banana comb neatly into place, so she decided to let the long wavy tresses hang softly around her shoulders. Before turning from the mirror and walking in the direction of several male voices, Leah paused to listen for the only voice familiar to her ear.

A smile appeared on her lips when she heard Thad's response to Taima's question. He was here! Even though his voice stirred her heart song, she could only hope he resembled the photo even a little bit.

When the words, *old-maid-school-teacher*, were uttered, Leah's eyebrows rose. It was time to make her presence known. She ran her hands quickly over her sweater and skirt to brush away any wrinkles or fallen hairs then walked forward with the angst of a school teacher who'd just caught some boys in their tomfoolery. There was only the hint of a smile on her lips when she walked into plain sight.

She saw a man in knee high muddy pants and boots looking at her like he was "seeing things". He was taller than she was by at least six inches and his beard and hair were the same dark brown as hers. His eyes were hazel colored--like the picture Leah carried of one gentleman by the name of Thad Tucker. However, this man didn't look like a freshman in college. He was older and much better looking than the old snap shot—if indeed he was Thad Tucker? Her heart pounded as she tried a smile of uncertain recognition.

There was instant quiet as the other men looked beyond the stalled figure of Wolfe Tucker to the lovely lady who approached them. Taima grinned when he saw Thad's statuesque reaction to Leah.

Rational thinking left Thad wondering why Leah Grant should be here standing in front of him. Surely, she should have been married by now. Even the school pictures she'd sent hadn't done her justice and he'd liked those pictures a lot!

"Leah?" he finally managed. She walked up to him and Thad thought she was beautiful.

"Yes." She verified.

"Thad?"

"Yes." He nodded and began talking until he realized how he must look in mud-caked garb. But Leah didn't care. He was standing in front of her and he was no longer just the silhouette in a phantom dream.

"I'm sorry I couldn't get to the airport to meet you. I hope you didn't have any trouble finding a cab." Thad was genuinely apologetic. "We had a motor burn out on the fishing skimmer."

Leah smiled forgiveness and Thad felt his calm, in-control demeanor waning.

"No, I didn't have any trouble," she assured, her gaze never left his face. "I just asked the ticket agent for some directions and she was very obliging. I thought perhaps something had come up." She glanced over at Taima with raised eyebrows and a humorous expression made its way across her face. He looked guilty enough but she smiled at him in friendship.

"Taima made me feel right at home," she said with a hint of tease in her voice. Thad glanced back at Taima with a frown of puzzlement as if he'd missed something.

"Why don't you introduce her," Taima quickly urged Thad.

"Yah! We'd like to meet the one that didn't get away!" Richard piped up as he and Don stepped forward, chuckling. Thad gave Leah a cautious glance to see how she would react to teasing. She winked at Thad.

"Gentlemen, this is Leah Grant, my friend and guest. Leah, this is Richard O'Brien and Don Ishioti. They're visiting the great fishing spots of Alaska. I say 'visiting' because they keep letting the fish get away." Leah laughed at Thad's barb.

"Gentlemen," she acknowledged graciously. "It's a pleasure to meet you. When you're not letting the fish get away, how do you earn a living?"

Laughter echoed around the large room.

"We develop new computer programs and software for educational instruction." Richard answered.

"What particular programs?" Leah was interested.

"School Nanny is one of them."

"Oh, yes. I've worked with School Nanny a number of times at my job." Leah assured them.

"Oh?" they both were surprised.

"Yes. I've spent many hours reviewing the programs on this software."

"You have?" Ishioti was curious.

"What's your line of work?" O'Brien asked, hopeful of some insights on their product.

"I'm an old-maid-school-teacher," she replied smoothly, then smiled in friendship. It was not her intention to be rude. Thad glanced at Taima and saw he was shaking his head and grinning.

"Oh, boy!" O'Brien sighed. "We walked into that one, Don."

A horn beeped twice outside and O'Brien and Ishioti made ready to leave, but not before they welcomed Leah to Alaska.

"I thought you took us to the best fishing places, Thad." Ishioti teased.

"He does, you just keep letting the right ones get away." Taima returned with a grin.

"Yah! That's the story of my life," the single O'Brien joked half-heartedly.

"I hope Thad doesn't let this one get away." Ishioti commented loudly as they left the trading post. He was a happily married man with two small children. Thad smiled at Leah and saw a blush of pink rise in her face. It was too bad the Anchorage plan hadn't worked out thanks to the boat motor. A phenomenon known as "Alaska time" had thwarted those earlier plans.

"Are you hungry?" he asked.

"I'm starved." Leah answered honestly. Though the airline had served complimentary meals, she had been too excited to eat much.

"So am I. It's been a long time since lunch."

Thad told her about the hike with the motor and then his return trip to help with the boat as they walked back to get her luggage. Leah told him about her flight across the continent to points north and the ride from Anchorage to Palmer with the taxi driver named, John. Thad knew John and was relieved that Leah's experience has been a good one. Taima was shutting off the lights and closing up the trading post for the evening. He helped carry some of Leah's luggage out to the sub and waited until Thad and Leah descended the steps to the vehicle before he went back to lock the front door. They talked to each other as if continuing a conversation they'd started as neighbors over a backyard fence. The awkward start of their first meeting subsided as they became accustomed to each other's presence. The familiarity their phone conversations produced over the past several weeks helped make it easier to be a couple. Taima recognized their formation as a couple, but Leah had not yet fixed his trust.

They left the trading post to check on Leah's accommodations for the night. She mentioned she hadn't been able to reach the missionary by phone as Thad drove to the specified address.

When they pulled into the driveway, there was no sign of anyone around except for several dogs that were each chained to small doghouses at various places around the place. They barked noisily at the intruders. When Leah knocked on the door, there was no answer. A rain drenched mail package was wedged between the storm door and front door. It looked like no one had been there for a few days.

"I think this is the right address." Leah ventured when she returned to the suburban.

"It is. I think they're away, Leah."

"Well, I did have a hard time trying to make arrangements with them." Leah admitted with a sigh of resignation. Plans were changing.

"I'll see what I can find out about them for you," Thad offered helpfully.

"Thad, I'll just have to make other arrangements." Leah was in a quandary as to what to do next. Thad noticed her furrowed brow and wanted to be her hero.

He sensed her obvious concern about accommodations and offered his own happy solution.

"Leah, I've already made arrangements for you to stay with us if you would like to." He felt like everything was coming out all wrong, but he plodded on anyway. "Taima, his sister Alma, and I go back a long way to when I came back to Palmer to take classes at the university extension here. I was working on the farms in this area as part of my university studies when I met Taima and eventually Alma. We've struck up a lifelong friendship and when Tyrone and I finally established the business here in the Palmer area, Alma, Taima and I decided to go in together and build a log cabin. He and Alma help take care of the place when I'm away on excursions or doing research work for the University of Alaska and Mat-Su Community College here in the area.

"His sister is also a better cook than I am, as you will soon find out. And…at this point, Taima and Alma will also be our chaperones." Taima leaned forward from the back seat to give Leah a nod like a policeman.

Leah could do nothing else but accept Thad's hospitality.

"Alma is planning on having you, Leah. She seems to think you'll be better company than we are," Thad added. "You already know that she is speech and hearing-impaired though she can read lips way too well at times." He chuckled. "She's excited about having another woman for gossip's sake."

"Okay! I'm convinced." Leah laughed light-hearted. "Take me to your humble abode!"

Thad could see Taima grinning as much as he was. This was a pleasing turn of events; exactly as he had hoped!

CHAPTER 10

HEAVEN AND HEARTH

THAD TURNED THE CHEVY SUB ONTO the Glenn Highway and headed south into Palmer where he turned onto Arctic Avenue towards the Lazy Mountain area. Several blocks of homes formed a neighborhood around elementary schools and churches. A view of Pioneer Peak was framed by many bay windows and Leah wondered what it would be like to live in the sun-glow of this mountain every day.

"Is someone in your family deaf?" Taima asked. "I was wondering where you learned to Sign."

"There is no one in my family who is either deaf or speech-impaired. I'd seen people signing in public and wanted to learn how to do it, but I knew nothing about signing until the first two weeks of my freshman year in college. My roommate was a deaf student. She was also a freshman. You might imagine how difficult it was for two homesick freshman to communicate when I couldn't understand a word she signed and she couldn't hear a word I said. Until the dorm supervisor rearranged us and put us with roommates where we could be more comfortable, there were two things we did well together. We both cried ourselves to sleep and we drove each other crazy," Leah paused to chuckle at the college memory.

"Because she couldn't hear me coming, I usually scared her to death when I'd just kind of--show up! Of course, she had absolutely no idea how to close a door without slamming it shut. And deaf people don't tiptoe either. Anyway, we began writing little notes to one another as a means of communicating. Our friendship developed to a certain degree. After we were relocated to other dorm rooms, she encouraged me to take a beginning sign-language course. By this time, my new roommate, Denise, and I decided to take the signing class together. We had so much fun learning sign language that we eventually became competent enough to hang around our deaf friends without embarrassing them or humiliating ourselves."

"Taima, is your sister speech-impaired from birth?" She asked as they passed a white picket fence that ran along the front of Pioneer Cemetery.

"No. A childhood disease destroyed her hearing and ability to speak when she was five. Our family never had the finances to do anything more about it and really didn't know if there was something we could have done for Alma anyway. She can and does read lips better than I'd like her to sometimes," he offered with a grin. "Of course, a person has to be facing her though."

"I understand. It's good to know." Leah nodded and watched the unfamiliar landscape pass beyond the safety glass. The road curved left and right alongside the Matanuska River past local farms with large signs advertising fresh vegetables for sale. In spots the trees opened to reveal the expanding muddy river as it curved beside the road and then moved toward a distant glacier. Leah was beginning to realize that Alaska was a land of contrasts flowing together in beautiful blends of wide space and towering majesty. Silently, she watched the views change as Thad drove on and realized her heart might be changing as well. It all filled her with a peace and assurance that her recent decision to come to Alaska had not only been a life altering one, but a right one. She smiled with joy at this thought.

"The cabin is just ahead, Leah," Thad mentioned as they turned off the highway and onto a gravel drive lined on both sides with tall thin evergreens. It made a natural arbor of beauty. Leah had no idea what to expect as she peered beyond the windshield. She didn't want to ask either. All she knew was that it was a cabin. Whether it was log or wood slat, Leah couldn't have guessed. Would there be enough room for the four of them in Thad's cabin?

The driveway ascended at a thirty percent grade and continued until the trees ended on one side and they drove into a clearing. Leah saw the cabin for the first time and her eyes widened in amazement.

Cabin wasn't the right word to describe the huge modern log home. It looked like a ski lodge aptly positioned at the base of a huge mountain. Surrounded by evergreens, aspen, birch, and scrub pine, it was a grand looking place! The light wood structure was some three floors from ground level to roof and sported two large decks extending at great length from opposite ends. A walkway ran along the front while steps led up to a large double door entrance. At ground level there was a two-car garage on one end and a large den behind the garage. Landscaping around the house gave it a nestled appearance against the backdrop of a rolling spruce forest then climbed upward to craggy cliffs.

Leah was speechless. Thad drove onto the cement parking area that led to the garages below the largest deck. She had been prepared for a tiny one-room cabin made with dark, fire scorched logs, rough cut lumber floors and a drafty fireplace. Thad's cabin was more than a pleasant surprise; it was breathtaking!

Thad couldn't resist a satisfied grin at the surprise he saw on Leah's face. Taima was already out of the Sub and heading to the back to get the luggage. He spoke softly under his breath.

"It looks like she wasn't expecting to see a place like this. I hope she can appreciate it."

Leah couldn't move, so awe inspiring was this first impression of Thad's home. She was a modest woman from ordinary if not simple circumstances where the smallest luxury was relished. Leah's eyes sparkled admiration for his home building skills. Thad took the opportunity to study firsthand what he had admired by letter and phone. It still amazed him that she was finally in Alaska.

"It's picture perfect. I've never seen anything so…so lovely? I was expecting…" she stopped. Thad saw the mirth rise in her eyes as she started to laugh. Thad shook his head and smiled as he exited the Sub and opened Leah's door. She was still laughing when he offered his hand which she reached to take while scooting across the seat and moving out of the Sub.

"Oh, Thad," she attempted to talk while standing beside him. His hand still held hers. They turned to look at each other as if trying to comprehend the other's features.

"I had such unrealistic ideas of what your cabin would be like. I remember telling Denise that homemaking in an igloo wasn't for me." Leah confessed. "Of course, when Taima called you 'Wolfe', I pictured a cave and mud floors." He cocked his head in amazement. Leah burst out laughing at this incredible idea. Her laughter was light and pleasant and Thad found himself grinning at the sound. Finally, she straightened and Thad could see the tears in the sides of her eyes as she took a deep breath and sighed.

"Oh, my!" she wiped the corners of her eyes quickly. "Thad, I am overwhelmed. It's like a dream."

"I can tell." He spoke for the first time since they'd arrived. Thad saw she was making an effort to keep from laughing again.

"Now what?" he asked with a smile.

"It would take a lot of packed snow to keep the drafts out of this cabin."

"What drafts?" He couldn't figure what she was thinking and wondered if he ever would.

"My friend, Denise, said log cabins are drafty in the winter and Alaskans pack snow around the outside walls to keep the drafts out," she explained. His eyebrows rose in understanding.

"Some of them are packed with snow, yes; but not this one. I'll have to show you that kind of log cabin when I return on Sunday," he promised. At once Leah was eager.

"I'd love to see it!"

"You'd love to see it, but I'm not sure you'd love to live in it... especially after staying at this cabin." Leah did something that baffled even her. She squeezed Thad's hand in affirmation.

"I think you're right. I'm sure once I've stayed here, the drafty cabin I imagined will seem ridiculous." She dropped her eyes from his to quell the strong feelings surfacing with this last mouthful. He saw her efforts to keep emotions in check and appreciated her candidness though it took him twice the effort to restrain his own.

"I'm glad you're finally here, Leah." What he wanted to add but didn't at the moment was, now that she was here, he could take care of her. The tone of his voice revealed concern.

Leah sobered and she answered quietly. "'Finally', that's a good word, Thad. I can't begin to tell you all the events of this past week that almost kept me from coming to see you. If I try to explain as tired as I am right now, I'll start crying, then you'll really think I'm strange."

Thad saw weariness in her eyes. He'd heard it in her voice over the phone Sunday and saw it now in her countenance.

Leah spoke slowly. "I am so very glad I came, Thad. Somehow, I know I'm supposed to be here."

"So do I, Leah." He held her gaze and realized she didn't seem to be in any hurry to release his hand or draw away. This brought peace and relief to Thad. It was good to know Leah was as warm and friendly in person as she was in letters and phone calls. When she spoke to him, she looked him in the eye. As a businessman, Thad liked this very much!

"You're hungry, tired, and overwhelmed." He smiled, using Leah's own words. "And I could be a better host by seeing to it that you don't starve."

"I'm not complaining." Leah grinned.

"You're too amiable for your own good."

"I'm too tired to complain at the moment."

Thad just grinned as they took the stairs to the second level and entered the grand cabin through double oak doors.

Alma came from the kitchen to greet them. At the age of forty-four, she was several years younger than her brother, Taima. She was about the same height as Leah with a slim build and an attractive face. Her black hair was shoulder length and pulled back in a George Washington with a hair clamp of Indian design. "*Mat-Su Valley*" was arched across the front of a white long-sleeved sweatshirt she wore with blue jeans. A picture of a red barn and a mammoth cabbage were screen-printed below the name.

"Hello! I'm Alma and we're happy to have you staying here with us." A smile appeared on Alma's lips as she signed to Leah and received the same in return. Alma's eyes twinkled with friendship and welcome, so opposite her brother's welcome! Thad watched the two women who both seemed eager for friendship and acceptance.

He wondered about Leah's past week and the events that had almost kept her from coming. During one phone call she'd told him in a whisper that she had to hang up. She'd called back at three o'clock in the morning, his time, to talk. Never had she done that before. Something major had taken place. The only thing to do had been to encourage her to stick to the plans.

Taima was taking Leah's baggage upstairs and Thad grabbed the other two items and headed up after him.

"I'll take these upstairs," he moved her way and was rewarded with a smile. When she smiled, Leah's eyes were soft and filled with warmth. Nobody had ever looked at him that way!

Alma and Leah exchanged information about the trip from Anchorage to Palmer. When the men returned, Alma signed that supper would be ready after Thad cleaned up. He took the hint smiling and moved to excuse himself.

"Leah, I'll take you up to your room and show you where to put your things." Alma directed as Thad turned and spoke before exiting down the hallway.

"You ladies take your time." Leah nodded and started for the steps but not before she saw the message Alma signed to Thad.

"She will have no trouble sewing your buttons on your shirts, Thad."

Thad smiled sheepishly while Leah bit her lip to hide the pleasure of acceptance.

Alma's bedroom was next to Leah's and she showed it to Leah, first. Off to the side of the spacious bedroom, she'd had a solarium built where she kept many plants and flowers with the aid of various sun lamps to assist green growth even in winter. It overlooked the Mat-Su farmlands. Leah spoke of the funny concepts she'd had of Thad's cabin before seeing it for the first time. Alma smiled at the happy exchange of another woman's banter.

When Leah followed Alma into the guestroom, her eyes widened in amazement at the elegance and comfort displayed in every detail of the room. Touch lamps illuminated the space and gave a soft glow to cream colored walls with floral boarders in mauves and greens. Leah felt pampered and special. Alma pointed to the private bathroom with a built-in beauty table. Beyond them, a double door opened into a large walk-in closet. The bedroom furniture was of a white contemporary design with gold touches. A chaise lounge was covered in a neutral fabric that contrasted with a maroon print bedspread. Decorative pillows in a variety of shapes, coordinating colors, and prints suggested both luxury and comfort for a home built in the rugged, arctic far north. Leah never dreamed she'd sleep in such a room. Then too, memories of what she'd left behind briefly overshadowed the joy of this moment. The bedroom she'd exchanged for this one was only ten feet square with a window that could hardly be budged open in the stifling heat of the summer and had to be stuffed with towels to keep drafts out in winter. Alma noted her melancholy and wondered if she found this room underwhelming.

"Thad often read your letters to Taima and me. I hope it does not offend you."

Leah's blinked the past away with a smile and signed a quick reply. "No! Not at all. I shared a few of Thad's letters with a very close friend of mine as well. She is perhaps the only person who understood my coming to see Thad and encouraged me to put one foot in front of the other and keep the rhythm going." There was a catch in her voice. Alma touched Leah's arm softly and smiled.

"I understand your courage, Leah. So does Thad. Even Taima does although he's **a pill** about it! Still, he doesn't carry suitcases up two flights of stairs for just anybody either." Alma's eyebrows rose meaningfully. "I can't remember him ever doing that!" They both laughed.

"Thank you, Alma. I'd love to hear more about you." Leah urged. Alma waved her hand off to the side.

"My story is old news. You're the one we all want to get to know."

"Well, don't expect perfection. I'm far from it in many ways."

"Thad doesn't think so," she replied with a wink.

"Wait until he finds out I come with a list of hazards."

"It won't make any difference, I'm sure." Alma smiled. "Let me know if you need anything. I'll be down in the kitchen finishing up meal preparations."

"Thanks, Alma. This room is...," Leah's voice caught with emotion as her hands moved to sign the message of her grateful heart, "so very lovely. I never dreamed anything could give so much comfort and welcome to this weary traveler." She finished smiling happily. "I'll just freshen up and change into clean clothes after the trip."

Alma smiled both satisfied and pleased.

Remarkably, Taima took the opportunity to freshen up with the use of an electric shaver to clear one-day's growth of stubble. He had a hunch Leah would be staying and after his cool welcome decided to make the best of it for Thad's sake.

Meanwhile, Thad was maneuvering a shower and a shave with transforming results. He started with scissors, then trimmers, and on to a regular shaver. Finally, he splashed some after-shave lotion on his hands and patted smooth tender skin. The pain of a thousand bee stings surged across his sensitive face and for a few moments all he could do was moan as his eyes watered. After a while, the stinging ceased as the alcohol evaporated. Checking the part of his hair in the mirror, he wondered what Leah might think of him now that he was cleaned up. It struck him that she had not seemed bothered by the beard other than not recognizing him at first. He reasoned she probably hadn't known what to expect, yet seemed too relieved and too happy to be in Alaska to mind. A smile revealed even white teeth as he turned from the mirror to pull a maroon sweater over his head and push arms through the sleeves. One last glance in the mirror with a hand through his wavy hair to smooth it and Thad left his room to feed the fire in the stone hearth of the large modern Great Room.

Leah decided on a quick shower then changed into a long forest green velour dress with a skirt that fell from the waist in fluted panels to just above her ankles. A multi-colored headband gathered her hair away from her face while bangs and little curls hung softly about her face. Shortly after Leah finished her make-up, she took one last look in the mirror, slipped a pair of black flats on her feet, and then left the lovely sleeping chamber.

Thad stood next to a wall of windows and gazed over the big valley towards the evening sun-glow. The sky was bright in colors of orange, gold, and purple. The mountains were black silhouettes hiding snow-capped peaks until the midnight sun dipped slightly beneath them to circle the evening sky and start a new day. Thad regarded the land as God's creation although only a few years ago he would have seen it as just earth and sky. As he'd grown older, he'd begun to read his mother's religious reflections in letters with a little more interest. In letters and phone calls, Leah said things that sounded very much like his mother's offerings, except that Leah was never forceful. She seemed to talk of such things as Bible stories without being pushy. Actually, Leah had to be pressed into talking about the Bible or answering questions he'd initiated to understand the level of her religious devotion. He figured she was timid about the subject. However, there was one thing that really puzzled him. She was a Christian and he wasn't. Yet, she was here and they both had voiced ideas about marriage during phone conversations. He knew Christians were not supposed to marry non-Christians. Even his mother had mentioned something about 'an unequal yoke', or putting an ox with a horse to pull a wagon. He knew that didn't work very well.

When Leah reached the entrance, she paused for a moment to wonder where Thad might be. Everything was quiet in the kitchen so she peeked into the Great Room before entering. It was the largest living room she had ever seen. Pictures of various sizes featured wildlife and landscapes of Alaska. Each invited study. Leah's eyes moved from one picture to another around the modern room until she gazed through the window panels to the mountain vistas outside the cabin.

The experience of moving from captive scenes in wooden frames to a living masterpiece beyond window frames stirred Leah's heart with the same wonder picture books of distant places had stirred her as a little girl. Her Grandpa Houck had kept a thick travel book entitled, *Around the World in Pictures* on a shelf in the TV room. Whenever she visited his home, she'd pull the book from the shelf and study the pictures wishing to step into those places of mystery and beauty. Today, she'd stepped into Alaska. This thought made her heart glad and she wanted to dance with glee until she saw the back of a neatly groomed man standing at a large bay window. He seemed to be surveying the land intently.

Leah considered the man at the window. It had to be Thad, but she hardly believed it was. He was clean-shaven and wore pressed black dress slacks and a long sleeved maroon sweater. Leah hesitated for a moment wondering if Thad had a twin brother. He hadn't mentioned one; but he'd never mentioned the grandeur of his cabin either.

Thad turned to greet her. Leah blinked in astonishment. She began to hope this handsome man was Thad because her heart was beating rapidly.

"Wow!" was all she could say as she tried to speak without swallowing and choking at the same time.

"Thad? I hope it's you!" Leah saw that Thad was amused. She couldn't help being confused because the only picture she had of Thad was a freshman picture from college.

"It's me," he assured with a wry grin.

"Whew!" Leah exhaled. "I wasn't sure how I was going to explain YOU to Thad." He looked like a man of quality and distinction. These characteristics had drawn her to him from their first letters. Those early letters encouraged more depth of person than surface attraction. Physical attraction often hid disappointing character flaws.

Thad smiled and shook his head at her odd humor. It was nice to know he had that kind of Prince Charming effect on her. It was obvious her trip to Alaska had been the biggest event of her whole life and he knew now she hadn't been prepared for all the changes. She needed time to adjust and he needed time to get used to her sense of humor.

"Oh, forgive me, Thad. I'm not myself. I feel like a fourteen-year-old on a first date."

Thad smiled, "Well, maybe some food and a good night's sleep will help you find a sense of balance. You've had quite a day, Leah. Come on. Let's eat," he encouraged taking her hand.

Thad lead Leah to a Dining Room just off the kitchen. It was a smaller private alcove with a dark mahogany table and matching chairs. This room was totally opposite the light wood color of the rest of the home furnishings. It had the ambiance of an English Tearoom straight out of *Victoria* magazine. Leah took it all in and wondered what Thad really did for a living.

Thad seated her then moved to a chair opposite hers. He was thinking he probably should have said a little more about the cabin. She looked a little apprehensive at the moment and he wondered what she was thinking as she surveyed the surroundings.

When he prepared to eat, Leah made a request that caught him off guard.

"May I give thanks for our food?" Leah faltered. Habit encouraged this prayer of thanks as well as her Dad's instruction that gratitude to God was the duty of mankind.

"Sure." he would be amiable. As she prayed simply, Thad recalled his mother's prayers at mealtimes and bedtime. He couldn't remember the last time he'd acknowledged God by giving thanks. It provoked questions he would ask Leah later.

"This looks wonderful," Leah commented as they served one another then began to eat without talking for several minutes. Both were too hungry for conversation.

"This is delicious. Alma is a fine cook, Thad." Leah dabbed at her mouth with a linen napkin. "I rarely cook myself because of my school and work schedule. My Mom does--did most of the cooking." Leah changed the tense from present to past as reality played catch-up yet again. "When I do cook, it's nothing to rave about."

"You'd still be a lot better than I am," he assured her. "I'm a can man myself. As long as I have a can opener and a pan, I can survive. Tyrone does most of the camp cooking and navigating while I do most of the book work and repairs for our business."

"You have a very good business?" Leah ventured. Thad wiped his mouth with a napkin before answering.

"It's worked out pretty good for us over these last-let's see, it's been almost ten years now." He saw the quizzical look in Leah's expression and expected more questions, but Leah didn't ask anything further—she just frowned as if processing data then surmised.

"I need a career change." Leah said matter-of-fact. She looked so serious Thad had to stifle a chuckle.

"School teachers don't make a good income in Pennsylvania?"

"Not the school where I teach-taught." Present to past, again! "I've taught for six years and I'm still listed on my income tax as a non-profit," she remarked dryly and shrugged as Thad laughed.

"What career would you consider?" he asked taking a bite of a buttered biscuit with strawberry jam.

"Horses."

Thad stopped chewing briefly and looked at her in amazement. They'd exchanged some stories and information about horses in letters, especially one letter she'd mentioned about a horse named Sunrise. But he'd never told her about the two horses he owned.

"What about horses?" he asked casually.

"I'd like to work around them again." Leah admitted honestly. "After Sunrise, I just…well, the memories were too much. But I think I understand some things a little better now than I did when I was a teenager. Everything in my life seemed so extreme then." They regarded one another for a few moments.

"The teenage years are extreme, I think," Thad reckoned.

"Yours were extreme, too?" Leah wanted to know.

"I spent more time and money on horses than girls," he guaranteed.

"No kidding!" It was Leah's turn to be amazed.

"No kidding." He saw her enthusiasm explode. The sparkle in her eyes brought the word "miracle" to his mind and heart like a lightning strike!

"Have you ever considered keeping horses here?" she asked all curious and hopeful.

"Maybe," he shrugged trying to show indifference though enjoying the secret surprise he had for her, if she became his bride. "It takes a lot of work and money to keep horses as you already know."

"Well, yes, it does and, of course, you do have the hunting and fishing business to keep going." Thad watched Leah's expression change from excitement to practical resignation. He hadn't meant to dash her dreams! Now he scrambled to the rescue.

"Of course, with what we both know about horses, maybe we could manage one or two," he offered rubbing his beardless chin in thought. Leah frowned.

"I don't know, Thad," she countered. "As you said, horses take a lot of time and money."

Thad cocked his head to the side and studied Leah. "Guess I'll have to teach you the hunting and fishing business so we can add some horses to your Alaskan experience." The fact that he already kept two horses in a stable less than a mile from the cabin made this moment more interesting for him, at least. The hopefulness in Leah's eyes cemented his decision to partnership with her in life, work and dreams.

"You better finish eating before your food gets cold," she urged gently.

"You sound like a wife."

"You wrote for one."

"And I recall you responded favorably."

"So I did. And I have a multitude of buttons to prove it." She stood to collect the dishes and take them to the kitchen. Thad reached for her hand before she could pick up a serving dish of vegetables. He did something only a year ago he'd have considered totally unlike himself— he kissed the palm of her hand gently. Leah was more than a little surprised, but this time she didn't giggle or laugh. Their eyes met and in those few moments their friendship blossomed into devotion to each other. The moment of peace amidst the chaos of love's discovery was unforgettable. Leah's smile spoke volumes of tenderness for him.

Thad knew if he'd have asked her to marry him right then, she would have said "yes". But he waited. He had a plan. Instead of a proposal, he squeezed her hand and released it.

"I'll leave the shirts that need buttons reattached on the couch for you." There was a confidence in the tone of his voice that made her smile with happiness. "You'll have to ask Alma where the sewing stuff is. I used to know where it was, but not anymore." He paused for a moment. "You really brought all the buttons?"

"I had to pay an extra fee for luggage." Leah chirped back.

Thad laughed. "You're fast."

"I worked with inner city kids in Chicago for four years and I've been a classroom teacher for a while. I've learned to be fast."

"I couldn't tell," he smiled and stood. "Here, I'll help you with these."

After the dishes were piled on the countertop, Thad asked, "Would you like to step out onto the deck? If we're lucky, we might be able to see a hint of the Aurora Borealis tonight. It's clear and much colder this evening. It *is* kind of early in the season to see them. Usually anytime in late October and November they can be better seen when the days are darker. I won't make any guarantees, though. Fairbanks and places to the far north see a lot more of the Northern Lights then we do!"

"That sounds good to me." She paused, thoughtful. "I've never seen the Northern Lights that I know of. The encyclopedia said that the Northern Lights are like a giant fireworks display across the sky."

"The encyclopedia said that?" Thad said slowly and regarded her with a grin she didn't see while putting dishes in the dishwasher.

"Yep!"

"Go figure." He shook his head at the *wonder* of Leah Grant and her encyclopedias.

CHAPTER 11

FIRSTS

"I'M SO IMPRESSED." LEAH SAID. THAD shut the refrigerator door and turned to see Leah staring at all the touch-sensitive selections on the dishwasher panel.

"The only dishwasher my mother ever had was me—after she wore my other two sisters out."

"You didn't have an automatic dishwasher in your house?" Thad faked shock.

Leah caught the sarcasm. "Not one plugged into an outlet. But I was automatic. After we ate, I automatically did the dishes!"

Leah stepped back and extended her hand toward the dishwasher in a sweeping gesture.

"Which buttons do I push?" she frowned. "I feel like Jane Jetson."

The more Thad was getting to know Leah, the more he was learning to relax and joke around, too. He'd never really been one to participate in such banter. Tyrone was the one who was good at teasing and joking. Over the last couple of weeks, Thad had endured quite a bit of teasing in view of Leah's coming.

"Does it make me George Jetson?" he tried.

Leah glanced at him wondering that he'd ever watched cartoons so serious a disposition he displayed most of the time. It stumped her.

"You know who the Jetson's—you watched cartoons?"

"No cartoons! I watched the old Westerns as a boy, but my Mom loved to watch the Jetson's on Saturday mornings. Since there was only one TV, Mom got first dibs. We watched George and Jane Jetson with bowls of Lucky Charms cereal. Mom always gave me the purple marshmallow horseshoes."

"That's so sweet!" Leah gushed delighted to know his little-boy side.

"Yes, I am." Thad winked, flirting.

"So I've noticed." Leah directed before glancing back at the display panel. Her last statement sailed smoothly into Thad's thoughts and anchored in his heart. He watched her study the panel and when Leah turned to ask for instructions, Thad moved a little closer.

"So, what else have you noticed?" he ventured while crossing his arms in front of his chest like Sinbad and leaning in enough to touch her shoulder. Thad already knew Leah to be as decent a woman as he'd ever known. But, he wondered how she would handle suggestive advances made toward her person. He hosted all kinds of clientele. He didn't want a woman who would compromise her own standards and flirt with his clients, nor did he want one who would offend them with Biblical rebukes either.

The simple gesture of folding his arms enhanced Thad's masculinity and created havoc in Leah's senses. She thought about returning his question with a daring remark, but caution seemed the wiser choice in this romantically charged atmosphere. Out of nowhere, her Dad's words about propriety encouraged a discreet response.

"I've noticed that you are a gentleman." She returned with sincerity, smiled then turned her attention back to the dishwasher.

"I'm a gentleman?" Thad dropped his arms and picked up a serving bowl that had been forgotten. He rinsed it under the sink facet then handed it to Leah for placement in the dishwasher.

"Have you noticed that I don't mind helping in the kitchen." It was a statement rather than a question. He barely managed to keep a straight face when he saw the confusion on Leah's. Leah wasn't sure he hadn't implied something else in his question after all. He was still smiling when he gave her directions for the dishwasher's operation.

"Press START."

"How do I press STOP, first?" she laughed and gave Thad side-glance. He had tested her.

"You know, Thad, my Dad liked to tell us girls about his teenage experiences every once-in-a-while. I'd like to tell you about one of his experiences. It's on the serious side of life." Leah looked at Thad for a nod to continue which he gave.

"When he was about fifteen years old, his family sold their ancestral farm land and moved to the city to make a better living. Dad made some new friends at school who introduced him to new ideas and activities. They were the kind of ideas and activities his parents would not have approved of if they'd known about them. He kept secret company with these friends. His parents noticed changes in his attitude, dress, and behavior. My grandpa decided to follow him to school one day and discovered my dad's secret association with a satanic cult group. Grandpa was shocked by what he saw, but didn't rush in to save my dad. Instead, he went home, got on his knees, and begged God to release my dad from this cult group even if it meant that God would take his son's life.

"When my dad came home that night, Grandpa Grant met him in the living room and made only one statement, 'Cole, what a man does in secret reveals his true character to an all seeing God.' Everyday grandpa would meet my dad as he came through the door and he'd say the same words, then he'd turn and walk to his room to pray. My dad was so miserable he ran away from home. He ran back to the old farm people he knew and they took him in until he made things right with God. He never went back to the city to live with his parents; but God spared his life and used him in ministry. Eventually grandpa and dad got back together. I've never forgotten grandpa's statement. Like my Dad, I struggle with faith, too. I know God sees me, even when I don't want to acknowledge Him."

"You're grandpa was quite a guy," Thad praised suddenly wishing he'd had a man praying for him in his teenage years.

"He's still quite a guy. He's seventy-eight and still turns cartwheels in the backyard with his grandkids." They both chuckled as Thad started for the doorway from the kitchen.

"I'll go get some jackets. It'll be cooler on the deck with the evening breeze." He left Leah to press the START button.

The display on the dishwasher turned green and Leah expected to hear noises of some sort coming from the dishwasher, but all was silent. When no sounds came from the machine, Leah surmised something was wrong and began to retrace the steps of operation. Without touching the panel, she moved through the steps again with a puzzled frown. Just as she got to the START button again, she began to smell something similar to burning garbage. Steam or smoke of sorts poured out from the top vents over the computer panel.

Leah's mouth dropped open at the horrifying prospects of a fire. She turned and flew toward the kitchen doorway just as Thad entered. Their collision sent him back peddling frantically with jackets flying in opposite directions. Resembling a tight-rope walker struggling to maintain balance, he finally grabbed the banister to stop the gyro effect created by Leah's mad dash and sat down hard on the steps. When he turned to check if Leah was okay, he was amazed to see she was still standing!

Sheer panic registered in Leah's eyes as she pointed to the dishwasher spewing steam and smelling of burnt food.

"I think it's on fire!"

Thad dashed past her towards the misbehaving dishwasher.

"I pressed the START button as you said and nothing happened. It didn't come on or make any noises." Leah was clueless. Thad was watching the dishwasher and checking the panel with a concentrated effort. Suddenly, he realized what was happening and relaxed. Taking a deep breath, he addressed Leah mildly.

"It's not on fire, Leah," he said trying to keep from smiling for her sake. He couldn't believe she could panic over such a thing as a dishwasher. Sometimes she defied understanding. "You haven't had much experience with dishwashers have you?" It was an understatement used to lighten the intense situation.

"None," was her poker-faced reply.

"Awe," he noted with raised eyebrows letting a smile escape.

"I've seen then in appliance stores and, yes, I do know what a dishwasher is and does. We just never had one in any of the church parsonages where we lived."

"Well then, I'll tell you about this particular dishwasher," he paused, "so you don't run over me when it smokes. Not that I minded!" Thad was making a sincere effort to keep from laughing.

"Go ahead and laugh," Leah rolled her eyes. "I'm not usually so mindless, although it's been a record-setting day for this Girl Scout!" Leah admitted with a chuckle. Thad agreed, laughing.

"You're not mindless, Leah, you're *amazing*," he emphasized then added, "and you're a pretty good tackle, too!" He rubbed a shoulder faking an injury.

Leah shook her head and made a face at him.

"Very funny, Thad, running into you was like hitting a steel pole. I'm still seeing double!" Leah crossed her eyes at Thad making him laugh out loud. "Just tell me about this smoke spewing beast!"

"The smoke is really just steam." Mirth still registered in Thad's eyes. It had been a long time since he'd laughed this much and this hard. "This dishwasher has a built-in food incinerator that keeps it clean. That's both the smell and the steam you've noticed. The dishwasher won't start the wash cycle until the incinerator is finished and cooled. It takes about fifteen minutes before it will start the wash cycle. So, if you don't realize what's going on, I guess it could cause some apprehension."

"SOME apprehension!" Both began to laugh as they picked up the scattered jackets and headed for the large double door to the deck.

As Thad helped Leah into her jacket, her curly long hair cascaded over his fingers. She was talking about her excitement at seeing the dusky skies over Palmer. However, Thad was thinking it was going to be difficult to wait until Sunday before asking Leah to marry him. This was a decision he'd made when the Anchorage plan hadn't worked. There had been an opportunity for a proposal, but with so many changes and new adjustments for Leah to deal with, he figured adding such a special event would be too much for what was, by now, a twenty-eight hour day given the time changes from Pennsylvania to Alaska. It was almost midnight for Thad. It was four o'clock in the morning for Leah!

He would be leaving in a few hours to take O'Brien and Ishioti out for more fishing and would not be returning until Sunday afternoon. It would give Leah some time to rest and acclimate to the surroundings. It would give him time to think through a better plan.

Over the last five years, he'd almost become a recluse as far as dating was concerned. Indeed, Leah's entrance into his life had been a pleasant adjustment in many ways. She was a wonder to Thad for drawing him willingly out of bachelorhood.

Thad had been wholly committed to developing the hunting and fishing guide business until he was able to cease working on local farms. Other periodic work he coordinated for the University of Alaska which included research experiments for forestry and agriculture. The income invested from the success of his joint business with Tyrone had provided the funds to build the cabin with Taima's and Alma's help...in his spare time. It hadn't started out to be this big and elaborate, but he'd had the money and Alma had directed the building of the cabin and enjoyed its construction. Alma's happiness and health returned as she worked on the project. The size and decorating had been left to her discretion. Leah seemed appreciative of Alma's labor of love. Indeed, Leah seemed to enjoy everything as though she'd rarely seen such comfort.

As they walked along the deck, Thad had no doubt Leah and Alma would get along well. This was interesting as well. Alma and Taima were part of the package if Leah agreed to marry him. He looked over at her profile as she gazed up at the dusky late-evening sky. Her presence filled him with a longing to make her a permanent part of his life.

Just then a spray of northern lights zipped across the dimming sky in frosty waves of varied lime greens. It shimmered in glorious curves arching above them. It was as if snowflakes popped and snapped in the cool air.

Thad blinked in surprise at the unlikely display for late August. It was indeed rare. Could this be some kind of sign?

"Oh! Look at that!" Leah said, astonishment filling her voice with delight. She moved closer to Thad to point out the magnificence of the charged sky. Thad enjoyed the scent of her light perfume. As they looked skyward his arm naturally moved behind her back and around her waist. Leah was talking.

"It's beautiful! I've never seen the…" she paused for a moment as her eyes widened when she felt his arm come around her waist, "…northern lights in my life." Her arms tingled with the pleasure of his touch. Her thoughts jumbled between the desire for his affection and moral propriety. Leah had little idea how to read this situation. At best, it was a judgment call on her part. Any dating experiences at the conservative Christian college she'd attended required strict observance of the infamous six-inch rule. This rule meant there had to be no less than six inches between a dating couple at all times. Leah hadn't dated enough since college to threaten that rule! Of course she understood certain things were wrong outside of marriage, but exactly what those certain things should be right now was a little fuzzy when his touch stirred her heart and emotions. There were questions popping up in her thinking processes that tested her trust of Thad. Physical presence was naturally going to be different from the impressions gathered by letter writing.

He'd held and kissed her hand and his hand was around her waist. She welcomed his attention but was it up to her to determine the limits? All her life there had been limits on almost everything. Always, she was made to feel responsible for the actions of others because she and her sisters were to be good examples. For a change, she wanted Thad to set the limits trusting that he was a man of character. Had their relationship progressed so much through letters and phone calls that these developments were a natural result? She felt they had. Did he really desire marriage? She sensed he did; but he hadn't told her he loved her, yet. Love was implied, but not spoken.

Leah managed to clear her thoughts enough to listen as Thad spoke.

"I am amazed, myself, to see them this early, this far south! Maybe we're going to have an early winter. There are stories native Alaskans tell about Eskimo children having a game they play when the northern lights appear. They whistle to them as if calling them down to the earth, then they run and hide before the noisy spirits reach down to grab them. If they are caught, they are taken to the heavens where they become stars and twinkle there forever."

Leah felt the tears gather in her eyes. The simple story seemed to speak to her present life. She was whistling at northern lights and calling them down to her, but she was afraid of them, too. She was afraid of ending up like her sister, Sarah.

"That's really interesting," her voice betrayed the emotional struggle underneath. Thad looked down at her with concern as he saw her blink away tears and smiled, thinking she, too, was touched by the display in the sky above. He had no idea of the emotional volcano building for an eruption. His hand tightened around her waist. A travel-wearied Leah began to cry. Tears spilled down her face making her feel totally foolish. The quick movements of both her pointer fingers pushed the tumbling eye waters to the sides of damp cheeks.

"Leah, what's wrong?" Thad asked gently. He was beginning to understand there was more to the tears than the beautiful sky blitz. She wanted to turn to him, to trust, but was unable to decide what to do other than remain still until it passed.

"Did I do something?" Thad began to remove his arm from around her waist, baffled by her tears. His eyes widened and he swallowed quickly when her arms came around his waist and she cried against him. This was an interesting development and for a moment he didn't know quite what to do except hold her until the tears subsided. At least she wasn't upset with him or she would have pushed away! His arms tightened around her protectively. This seemed to bring about some calm until she stood quietly. As suddenly as the northern lights had appeared across the cold evening sky, they departed in the twinkling of an eye.

The aurora borealis had vanished from the sky and the crackling noise it had made was replaced by the sounds of noisy night bugs and hidden nocturnal creatures.

"Do you ever get tired of seeing the aurora borealis?" she asked.

"Not when I see the pleasure it gives to new people; especially to you, Leah." His voice was tender and Leah felt the warmth of his gaze.

"I would never tire of seeing them if I could always share their beauty...with you." She smiled honey-eyed at Thad.

"I love you." Thad promised.

Leah's eyes watered again. Thad wondered.

"Are you going to cry again?"

"These are happy tears." She reached up and touched his smooth face.

"You didn't have to shave your beard off for me. I loved you the moment I saw you at the Trading Post." Thad's arms came around her and Leah responded to his kiss with matching fervency.

"You know!" A voice with pronounced volume spoke behind them and broke their romantic reverie. Actually, it startled both as they parted a little off balance and fuzzy. Taima had walked into the great room to pick up reading glasses and observed the couple with interest. Their romantic discovery of each other refreshed some old memories of his, too. Thad and Leah now turned to regard him sheepishly. He continued to speak checking the lens of his glasses for smudges. A small grin on his face showed relief at seeing Leah's response to Thad.

"They say that if a man kisses the woman he loves on the night of the aurora borealis, he will marry her before the first snow of winter." Taima shot a warning glance at Thad, a grin still holding true to form on his face.

Thad smirked warily. "There are a lot of things that are supposed to happen when the aurora borealis stirs across the night sky. Where did you hear this one, Taima?"

"A great voice whispered it to me." Taima tried to sound ominous.

"That great voice must have been my Dad's." Leah nodded knowingly. Thad still gazed at her. The memory of her returned kiss still wreaked havoc. Taima laughed out loud.

"Actually, I think it was the spirit of bachelorhood calling out to me and telling me to warn Wolfe about his coming marriage." He chuckled and Leah checked Thad for a response.

"Thanks for the warning, Taima, but this bachelor was won to the idea of marriage the day he received the first rose-scented letter. I'm glad you ordered me to go to that dating service to find a wife."

Leah wondered when the proposal would come and how it would come. If Thad had plans, he wasn't sharing details with anybody!

"I guess I did push you out the door, didn't I?" Taima chuckled as he remembered the occasion with relish. "Well, I'm going back by the fire to read for a while before bed." He left them after glancing meaningfully at Thad to do likewise.

The thrill of all that was happening caused her to shiver. Thad saw it and moved Leah inside the cabin and over to the fireplace.

"You're chilled."

"It's a thrill chill," Leah smiled and warmed her hands from the glow of the fire. "I think it's the change from ninety degree heat and humidity to a fifty degree cold that's a little bit of an adjustment." Thad nodded in agreement.

"It will take some time for you to get used to it." The assurance in his voice seemed to suggest a permanency and Leah found joy and comfort in his guarantee.

Alma had just come from the kitchen and was heading for the stairs as they took off their jackets. Leah was warming quickly. She signed to Leah as Thad took the jackets and hung them in the hall closet.

"Are you ready for some sleep, Leah? I'm heading up now and I'd be glad to help you unpack if you want help."

"Yes. On both accounts," Leah admitted with an escaping yawn. She looked at Thad. "Will I see you in the morning before you leave?"

"I doubt it. I've got an early start at 4:30 tomorrow morning, so I'll say 'good-night' now and I'll see you on Sunday afternoon." Alma was already halfway up the stairs by this time and Leah turned to head in that general direction when Thad stopped her mid-step.

"Leah?" She knew what he was asking.

"Yes," she answered and he kissed her quickly.

"Sleep well," he encouraged and turned to walk in the opposite direction.

Chapter 12

Favorites and Friends

Alma met Leah in the hallway as she came out of her own room with extra towels and another comforter. She saw the happy smile on Leah's face.

"I can help you unpack your suitcases after you get some rest. You've had a very long day."

"Yes, it has been, thank you. I'll just pull some pajamas out for now." Leah paused, "I tried to think of clothing which would be the most useful and appropriate for the weather."

"We mostly wear casual clothes in layers; like lots of sweaters and warm pants." Alma signed as Leah unzipped a travel bag and retrieved warm flannel PJs.

"That's what I brought the most plus a few dresses for church or special occasions."

"Don't worry about it too much. If you need anything, Thad will take care of it." It sounded almost as if this was the usual way of doing things. Leah wasn't sure about this idea. She wasn't used to being waited on or pampered. Everybody earned their own way in her family, mainly to help with expenses. What luxurious surroundings these were for a girl who thought the dishwasher was going to burn the house down!

"I'm planning to go to church on Sunday so I'll need to put some dresses and jackets on hangers to let the wrinkles fall out or use an iron." Leah yawned suddenly. She noticed that the mention of church received a frown from Alma.

"I haven't been to church in a long time," she signed slowly.

"Would you like to go with me?" Leah invited. "I'm not sure Thad will want to go when the opportunity comes. I have no intentions of making him feel he has to go, either; but I don't relish the idea of going alone either, so you would be welcome company."

"Then we'll go together," Alma decided with a flourish and smile. "I'm looking forward to going."

"So am I. It will be nice having a friend along."

"If you need anything, let me know. I'm right next door." Alma encouraged as she turned to leave. "Good night!"

For a while, Leah relaxed under the warm comforter. There was a smile of contentment on her face as she lay in the silence and thought about the events of the day—of their first kiss.

The whole idea of coming to Alaska as a prospective bride had at one time sounded too fantastic and even more than a little risky. Leah was not unaware of a society that practiced open relationships as an accepted lifestyle. Her work in inner city Chicago had opened her eyes to life beyond an ultra conservative background.

One memory came to mind of a young woman waiting at a Chicago bus stop early one Saturday morning. Leah and some college mates had stopped for hot chocolate and sandwiches at a corner deli. From the deli window Leah and her college-mates could see the woman's face was swollen. Her makeup was smudged in an unsightly mass on her emotionless face. It had startled Leah to see the bruises on the woman's arms where the long sleeves of her short party dress had been torn away. One heel on her shoe was broken while her black nylons were frayed and bagged around her ankles. Leah's heart had registered what her mind fought to accept. This woman didn't look like the movie stars on TV after a night of business calls to paying men. Her beauty was marred and her face ghostly. Suddenly, the woman had turned and looked directly at Leah. Dark eyes revealed a deadness that had shaken Leah. After a few intense moments, she turned away from Leah and stood with the crowd of people who seemed not to notice she existed except to check their distance from her. Leah's friends had pressed closer to look at the prostitute and snicker. Their self-righteous judgment bothered Leah and she moved away from then, embarrassed by their lack of mercy or care for a lost heart and soul. She had seen a woman the morning after a hard-spent night. In that moment of truth, Leah understood that morning always comes with a new day's promise or regret.

There had been some apprehension before she opened Thad's second letter which was much longer than his initial entreaty. One particular paragraph had encouraged her to continue to write with ease of heart and mind. This special letter she carried in the zippered lining of her purse though it was committed to memory.

"I live in a cabin where from one window I can see the snow-capped mountains reach to the sky. From an opposite window, I can view a rich green valley that extends to meet the Matanuska River along its banks. From the river's cut through the valley, the land merges into the sky again. On all sides I am surrounded by the ageless evidence of a Creator whom I do not know and cannot see except for the witness of this great land and endless sky."

At first, the words had seemed too philosophical for a bachelor from rugged Alaska. But Leah found the honesty of Thad's words to portray a man who acknowledged someone greater than he was even though he didn't know God personally. But then, Leah didn't either, though she'd heard the gospel since childhood. Whether Thad Tucker might be searching or not, she didn't know, yet. She was only just beginning to give God serious consideration.

Snuggled warm and comfortable beneath the soft bedding, Leah reckoned thoughts of God were also the reason for her trip to Alaska. There was a longing to know God for Himself away from the people whose expectations were too high for her to live up to and too rigid for her to accept. She reasoned that she had been surrounded by Christianity and yet had felt lost in the middle of it. Her courage and determination to step away from all of it had shocked her family and a good many other people. Never had she been made to feel so guilty. Instead of an

"A" placed on her chest, people had placed a "B" for backslider. Their disparaging whispers and judgment had hurt. But Leah reasoned that she wasn't a backslider. She was just Leah Grant. When the plane left Pittsburgh, a sense of discovery energized her as old hurts and rebellions seemed to fall away. Indeed, she anticipated a future faith that would be genuine and soul filling. There was peace in this sleepy thought.

Leah yawned and moved to rest on her side. Shortly thereafter, she slept…until 2 a.m. After just three hours of sleep, Leah was wide-awake! She looked at the digital clock display and moaned in disbelief.

"What's going on?"

CHAPTER 13

JET LAG

IN THE DISTANCE THE FAINT BLAST of a whistle signaled a train's approach and then its passing a short distance away from a slumbering Palmer. The Midnight Fox of the Alaska Railroad broke the pristine silence of the landscape as it glided through the summer's light blue evening shades into dawn's light. The sound of the train's lonely travel reminded her of the home she had left and the old train tracks behind the church. Restless thoughts encouraged her to get up and read for a while.

She reached and touched the base of the lamp on her nightstand. The blinding light made Leah squint until her eyes adjusted. After a quick glance around the twilight shadowed room, she located the cosmetic case that contained her Dad's Bible. She drew this out of the case and held it for a while, noting the significance of the gift her Dad had made her.

Leah knew it to be her Dad's "preaching Bible." It contained carefully notated sermon outlines in the margins. Though well used, the Bible was in immaculate condition, reverently handled in study and practice. Dad had wished her God's peace and grace as she went. Even though she knew he was disturbed by her decision, Leah sensed he had accepted it believing God would work in her life in His time. As her hand brushed the smooth black leather surface, she realized she'd never touched this Bible. The lamp by the bed was not a lamp to read by so she decided to go downstairs to the great room. Leah hoped she could get there in the dim light of the quiet cabin without waking the household.

Quietly, she descended the stairs and walked softly towards what she hoped was the large living space. Cautiously, she felt her way along an inside wall until her feet felt the change of the floor from tile in the entrance to the lip where the carpeting started. The floor was cold and Leah bit her lip in chagrin for forgetting slippers. For a moment, the idea of going back and retrieving them was tempting but she didn't want to waste time and effort.

She rounded a corner and clearly saw the last flames flickering in the fireplace...in the great room. A sigh of relief escaped at the warm sight where orange embers glowed like a lamp for her feet and a light for her path. When she misjudged the size of a piece of furniture with a bump, she stopped and remained completely still hoping nothing would crash to the floor.

At last, she was close enough to blow on the embers. When she did, a flame popped up from the coals and danced upon the unconsumed remnants of a Yule log. The fire blazed back to life. Leah was surprised and a little pleased at the result. She had no idea how fireplaces worked. At Christmas, her Dad had always put up a cardboard fireplace to hang stockings and that had been a real treat for her sisters and her. Slowly, Leah turned and reached carefully for the arms of a wing chair close to the fireplace. She found it and felt for the lamp table beside the comfy seat. The touch lamp automatically came on when her fingers bumped it and the bright light blinded her again for several moments. When at last she could open her eyes, the inevitable bright yellow spots danced around her vision. She squinted and blinked trying to clear them, but they still blocked her eyesight. Gradually, Leah moved forward with her right hand extended toward a large cream-colored sofa. She still held the black Bible firmly in her left hand as she negotiated the distance with a guess. But, alas, she guessed wrong. Her toe hit the edge of the hidden sofa leg with a faint snap and she winced in pain!

"O-o-o-o-h! Ouch!" she exclaimed irritated by the pain and her own clumsiness. Suddenly she stood perfectly still, hand clasped over her mouth fearing the slightest noise would awaken others. She managed to sit down without further stumbling then listened for sounds of movement. When it seemed all was well, Leah relaxed, noting that the spots before her eyes were now tiny yellow specks. As a child she and her sisters had thought it great fun to try to catch the spots. On impulse she reached out and attempted to catch one, two, or three of these illusive little beamers. What else was there to do anyway? She still couldn't see clearly enough to read, yet.

Just then, Leah heard what she thought was a release of air. She froze in place. Her hand still poised in mid-air to capture a fluttering yellow spot. She turned slowly around and peered into the darkness at the far end of the large room. She saw nothing though it gave her the willies and stirred her imagination with all kind of frightening possibilities. Leah jumped up and grabbed the first handy object which happened to be a small broom from the fireplace. She started in the direction of the phantom noise. Memories of being followed by gang members in a rough Chicago neighborhood fueled the desire to defend her wellbeing. There was a determined look on her face as she held the broom like a baseball bat for a quick and decisive wallop!

When Taima saw her grab the broom, he looked at Thad, waved his hand as if to say, "She's all yours!" then scooted noiselessly back to his room before he chortled with mirth. There hadn't been this much excitement in the house since the fall of '95 when the chimney caught fire! This was just short of chaos. Alma, he was used to. Leah? Well, he'd hoped for a unique wife for Thad and, so far, Leah was proving to be one-of-a-kind.

Thad started for her with the hopes of making his presence known before she let him have it with the fireplace broom. But she moved so fast he couldn't do anything to stop her attack. Instead, he tried to speak without frightening her further.

"Leah, stop! It's me, Thad!" He flipped the light switch on.

THWACK!

"UH! Crash! Silence.

"Too late!" Taima remarked after he heard the connection of the broom with the human object it hit. "I hope she never meets up with a bear. I'd feel sorry for the bear." He mumbled and chuckled then lay down to sleep once again. All was well!

Meanwhile Thad was nursing a sharp pain to his left forearm. Leah was still holding the broken half of the broom in both hands. The whisk end of the broom lay several feet away surrounded by a fallen shelf of porcelain knick knacks now resembling Humpty Dumpty's great fall! She clearly saw it was Thad she'd vanquished and not the horrible "Zillah" of her wacky imagination. A wide-eyed Leah faced a quietly contemplative Thad Tucker with open-mouthed mortification. Finally coming to her senses, she began to apologize.

"Oh, Thad! I…I'm so sorry!" Her voice shook. She rubbed his arm gently as a mother would to comfort a hurting child.

Thad didn't say a word. The expression on his face was placid enough thought he regarded her thoughtfully. A few pieces of information registered in his thoughts. He wasn't sure if he'd call it courage, but she had it! Two, she was fast. Three, she had a wicked swing. And four, she didn't miss! He listened as she attempted to explain, apologize and scold herself all at the same time!

"I thought all kinds of wild things were coming to get me. I'm really sorry. I wasn't thinking clearly. How could I be so stupid!"

When he didn't make any effort to acknowledge her apology, Leah's heart sank. He still had the same sober, tolerant expression on his face, but the squint of his eyes made Leah drop her hands from his arm and clasp them together in front. When he saw her eyes drop, he quickly spoke up.

"It's jet lag, Leah. Come with me. Let's go put some wood on the fire." Thad said cheerfully as he reached for her hand then led her over to the sofa to sit.

"Don't move, now," he instructed with a teasing smile. Leah tried a sheepish grin. Thad winked at her and turned to rebuild the sputtering fire. She watched his practiced efforts to rebuild the blaze in the hearth with quick results.

"We should have stuck to letter writing the rest of our lives," she reckoned with a nod.

Thad turned just then and realized Leah was taking his thrashing with a broom harder than he was. He walked over to the sofa and picked up the Bible still lying next to her then sat down taking her hand in his.

"My Mom is a Bible reader, too," he attempted a familiar subject as a means to make a connection between both their backgrounds. "I think I may have told you she attends church all the time and prays a good deal, too. She still prays for me, I know. I never had too much interest in religious things as a teenager; but I learned about God in Sunday School when I was a young boy. I do believe there is a God, but that's about it."

"Me too." Leah returned honestly. She appreciated his efforts to wave aside her last offensive act of chaos figuring he would be glad to see her go at the end of the visit. So, she might as well confess her own spiritual delinquency, too. Thad looked surprised. He had expected she knew God by her knowledge of the Bible and because her Dad was a minister.

"Many people think I am a Christian, but all these years, I've just gone through the motions. I don't know God in my heart like Christians are supposed to know. I know all the Bible stories and all the right words to say, but I can't seem to trust God. I have tried to pray, but there is always silence." Leah was thoughtful. Thad was thinking about what she said and understood the silence, too. At one time, he'd given great effort to prayer. As a boy, he'd prayed that God would bring his Dad back home. But there had been only silence and after a while, he'd given up on God. After returning to Alaska to attend the University of Fairbanks, his mother's influence waned and he'd hardly given any thought to God over the passing years. Only the brief statements in Leah's letters about religious things had stirred such thought of God again.

"I want to know God," Leah acknowledged.

He regarded Leah in a new way. "How will you know when you find God?" he asked.

"I don't know," Leah sighed. "I know the answer is in this Bible and I want to find it." Leah focused on the black leather cover of the Bible then looked up at Thad curiously.

"Do we find God or does He find us?" The question was difficult for Thad to contemplate. He remembered the talks with his Mom about heaven and hell but didn't understand why these talks make him feel uncomfortable. Such thoughts challenged his ability to control his own life.

"Sometimes I think I'll always be lost," Leah said candidly.

"No, you won't, Leah," he said frankly and suddenly wanted to end this touchy subject. "You'll be found because you want to be saved." He paused. "You just have to figure out what's holding you back from knowing Him. As for me, I've chosen to ignore God. Being lost or saved means nothing to me." Leah was startled by his detached reply. It somehow pierced her heart that he didn't seem to care.

"You know about the gospel?"

"Yes. My Mom witnessed to me often. But I figured I didn't need God. I could get along without Him just fine. I had my own plans and I knew God would probably ask things of me that I didn't want to do if I became a Christian. You see, Leah, one day I heard my Mom praying that I'd get saved and be used of God. The phrase, *used of God,* scared me to death. I knew she really meant maybe someday I'd be a missionary or a preacher or something like that. To tell the truth, the idea sickened me then. Still does. No offense to your Dad." He corrected.

"None taken," Leah assured him with a nod.

"So, we're both heathen?" Thad joked. Leah frowned at his inference. She'd never viewed herself as a heathen. He laughed at her expression, but stopped when he saw she didn't see the humor. This subject had run its course for him.

"Well, I have only one question to ask you before I leave to get back to bed." Thad raised a hand to count on his fingers as he stood and moved over to the fireplace. At that moment, he reminded Leah of her Dad and she was amazed at the similarity of the two men she loved. When her Dad lectured her for some infraction or catastrophe, he would always use his fingers to list the points he wanted to cover for her benefit.

She considered the man standing before her with wonder as he held up one finger than another.

"You didn't recognize me after I shaved off my beard. Then you nearly knocked me to the floor when the dishwasher scared you, and, just a few minutes ago, you hit me with a broom--and broke the broom, I might add!" A smile stirred on Leah's face. "Now, I don't recall deserving any of it." He was enjoying this too much.

"You said you loved me, and I believe you, but do you like me at all?" he asked. "There is a difference, you know."

Leah covered her mouth to cover a merry twitter.

"Oh! I forgot. I showed you this house that I built with these two hands and you laughed hysterically." Thad crossed his arms and cocked his head to the side waiting patiently until Leah finished laughing. It was good to see her lighthearted again. He enjoyed the fact that he could cheer her up and make her laugh when things got too serious for both of them.

"Well, I have to admit that I do like your house, Thad Tucker!" She dodged coyly.

Thad came over and sat down beside her again. He wouldn't sleep anyway. There were questions he wanted to ask her about events in her life from this last week. He'd tried to get her to talk about these events over the phone, but she seemed reluctant to talk.

"You mention that you almost didn't come. Why?" he asked gently but determined to have an answer.

Leah's brow creased in reflection. They were unpleasant memories to say the least. She expelled a breath and began.

"We've known each other since the end of February, first of March. My parents knew nothing about my writing to you and our plans until last Saturday afternoon." Thad's eyebrows rose. His mother had known about Leah since July when he'd been to the Weston Ranch outside of Phoenix visiting his old boss on business. Leah saw his surprise and continued quickly.

"I had planned to tell them right after we made our final plans. But, the summer was so hectic…it seemed one thing and another happened to keep our family in turmoil." Leah waved her hand aside. "There's too much to explain."

"Try me!" he said expectantly. Leah's voice caught.

"Its church related, Thad."

"Okay. Tell me about the church."

"I can't." It was the first time she had responded negatively to him and it had to do with religion.

"Why?" he asked. "Were you embarrassed to tell your family and church friends about me?" Leah blinked.

"No! Not embarrassed. Just cautious."

"Were your parents in favor of your coming to see me?"

"No." Leah's voice was soft. Thad ran a hand through his hair and rubbed the back of his neck as if it ached. Alarms were going off in his head as he thought about the consequences. She might be twenty-eight and old enough to do as she pleased, but he didn't want an irate father and mother-in-law to visit for the next thirty years or more!

"Should I be looking over my shoulder?" he asked frankly. There was a tinge of irritation in his voice.

"Huh?" Leah didn't understand what he was asking her at first. Then it made sense and her brown eyes widened in astonishment. He was wondering if there might be the possibility of a shot-gun wedding in the future!

"No." She shook her head quickly. "My Dad understands."

"But your Mom doesn't?" He saw emotional pain in her eyes and put an arm around her shoulder.

"What church problem?" He returned to the topic that received the same reaction as his question regarding her Mom. Leah began to refuse.

"Leah." His voice was firm but compelling. "As long as you stay here, you can say anything you want to say, anytime you want to say it, anywhere you want to say it, and nobody will use it against you, me, or us." Leah frowned at him.

"How did you know?"

"My Mom always told me that what I said and did was a reflection on her and on us. This included my Aunt Anna and Uncle Peter," he added. "My uncle was at one time a missionary pastor in Arkansas before he returned to Arizona when my aunt became ill from respiratory disease.

That was when my Mom ran off with my father against her parents' wishes, too."

Leah flinched a little at this revelation and Thad saw the connection.

"Leah, please tell me what happened. I can't begin to understand what you went through unless you tell me. I want to make it easier for you and better for us," he encouraged. "You probably don't realize this, but there are a few people up here who are amazed you actually came to visit me. A lot of so-called prospective brides don't make it this far. Most of them think Alaska bachelors will come to visit them first. That's not necessarily how it's done up here." He removed his arm from around her when she stood and moved over by the fireplace to consider him further. She was working on trusting him. He wondered why trust was so hard for her.

She turned from him to stare at the blazing fire for a few minutes. Thad waited, a slow dread filled his thoughts and heart as she turned away from him.

Leah's thoughts were jumbled. Would Thad understand she was trying to change directions because she couldn't stay in the same rut any longer?

"My sisters and I have always lived in church parsonages. Our mother told us we had to be careful of what we said or did because it could hurt or ruin our dad's ministry. We didn't understand that this was a control button Mom used to get good behavior. Because my Mom felt pressured and insecure, she used this method to great advantage. Leah paused to check the root of bitterness sprouting in her heart.

"Thad, this is not easy for me to talk about."

Thad listened carefully. He'd never dated a preacher's daughter before-at least not that he'd known. Even if he had known one, there probably wouldn't have been a second date!

"As preacher's daughters, much was expected of us. It seemed like the slightest mistake or misbehavior was noted against us. Sometimes people tried to get information out of us about church matters or life in the Pastor's home. Because we didn't talk about our family life and dodged questions about church matters, we girls were labeled as being contrary and distant." Leah took a deep breath and expelled it as if turning a corner. "Not all the people were like this; but in close knit circles, gossip spins webs of lies faster than goodness can justify." Leah shrugged as if this was a normal way of life. Thad found this more than a little disturbing.

"So, when you and I began to make plans of our own, I didn't want it to become the subject of gossip, which it did anyway. I wanted to protect the goodness of our friendship without the skepticism of others. And, I chose not to renew my contract to teach at the academy for this coming school year figuring that, if things didn't work out with us, I would find a job here in Alaska and stay to make a new life anyway. Usually contracts for the next academic year are signed by the first of June at the very latest. Most teachers sign by the end of March so that vacant teaching positions can be filled in good time. No one took me seriously when I declined to renew my teaching contract."

"By the end of June, the academy board was getting nervous. They and my Mom kept after me to renew my contract. They wanted a reason why I wouldn't renew and I didn't think it was any of their business. Yes, the more they insisted, the more stubborn I became. Finally, I adamantly refused to renew the contract at a special board meeting called on my behalf. In the heat of it, I said some things I shouldn't have. I felt backed into a corner for letting the school down by leaving the deaf program without a supervisor. This was before Denise decided to take on the program and teach this year." She stared blurry eyed at the sculptured carpet design beneath her feet. After several quiet moments she looked up. Thad saw a well of hurt gathered in her eyes.

"My Mom was angry with me. The school board was angry and then everybody at church was upset. Then Saturday, my plans to visit you became known before I had the chance to talk to my parents, first. Of course, everything got blown out of proportion!" Leah paused, blinking away tears that threatened to fall. Talking a deep breath she continued, her jaw tight with determination to be in control. Her eyes found Thad's for support. For all the mayhem she embodied, Thad saw a woman of steel and grace standing before him.

"This past Wednesday night, the church called a special business meeting and voted to administer church discipline on my behalf. I guess they figured I was living in rebellion because I didn't want to do what they thought I should do. And, my trip to visit a bachelor in Alaska was not exactly the kind of missionary endeavor they could sanction wholeheartedly. They probably figured that public humiliation would change my mind. Obviously, it didn't."

Leah saw a triumphant smile edge its way across Thad's face. The distraction made her heavy heart feel lighter.

"Anyway, I stood in front of the congregation and all my wrong doings were brought out into the open. There were reports given of things I'm supposed to have done I didn't even know I'd done." Leah frowned confused as she bit down on her bottom lip. "One elderly lady asked me if I was planning to come back after my confinement. I had no idea what she was talking about until my sister pulled me aside later to tell me that rumor had it I was pregnant and that was the reason why I couldn't renew my contract." Leah paused to frown at that one and then realized what she was saying.

"Mail order pregnancies, now that's a new one!" She snapped her finger as if a light bulb had gone on in her mind. "That's why old Mrs. Grayson was so offended when I told her I had no intentions of being confined anywhere for any reason. I told her I was planning on enjoying myself." Her voice rose in pitch and intensity. "She rebuked me for having no shame and then quoted scripture at me!" There was a snarling mother-bear quality to Leah's voice that made Thad regard her present flare of temper with interest.

"I can't believe it! They twisted everything I said and used it against me when I didn't even know why they were so upset. Not one person checked the rumor for truth or defended me." Leah was clearly steamed by the injustice. Thad noticed she looked like she might need something to throw. He quickly spoke up.

"I'd hand you the broom and a rug to beat, but you broke the broom already." He wondered if that was the right thing to say. She looked at him and blinked. There was utter confusion on her heated face. Then the humor of Thad's remark registered along with the stupidity of gossiping tongues and Leah calmed to chuckle. This broke the tension and returned Leah's serenity. They laughed together for some time. One would stop and look at the other and then start laughing again. Finally, the mirth subsided until Leah could speak genuinely.

"I'm not angry anymore, Thad. It's over." She shrugged. "I'm still a little hurt, but I'll get over the hurt eventually, too. It's just that so much built up over these last several weeks and I had no outlet for any of it." She hastened to add, "Not that I came here to vent my frustration on you. When I called you Wednesday night, I just needed to hear your friendly voice."

Thad came to stand in front of Leah, looking full into her eyes. Leah melted into his gaze as she spoke.

"People thought I was foolish to come all the way to Alaska to meet you. They obviously thought a lot of stuff that was not true." She nodded and moved around Thad to sit down on the couch. Her expression was unreadable. He searched for bitterness but didn't see any. She seemed relieved and peaceful at last. Thad, however, wasn't exactly sure how he felt.

"I had no idea," he said simply.

"Does it change things?" Leah asked, not knowing what to expect.

"Why would it change anything?"

"Well, I'm kind of a woman without a country right now. I can't go back. There are cannibals back there that think I'd taste good in their soup. I can't go forward, because I don't want to ruin your view of the country they live in—namely church. Can you understand what I'm saying?"

Thad frowned and came over to sit down beside Leah. This time she did not move away from him.

"Not really," he admitted. "You lost me with the cannibals-in-the-soup statement." He was having a hard time following her unique logic which he'd also found humorous in her letters. He could laugh out loud while reading her letters, but in her presence he struggled to keep laughter in check not knowing how she would react. He saw that she remained serious and wondered at their differences.

"Well, some consider me to be in rebellion towards God, so they don't want to have anything to do with me. I'm not welcome, except if

I return and plead for their forgiveness on their terms. Even then, I'm still open for 'pot shots' anytime I mess up…and I mess up a lot!" Leah nodded and sighed.

Thad regarded the last statement with a smile.

"It's not the church, Thad. I like going to church because usually it gives me a good feeling about myself even if sometimes the sermons are boring. I don't understand how it all fits together." Leah shrugged. "I just want to learn about God without others expecting things of me they don't expect out of their own family members." There was a quiet pause as Leah thought carefully. Her eyes squinted in contemplation as if she was determining that her next works would be critical in their relationship.

"There is one other thing I want to say." Thad couldn't guess what that could be, but she spoke with such conviction that it earned his further admiration. "I don't want your views of church to be tainted by my personal grievances. If you allow me to influence your thinking, it will naturally encourage your disgust of the church and of God. This would be very unfair to you." Leah's eyes softened. "I want you to have the freedom to choose for yourself what you will believe without being influenced by my experiences." Leah was thoughtful as Thad watched a transformation take place. "I'm beginning to see that I've been wrong about a few things and I'm trying to make some changes." She took Thad's hand and held it firmly. "Besides, I'm here with you…and Taima and Alma. You've given me a new beginning. I have to leave that old stuff behind or else I'll ruin something special we have right now. A distant relative once sent me the page from a devotional booklet which encouraged me so much. The quip at the bottom of the page read, 'If your vision for the future is greater than your memory of the past, you can go forward.' It's time for me to catch the vision forward."

A smile edged Thad's lips. The anger he had felt for a lifetime against the church was vanishing and slowly being replaced by a greater desire to move forward in discovery of God's person in both of their lives. Leah had allowed him this privilege and was offering him the leadership role.

"Well, I had to drag it out of you, but it's kind of nice to know you'd go to all that trouble just to sew my buttons back on my shirts for me."

Leah couldn't help laughing.

"Well, Mr. Tucker, where are those shirts? I'm wide awake!"

Thad pursed his lips together thoughtfully. "I was going to put them out for you, but I've decided not to."

"Why not?"

"We're not married yet."

Leah regarded him with surprise.

"Besides, I haven't asked you to marry me yet."

"I know and why is that?" Leah ventured with more daring than convention.

"I have a plan." He smiled and didn't continue.

"Oh?" At that moment Leah looked like a child surrounded by a multitude of Christmas presents. All of them had her name on the gift tags. He relished her enthusiasm for marriage, but he wanted to orchestrate a proposal in a special way that would honor her sacrifice and courage.

A large piece of charred log fell from its perch and landed against the fire screen. Thad got up, picked up a poker and adjusted the chunk before adding more wood. The fire enveloped both the charred piece and the new fuel producing a warming glow. He turned and sat down in a wing-backed chair across from Leah—a pleased grin played across his face. His pen pal was some kind of miracle!

Chapter 14

Morning Devotions

"I remember one of your first letters to me, Leah. You asked me if I'd ever lived in an igloo. I think I know why you laughed so hard when you saw this cabin for the first time." He smiled and leaned forward to confide in her.

"The summer after I returned from the ranch in Arizona to attend the University of Alaska, I remember stepping off the ferry in Seward and thinking this land was big enough for me. I thought I was one tough cowboy even though I'd slept through the port call at Whittier and had to pay the extra fee to get off the ferry at Seward. I was so ticked that I decided to hitch-hike to Anchorage just to prove I could do it." Thad chuckled. "But I was soon reminded that this land was a whole lot bigger than I was MAN enough to handle. About three miles out of Seward, I met a bull moose with a bad attitude grazing by the road. I don't think he liked the smell of horses on me. I backed off slowly then walked all the way back to the train depot in Seward and bought a ticket to ride the tracks to Anchorage." Thad said dryly. Leah was trying to picture Thad as a tough cowboy. It came across as odd and she stifled a smile. He did not seem the type...at least as she knew him now. Thad noticed her effort to keep serious.

"I was in a hurry to do great things. I had plans of building a big horse ranch someday. But, as you will come to find out for yourself, there is definitely one kind of time here that is known as Alaska Time. I've come to believe that *hurry* around here is a miss-typed *flurry,* as in slow falling snow! Nobody messes with Alaska Time either." Leah laughed outright. She was still trying to picturing him as a tough cowboy while dealing with the *hurry-flurry.*

"Did I say something funny?" he frowned.

"I'm sorry, Thad. I just can't seem to picture you as a tough cowboy at the moment. The *hurry-flurry* thing didn't help. But it's late. I'll settle down, you just keep talking. I am listening." Leah said sincerely. Thad smiled at her concentrated effort to give full attention before proceeding.

"All I had was a letter of acceptance from the University and a blank check for room, board, and tuition from my Uncle Peter. All the clothes I owned were stuffed into one duffel bag. I knew I had to complete a freshman year in Fairbanks before really getting involved with the Agriculture and Forestry program here in Palmer and I was glad I didn't have to stay with my Mom. I was cocky and stubborn. When I left my Mom at our small apartment in Palmer that August, she cried. Not because I was leaving for college, but because I was leaving, period. You see, after graduation from Colony High School, I left immediately for the Weston Ranch in Arizona so she hadn't seen me all summer." Leah listed with growing interest. Both had been eager to leave home for a similar reason.

"That first semester at UA was awful. I can smile about it now, but then…well, I endured that first semester of college out of sheer stubbornness. I missed Arizona a great deal and college life was a whole lot different. For one thing, I was a nobody!" Thad emphasized. "And, second, it was cold, dark, and lonely, because I'd always been surrounded by friends, family, or horses. Now, I had to make friends." He saw a little smile etch the corners of Leah's mouth as she nodded in mutual understanding.

"There is one reason…well, actually two reasons, why I stayed and stuck it out." He put two fingers up. "Second semester, I got a new roommate. A black fellow named Tyrone Johnson. I don't think you met him at the Trading Post." Leah shook her head from side to side. "He was born in Alaska and his father had served as a jet pilot at Elmendorf Air Force Base during the Vietnam War. After the war, he worked for the Alaska Railroad until he retired. Anyhow, Tyrone and I became good friends and then business partners. He helped me find work locally to pay off college bills. Thankfully, his family welcomed me into their home on many occasions. His parents are also strong Bible people, but both of us were uninterested in religion, though Tyrone seemed warmer to religion than I was." Thad took a momentary sidetrack. "He's a bachelor too." He stood and shoved his hands into his jean pockets and yawned. "The second reason I stayed was for Taima. Sometime, I'll tell you how Taima and I met. But I'm too tired right now." He yawned again.

"I've told you some of my life's story because I made it a point to ask about you; but never offered much information about myself. I did that purposely, Leah. I needed to know your motives for writing to a man who lived so far away from everything familiar to you. You're here because I liked you from the very first day I received your Bio along with that rough FAX picture from the dating service." Thad came over and sat beside her. He reached up and ran his hand gently along her soft smooth cheek. There was a fondness in his eyes that melted Leah's heart.

"There were moments after the arrangements were made for you to visit that I wondered if it was really a good idea. People are masters of disguise and even though I felt confident you were honest, I still had doubts about the whole idea. Pennsylvania is such a long way away. It seemed like another world." He took her hand in his.

"When we met in the store, the first thing I thought was that you were ten times prettier than your schoolteacher pictures. I made a decision right then. If you'd made all the effort just to come up and meet a bearded man in muddy pants and boots when you could have stayed back home and married someone from your hometown...well, I just figured you had to be some kind of special." He gave her a cocky grin.

"You are, Leah," he assured her than added, "I just want to know that you're not a dream or too good to be true." He still held Leah's hand. She stood to face him as well.

"I need you to be true."

"I want to be true."

"I know that now." He squeezed her hand and released it. "I need to get some rest. I know you're still operating on Eastern Time Zone so there's no use telling you to get some rest until your brain adjusts to this time zone. I'll put another log on the fire for you. Maybe you'll doze off later." Thad moved to care for the fire.

"I did wake up thinking it was time to get up and get going. But, how did you know I was up? I tried to be as quiet as I could."

Thad chuckled, wiped the wood bits and ashes from his hands and turned to regard her with a little smirk.

"You remember my living depends on employing skills as an experienced hunting and fishing guide. Disciplined sensibility, natural and acquired instinct, the necessity to be keenly alert to every sound, sight, smell, touch, and even taste is essential in my line of work." He winked at her. "I knew you were up and 'lurking' around when you started down the steps." Leah was wide-eyed.

"Why didn't you tell me you were there?" she asked and Thad paused before smiling and answering.

"Because I was so engrossed in trying to figure out what you were doing that Taima came up behind me and SCARED THE LIFE OUT OF ME!" he confessed frankly. "He's good at it, too! Anyhow, I was afraid if I let you know I was there, I'd frighten you and cause you to fall down the steps. So, I just watched to make sure you were making your way safely." He rubbed his forearm under the T-shirt gingerly as if it pained him.

"I should have been more concerned about my well-being than yours."

Leah groaned but Thad slyly smiled.

"After you broke the broom handle on me...and left marks," he emphasized, "I took a couple of seconds to think about what you might have done if you had known I was there."

Leah couldn't resist a merry laugh at Thad's expense. He waited enjoying the sound of her mirth then carried on some more.

"I must admit, there are a whole lot of wild animals out there," he pointed out the window, "that frighten me much less now than you do." Leah bit her bottom lip to squelch the laughter that bubbled up and escaped.

"You haven't met my best friend, Denise." Leah said knowingly.

"Don't change the subject," he protested mildly. Leah's eyebrows rose. "I have to leave in a few hours to take those two gentlemen to their next fishing destination and I won't be back until Sunday afternoon. So you and Alma will pretty much have the place to yourselves." He hesitated. "I know you'll protect the place," he rubbed his arm meaningfully. He wasn't going to let her forget the punishment. "Just don't burn the place down, please."

Leah peered around him as if looking for something. Thad stopped chuckling in efforts to understand what she was searching for.

"What?" he asked. Leah took a step to the right.

"I was looking for another broom."

Thad laughed, "I hope you're not the type that uses a broom to solve all your domestic problems. One sore arm is enough." He stepped toward Leah, relishing her closeness, then bent and kissed her forehead before turning and saying a clipped, "Good night, Leah!" He was at the end of the room when he turned and smiled at her. Leah was bewildered. She had expected…something a little more than a kiss on the forehead. 'Babies get kisses on the forehead,' she thought.

"My Mom drilled something into this thick brain of mine a long time ago," said Thad. "Her only words to me about the birds and the bees was this, and I quote, 'If she hasn't put a ring on your finger, said I DO, and signed on the dotted line, you don't!' And right then, I was teetering." He smiled before disappearing into the semi-darkness.

Leah peered into the darkness for a few moments before turning to catch the reflection of the fire lights dancing on the walls. Many thoughts and emotions made it difficult to think clearly until her gaze returned to the orange embers of the fire crackling and snapping happily in the hearth. The fire's sounds were calming and she returned to sit on the couch to ponder her runaway heart. The Bible lay beside her and with a gentle hand her fingers slid over the leather binding noting its well worn cover.

Bits and pieces of the recent conversation with Thad came to mind, especially the astounded look Thad had given her when she revealed to him she was not a Christian. The word "heathen" charged into her thoughts.

What was wrong with her? Why couldn't she trust God to be more to her than what she saw of Him in people who claimed to believe in him? She'd known about God for so many years and at times tried to please Him. The Bible opened to the Psalms where Leah scanned the song for one verse to answer her many questions. But phrases of words weren't connected. It was as confusing as classic literature without an interpreter.

Even as she turned page after page, she realized the futility of this process she had so often used. At last, she made up her mind to stop and read the very next Psalm in its entirety. It was Psalm 143.

"Hear my prayer, O Lord, give ear unto my supplications; in Thy faithfulness answer me, and in Thy righteousness."

This verse said exactly what she desired in her heart. It amazed her that the person who wrote this Psalm had asked the same request of Deity. She wanted to know God's faithfulness to her. People weren't perfect. She wasn't perfect.

"And enter not into judgment with thy servant; for in Thy sight shall no man living be justified." Leah identified completely with the Psalmist. She felt unjustified in God's eyes and she felt the judgment of God towards her to be rightfully deserved; but she wanted something other than judgment. There had been so much of it all her life.

Verses three, four, five and six were a revelation of her struggles, "the enemy hath persecuted my soul." Who was the enemy of the soul? She knew from childhood it was Satan. "...he hath smitten my life down to the ground; he hath made me to dwell in darkness, as those that have been long dead."

Leah had always felt dead and lifeless to the teachings of the scripture about salvation and eternal life. She realized her soul dwelled in darkness. There was no light of love, no joy, no peace, only the longing for the true God others spoke of knowing...like Denise and her sister, Sarah, and her Dad.

"My heart within me is desolate." A picture in her mind revealed an empty, run-down shack with dirt and cobwebs. In this shack silence and fear greeted the explorer instead of life and peace. There was no Savior to reign triumphant in her heart and no hope to fill the cracks where death threatened to carry her away to a lonely eternity for more judgment.

She read on through verse five. "I remember the days of old; I meditate on all Thy works; I muse on the work of Thy hands." Leah had grown up in a Christian home knowing the stories and people of the Bible by heart. She enjoyed God's creation. Honestly, she had seen God's power work positively in the lives of others also. Denise came to mind for a moment and Leah missed her best friend a great deal. She could hardly fault Denise for her failings as a Christian where Jack was concerned. She knew her friend was trying to find answers as well.

Verse six read, "I stretch forth my hands unto Thee; my soul thirsteth after Thee, as a thirsty land. Selah!" Think about that. Leah defined the last word as her father had defined it for his congregation.

"Oh, Lord." She stopped and looked up somehow thinking that God would turn an ear to her request. "I do thirst for You, God." Her eyes dropped to verse seven and she recognized the cry of her soul.

"Hear me speedily." As a little girl, Leah had seen a movie where a man had been swallowed up in a pit of quicksand. She had dreamed this nightmare often over the years. Always, she saw herself being swallowed up in that pit. It had terrified her then, and still did. The vivid picture of the next words awoke a dread in her heart and soul for fear that when she next slept she would dream it again. "...lest I be like unto them that go down into the pit." Leah wondered if any of these verses had hope! They were the perfect parody of her life. She was tempted to leave this depressing passage and find another more pleasant one to read; but she kept her promise and read on to the end. Gladness filled her heart as she read verse eight.

"Cause me to hear Thy loving kindness in the morning: for in Thee do I trust; cause me to know the way wherein I should walk, for I lift up my soul unto Thee." Leah stopped reading and thought about this beautiful request. The word *loving-kindness* was a cool drink of water to her soul. Leah wanted to hear the words of loving kindness from God. It was a magnificent wonder that God should love her, Leah Grant!

"Show me which way I should walk to you, Lord." Tears gathered in her eyes as she lifted her soul to the Lord. Leah finished reading the last four verses of the chapter and read verse eight again. For some time she sat still thinking about the verses of scripture which so clearly described her own need. After a while the exhaustion of travel and emotions overwhelmed her and she lay down on the couch. The Bible remained opened beside her as she drifted off to sleep. Dreams of unrelated events coursed through her subconscious at lightning speed until once again the nightmare of the sand pit played out in slow-sinking motion.

The August sun was already up when Thad and Taima awakened at 5 a.m. Thad was meeting O'Brien and Ishioti to take them to a place called Cantwell where they would meet another fishing guide to fish the lakes and streams along the Parks Highway, about two hours northeast of Palmer. He would stay overnight at the hunting lodge in Cantwell and leave on Sunday morning with three other clients who were returning to Anchorage to catch flights back to Seattle then on to Bellingham, Washington. Thad hoped to spend some time with Leah Sunday afternoon. His hope was to be engaged by the end of the day whether or not everything went as planned!

At the last minute, Taima remembered he needed to leave a note for Leah to be ready to go with him to the trading post after lunch. After last evening's meeting with the couple on the deck, Taima decided he might as well show Leah around the place. He'd considered their threesome household and reckoned they had room for Leah. Beyond that he was not willing to contemplate just yet.

Thad fixed mugs of coffee for both of them and followed Taima through the dining room and into the warming rays of rising sunshine coming through the large windows. He greeted another beautiful day with a long gaze at Pioneer Peak. Its massive height and breadth shaded the still sleeping city of Palmer until the sun crept slowly over its jagged summit to brighten potato fields across the fertile valley. High winds passed over it and around it like invisible wings fanning lazy clouds north to south. The famous peak was a testimonial to the perseverance of early pioneers to the region. Only those who studied it for a lifetime might notice changes in its granite face. Each new day marked the passage of ancient time.

Thad went over to stand by the fireplace where tiny embers still flickered beneath the pile of charred black ash. He looked over at the couch and saw Leah sleeping soundly. Taima smiled when Thad showed him her sleeping repose.

Leah lay on her side with her feet tucked up under the long chenille robe for warmth. Her hands lay together under her cheek to support her head like a pillow. Dark curly hair lay in chaotic array around her face and shoulders. She slept peacefully like Susitna's maiden. Taima watched the expression on Thad's face and grinned when he reached to stroke a beard that wasn't there anymore!

Thad studied her quiet repose as if to etch this picture in his mind. At some time in his travels, there would be time for reflection when he would bring this picture of loveliness to mind. Of course, there would be a few moments when he would have to concentrate on pertinent things like hunting and fishing. At least this vision of her would be some small respite for the absence of her presence.

"Sleeping princess," Taima teased. Thad nodded as he continued to look at her. He sipped coffee more out of habit than for the taste or need of it. Setting it down on the fireplace mantle, he reached for an afghan on a nearby rocking chair and was about to lay it over Leah when Taima stopped him. He followed Taima's gaze and saw that Leah's sleep had changed from peaceful to troubled. She stirred restlessly; her breathing irregular and staggered. She seemed to be trying to say something but couldn't. Thad moved to awaken her, but Taima put out a hand to stop the advance.

Just as quickly, Leah relaxed. Her breathing returned to normal and once again, she slept peacefully. Thad waited for a few moments before gently laying the afghan over his sleeping princess. He thought of the mountain called Susitna and understood the warrior's temptation to remain by his beloved's side. But Thad resisted the urge to remain or to kiss her forehead fearing it would awaken and startle her. He had no intentions of robbing her of any sleep, so he left her and quietly walked out into the front hallway where Taima was putting on his carhartt jacket to leave. In low voices they talked about the arrangements for this day and the next. Then Taima spoke about Leah.

"She had a bad dream, you know. Something troubles her a great deal," he said matter-of-factly." Thad considered the statement before commenting. Taima's native background played deeply into the spirit world of superstition and omens. Most of the time Thad didn't take Taima too seriously; nor did he make light of his musings. He respected Taima even if his old friend seemed to make use of this background to tease him.

"Maybe it was just a result of all the changes." In the nearly five and a half months he and Leah had corresponded, he thought he had learned a great deal about his pen-pal, bride-to-be. But in just the few short hours since her arrival, he'd discovered there was a whole lot more to learn about one Leah Annette Grant! Her presence struck several emotional nerves he had not expected or even known existed. Taima shrugged his shoulders.

"Maybe her nightmare was about wolves." His voice almost cracked like an adolescent.

Thad glanced in the direction of the couch then he shook his head at Taima who was grinning at his own humor.

"Nice try."

Taima sobered. "Don't worry, Alma and I will look after her while you're gone. I had to look after you until you straightened out." A sly grin appeared on his weathered face. Thad reached for his camera equipment then fixed his eyes on Taima.

"No stories about me, Taima. She'll hear enough of them from Tyrone…if he meets her before I have a chance to tell her a few stories myself." This last part he mumbled under his breath, then emphasized, "No stories!" As they took the steps down to the vehicles, Taima chuckled and Thad glanced back at him, but Taima didn't share the joke. He just shrugged his shoulders and smiled.

He was remembering one of Thad's first clients who had been from a small Pennsylvania town called Clarion. This guy had spoken to Thad about a forest animal called a "snipe." He had described it in such glowing terms that Thad had agreed to look for one of the creatures in Alaska. Arizona had no such animal and it was doubtful Alaska had anything like it either! But Thad had humored the guy anyway. About the time Thad figured out the intricacies involved in snipe hunting, the guy took off leaving Thad to search for him in the Alaskan wilderness. The client probably thought he was pretty clever to pull off such a neat caper with an experienced guide, but he had underestimated the Alaska frontier and became miserably lost. Thad searched and found him with a broken ankle due to a fall over the side of a slippery rock ledge. Long on fatigue and short on temper, Thad had carried the man back to Palmer over his shoulder. That was eight years ago. It was one story Taima frequently told Thad's clients and one he repeated to old friends who sat around the pot-bellied stove at the trading post musing over youthful days of folly.

Chapter 15

Taima Knows!

Leah slept until the sun awakened her around noon. A little groggy and confused by new surroundings, it took a few seconds to remember where she was and how she'd come to be in this new place. The sun was out in brilliance and was casting long rays across the room in warming waves of welcome. For a few minutes, she sat looking about her at the lofty ceiling beams above then stood and looked ahead at the landscape beyond the large glass deck doors. The majesty of the distant Talkeetna mountain range gave a feeling of exhilaration as she viewed the limitless expanse of earth and rock from the wall of windows. There was room for her in Alaska. Still dressed in pajamas and robe, Leah easily pulled the glass door to the side and stepped out onto the deck. The mild 50 degree temperature seemed chilly though it was pleasantly warm for Alaskans. The fresh air filled her lungs as she breathed deeply and exhaled.

After only a few minutes, Leah decided it was too cold to stay outside even thought she longed to enjoy the peace and quiet. Her body was not yet used to the cooler temperature after the ninety-degree weather of her distant home state. She wrapped her arms around her chest and walked back into the cabin shivering as she entered. It had been so warm under the afghan. A glance at the afghan caused her to wonder if Alma had covered her earlier.

Alma came into the room and smiled a greeting as she signed a "good afternoon."

"Hi, Alma," Leah responded. "I'm afraid I've slept half the day away. Thank you for covering me with this warm afghan. I slept like a baby."

There was a frown on Alma's face. "I didn't cover you, Leah. Thad must have before he left with Taima," she replied forming the letters "T-A" in short for Taima. Thad was just "T". Leah was addressed with the letter "L" formed with the right hand index finger pointing up and the thumb at a right angle like a printed "L".

"Oh." Leah nodded wondering when Thad had made the kind gesture. It embarrassed her a little, but Alma didn't seem to think anything of it.

"Taima will be in for lunch soon, so you may want to shower and dress before we eat. I think he plans to take you to the Trading Post this afternoon and show you off." Alma's eyes were large with meaning. She smiled mischievously at Leah who at once felt shy and a tad apprehensive.

"Well," Leah said with more confidence than she felt, "I'd better get busy right away. This could take some time." She lifted a tangled bunch of curls and frowned at them. Alma waved her hand and made a face.

"You're young and I know someone who thinks those curls of yours are beautiful," she assured, a thumb lightly brushing the side of her face meaning "beauty." Leah pressed her lips together and blinked her gaze down.

"Thank you, Alma," she said simply. "Sometimes it's just nice to know someone thinks so."

Alma understood and nodded her agreement. Leah picked up the afghan and, folding it in half, laid it neatly over the back of the couch. Alma noticed the placement of the afghan and pursed her lips in satisfaction. Leah didn't realize it, but that single action earned Alma's respect because it revealed that Leah cared about neatness and order, even if it was someone else's place and responsibility. Alma didn't really care where the afghan was placed, as long as it was placed neatly. She had labored over this home for Thad with the hope he would one day bring his bride here. She had hoped his future bride would care and was pleased to see Leah's thoughtfulness. There would be human faults and failings, but Alma felt comfortable around Leah. Perhaps it was because of the communication between them. Alma also saw kindness reflected in Leah's sincere desire to be helpful, and it spoke clearly of her inner character. If Leah went to religious services, Alma wanted to find out what kind of religion Leah practiced. She had noticed the Bible Leah unpacked and wondered that anyone could understand it. She had grown up in the Russian Orthodox faith. The priests seemed to be the only ones who could interpret the scriptures. Leah's reading of the Bible puzzled Alma because it seemed as if it was common to have the Holy Book—like having a library book to read. Their differences had made her both uneasy at first and then eager to know more about Leah's religion. When Alma was only a baby, she and her brother, Taima, and their family had been displaced from their village on the Aleutian Islands and moved to the Alaskan Panhandle to an Internment Camp for a period of time during World War II. The sight of the Bible stirred sad memories of her mother's death from disease while at the camp. Pushing these thoughts out of her mind, Alma went back to the kitchen to finish lunch preparations while Leah made her way upstairs to dress for the day.

Once showered and dressed in a pair of navy slacks, Leah pulled a white turtleneck over her head. Over that, a red sweater with gold music notes printed randomly around the yoke shimmered as she checked their sparkle reflected in the mirror. She pulled on navy crew socks then laced up a pair of dark brown leather ankle boots. A banana comb was secured in her hair after she thoroughly brushed the tangled strands into some semblance of order. After a creamy foundation of liquid makeup was applied, a light brushing of rose blush tinted her cheeks. A touch of velvety mascara highlighted soft lashes before some lip-gloss smoothed dry lips to complete the cosmetic routine. A small case containing several sets of pierced earrings was pulled from the drawer of the nightstand beside her bed. Many of them were new while a few of them had been gifts or long time favorites. Leah selected a small gold ball set and secured them in place before checking her appearance in a full-length mirror. Curly ringlets of brown hair were gathered in a mass and fell gracefully below her shoulders. Leah turned from the mirror with a positive sigh and began cleaning up the room by quickly unpacking clothes and putting personal items away before going downstairs.

Taima came in the door just as Leah came down the stairs. She greeted him politely wondering what he thought of her "visit". He glanced at her as if not used to her being a member of the household, yet. Offering a quick nod of acknowledgment he moved toward the kitchen and took a seat at the round table.

Leah felt awkward all at once but managed to take a seat without any catastrophes. Alma was sitting down as Leah adjusted her chair. Taima began to make a sandwich from the plate of bread and meat when Alma gently touched his arm and signed for him to wait until Leah said a prayer. The irritated expression Taima gave his sister was one Leah could not help but see. But, in deference to his sister and "Thad's mail-order bride", he managed a polite nod and bowed his head. After all, he'd been telling his customers about "Thad's mail-order bride" all morning, especially the broken broom incident. It would be a busy afternoon at the trading post!

Alma nodded her head for Leah to give a prayer of thanks for their food. At once, Leah felt insincere and false, but she managed to utter a simple prayer of thanks to God and to request Thad's safety. When she said, "Amen" Alma devoutly made the sign of the cross over her heart. Taima remained poker faced but Alma lipped a "thank you" and they began to eat the soup and sandwiches. If Alma hadn't encouraged the prayer, Leah realized she probably wouldn't have initiated one. The word "heathen" raced across her subconscious in a flash of conviction.

"Would you like to see a bit of Palmer by way of the Trading Post, Leah?" Taima asked Leah cordially enough. Almost too cordially! She sensed he was making an effort to get used to her. It was the first time he'd used her name. Leah felt exactly the same way about Taima. His stoic, often sarcastic expression was hard for her to read or respond to without feeling like a misfit. If she was to understand Thad better, she would have to try to understand Taima because he had Thad's respect as a confidant.

"Yes, I'd like to, very much."

"Good, we'll leave right after we've finished lunch." Alma winked at Leah from across the table. Leah returned a nervous grin that played uncertainly across her face. Taima told her about some of the local people as they ate. When Alma wasn't eating, she was smiling. Her brother was doing a lot of talking. This was very unusual for him!

After they finished, Alma shooed them out of the kitchen. As they prepared to leave, she came up to Leah. Taima was already at the door.

"Don't be nervous, Leah. Taima likes to play at being intimidating, but he's really a kitten," Alma snickered, still signing rapidly. "I've never heard him talk so much in his life, especially when he's eating. I think he was trying to make you feel at ease. Help him," she requested. "My brother wouldn't show you off to his friends if he didn't like you."

"Unless it's to humiliate me,' Leah teased. Alma grinned and shook her head. She patted Leah's arm before waving her out the door.

"Thank you," she said and hurried out the door and down the steps to the sidewalk beside the cement driveway.

When Leah reached the cement, she stopped in her tracks with mouth open in astonishment. Taima sat on a Harley Police Electraglide which dated back to the early 1960s. The only reason she knew about this motorcycle was that Denise's Dad had one he prized and protected in his collection in the garage. He'd have kept it in the house if Denise's mother would have permitted it. It had a notorious heritage with the California Highway Patrol. Taima had one, too! And, he was laughing at her! Having never been on a motorcycle in her life, the opportunity to ride one challenged every imaginable inhibition. The Harley revved powerfully. Leah stepped toward the cycle, knees wobbling like jello.

"Loud and leakin'," Taima shouted proudly. He turned the Electra glide off to tell the history of the classic bike. Though Leah knew the history she listened realizing this was his way of showing acceptance or maybe testing her for a negative reaction. It was an important hallmark in their relationship and Leah paid attention to his every word.

"The year I bought my very first motorcycle, I was nineteen and it was the year Alaska became a state in 1959. I tore that bike down and built it back up. It didn't run very long—about three minutes total before it caught fire and burnt to a crisp. But that didn't stop me. I saved up about eight hundred dollars over a period of six years and was just about to purchase a used bike when I heard that the California Highway Police department was auctioning off their old Harley Electraglides in 1965. So, I hitchhiked all the way to Sacramento and bought two bikes for only $250.00 a piece. I had to stay long enough to tear them both down and rebuild one that would run me back to Alaska, at least. It didn't burn up this time," he chuckled. "I gathered what extra parts I could use, especially the chain, and packed them on the bike, then sold the other parts off for gas and food. I returned home with this particular bike. If you look closely, you can still see the CHP's emblem on the gas tank." She could hear the passion in his voice as he pointed to the faded emblem. Leah bent to examine the dark blue trim which had been polished to a glazed shine over thirty years of care. Taima had just given her a unique glimpse into his past and into his heart.

"This is the best maintained Electraglide I've ever seen, Taima."

Taima blinked his surprise at her statement.

"You've seen Electraglides?"

"Only one. My girlfriend's Dad is a Chicago Policeman and has one about the same year as yours, but it doesn't run. He just keeps it in the garage with some other old motorcycles," Leah replied then added, "My Uncle Sam rides with The Road Ranger's Harley Club in upstate New York. Once, I remember him telling my sisters and me that there are three rules to owning a Harley. One, you can't ride until you can pick it up. Two, it's not your ride until you've torn it down and built it back up. And, three, you have to be able to lay it out to avoid an accident." Leah chuckled, "I memorized the rules just to aggravate my Mom at the supper table and irritate two cousins who were boys. They got to ride with my Uncle Sam once at a family reunion and I didn't. Mom wouldn't let me ride."

Taima regarded her keenly with a grin of satisfaction.

"Your Mom isn't here, now. How about a ride?" Taima queried.

"Sure! There is one thing, though," she started shaking her head slowly from side to side, "I have no idea how to ride. I don't know how to get on. I don't know how to sit on it and I have no idea where to put..." she put her hands in the air, "...hang on," she finished with a dubious expression. Taima roared with laughter. Leah blushed, embarrassed by her own ignorance. When Taima's laughter mellowed, she shrugged her shoulders and he laughed again as he got off the bike and began to explain the process. She listened and nodded in understanding. He regarded her for a moment and suggested they could take the pickup if she wanted to. Leah considered the option briefly.

"No. I don't want to go in the pickup," she decided. "You've told me what to do and how to hang on. So, we'll take the Harley."

Taima smiled and handed her a helmet then helped her put it over her head. She awkwardly mounted the bike after Taima mounted and waited while he started the Harley. Leah held on securely and loudly shouted, "I'm ready!"

Off they went down the driveway and onto the macadam road. All Leah could say over and over again was, "Oh, my goodness!" She couldn't help the nervous giggles that escaped between the repeated phrases. For a few minutes she felt overwhelmed until she began to gain her equilibrium and confidence. Breathing became slower as she focused on the rugged countryside which flattened and opened into the wide expanse of pre-winter fields and sporadic wooded patches of birch tree, small pine trees, and a variety of bushes of all sizes. Always, the gray line of mountains rose in snow peaked grandeur where the fields stopped to give way to wilderness.

"Thank you, God," she said aloud and wondered at this infant regard for the Creator.

It was a short distance to the edge of Palmer where Thunder's Trading Post was located. As they came to it, Taima steered the Harley around to the back of the store and drove into a long building which had several automobile storage stalls. He proceeded into one of them and drove the Harley between the opened doors. Once the kickstand was down, he slid easily off the bike seat then helped Leah off checking to see how steady she was on her feet. Noting that she seemed sure footed, he took his helmet off and laid it on the bike seat. He took the helmet Leah had just removed and set it down as well.

As she removed the helmet, the banana comb sprang open releasing a mass of tangled hair. Taima saw something about Leah he would always remember. Her eyes were moist as if tears had gathered only moments ago. There was a joy in her expression radiating the pleasure of the most recent ride. It was as if she had been reborn. What he sometimes took for granted he somehow knew was keenly unique to Leah. It was freedom. Taima wondered about her life back home. She had called no one back there to say she had arrived safely. Then again, he reasoned she was not a child at all, but a grown woman who had made a choice to come to Alaska to meet someone she'd never seen face to face until yesterday.

Thad had mentioned that her father was a minister and he figured she'd struggled with the decision to come on that particular account. Of course, the disappointment of others and their condemnation might have figured in there, too. Maybe this explained why there was a sense of freedom and release he'd noted in her eyes. That she'd left home behind and didn't seem to miss it at all would be understandable. But there was another thing that nagged at him concerning her supposed Christianity. He wanted to know why she would pay attention to a man like Thad who had nothing at all to do with church or religion. He decided to wait and see what direction their relationship would take. He was beginning to like Leah as a person.

"I'm glad I decided to take you up on your offer to ride the Harley," Leah said with shinning eyes. "I never imagined how close to nature it puts a person. It's completely different from being surrounded by the steel and glass of a regular vehicle."

Taima pulled his jacket sleeve up a short way past his wrist to reveal a massive scar from the middle of his palm to about three inches past his wrist. "I got a little too close to nature once," he said, "and a little too careless." Leah grimaced at the scar. She pushed her bangs above her forehead and pointed to a one inch scar.

"Tricycle accident--sidewalk racing at age four."

Taima nodded, smiling. She was a kindred spirit after all!

CHAPTER 16

MAYHEM AND MOONLIGHT CHATS

ONE OF THE GREATEST EVIDENCES OF acceptance is friendship. Both Taima and Leah needed friendship. One needed a new path, the other needed to show the way.

"Have you ever taken Alma for a ride on the Harley?" Leah asked. Taima didn't answer right away.

"I used to take her for rides all the time when she was younger. But she left home when she was eighteen and lived in California for several years. When she came to live here about eight years ago, she was too sick to care much for anything, especially riding a motorcycle." The tenor of his voice was deeply reflective. Leah sensed conversation about Alma was a delicate topic with Taima. She wanted to ask him more, but didn't want to pry.

"Maybe she'll ride again," she offered mildly.

"I hope so," Taima agreed.

"I'll never forget the smell of this store. When I first arrived yesterday evening, I thought I'd entered an era of time before automobiles and telephones." She glanced at Taima to check his reaction. "I hope that didn't sound like criticism."

"I wouldn't take it that way." He said as they moved from the back of the store to the front where he unlocked the door and turned the "closed" sign to "open".

"I mostly sell hunting equipment and supplies, plus sports equipment, sportswear and camera gear." Taima walked behind the counter. "Usually, we just talk about news here, though. It's sort of a meeting place at times." He looked out the front display window and saw some friends walking toward the store.

"Looks like you'll get to meet Joe Dorance and his little daughter today. Joe's a second-generation vegetable farmer in the valley. His mother is well known for her greenhouse plants and flowers which are some of the hardiest grown. Years ago she would start the cabbage plants for two local gentlemen who vied for first place in the giant cabbage contest at the Alaska State Fair. Of course, neither man knew that fact for a long time. Some of their cabbages weighed as much or more than seventy pounds. One head of cabbage would fill a wheelbarrow. They still grow them big up here. Many vegetables grow to gigantic sizes in Alaska due to the longer hours of daylight in the summer. Joe is in the wholesale business now. He farms some of his family's land plus his own. His mother still has her green house business over near the Butte. He's a widower and little Michelle is his only child," he confided. "Judy Dorance died in child birth. It was a miracle the baby girl there survived. She's real shy and backward. It's tough for Joe, though." Father and daughter walked up the steps to the front door and entered. Leah smiled a greeting to them then moved over to look at some cameras on display. Michelle walked at her father's side, but Leah could sense the little girl's eyes watching her every move. She looked over at Michelle again and smiled quickly before returning to study the cameras. Michelle's long blond hair was pulled back into a neat ponytail with a pink ribbon. The little girl was dressed in casual play clothes and looked freshly groomed. Her big blue eyes captivated Leah's attention and revealed a depth of curiosity sparked by youth.

Joe Dorance spoke to Taima about general news for a while before he inquired about ammunition and skeet disks. It was obvious he enjoyed the sport as he talked avidly about his scores at a nearby shooting range.

Leah had picked up a camera and was looking through the eye gate. Everything was blurry, so she automatically stepped backwards while adjusting the focus to see if distance would produce an image. Slowly she stepped back, taking one step at a time while turning the lens. Just as the focus adjusted, Leah bumped into a display of hockey sticks and they fell one after the other in a kind of rhythmic pattern. She tried to catch them with one hand but it was too late. By the time she reached for one, another would lean and fall in domino style. At last, all eighteen hockey sticks were in a pile on the floor. Taima had been showing Joe the skeet disks and stopped to check the mayhem. Leah turned around slowly. The camera still clutched tightly in her hand. When all was finally quiet, she released a weary sigh.

"Oh, no!" she said simply and frowned while returning the camera safely to the display case. The silence was broken by the eruption of a girlish giggle. Little Michelle Dorance had stepped away from her father to check out the smiling lady. She had watched Leah with the camera and seen the inevitable bump that sent hockey sticks tumbling in all directions.

Leah looked apologetically at Taima, uncertain of what kind of damage she might have done to the sticks and display. He looked as surprised as Joe; but they weren't looking at Leah. They were watching Michelle who continued to giggle while Leah stopped to pick up the fallen sports equipment.

When Leah tried to set the hockey sticks back, they threatened to fall again because she could only put one stick at a time back into the slots. When they tipped again, Leah tried to catch them, but they all tumbled again. This sent Michelle into a ripple of giggles. Leah looked over at her and smiled as did Taima and Joe. They still seemed astonished by Michelle's outburst. Leah approached Michelle slowly.

"Would you like to help me put the hockey sticks back on the display? I'm not doing very well by myself." Michelle stopped giggling to consider Leah's request. The smile of friendship encouraged the shy little girl to help.

"I'll help you," she said softly and started towards the hockey stick display. Joe Dorance could hardly believe what he was seeing. His little girl laughed and talked to him all the time, but rarely to anyone else. He had been concerned that she would have trouble adjusting to school because of her shyness. For a moment the tall, thin man of forty-five paused to thank the Lord for an answered prayer.

Taima glanced from Joe to Michelle then made introductions for Leah. "Thad has been writing to Leah these past few months and she's here for a visit." Joe welcomed Leah cordially then asked her how Alma was doing. Taima smiled to himself. It was no secret Joe Dorance admired Alma.

"Alma is fine." Leah reported then shot a quick glance at Taima in puzzlement. Taima spoke up.

"Michelle is a good little helper. She'll do a fine job helping you… fix the hockey sticks." He barely suppressed a chuckle as he returned his attention to the box of skeet disks. Joe smiled at his busy daughter. There was a grin on his face and for once seemed lighthearted. Taima gave Leah a look of gratefulness but saw she was busy resetting the hockey sticks.

"You're a pretty good helper, Michelle," she praised. "Thanks for helping me put these back and getting me out of trouble with Taima."

"You're funny."

"Lately, I've been funny a lot!" admitted Leah with a nod. Michelle giggled.

"Where do you come from?" Michelle asked tilting her head to the side.

Leah straightened up and brushed a hand over her pants to adjust the hem to the top of her shoe. The static from her pants and socks kept driving the hem above her ankle.

"I'm from what you would know to be the Lower Forty-Eight," replied Leah, "Pennsylvania to be exact."

"Let's go sit by the stove to talk. That's what the old people do when they come in here to get stuff. What do I call you?" she asked and Leah smiled at the voice of attempted maturity.

"My students in school called me Miss Leah."

"Miss Leah. That sounds okay to me." They each found a chair beside the warm pot-bellied stove. Only a small fire burned because the day was warm.

"You are a teacher, Miss Leah?"

"Yes, I normally teach deaf children at a church school. I also teach art and music in the academy at my home church."

"Church?" questioned Michelle.

"U-hum."

"Have you ever taught in other schools?" Michelle asked and Leah gathered that she meant a public school.

"Yes. I substituted in public schools many times before I began to teach at the church school." Leah answered noting Michelle's large blue eyes. Leah figured there was a reason for all these questions.

"Did you like it?"

"Yes." Leah nodded positively. "I met many nice teachers and enjoyed working for them as their substitute. Are you going to school this year?" Leah asked, guessing Michelle to be near school age.

"I'm supposed to go this September. But I'm not sure I want to go to school."

"I know how you feel," Leah assured.

"You do?" Michelle was surprised.

"Yep! Going to school is a little like going to a brand new place where you don't know anybody and there's not much that reminds you of home—except one thing." Leah suggested raising her pointer finger.

"What's that?" Michelle was eager to hear the answer.

"Kindness," Leah smiled. "There are always people who are kind to us and want to help us get used to new places and things. You were kind to me just now when you helped me with the hockey sticks. Your teacher will help you, too, Michelle, and I know she'll be kind to you. I was a Kindergarten teacher at one time and I know that we are the kindest teachers in the world!" Michelle was thinking about this. Her eyes squinted as she studied Leah.

"Did you ever yell at your kids?" Michelle was very serious. Leah smiled at the unexpected question.

"Yes, I've *yelled* a few times," she used Michelle's own word to answer. "But it was because I didn't want my students to get hurt. I wanted them to be safe and to learn to do things the right way. I had very good students, though, Michelle. Usually, I only had to remind them once-in-a-while to be careful and to think about what they were doing."

"Oh." She nodded in understanding. "What does your dad do for a living?" Again, the question was such a complete change from the subject that Leah couldn't resist a smile.

"My Dad is a preacher of a Community Church in the small town where we live." Michelle's eyes blinked in surprise.

"Wow! You're lucky!" It was a wonder that Michelle would be impressed by this fact. Leah had never thought that others might think she was privileged to have a preacher as a Dad. Perhaps she'd never considered the sacred honor of her Dad's commitment to ministry before. After all, she'd never honored him or his faith. This thought pricked her conscience.

"We go to a church here in town." Michelle put in and Leah blinked back attention. "My Daddy is on the deacon board." She said rather importantly, sitting up a little straighter. The pride showed in her bright eyes.

"He has an important job, doesn't he?"

"You should come to our church while you're here visiting Wolfe Tucker, Taima, and Alma," Michelle used Thad's nick name too! Leah wondered if the conspiracy had enveloped the little girl as well. "I know them all. Alma's nice to me like you are. Sometimes she works here in the trading post, too. Daddy always stays at the store longer when she's here. I think it's so I can learn how to talk to her. We talk with our hands and lips. I teach my Dad so he can talk to her, too." Leah accepted this last confidence with interest on Alma's behalf. She moved the conversation to another area.

"What's the name of your church?" Leah asked.

"Homestead Chapel and it's just down the street from here," she directed by pointing her finger in the general direction past the front door.

"I'll try to find my way there tomorrow," Leah promised. "At least I'll know you, Michelle. And I won't be by myself either. Alma is coming along to keep me company, too." Leah saw that Michelle was pleased by this information.

"Michelle." Her father called to her. "I'm ready to go now." He approached them and, taking Michelle's hand, he smiled briefly at Leah and left. Two girls of varied ages waved at each other as if they were old friends.

"Daddy, Miss Leah and Alma are coming to our church tomorrow." Michelle spoke as Joe nodded to Taima and they left the store.

Taima was busy putting the ammo back on the shelf when Leah approached the front counter.

"Is there something I can do?"

She felt a little useless and was missing Thad to such a point that time seemed to be dragging with nothing to make it pass faster until she saw him again. Just the thought of him stirred her heart and brought a smile to her daydreams.

Leah was so engrossed in her thoughts of Thad she didn't hear Taima's response until he was a few words into a sentence.

"...need dusted." He directed her way.

"Pardon me?"

"You don't dust shelves?" He asked curiously.

"Oh, yes! I do. I just didn't hear what you said. My mind was somewhere else." Leah finished lamely. Taima grinned.

"He'll be back by this time tomorrow." He saw she immediately looked above him at the large wooden clock on the wall. It pleased him to see that Thad was missed.

"There are some dusting clothes under the counter. Start anywhere, it all needs it."

Leah picked a spot and went to work as Taima welcomed other customers. All afternoon he introduced his customers to Leah as Thad's pen-pal, but she wondered if they were really referring to her as Thad's mail-order-bride! Taima had let this slip a few times.

It was late afternoon when Taima turned the "Open" sign to "Closed". The sky was still bright with sunlight as Taima began to put things under the counter he had been working on and fixing. Leah was in the rear of the store wiping down a display of binoculars when she heard the front door open. Two loud male voices boomed from the front of the store before the door slammed.

Leah heard their vulgar language as they entered. She was standing behind the pot belly stove so her view of the two men was blocked. She stopped dusting to listen realizing she hadn't heard that much filthy language since working at a hotel restaurant while in college. She cringed at their mindless profanity.

Taima greeted them with tight-jawed tolerance. Leah could tell by the tone of his voice he was also repulsed by their crude talk. The first voice hinted a Russian accent. He did not seem as vulgar as the second man, but Leah didn't understand a word of Russian to know the difference!

"Hello, Taima. We have a few supplies to purchase—

"Hey, Taima, we hear Wolfe's **bride** is here," he emphasized suggestively. "I thought Kroft and I would stop in the trading post and see what kind of. . ."

Leah's face became hot at the vulgarities used to describe her female person. Both men laughed coarsely.

"I'll tell Thad you'd like to be introduced when he gets back." Taima made no effort to hide his disgust of them.

"We were told she was here at the trading post." Sneered the man called Charlie. In Taima's opinion, both men looked like the filth they spoke and smelled worse than the varmints they claimed to hunt and trap. He just shrugged and turned slightly to see where Leah was out of the corner of his eye. He hoped she would stay where she was—hidden. There was a steadiness in his voice and calm on his face masking a powerful reaction for a fast and decisive response if needed.

Taima knew these guys, especially Charlie. The other man called Kroft was usually the silent partner, but he was just as much a menace as Charlie. They had a reputation around the borough that was anything but nice and most people tolerated them from a distance. Their small shack was about a ten hour hike further inland. Every so often they crawled out of their wilderness stake and bought supplies in the Palmer/Wasilla area. He figured news of Leah's arrival via town gossip was the reason why they had chanced coming to the trading post today. They were not welcomed here and knew it. On one occasion he and Thad had made their visit to the trading post a very unpleasant one. Apparently, they were testing Taima's good graces to see how far they could push. Taima was ready, willing, and able to remind them of that last memorable visit, even without Thad.

There was a look of steel in Taima's eyes as he spoke ever so calmly. "She's not available right now, but Thad will introduce her…" Charlie started to look around and took one step towards the rear of the store. At that precise moment Leah knew what was about to happen. She'd seen a few street-gang fights start in her experiences in Chicago. No doubt, Taima could handle them, but not without receiving some punishment himself before calling for police intervention. The injustice of two men against one angered her significantly. The flagrant vulgarities directed at Thad and her a while ago had sickened her and had given her a resolve that presently sent her into action without thought to her own welfare.

Before Charlie took the second step that would have required a blast of action from Taima, Leah walked up the middle isle towards Charlie and Kroft and extended her hand in a ladylike fashion to Charlie. She smiled tight lipped while glancing over at Taima only to note he was glaring at her in anger. Leah steeled herself to keep from showing fear. Seemingly out of nowhere a Bible verse pulsed through her mind and Leah moved forward at the wonder of the promise, 'For I have not given you the spirit of fear, but of power, and of love, and of a sound mind.'

"Hello, gentlemen. My name is Leah Grant and as you know by now I am visiting your lovely Alaska as Thad's perspective bride. I want you to know I've found Alaska to be even more beautiful and majestic then even I had imagined. Taima, would you introduce me to these gentlemen, please? I wasn't available when they came in." Both shaggy men seemed shocked speechless by her charm. She smiled encouragement to Taima who unwillingly made introductions with as much courtesy as he could force into his voice.

"Leah, this is Mr. Charlie Bachman and Mr. Lance Kroft."

"I'm pleased to meet you, Miss Grant." It startled Leah that Kroft spoke properly and bowed slightly as though he had training. Charlie was compelled to follow suit and greeted Leah as graciously as his stumbling speech would permit.

The man, Kroft, seemed most affected by Leah's presence. He could not stop staring at her. The startled expression on his face made him look like a lost little boy though built big and burly. Leah guessed him to be about the same age as Thad if not a little older, but his appearance was so shabby that Leah really couldn't tell. His black beard was gray streaked and covered what face he did have. The only fine features he possessed were brilliant blue-gray eyes.

"What do you fellows do up here?" she asked interested.

"We hunt and trap mostly," Charlie offered almost eager to please the grace and beauty speaking to him. He was a tall, thin man with sandy hair and beard. He seemed wiry and unable to sit or stand still. Mischief radiating from his brown eyes, catching one's wary attention. It made him look too eager for a fight and too lanky to stay standing. Charlie's eye twitched with excitement. All at once he seemed eager to leave.

"Well, let's go, Kroft. We've got other supplies to pick up before the town closes up to us two gentlemen for the evening. We got a police cruiser checkin' up on us, again." Kroft wasn't in a hurry. He seemed spellbound by Leah; but Charlie had an idea and he wanted to get busy on it right away. Kroft finally turned away and the men tipped polite "good-byes" to Leah before leaving the store. An excited Charlie was already talking.

"Say, Kroft. If we cleaned up a bit and each wrote for a bride for ourselves maybe we'd have two nice ladies like Wolfe Tucker's, Miss Grant to come be our wives." His left eye was twitching like crazy and he rubbed it gingerly. Kroft glanced over at Charlie with a disgusted look on his face.

"No decent woman in her right mind would want to bother with the likes of us," he snorted, bitterness evident in his tone. Charlie, however, continued on and on with his idea while Kroft was remembering someone who reminded him a great deal of Leah Grant. Namely, one Sarah Kroft!

Leah and Taima both watched them go. They were almost as docile as puppies by this time. When Leah turned to check Taima's reaction, she could see he was still disturbed. She drew a long breath and exhaled before speaking.

"I know it wasn't a very bright thing to do, Taima, and I wasn't trying to be funny, either. The truth is my hands are still shaking." Leah showed him that they were. "I haven't heard some of the words they said in my whole life, but I know they are wicked men who are as unpredictable as—

"One Miss Leah Grant." Taima supplied. He moved around the counter to lock the door and change the sign to *Closed*.

"I hope I'm not that bad." Leah countered.

"Look at the effect you had on those two *gentlemen*." Taima emphasized.

They left through the back door of the trading post and walked to the garage. "They looked like they'd seen an angel," he joked and Leah laughed.

The sun was low in the sky as they drove up onto the cement drive on the Harley. Soft amber light showed from the window of the cabin as they approached the steps to the front doors. Leah paused for a moment to look down the length of the cabin. Its size and grandeur marveled her as it had last evening when she and Thad had briefly observed the northern lights. The sun and moon were making their appearance opposite each other in the same sky. She wondered if Thad was thinking of her as she was thinking of him.

It was almost quarter to two in the morning and Thad Tucker couldn't sleep at all, so he decided to step outside the large hunting lodge and consider the gray night light. However, his thoughts turned once again to Leah. It was still hard to believe she was here in Alaska. She might as well have been from another world until he had seen her standing right in front of him at Thunder's Trading Post. He smiled as he remembered her charming entrance. It was like she had walked out of his dreams. She had little idea what he looked like or that he was sometimes called "Wolfe" by some people. He'd never told her his nickname because it wasn't all that important to his thinking and he was used to this address.

"Taima must have used my nickname, first," Thad guessed out loud. He could only imagine what Leah must have thought! Then, seeing his beard and clothes caked with mud, she might well have reconsidered her decision to come to Alaska. But he remembered her telling him she loved him the moment she'd seen him. This thought made him fidget and he accidently kicked the porch post beside an empty chair. A loose piece of a wood shingle slid from its dangling perch and dropped with a thud. He jumped away in surprise and sat down heavily in a rocking chair. The awkward movement threw him backwards until the rocking chair hit a large flower pot of red-stripped petunias. It threatened to overturn from the rocking chair's attack, but Thad grabbed the pot to steady its wobble. After Thad regained his balance and his senses, he sat quietly musing over the fact that Leah's lively—if not accident prone nature—could be catching! He wished to be back standing with her watching the midnight sky and enjoying her presence. The mild bruising he'd received as a result of her defensive broom brought some comfort when he checked the purple spot on his skin again. It was evidence she really was in Palmer and would be there when he returned tomorrow afternoon. This made him particularly glad.

He thought of his mother and recalled her gospel witness and the concern Leah had for their lack of faith in Christ. She desired to find faith and Thad was not opposed to her search because he didn't want religion to divide them.

Considering their present progress towards marriage from their first contact a few months ago, he realized their relationship had proceeded faster than he figured. He'd thought it would be a slow process over a couple of years, but Leah seemed to be fanning the flame and he was glad! Tomorrow, or rather today, he planned to take her up to the original cabin where he had lived when he'd first moved back to Palmer after college graduation. That drafty, rustic old heap of logs was probably what she had envisioned. Indeed, if they'd met just two years ago, that kind of cabin would have been her welcome to his home. He looked forward to her reaction, wondering what she would say about the dilapidated hovel!

"It would just be nice to hear her voice," he mumbled aloud, stood, and entered the quiet lodge. Walking over to the phone booth, Thad pulled a chair over to a corner phone and sat down. He propped a foot on the lamp table next to the phone, then dialed his home phone number while preparing for a long chat. The only sound heard in the lodge was the drumming of his fingers on a desk nearby as he waited for a feminine greeting; but it was Taima who answered somewhat groggily.

"Taima!" he said enthusiastically, "can you get Leah on the phone?" Thad asked as he noticed the time on a nearby wall clock. He blinked surprise realizing it was two fifteen in the morning. He frowned. There was silence for a few moments.

"I think she's asleep, but I'll check," he groaned throwing covers back and stirring out of a warm comfortable repose.

"Sorry, Taima. Maybe I'll wait and talk to her later," disappointment sounded in Thad's voice.

"No, I'll get her on the phone. She's been dull company without you around, Thad," he snickered. Thad smiled.

"I'll bet she has. Thanks."

"Yah," Taima huffed as he left his room. The phone receiver slid off the nightstand and fell to the floor making a loud THUD. Thad pulled the receiver away from his ear with a jerk and cringed.

Before Taima went up to Leah's room, he checked to see if she was on the couch in the Great Room. Sure enough, she was--with the afghan snuggly wrapped up around her chin.

"How one woman can create so much chaos..." he mumbled and yawned before gently shaking Leah awake. Her eyes fluttered open in confusion.

"Leah, Thad is on the phone. He wants to talk to you. The phone is over on the desk." He turned the light on as Leah groaned and covered her eyes with her arm.

"Not the spots again," she moaned, fumbling her way to the desk and chair. Leah quickly blinked several times to clear her vision. Taima handed the afghan to her before shuffling off down the hall and shaking his head from side to side. She was wearing a pink adult-sized Dr. Denton pajama suit. The attached slippers were over-sized and flopped when she walked. Nobody would believe him, but Taima had seen the Easter Bunny!

"Thad?" Leah asked, happy to know he was on the other end of the line when she heard his voice.

Even the sound of her muzzy voice bought happiness.

"Hi, Leah, I didn't realize what time it was when I decided to call you."

"Oh, that's okay, Thad. Last night I woke you up, so now it's your turn to wake me up," she teased. He laughed when she yawned at length.

They talked for two hours. Leah told him about her escapades at the trading post with Taima and her plans to go to church with Alma. Thad talked about some of the experiences he'd had with clients on hunting trips. Both kept the conversation going just for the sheer enjoyment of hearing each other's voices and just because they had the freedom to continue without inhibitions.

Whey they said good-night, Thad encouraged Leah, "I'll see you in a couple of hours."

"I'll be waiting at the window," Leah promised cheerfully. Thad shifted in his chair.

"We'll take a trip up to the old homestead when I get back. It's just a short hike."

"Okay, I…miss you," Leah ventured awkwardly. It was quiet for a few seconds. Leah waited for some response then began to hope for one when the silence continued.

"That's nice to know. It's been a while since someone missed me or waited for me to come home. Thanks, Leah, catch you later." There was a click as Thad replaced the receiver.

"Good night," Leah said softly and pressed the "off" button on the cordless. The happiness in her heart put a smile on her lips even after she lay down on the couch to sleep further into morning.

CHAPTER 17

SUNDAY BEST

ALMA AND LEAH LEFT FOR CHURCH in Thad's old Chevy pick-up. He'd purchased it from a farmer in the area about nine years earlier to carry wood and building supplies. As they walked from the cabin to the pick-up, Alma signed that she preferred the pick-up over the new Chevy Suburbans used for the business because the old Ford pickup was simpler to drive without all the fancy doodads.

"I'm not that good of a driver," she admitted. The truck had several dents testifying to poor judgment.

"I never learned to drive a stick shift," Leah returned. "My Dad tried to teach me, but I just wasn't coordinated enough to get the car more than a few inches forward or a few feet backward. The last shifting lesson ended IN the garage when I put that little Corvaire through the steel garage door. Dad eventually had the car hauled to the junkyard. He used a five-pound mallet to pound the garage door back into a workable shape. We walked away from that one." Leah affirmed.

The two church ladies made quick steps up into the truck and soon were moving down the driveway from the cabin. As Leah glanced over at a smiling Alma, she noticed that Alma chose to wear a skirt and blouse in tan and brown colors that suited her well. The blouse was cream colored and had fall colored leaves embroidered on the western style yoke. As usual, her black hair was pulled back into a George Washington with a large gold hair barrette. She didn't look "forty-something" to Leah because her complexion was smooth with only a hint of crow's feet at the side of dark brown eyes. She was about the same height as Leah, but somewhat thinner. An attractive woman in her own right, the remnants of youthful beauty could be glimpsed when she smiled or worked in quiet exuberance around the home she had created. As Leah became more acquainted with Alma, she wondered about the native Alaskan woman's life.

"Alma, you'll have to tell me about yourself sometime?"

Alma only nodded as she drove, keeping both hands on the steering wheel.

Leah turned to view the scenery and exclaimed about the V-shaped flight of geese just above the truck. "Each time I look out a window, I find something new to surprise me about this area."

Alma smiled at her as they approached the church a little distance from Taima's Trading Post--just as Michelle had directed yesterday.

It was almost eleven o'clock when they entered through the double glass doors of the mid-century vinyl-sided building. Leah noticed at once the familiar smells of the church she'd known since childhood. It was the smell of well used hymnals and furniture polish mixed with the odors and fragrances of people over decades of worship together. Leah welcomed this small reminder of home as she and Alma proceeded into the larger sanctuary. Folding chairs were set up in two long sections with rows of six chairs on either side from front to back. There was a shield shaped wood pulpit on a platform with a small organ on one side and a huge covered object on the opposite side. They proceeded to the middle row of seats in the center of the sanctuary and sat down after picking up the blue hymnals that lay on each of their seats.

Leah studied the simple wooden pulpit then returned her gaze to the large covered object. That a grand piano should be under the cover was at first unfathomable to Leah in this modest sanctuary in Alaska. For some reason she couldn't quite picture such an instrument in this far northern frontier. Igloos and icebergs were still foremost in her concept of Alaska though she was daily learning that life in this farm community was somewhat similar to what she had known all her life. Replacing incorrect ideas with reality took some time for adjustment. Curiosity spurred the desire to find out what was under the cover and it also overcame her better sense of good manners.

"Alma, I'm going to see what's under that blanket."

"Under the blanket?" Alma signed, puzzled.

"I just can't resist a look at what's under that cover."

When Alma moved to let her pass, Leah headed for the front of the sanctuary without any hesitation. In Alma's strict orthodox upbringing, it was not proper to go exploring in a church, especially an unfamiliar one. When others started to move into the sanctuary, apprehension gathered in her eyes. Alma already felt very awkward in this Protestant church. She wanted to motion Leah back to the seat but didn't want to draw any attention to herself so she sat and watched the drama unfold with stoic reserve.

Gingerly, Leah began to pull the thick black cover from the keyboard. The more she uncovered, the more astonished she became. It was a shiny black Bosendorfer grand piano! Leah moaned in awe. The black sheen and beautiful condition of the piano beckoned Leah to discover the unique tone and quality of this special instrument.

Reverently, Leah lifted the lid of the keyboard and instinctively touched the white middle C key twice. She smiled broadly then struck a C major chord. The sound of ascending tones rose clear and melodious in the sanctuary. She looked up at Alma with raised eyebrows and nodded positively. Alma's doubtful expression did not dissuade Leah from pulling out the bench and sitting down at the piano. She spied a hymnal on one of the folding chairs nearest the piano and, stretching precariously; she grabbed it, opened it up, and smoothed the pages back before setting it against the music stand she'd moved into place.

"Rock of Ages" was played in simple fashion to enjoy the purity of the piano's tonal qualities and action. Leah came to the third line of the refrain and began to add embellishments to the favorite hymn. It was as if a bird had taken flight and was rising ever higher to soar wide winged to the heavens. Alma was so captivated by the music she did not realize others had entered the sanctuary and were listening as well. When little Michelle Dorance patted her on the arm, Alma jumped a little in surprise, then smiled warmly and saluted a "hello" to the little girl who greeted her with a smile of childish pleasure. Then she noticed the group of people who had gathered and wondered if Leah knew others listened, too. But Leah played on, unaware of anything but the musical response of the keys to the touch of her fingers. Time was no longer measured in equally spaced seconds and minutes; it was simply passed in measures of inspiration for the heart and soul.

Before Alma could get Leah's attention, Joe Dorance approached the piano and stood waiting quietly for Leah to conclude the hymn, "Pass Me Not, Oh Gentle Savior."

"Hello, Miss Grant."

Leah immediately turned to acknowledge the man and saw that several others were looking her way curiously. Embarrassment washed over her person and colored her face crimson.

"Oh, I'm sorry, Mr. Dorance," she fumbled. "I guess I forgot where I was for a while. It often happens when I'm playing the piano. It was such a surprise to see this piano here that I couldn't resist the temptation to play. I hope I haven't been impolite, Mr. Dorance." Leah offered sincerely though guilt remained for taking liberties without permission.

"No. Miss Grant. You haven't." He seemed to be choosing his words carefully. "My wife, Judy, Michelle's mother, played this piano. I purchased it for her a few years after we were married and she enjoyed playing it so very much..."he paused, "after she died, I couldn't see it sitting unused in our home, so I gave it to the church in her memory. I hoped someday Michelle would take an interest in playing the piano or that someone would be blessed." He seemed to brighten. "You have a similar technique, Miss Grant, to that of Judy's." He hesitated, willing loss and pain away. "Would you play the piano for our service?"

"Sure. It would be an honor." Leah said sincerely.

"Thank you." He nodded and withdrew in quiet dignity.

Leah glanced at Alma and signed, "Alma, would you like to sit with me? I'll have to sit closer to the front." Feeling awkward but eager to stick close to Leah, Alma moved to the front of the sanctuary to sit near the piano.

Pastor Paytor came up to the piano as Leah was about to play a short prelude. He was a tall, big-built man about sixty and was bald except for gray hair around the sides of his head. There was a quiet dignity about him that was not borne of professional humility, but of the Spirit of Christ lived out in his life. He reminded Leah of her Dad and she pondered this thought with the significance of how God had directed her to this particular church assembly.

The hymns were enjoyed by everyone. Alma read the words of the hymns from the lips of the song leader as faith formed in her heart. No one seemed eager to stop singing, so they continued on for several more minutes with people from the congregation selecting favorites. Leah's accompaniment made for lively, soul-stirring singing and encouraged hearty participation. As she played, thoughts of her older sister, Sarah came to mind. Sarah could play anything in any key after hearing it only one time while Leah had to have the music in front of her at all times or she was miserably lost!

The thought of Sarah stirred some homesickness in Leah's heart. She missed her sister for her gentle, steady ways; and, even more, she missed Sarah's common sense counsel.

The Offertory Leah had chosen to play was, "*Tis So Sweet To Trust In Jesus*". It was while she played this song and followed the music notes that the words of the song reached her heart.

"*Tis so sweet to trust in Jesus*
Just to take Him at His Word.
Just to rest upon His promise,
Just to know, "Thus saith the Lord."
Jesus, Jesus, how I trust Him,
How I've proved Him o'er and o'er!
Jesus, Jesus, precious Jesus.
O for grace to trust Him more."

'O for grace to trust Him more,' repeated itself in her mind as she finished the last measure of the song with an arpeggio up the keyboard and gently lifted both hands off the keyboard.

Pastor Paytor read scripture from John 4:40-42, then began his message as Leah settled in beside Alma. For once, she didn't read Thad's letters during church as she had before her trip to Alaska. This new place and the changes it presented stirred a desire to be still and know God.

"I have entitled today's message, 'Christ, the Savior of the World,' from the last part of verse forty-two. To get a full picture of this verse, it is necessary to read the verses within the context of this chapter. We consider the account of the woman of Samaria beginning in the sixth verse and concluding with this great testimony for Christ in our theme verse. Leah shared her Bible with Alma as they followed along while the pastor read the passage aloud. When they read further through the chapter, Alma became troubled by the seventeenth and eighteenth verses.

"The woman answered and said, 'I have no husband'. Jesus saith unto her, 'Thou hast well said, I have no husband. For thou hast had five husbands, and he whom thou now hast is not thy husband; in that saidst thou truly...'"

Alma placed her hand on the Bible and then began reading ahead of Pastor Paytor by following with her index finger. Leah could see she was reading intently until her finger halted after verses twenty-five and twenty-six.

"The woman saith unto Him, 'I know that Messias cometh, which is called Christ: when He is come He will tell us all things'. Jesus saith unto her, 'I that speak unto thee am He...'"

Alma looked up at the pastor. There was an expression of deep thought on her face. When Pastor Paytor read that verse she looked down and continued following with him to verse thirty-nine.

"And many of the Samaritans of that city believed on Him for the saying of the woman, which testified, 'He told me all that ever I did'."

Pastor Paytor stopped there to comment. "Beloved, here in this passage of scripture is demonstrated the mercy and grace of our Lord Jesus Christ. It was shown to a woman who was of a nationality despised by the Jews. Truly, there was no love lost between the Jews and the Samaritans. An ancient offense kept the smoldering resentment alive from generation to generation. Yet Jesus talked to her when others would have shunned this Samaritan woman. There was more to her story than a mere walk to the well to fill a water pot. This woman had been married five times. Even now, she was living with a man who wasn't her husband. She had become a prostitute. We might imagine her astonishment that a stranger could give account of her marital history, especially one who was a Jew. And wouldn't we all be astounded if someone came up to us and shared all our flaws?"

Both Leah and Alma sat perfectly still.

"I don't know about you, but I'd not like to have my dirty laundry hung out on the line for all to gawk at. Gossip is one thing because it's made up of misconstrued information and half truths, but an eye witness testimony of my life would be quite another devastating matter." Pastor Payton's voice was quietly reflective. "Nobody relishes the idea of others exposing all they know about a person's sin. But Jesus did this for the purpose of showing that forgiveness is available to anyone, anywhere, and at anytime in their lives. His love and forgiveness are unconditional.

"Can we make application to the believer in Christ? Maybe you have un-confessed sin in your life as a Christian. We call these sins, 'secret sins'. Nobody else knows about them, except you and God and you wish He didn't know about them either. But He knows your rises and falls and how they stifle your fellowship with Him. I can tell when I have un-confessed sin in my heart." He held up one finger. "My Bible reading and prayer life diminish." Two fingers were raised. "I think more about myself and my own life and less about God and others." Three fingers were raised to the ceiling of the Sanctuary. "I squirm when others talk about the Lord in my presence." Four fingers stood tall. "I am quick to judge others to be worse sinners than I." He looked at the small sea of faces in his congregation. "Can you agree with me?" There were several nods of quiet agreement. "Not to worry, Beloved, we all wander and stray like Dall sheep." He smiled as others chuckled at being compared to the willy-nilly antics of mountain sheep. "We all become calloused to our own sin. But, we have God's Spirit to convict us of sin. We have His divine forgiveness available because His Son's atoning blood cleanses all our sins and puts us in a right relationship with Him. Though we sometimes bear the earthly consequences of our sins in pain and regret, we have the promise of hope in Heaven where there will be no more pain or tears ever again. Then too, God takes every circumstance and makes it a testimony of His grace to us in working all things together in marvelous ways. For this we give God the glory. Amen!"

"Amen!" sounded around the listeners.

"The Samaritan woman was excited. She was forgiven! If you have realized that you are a sinner in the eyes of God, verse twenty-nine is for you. This Samaritan woman was wonderfully converted to Christ! Her enthusiastic testimony is the evidence of a changed heart and life because she went and told everybody! 'Come, see a man, which told me all things that ever I did; is not this the Christ?'

"Can you imagine what her neighbors thought?" Pastor Payton paused and whistled in astonishment. "Can you imagine what those former husbands and the new guy thought? Lots of guilty people live around us when Christ enters a neighborhood. Perhaps this is why there are sour feelings towards the church until the love of Christ is demonstrated by the people of Christ sharing the gospel and helping in the community." He paused to allow a few moments of contemplation.

"Come to Christ, my friend. He knows all about you and yet He says, 'Come.'" He looked down at his Bible. "In verse thirty-nine, we see the revival in Samaria as a result of this woman's testimony, '...for many in that city believed on Him, Jesus, for the saying of the woman.' The Lord Jesus Christ is able to forgive the sins of any sinner who calls on Him for forgiveness. He is more than able to save all who by faith will believe on Him as Savior of their soul. Don't delay, Beloved. The Samaritan woman's salvation experience was immediate and dynamic. She didn't put it off and wonder what people would think. Of course we all have reputations that haunt us. There are some who are morally good people whom others would think were very dedicated Christians by their good works. Yet wouldn't it be shocking to find that those very same people need to personally meet the Savior for the first time?" Leah understood this clearly. She felt her own hypocrisy keenly.

"Even some here who have come to know Christ, remember the wickedness of their past when Satan brings it up to haunt them at times;

but, they're forgiven for Christ's sake. And dear sinner, you may feel your sins are unforgivable and you want to hide from God's all knowing vision; but be thankful He knows all about you and still offers you love and forgiveness through Jesus. He desires to rescue you from sin's own death penalty and from Satan's eternal hold on your soul. There is peace and joy He will freely give you in exchange for a condemning heart." He looked down at his pulpit for several moments. There was a solemn stillness that enveloped the congregation as each pondered personal meanings.

"Christ, the Savior of the world. Is He your Savior? Why do you wait to trust him? Shall we pray?" Leah struggled with this last question as Pastor Paytor prayed.

"Father in Heaven, who is it in this group of souls that needs to know they are loved by You regardless of the fact You know all about them? I pray for the Holy Spirit to move in their hearts and bring them to faith in Christ. Amen."

"Why do I wait?" Leah asked herself, but would not answer her own question.

After the prayer, Pastor Paytor announced they would sing the second verse of *Tis So Sweet To Trust In Jesus* in closing.

While Leah was opening to the hymn's page and preparing to play an introduction, the Pastor spoke.

"The message was not long this morning. We spent much time worshipping the Lord in singing hymns and giving praise to Him. Jesus Christ's conversation with the woman of Samaria was not an eloquent sermon. It was very simple. It was the plain message of Salvation from a faithful Savior to a needy soul. 'Is this the Christ?' or 'This is my Christ, my Messiah, my Savior,' she proclaimed. Can you agree in your heart and soul with the Samaritan woman today?

"Beloved Christian, have you shared the message of Salvation with someone even once this week? Or do you despise the sinners around you and ignore their spiritual need by remaining silent and unconcerned about the eternal destiny of your fellow neighbors? Why are we so insensitive? I know this sounds harsh, but we must love sinners for Christ's sake.

"Shall we sing the second verse as Miss Grant plays for us? Turn to hymn number 534."

O how sweet to trust in Jesus,
Just to trust His cleansing blood,
Just in simple faith to plunge me.
'Neath the healing, cleansing flood!
Jesus, Jesus, how I trust Him!
How I've proved Him o'er and o'er!
Jesus, Jesus precious Jesus!
O for grace to trust Him more!"

The words echoed in both Leah and Alma's hearts. One found joy in the newness of faith. The other one still struggled to accept faith without expectations.

After the service Pastor Paytor greeted Leah at the piano and thanked her for playing.

"I believe you're new to Palmer," he said. "Where are you from?"

"I'm from a small town north of Pittsburgh, Pennsylvania, called Limestone." Leah replied as Alma came to stand beside her.

"I assume you attend a church there?"

"Yes. My Dad is Pastor of the church in the village there."

"Fine. Fine." He replied then greeted Alma as she moved closer to allow an elderly lady to pass.

"Hello, Alma. It's good to have you here with us today." He said kindly.

Alma's face was glowing as she signed for Leah to interpret.

"I came with Leah today. She is Thad's friend and maybe will soon be his bride." Alma winked at Leah who colored noticeably. Pastor Paytor knew Thad. He'd gone fishing with Thad and Tyrone a few times. He also knew Thad had very little time for religion. He shot a concerned frown at Leah. Alma's eyes sparkled with happiness as she continued.

"Pastor Paytor, I want you to know that I have trusted Christ as my Savior. He has forgiven me of my sins." Leah could not help the tears that came to her eyes as she heard about Alma's salvation experience. She hugged the happy Alma and wondered how faith could be so easy. Joe Dorance and Michelle came up and greeted them. Pastor Paytor related Alma's testimony to Joe and Michelle and the little girl wrapped her arms around Alma's skirt. Joe's expression was a mix of surprise and wonder as he gazed at her before offering a hand of fellowship. Alma seemed somewhat shy about shaking his offered hand. She looked down at Michelle who regarded her with the same admiration as did her father.

"Can I walk with you out to the car?" Michelle asked Alma. Alma smiled and nodded her head. They started back the aisle hand in hand and walked out the door into the fledgling sunshine. Joe preceded them to open the door as Michelle chattered away.

Leah and Pastor Paytor followed. There was an awkward silence as they walked to the door before Pastor Paytor spoke.

"I know Thad Tucker, Miss Grant, and I'm afraid I don't quite understand…"

"Pastor, I am not…" Leah stopped and started again. "I have never committed my heart to Christ. I know the gospel, but I don't seem to have the faith needed to believe. I feel like I will always be lost."

Pastor Paytor regarded this statement with concern. He could see she was struggling. A smile of confidence crossed his face as he spoke kindly.

"Miss Grant."

"Leah, please," she encouraged with a polite smile.

"Leah, faith is not something you have to have enough of to give to God. He gives faith to you as you open your heart and trust Him to be the way, the truth, and the life. Do you remember the acrostic for faith? Forsaking All I Trust Him?" She nodded affirmative.

"Do you realize the Samaritan woman left her water pot at the well to tell others about this Christ, the Savior of the world? She forgot all about her physical need for water, because her thirsty soul was filled with the living water of faith that Christ had poured into her heart. Oh, she'll get thirsty for a drink of water eventually, but the spiritual drought is over for all eternity." He stopped to think before asking Leah a question.

"Is there something you've been told that makes you think you cannot be saved?" Leah looked at him carefully. "It is a false teaching.

You have just as much opportunity to belong to Jesus Christ as anyone else in this world. You have the choice to accept Christ or turn your back on Him. Nobody else decides this for you and nobody else has the right to determine your future life after this earthly one is finished. God gives the choice to you alone. He wants you to chose Him out of love, not out of fear and not out of obligation either. Leah, you need to let go of what other people have judged about you. It's just you and God. He doesn't see you as a preacher's daughter. He sees you as a person and one in need of forgiveness and acceptance." Pastor Paytor considered the young woman before him.

"Mark 8:34 is a good verse to ponder on this matter, Leah."

"And when he had called the people unto Him with His disciples also, He said unto them. 'Whosoever will come after me, let him deny himself, and take up his cross, and follow me." He quoted.

"Notice, Leah, He spoke not only to the people, but included the disciples because some of them were struggling, too. He gave four instructions; come after me, deny yourself, take up your cross, and follow me. There is a particular order here. Not because salvation comes in steps, but because men must process information in an orderly manner to understand anything important. When we come after Christ, we show a desire to know Him. You have that desire. But you're stuck here." Leah agreed.

"Many people are stuck here," he continued. "A lot of people believe there is a God and they try to do good deeds to please Him. But that's it. Good deeds are commendable, but God saves us by grace, not our good works and deeds. He does all the saving! What kind of God would He be to put man on a troubled Earth and then leave man to work all his life doing good deeds when Heaven demands sinless perfection. No man can obtain sinless perfection in this life, because he is born with the sin nature. If sin is a part of man at his birth, it is part of him in death unless he humbles himself in the sight of God and believes that Jesus Christ is able to forgive him and make him fit for Heaven. The question is, Leah, can you ever do enough to please a Holy God without offending Him with your thoughtless failings?" Leah knew she couldn't. "I can't either." Pastor Paytor agreed.

"To deny one's self is to forsake your own thinking about how God will save you. You can't do it yourself. You cannot save your own soul or allow anyone else to take responsibility for your eternal destiny other than Christ. This is the work of the Divine. Your directive is simply to hear what God has to say about His Son as Savior and to choose whether you will put your whole trust in Him or go on doing it your way. And, as you said, feel like you will always be lost because you can never do enough right to please Him?" He asked.

"Yes, when I was a little girl, I tended to get into trouble a lot. It seemed like I was always offending church people whose expectations were way higher for me than I thought they should be. I overheard some ladies saying that I would be the lost sheep of their pastor's family and..." Leah hesitated, embarrassed. Her excuse was juvenile. Pastor Paytor took up the conversation again. He spoke in earnest. There was no condescension in his voice; only a desire to help Leah think through her course of action.

"Why would you believe anything those gossips said, now? You're an adult. Surely, you know the truth that God wants all men to come to repentance and faith. God doesn't pick who will be lost, He saves all who come to Him. Yes, He knows who will be saved because He is God and He knows all things; but He is not willing that any should perish. Think of what God has done in your life to reconcile you to Himself in salvation, even today. He provided a preacher Dad for you, Leah. Your Dad is a servant of Jesus Christ in the greatest sense of sacrifice to the cross. I grew up in a drunkard's home. I didn't come to Christ until I was thirty-seven years of age and a gutter drunk myself. Don't let what a few hard-hearted women said destroy all the wonderful things God has done to bring you to faith in Christ." Pastor Paytor opened the door for Leah and they left the church building.

"Be willing to forsake all that would keep you from becoming a follower of Jesus Christ." He shook his head in concern for her. "It won't be easy, Leah. You may have already made some choices that will take you away from God. Be careful. I know Thad. He's as good a man as there ever was made by God, but he is resistant to the things of God."

Leah thought about Thad right then. It was a choice that made her heart ache.

"My wife, Betty and I are more than willing to talk with you about anything. Just give us a call. Our number is in the Sunday bulletin you have in your hand," he encouraged as they walked up to Alma, Joe, and Michelle. Alma was signing to Joe and Leah was amazed to see he understood.

"Hope to see you again, Leah." Frank Paytor waved and moved towards his wife, Betty, who was talking to an elderly Native Alaskan lady named, Sarah. She wore a beautiful Eskimo fur parka called an *anorak* that had colorful embroidery strips around the cuffs and an attached gathered skirt. Leah had never seen anything so unique and couldn't help admiring it. Sarah turned and smiled knowingly at Leah's gawk. *Cheechakos* always stared when she wore her ancestral coat!

"It's lovely," was all Leah could manage.

"Thank you, Miss. It's very warm, too." She smiled with polite deference.

Leah felt awkward at being treated as a better instead of an equal. Later Alma would share her story and Leah would understand a little more about the history of native Alaskans.

A quick glance at her wrist watch told Leah it was almost one o'clock already. She wondered if Thad was back to the cabin yet.

Alma was smiling and Leah could tell she was about to burst with excitement over her new faith. However, Leah had much to think about as they drove away from the church. She could not rejoice with Alma as a fellow believer. Somehow, she felt like they had lost some common ground. Then Leah wondered what Thad and Taima would think?

CHAPTER 18

TAKE A HIKE!

TAIMA WAS SURPRISED TO SEE THAD walk through the front door about twelve fifteen.

"You're home early. Alma and Leah are still at church."

"I know. I saw the truck parked at the church and stopped in for a while." Taima frowned at Thad.

"You didn't stay to talk with Reverend Paytor?" he asked with sarcasm which Thad chose to ignore.

"I walked in when Reverend Paytor was finishing his sermon." Thad remarked dryly. "I left after Leah played the final hymn on the piano." A deep frown creased his brow. "I didn't know she played the piano." He unloaded the camera gear onto an office chair off the Great Room and dropped a heavy backpack on the floor. The thud of the backpack hitting the floor matched Thad's mood.

"How did you manage to get back so soon?"

"I left two hours earlier," was Thad's sullen reply.

Taima detected the irritation in Thad's voice and knew life was going to get interesting. He saw the pick-up coming up the drive and walked out onto the deck. He'd seen Thad in this mood before, but Leah hadn't.

Thad glanced out the bay window and studied the approach of the truck as if studying its metal frame for new rust spots. He checked his mood and realized he was almost too tired to be cordial. The few words said about Salvation reminded him of his mother's urgings. Then Leah had played the familiar hymn. He'd heard the words as they sang them and they made him uneasy. But the song wasn't really what was irking him. It was the fact that Leah had participated in the service. To him, this reeked with hypocrisy. Although he knew she was searching for the truth, she was still giving the appearance she belonged with those who claimed the faith. He hated deceit of any kind. He hadn't attempted to be religious or to participate in religion in any way. At least he was an honest heathen!

After expelling a long breath and turning from the window to walk toward the front door, he looked for Leah in the approaching truck. The sight of her stirred him significantly. Everything had been so clear and perfect last evening. He thought about their conversation over the phone encouraging her and Alma to attend church. But, once again, this church thing riled him. It brought back a lot of unpleasant memories of past battles that had hampered the peace and happiness between him and his mother. Now Leah had entered his home and the religious conflict was back to threaten the harmony. Yet, it really wasn't Leah who had perpetrated this threat. It was his battle with God alone. Then the thought struck him that maybe Leah's participation in the service meant she had become a Christian; but without him? This did not sit well with him either. After their conversation of Friday night, he had been willing to find answers about God together.

Taima had already walked onto the driveway to meet the pick-up as Thad descended the steps to the driveway. Both men resembled expectant fathers, though the expectations of each were different. Taima expected to meet the same sister who had left the cabin two hours earlier. Thad expected to meet a new Christian. The expectations of both would test loyalties.

Leah had been looking at the mountains rising to great heights behind the gracious cabin. At first, the cabin looked dwarfed and miniature in comparison to the rugged snow capped peaks. Yet, there was elegance in the architecture that befitted the surroundings. It seemed like a lovely flower had blossomed and flourished in the riches of the mountain valley. Leah thought about this. The truck bumped gently along until it came onto the smooth cement. Taima was already walking toward the pick-up to greet Alma. He was curious to ask about her church visit. Before he was alongside the pick-up, Leah signed to Alma.

"You know, Alma, if I had the privilege of naming this cabin, I'd call it, 'Rose Glen', which means 'Rose in the valley'. What do you think?" Alma smiled and nodded positively, then she patted Leah's arm and pointed to the Suburban. Leah was surprised to see Thad was back an hour earlier than expected. Her heart skipped a beat when she saw him standing on the deck. It was still hard to believe they could see and talk face to face.

"I think 'Rose Glen' is a fine name, Leah. Thank you for inviting me to come to church with you. I'm so happy I went. I'll tell Taima all about the church service this afternoon when I can talk to him alone." Leah nodded agreement, but not without some apprehension apparent on her face. Old fears of what others would do and think surfaced. Alma assured her, "Don't worry. My brother's bark is worse than his bite!" The movements she made with her hands expressed this statement in humorous fashion and Leah couldn't help but laugh at Alma's picturesque description of Taima.

Thad had moved off the railing where he'd been sitting and was headed down the steps toward her side of the pick-up. She opened the door to greet him, but saw he wasn't smiling. Leah frowned at him curiously while attempting to maneuver the high step from the truck to the ground. She was not used to the height of the four-wheel drive vehicle and had worn a long straight black skirt and a black plaid tailored jacket with a white blouse. While it was cooler outside, the jacket provided enough warmth so that a coat had not been necessary. The impractical two-inch heeled shoes now dangled in mid-air. It had been too late to change them before leaving for church this morning when she had found out they would be taking the truck to church. In the first place, Leah had been forced to pull the straight skirt up above her knees so she could hop up into the truck. Now she considered this present dilemma. In slacks, it wouldn't have been an issue! Thad stood holding the door open for her. He extended his hand and Leah took it surveying the distance to the ground from her perch while assessing a "jump" without embarrassment.

"What's wrong?" he inquired as if it was becoming a natural thing to ask.

"I'm afraid of heights," was her all too quick reply.

"What?" his tone was short, "I don't understand." Leah met his eyes and noted they were hard and calculating. There was something in his mood that made her wary. He seemed irritated and Leah had no idea why he would be upset.

"I can't get down from this truck very easily because of this skirt," Leah blurted. This was one problem she had not anticipated. Some women wouldn't have been bothered in the least, but Leah was and it made it a bigger problem than it needed to be. It was a moment when she needed to confide a personal need to Thad and hoped he would be considerate and helpful. Perhaps some men would have taken advantage of an opportunity like this one. Leah fully expected Thad to be chivalrous.

Thad's eyes widened with comprehension. This was an interesting situation for him. A smile escaped before he could stop it. He also didn't stop to contemplate his next words which sent the situation further "south!"

"I always meant to put a running board on this truck for Alma," he said with lighthearted candor. "But I'm kind of glad I didn't." He reckoned as he folded his arms in front and gave Leah a large smile of amusement. His eyes fell to the hem of her skirt and moved up her person to her warming face. His censure reminded her of Rusty Glick and it fired an offense!

Leah met Thad's smile with a glare of irritation that encouraged his response.

"Teacher's ugly looks won't work on me," he said waiting expectantly. He knew he was wrong, but he wanted a fight.

"It's not a teacher that's looking at you at the moment." Fire danced in her brown eyes charging Thad's emotions.

"A Christian?" he mocked and saw her fight dowsed like water poured on a campfire. Leah pulled her hand back.

"No. Not a Christian either," was her cool response as she slid towards the edge of the seat to jump without his assistance. Thad blocked her progress.

"Just ask me to help you get down," He saw the silent anger seething from her heart through her eyes and realized he'd misjudged her hypocrisy for the exercise of a talented musician. She was mad, but Thad wasn't sure if she was mad at him or something else. His mood altered when he saw the fire fade in her eyes and change to cold silence.

"I'll help you down, Leah." He offered extending his hand again, hoping she would take it. Leah looked at the offered hand and then raised her eyes to meet Thad's. This moment could send her packing to Pennsylvania. Pastor Paytor's urging to be careful threatened her relationship with the man she loved, but challenged her resolve to form a relationship with God. There was no sense moving ahead until this moment was reckoned between them.

"There's no reason for you to be insulting, Thad Tucker. Church has been my whole life, to this point. It's who I am even though I don't have everything figured out, yet. If this is a source of irritation for us, then we shouldn't go any further. I won't live with mockery against myself or my background."

Her words hit his heart like arrows piercing a thick wine skin. The sour juice of bitterness began to seep from years of containment. Without knowing it, Leah had pinpointed Thad's umbrage with God. It was Thad's turn to navigate the silent way before speaking.

"Leah, I apologize for my lousy attitude. Can you be patient with me and forgive me for misjudging and offending you?" Leah smiled forgiveness and took his hand.

"Help me down." She commanded playfully.

"Your wish is my command," Thad smiled mischievously and reached for her waist. In one swift movement she was in his arms. At the same time the back of her skirt came up. Leah tried to push away from Thad's amorous embrace, but her feet weren't touching the ground at the moment! Once again, the unexpected action sparked a defensive move on her part.

Taima and Alma were already inside the opened garage and heading for the steps up to the main level. Alma was telling Taima about Leah's ability on the piano, so they were not aware of the two out by the truck. Taima had helped his sister step down from the truck, but Thad wasn't regarding Leah as a sister and that made a big difference. Of course Thad was a bit unhinged from tiredness. Then again Leah's "jet lag" wasn't helping matters either.

Taima had come to stand at the glass doors of the Great Room to look out at the changing weather. Alma came over to stand by Taima as he happened to see Thad reach for Leah.

"She will make Thad a loving wife." Alma commented to her brother in sign. Her expression was cheerful.

"Too much, too fast!" was Taima's instant retort as he growled and turned from the window. Alma was confounded by her brother's uncharacteristic outburst of anger. He was headed for the front door. Alma hastened after him flabbergasted. She thought it was the first time Thad had kissed Leah. She didn't think it was so bad; but obviously Taima was not pleased! Alma wondered as she shrugged and followed Taima.

As Taima walked out onto the deck and headed for the steps in a steam, Leah was coming up the steps in an angry stomp! She brushed past Taima in a gust of fury. He turned to look after her with concern then directed a frown at Thad as Thad rubbed the side of his cheek gingerly and approached the steps. Regret was written across his face. A groan escaped his lips as an angry Taima approached.

"I'm not even going to ask what happened! But I can guess it had something to do with your ugly mood." Taima barked. Thad had never seen him this angry...or protective...and it shook him even more than had Leah's slap. He could tell Taima was trying to control his anger, because he was pacing. The fact that he blocked the steps told Thad he had something to say. After some tense moments, Taima took a deep breath then exhaled. His face relaxed, but the tone of his voice was no-nonsense.

"You've only known me about ten years. So you don't know a whole lot about the years before we met and I haven't told you too much about them either. I had a wife, a common-law wife for almost seven years," his voice caught and he cleared his throat. Thad blinked surprise.

"She was sweet and decent; much like Leah. We met at a restaurant where she was working as a waitress. In a short time we fell in love. But I was stupid! A girlfriend was one thing, but a wife was another thing all together to me and I didn't want a wife, yet. I thought it was a nice idea sometime down the road to get married, but not then. We kept seeing each other until we were together more than we were apart. Naturally, her parents began to complain, so I convinced her to come live with me, telling her that we'd get married eventually. It was ideal for me. I had all the benefits of a woman but no responsibility to her. But, after a while, the arrangement went sour. She became somber and quiet. I ignored it and went on with life doing what I wanted and taking her for granted. When she became unresponsive," Taima paused, "I treated her mean and hurt her. She left me and went back to her parents in Anchorage," he lamented.

"When I finally realized what a fool I was, I went to her home to make things right and marry her. I had the ring and everything. But her father met me at the end of the driveway with a double-barreled shotgun. He knocked me to the ground with the butt of the gun and put the barrel against my head. I heard the click as he pulled the safety back. It's the one sound that scares me to death to this day," Taima shuddered, "and I sell guns everyday! If Sonya hadn't pleaded for her father to let me go, I'd have been dead!" he assured.

"That happened eighteen years ago. Sonya and our seventeen-year-old son still live in Anchorage. But that's done the three of us a lot of good, hasn't it?" Taima's voice dropped its intensity and became morose. "I'd give anything in this world and the next to do things differently." Taima looked directly at Thad.

"Leah's a real nice girl and I think she wants to be somebody's bride. Think about it," Taima growled, "or send her home!" He turned and started up the steps.

"Taima's words echoed like hammer blows in Thad's mind. He never would have guessed Taima had a wife and son. Suddenly, Taima turned and took a few steps down to Thad again. Thad's eyes grew large.

"I'm going to tell you something else," Taima confided. He made eye contact with a sheepish Thad.

"Yesterday, I took Leah for a ride on the Harley." Thad's eyebrows rose in astonishment. "I showed her how to ride safely. When she asked me how to 'hold on', I gave her a few options."

Thad nodded in understanding. Taima relaxed and even started to laugh.

"It's the first time I ever had my belt turned almost completely around!"

Thad managed a grin and shook his head in wonderment. "How does she do it?"

"What? Turning my belt around or creating chaos?"

"Both!" Thad said with a sigh and kicked some gravel off the pavement.

Taima grinned broadly, "I think it just comes naturally for her."

"She'll make a good Alaskan," Thad guaranteed then frowned, "if she stays." He thought about the events of the last few minutes and groaned.

"You're a good man, Thad," Taima encouraged, "I knew that when I pulled your broken body out of a ravine ten years ago and nursed you back to health." He shifted his weight to his other foot and put his hands in jean pockets.

"You're thirty-four years old and you've waited a long time. I can understand that. I just don't want you to make the kind of mistake that could ruin something beautiful." Both were quiet.

"She really enjoyed the ride on the Harley," Taima offered to lighten the mood. "She had tears in her eyes." He grinned all proud.

Thad gave Taima a long tired look. "She may have enjoyed it, but I can't buy a Harley, Taima. I already have two horses in the corral just below here that I'm working hard to keep alive."

"When are you going to show Leah her horse?"

"On the day we get married. IF we get married!" he stressed with gloom.

"You will, Thad." He assured then countered, "she was really steamed at you, though?"

"You might say that." Thad rubbed his cheek in remembrance.

"That's a good sign." Taima was pleased while Thad gave him a puzzled look.

"Whose side are you on?"

"Yours, of course!" Taima affirmed then added, "and hers, too."

"Fence sitter," Thad piped up and laughed at his older friend who shrugged as he turned to go up the steps.

"I cooked dinner today," Taima announced, "and that ought to be punishment enough for all of us."

"Not that terrible Road Kill Stew, Taima," Thad objected. "You know what that stuff does to first timers." Thad looked up at the cloudy sky. "Not today!" He had plans. At least Thad hoped he still had plans for a proposal.

Alma was upstairs consoling a distressed pen-pal. Angry tears ran down Leah's face. She rubbed the hand still stinging from its connection with the side of Thad's face.

"Oh, Alma," she blurted and signed, "how could I have done that to Thad? I can't believe he would...I can't believe I..." she couldn't finish.

Alma put her arm around Leah and patted her hand gently to get her attention before signing some encouragement.

"Until you came into his life, Thad tolerated women-politely. But I could see the minute you walked through the door Friday night that Thad's heart was captured by you. He doesn't know what to do about you just yet." Alma smiled broadly. "You've managed to upset his whole world and he's actually okay with it. But he's making some mistakes and blunders just as you are." Leah rolled her eyes as tears formed again. Alma reached for Leah's hand and squeezed it.

"If Thad did something that offended you or you felt was wrong, then he deserved what he got." Alma's expression was firmly supportive. "But make sure you're not giving him signals he misinterprets. We both know passion is strong, especially between a man and a woman who are discovering they love each other with the *ever-after* kind of love. It must be wonderful." There was regret on her face. "I have not known that kind of love in my life, yet. You and Thad have something special. Be patient and kind."

Leah reached for Alma's hand. "What would I do without you? Right from the start, you've been such an encouragement to me."

Alma smiled. "I could tell you needed some help with all of this adjustment. I've seen your type, Leah. We'll talk about that later, I promise. Right now, I am enjoying the peace and happiness of knowing Christ as my Savior. I am thankful He has forgiven me and now we are both Christians." Alma smiled, but Leah's face sobered.

"No, Alma, not yet." Leah replied softly. Alma was puzzled and Leah was weary of making the same old explanation again and again.

"All my life, people thought I was a Christian but no one ever asked me personally if I had Jesus in my heart." Leah paused to consider she was yet again blaming others just as Pastor Paytor had challenged. "That wasn't their fault," she corrected. "It was mine. I've used them as an excuse; but I can see I've just been rebellious. Pastor Paytor has given me much to think about." Leah looked directly at Alma.

"Alma," she was earnest, "will you please pray that God will help me to figure this all out? I'm so confused." Leah acknowledged wholehearted. Alma smiled.

"I already am, and I'm praying for Thad and Taima, too." She assured with a nod. "I think we'd better go downstairs to the kitchen. Taima has made lunch for us." Alma shook her head in disgust. "It's that Road Kill Stew of his." She seemed perturbed but Leah had no idea why, except to think perhaps Alma didn't particularly care for Taima's stew.

"Road Kill Stew?" She asked and Alma turned around to respond. The name of the stew sounded rather odd and uninviting.

"He puts all kinds of things in it. One never knows. He won't tell anyone the ingredients that are in it either, so thankfully, there's no recipe. We just survive it as best as we can."

"I'm not so sure about this stew." Leah hesitated.

"Just eat a little to be polite, Leah." Alma suggested and they headed down the steps. As they entered the kitchen, Taima was just putting the pot of stew on the table and wiping his hands on a towel.

"Do you need any help?" Leah ventured.

"No. Everything's ready. I just need people to come and eat."

Leah looked around to see if Thad was near. She was about to ask Taima when he gave her directions with a nod of his head.

"He's out on the deck. Why don't you go tell him we're ready to eat," he encouraged and Leah left, glad to have a chance to make things right with Thad.

When she stepped onto the deck, Thad was turned away from her looking over the valley and mountain ridges. He heard the light tap of her heels and turned to acknowledge her. A timid smile on her lips brought some relief to him. He smiled as she approached.

"I'm sorry, Thad. I…" she hesitated and looked away.

"I deserved it," Thad confessed, "again." He smiled lamely. "Leah, I shouldn't have…kissed you that way." Leah blinked in surprise.

"It wasn't the kiss, Thad. You seemed upset about something and I was angry about something else and…it was…I felt the back of my skirt come up and thought…" Leah stammered. Her face became hot with embarrassment. Thad frowned at her in confusion. He hesitated for a moment until it dawned on him what she was suggesting.

"No, Leah," he said with gravity. "I'll admit to kissing you every opportunity I can get; but anything more than that, I wouldn't feel was right by you. I hope you don't think—"

"—No, Thad," Leah interjected quickly. "There must be some other explanation."

He could see she was miserable. In efforts to cheer her up, Thad handed her the binoculars and changed the subject.

"Here, check the view of Pioneer Peak with these, Leah. There are often a variety of birds that fly over the seed fields next to the mountains looking for food," he directed with an outstretched hand pointing to the swooping scavengers. "You might see some Ptarmigan near the ground." She managed a grateful smile and accepted the binoculars wishing her Calamity Jane bent would just quit!

Leah raised the binoculars to her eyes and suddenly brought them down again. A startled look was on her face because her skirt came up in the back again! Thad looked down and grinned at the funny face she made. He began to talk about the various birds in the area in an informative tone of voice. His next remark didn't help matters.

"Those binoculars bring the mountains up so close, you think you can reach out and touch them." Leah's mouth opened in astonishment as she looked up at his profile. However, before reacting, she noted he was observant and thoughtful as he leaned against the deck's railing and watched the flight of other birds above.

Again, she slowly raised the binoculars and again the back of her skirt rose. It was then she felt a little tug on her jacket. When she brought the binoculars down, the skirt moved down. A frown was frozen across her face when Thad turned to check her interest in the bird life. He smiled thinking he'd seen this same look on the faces of many newcomers. However, it wasn't the scenery or the wild life that transfixed Leah.

"They are something to see, aren't they?" He exclaimed then halted when she didn't reply.

"Thad," Leah started slowly while handing the binoculars back. Her face was so serious Thad was beginning to be uncomfortable.

"I think I know what happened and I'm such an idiot." She groaned unbuttoning the fitted jacket. Thad's eyes widened as he stepped back, clearing his throat nervously.

"My jacket lining is caught on the waist hook of my skirt. Could you please help me take this jacket off to check?" Thad's eyes narrowed warily at the request for aid. He moved carefully toward her hoping it wasn't going to be against his better judgment. The hook on her skirt was indeed snagged in the tangled mass of threads from the jacket lining. Working gingerly to release the snag, it reminded Thad of tangled fishing nets.

"I must have ripped the lining of the jacket when I reached up to get into the truck this morning. It must have caught and snagged when I moved around." She guessed as the hook finally came free from the tattered lining. Thad handed her the jacket with a smile of heroic relief. "I wouldn't have known it until…"

"Uhuh." Thad agreed.

"I'm sorry, Thad. Can you forgive me?"

"Sure." It was instant!

"I really do love you." Leah said sincerely. Thad could tell she did. Her eyes reflected it so very well.

"I know. Just keep telling me. I'm finding I need to be reminded often," he teased. "I forgive you and I'll always love you, Leah." He assured. For some reason, his pledge triggered an understanding of God's everlasting love deep within her heart. No matter what wrong she had done or would do, forgiveness was available right along with unconditional love. She hadn't always felt that way around other people. A great relief flooded her heart to know Thad was committed to her and accepted her for herself. He saw her anxiety disappear as a smile formed at the corner of her lips.

"Wow! That's just what I needed to hear you say," Leah exclaimed. Thad regarded her with an amused grin.

"I'm glad I finally did something right," he teased. Leah laughed enjoying his ability to joke and be lighthearted. Thad's letters had always been straightforward and business-like to the point that Leah wondered if he had a sense of humor. They started for the kitchen. "Thad, you do everything right."

"I hope you think that thirty years from now," he tried skepticism.

"Oh?" her large brown eyes met his with such hope that Thad's plan for a marriage proposal up at the old cabin was in jeopardy; but he didn't propose. He had plans!

"How did you get out of the truck down at the church," he took the conversation a different way and saw a flash of mild frustration spark in her eyes.

"I looked and leaped," Leah answered flippantly.

Thad stifled a smile and moved ahead to open the deck door for them to pass through and into the pungent aroma of Road Kill Stew. He winced as Leah took a quick breath in and wrinkled her nose.

"I'll have running boards put on the truck by the end of the week for you ladies," he determined. Leah was about to protest, but Thad's ardent gaze stopped her as her eyes watered. The air was spicy.

"When I'm not there to help you down, I want to make sure you can get down by yourself without somebody else getting ideas." He winked at her. Leah smiled and nodded agreement. He took her hand in his and walked into the kitchen where Alma and Taima waited around a bubbling pot in the middle of the table. Leah wondered if it was tempting fate to eat the strong-smelling stew.

Thad seated her before sitting down while his bowl was filled with the notorious concoction.

"Somebody better pray over this stuff," Thad advised with a long look at Taima.

"Leah should," was Taima's quick reply. Leah looked at both men and couldn't understand why they seemed so interested in prayer all of a sudden. Alma nudged Taima and gave him a warning look before bowing her head for the prayer.

"Lord, bless this food to the nourishment of our bodies. Thank you." There were snickers around the table she did not hear.

"Amen," Thad uttered when Leah finished.

Taima noted the Thad's prayerful assent and thought, 'His heart's taken and his mind is gone!'

"I enjoyed going to church with Leah today," Alma began their dinner conversation. "I learned many things that helped me." Joy radiated from Alma's face so much Taima glanced at her with interest. Thad looked at Alma and understood her happiness had something to do with the faith his mother had spoken of so persistently. He saw the change. Leah saw the joy of faith and was beginning to understand the wonder of Salvation. Both longed for Alma's joy in Christ to be experienced in life.

It was silent around the table as they focused on Alma. When she began to eat again, everyone else resumed eating though the room was thick with unspoken comments.

A few moments passed before Leah spoke up.

"This stew isn't too bad, Taima. Actually, it tastes pretty good."

"You seem surprised," Taima teased.

"Do I understand it's called Road Kill Stew?"

"Yep," Taima exclaimed and said nothing more. Thad and Alma looked quickly at each other in amazement! When Leah requested seconds, Taima gave Thad and Alma a look of justification.

After a while conversation about plans for the afternoon were disclosed. Thad looked over at Leah to see how the stew was sitting with her. She seemed to be doing just fine, so he decided to go ahead with his plans. Her resilience to the stew amazed him and he thought, 'maybe they have this kind of stew in Pennsylvania.'

"I'm going to take Leah up to the old cabin this afternoon. She wants to see what a 'real' Alaska cabin looks like," he teased happily. Taima and Alma looked puzzled. They wondered why Thad would want to show Leah a run down old shack in the middle of nowhere!

"Where does he get his sense of humor?" Leah chuckled.

"I don't know." Taima replied with a glance at Thad. "He didn't have one until you came." Then he added with sarcasm, "The whack with the broom must have knocked some humor into him instead of sense if he wants to show you that pile of rotten logs!" He laughed out loud at the memory of Thad's attack by a panicked *Cheechako* with "jet lag"!

"Go take a hike!" Alma encouraged with a flourish as she moved to clear the dishes from the table.

CHAPTER 19

LAST DATES

LEAH WENT UPSTAIRS TO CHANGE INTO some brushed navy jeans and a bulky hunter green sweatshirt with white printed evergreen trees designed across the front. A pair of white crew socks would keep her feet warm while her ankle boots were pulled on to keep her feet dry. It was cooler out today and the low clouds threatened rain. She was prepared for any kind of weather or so she hoped.

A few brush strokes through her hair gave order to the mass as she pulled the sides up and snapped a decorative barrette in place. After touching up her make-up, Leah glanced around the comfortable room to see that everything was in order. A small shoulder-strap purse was picked up to take with her before heading downstairs to the roomy entrance.

Thad was waiting to help her into a rain jacket. When her hair fell over his hand again, he gave consideration to the fact this was their first opportunity to spend time alone.

"We'll be back in a couple of hours." Thad told Taima as he opened the door for Leah.

"Okay. I've got to go to Wasilla and pick up a pair of boots at Cottonwood Mall. I think Alma has some shopping to do at the stores, too. We'll catch you two later," Taima waved them away and went into the kitchen to help Alma finish clearing the table.

"There's a shopping mall in this area?" Leah asked once they were out the door and headed down the steps.

"Yes. There are several more stores and businesses of all kinds in Wasilla. Alma likes to shop there for more of a variety. It saves on trips into Anchorage. Right now, it's a boomtown in Alaska with lots of traffic. You'd probably like it, Leah. It might remind you of small towns back home in Pennsylvania."

"Back home," Leah repeated quietly, "I haven't thought too much about home."

"You've been busy discovering Alaska," Thad reasoned.

"And you've been busy dodging my crazy discoveries."

"Dodging?" he gave her a side-glance. "I wouldn't say dodging. Targets usually don't have the opportunity to duck."

"Targets usually don't get as much affection either," Leah murmured as she reached for Thad's hand and squeezed it. His smile was followed by a tender kiss aimed to convey his pleasure at being the soul target of Leah Grant's affections.

"Practice makes perfect." Thad quipped with a wink and moved them to the Suburban. A few sprinkles of rain dotted the windshield as they entered the vehicle and buckled seatbelts.

"Leah?" he paused before blundering ahead, "when was your last date?"

"What?" she blinked and studied Thad a moment, trying to figure out where this question was coming from.

"I was just wondering. My last date was..." he thought for a while, eyes squinted in deep concentration.

"Too long ago!" she answered for him and they both laughed. Just as suddenly as the raindrops had appeared, they vanished and the sun peaked through the clouds as if pushing the rain clouds to the side. A gust of wind stirred the tops of the birch trees and turned the leaves in dancing waves of green and yellow. As Leah began to answer Thad's questions she noted the early arrival of autumn to this Alaskan valley.

"My last date was about a year ago." She started. "I went to a church picnic with a guy named Rusty. It had been an *arranged* date." Her voice revealed a lack of enthusiasm.

"His family had just started attending our church and both our mothers thought it would be nice for their single adult children to meet. He seemed like a nice guy so I agreed to the date...under pressure. I didn't look forward to the date because he just didn't have any real positive effect on me, but I felt obligated for the sake of pleasing my parents. I'd declined so many other guys that one person asked if I was normal and liked men." Leah frowned in annoyance. "Anyway, he picked me up and we went to the picnic. Bless his heart, he tried to make conversation, but we just couldn't seem to connect on any topic. After about an hour of awkward attempts to find common ground, I was ready for the date to end. I asked Rusty to take me home and we left the picnic; but by a different road. I didn't think anything of it at the time because I was selling Avon beauty products on the side to help with personal expenses, so I knew every highway, road, path, and ditch for miles around my home. When he took a turn onto a dirt road away from the general direction of my home, alerts sounded in my mind! I knew this dirt road was only four miles from the Ohio state line. One good thing was that I had customers along this road who knew me well." Leah guaranteed. "It took every bit of courage to remain calm and keep from panicking. I thought maybe he was unfamiliar with the area being his family had just moved to a new location. He was very quiet and seemed preoccupied when I tried to initiate conversation.

"When I got over the initial panic, I became angry that Rusty would try anything." Leah pursed her lips together then parted them to continue. "I had a lot more spit than brains. I couldn't think what to do except to talk to hide my panic until I could come up with a plan. As we passed houses and farms I knew, I named their residents and spoke of my friendships with my Avon customers. This got his attention. When I told him this road was part of my sales route, the car slowed noticeably. As we passed a farm house, a customer turned and waved at me in recognition. Rusty then mentioned he must have taken a wrong turn.

Amazingly, he was able to find his way back to the main road without any trouble!" Thad's eyes narrowed.

Leah smirked. "When he dropped me off at my home, I told him it was a good thing he'd decided to turn around. I also told him my friends had large gun cabinets and were good hunters, but he didn't take the hint. For the last year and a half I've dodged his invitations for dates repeatedly." Leah shrugged, "And that was my last date with one Rusty Glick." When Leah had told her parents about the picnic incident later that evening, it was met with a yawn and a reproach for trying to bring shame on a nice guy. It had seemed like she didn't have her parents support or protection anymore.

Thad mentally put Rusty Glick on his black-list.

"I'm grateful you were safe, Leah, and I'm glad you're here with me now." His simple statement helped heal the emotional wounds of her memory.

"Thank you, Thad. What a difference one year and a few letters makes. I feel safe here with you."

"Good. I hope you still think that when we get to the cabin."

"It's your turn to tell me about your last date." Leah encouraged. Thad didn't relish telling about his last date either. When there was a sufficient time lapse, Leah reached for Thad's hand.

"You don't want to talk about it, do you?"

"No, I don't," was his honest reply.

Leah considered the man beside her. He seemed well respected by all who knew him.

"Okay. I'll ask the questions." She saw Thad glance over at her. Just as he had been so open to her story, he was closed to relating the events of his last date. This was a side of Thad Leah did not know. He seemed suddenly cool. Leah ignored this intimidation.

"I'm going to guess what happened." Leah nodded slowly. Thad remained silent.

"Was your last date a set-up, too?"

Thad made no reply. Leah took that as a "yes".

"Was it set-up by so-called friends?"

"Tyrone wasn't involved. He was out of town for the week." Thad defended. Leah received the clipped response as further evidence she was right about his last dating experience.

"You're a handsome man, Thad, and a good catch for some ditzy woman with ideas on how to spend your money for you. Or, your friends thought it was about time you left the wild wilderness for some wild times in town. Somehow your date was arranged or hired for the night. They probably thought it would be humorous, too. Denise's brother had a similar experience. Anyhow, that's how it's done to some unsuspecting person who's in the "over thirty crowd of singles. It's supposed to be funny. Not!"

Thad spoke sincerely. "Nothing happened, Leah. When I figured it out-which didn't take long-I just left the woman and signed the bill to Frank! It made me sick." Thad was disgusted, then chuckled, "Come to think of it, I haven't heard from Frank since!"

"Well, we've both had similar experiences with people setting us up with unwanted dates, Thad. People try to be matchmakers." Leah traced the top of his hand with her index finger. This little gesture was meant to offer comfort but it stirred his senses. "Even those whose intentions are meant for good have no idea of the trouble they can cause when they interfere with stupid matchmaking plans." Thad saw her peeve and smiled.

"Dating Services not included." He offered the exception with rising interest at the light touch of her finger.

"That's another fiasco for the most part. Did you ever read some of those statements on the bios?" Leah asked wide-eyed and stopped tracing his hand to brush a strand of hair behind an ear. Instantly he missed her gentle touch.

"I've seen enough of them and they certainly cover the ridiculous pretty well." Thad took a deep breath and released it. Leah was relieved to see he relaxed.

"You were the very last bio I read. I almost gave up," she pointed to him and smiled brightly.

"Yours was the last bio I picked up from the dating service before requesting my name be removed from the active list." Thad said this with amazement. His hand moved to enfold hers securely. They regarded one another with wonder.

"Miracles really do happen," Thad said with a smile. Could it be that God really answers prayers?

CHAPTER 20

THE HOMESTEAD

THAD AND LEAH DROVE AWAY FROM the large comfortable cabin with a greater sense of harmony in their courtship.

"The original cabin we'll see is what you might have stayed in about two years ago if we'd met then," Thad told her as they left the pavement and descended the gravel driveway to the road below.

Thad turned left onto a two-lane highway and drove away from Palmer. The Talkeetna Mountain Range grew closer until it shot up to great heights along the curvy roadway known as the "Old Glenn Highway". Two parallel bridges came into view. One was of steel construction while the newer one they crossed was constructed of concrete. At the end of the bridge, Thad turned onto a dirt road that followed the Knik River for a short distance. They talked about the landscape and avalanches that occurred in this area the past winter. After a few moments of comfortable silence, Thad commented about Leah's abilities as a pianist.

"You're very good."

"Thanks, but when did you ever hear me play the piano?" Leah wondered.

"I stopped at the church this morning when I saw the truck parked there. I think you were playing the last song," he answered. Mild surprise registered on her face.

"Did you get to hear any of Pastor Paytor's sermon?"

"Just the last of it," he replied blandly and wondered what she might say, but Leah was quietly reflective.

"Did he say something that interested you, Leah?" Thad encouraged when she did not immediately continue the topic.

"Pastor Paytor made a statement that made me think about my own spiritual life. He said some of us are good people whom others would be shocked to find are not believers," Leah was thoughtful. "He was talking about me. Even though I have a desire to know Christ as Savior, it's not enough. I just can't seem to get any further," Leah was puzzled.

Thad participated, "My mother often told me that I knew the truth, but my problem was rebellion against God. I never let it bother me too much, though."

"That's my problem, too." Leah confessed with a slight tremor. Thad glanced at her. Apparently she thought rebellion was very serious.

"You don't have a rebellious bone in your body, Leah," he offered.

"It's not my bones that are rebellious, Thad. It's my heart." Her honesty pricked Thad. "I rebelled as a child because I resented being raised in a Pastor's home." Leah stopped abruptly. "We both rebelled. You had a choice to believe and you refused. I was expected to believe and I refused.

Thad pulled the Suburban over to the side of the narrow dirt road, parked, and turned off the engine. He was thinking about what Leah had just said. He understood what she was saying but he still wasn't sure about his desire to make a commitment to Christ. The last thing he wanted to become was a Bible hugger.

"What are you thinking?" Leah asked as her stomach rumbled and rolled. She figured it was probably a gas bubble or something. He looked over at her.

"I think of God as being a man's kind of guy." It came out sounding awkward. "But Christ…I have a different picture of Him for some reason. Why? I don't understand. He never stuck up for Himself. He seems weak and soft to me." Thad confessed.

"He stuck up for His Father," Leah suggested. "Do you remember the story about the money changers in the Temple? It's one story I vividly remember."

"Vaguely," Thad replied. "You'll have to refresh my memory."

"When Jesus entered the Temple in Jerusalem, he became angry with the money changers who were charging people extremely high prices to buy animals and other items for their sacrifices. It was hard enough to get the nation of Israel to remember God in the first place. These greedy men worked the people for money. Instead of a House of Prayer, they made it a den of thieves. Jesus' angry reaction defended every man's desire to worship God without being robbed and manipulated. It says he turned over the money tables and threw the moneychangers out of the temple. You know? That sounds like something Sampson would have done. Jesus wasn't weak or soft-spoken when the true worship of God was threatened by corruption in the place of prayer."

Thad watched her. "You know this stuff backwards and forwards, Leah, and live it better than most so-called Christians, but you refuse to be a Christian in your heart although you know it in your mind? I don't understand that at all," he shook his head in total bewilderment. "At this point, I'm more convinced of what you just said then you are because it is beginning to make sense," Thad confessed.

"It's beginning to make sense to me too, Thad. I've turned away from God so many times it just got easier to refuse Him, until now. Now I have to make a choice." Leah said seriously.

"WE have to make a choice," Thad reiterated. Leah nodded quietly and smiled.

"We. I like that," Leah winked and Thad laughed. He was beginning to think she would propose before he could carry out his plan.

"Let's walk up to the old cabin. I have some questions to ask you about redecorating the old place," he said eagerly pulling the door latch to release the lock.

"Decorating ideas?" she frowned but Thad gave no hint he had anything else on his mind. As she stepped out of the Suburban, he took her hand and spoke with a gravity that comes with the making of a vow. A seagull screeched above them and another answered from a distant wind current that moved the treetops and sent a cascade of yellow leaves to the earth around them.

"Leah, when you started writing to me about your religious background, I began to remember some things my mother said to me. One of her many quips was often repeated. 'What you do with the Bible, son, will determine what God does with you.' I don't know what it is about that statement, but it always made me uncomfortable every time I heard it. I've never given the Bible any serious thought other than thinking it was a book of fables for people who enjoyed narrow-minded thinking." After closing Leah's door, he started their ascent up a steep incline. Only a four-wheeler would maneuver such a path and it looked like several ATVs had made the climb and left a well-worn path. There were many deep ruts on either side making it necessary for Leah to walk carefully as Thad guided her along. He continued to talk as they climbed.

"It was always easier to ignore the Bible in favor of another creed that allowed me to live my own way and be my own boss without accounting to a Higher Authority. It eliminated the dependence on someone else for anything more than friendship or mutual aid. Since I chose how I would live here and now, I figured death was nothing to worry about. If there was a God, my mom would see to it I made it to the right place," he joked. "She'd pester God until I was placed in a mansion beside hers or put on a distant star if I needed a proving ground for a while."

The easy way Thad referred to God make Leah cringe. Reverence for God and His holiness had always earned her fear of Him but never her faith in Him.

"How do you picture God, Thad?"

He stopped to check Leah and regarded her with admiration. Her cheeks were rosy from the exercise of the climb and the chill in the pure mountain air. All he wanted to do at this moment was to gaze into her soft brown eyes and find he was cherished in her heart.

"I guess I picture God as just another guy with a higher social standing in the universe. Everything He does is right according to how He sees things. Some try to please Him to get what they want. Others, like me, would rather muddle through the best we can and appeal to His mercy at some future judgment or such. To be honest, that seemed to be a good idea until you came along, Leah. I only had myself to consider." He took a deep breath and let it go. "Mom's statement comes back to me and I have to consider the 'us' if that happens." Thad was thoughtful, "What we do with the Bible determines what God does with us," he repeated. "I'm unsure about this for your sake. It makes me responsible for you somehow and it means my view of God might need to change."

The incline of their hike gradually leveled out ahead making the ascent easier as they walked on. "Ignoring Him doesn't seem to be a wise choice anymore and I don't like the idea of being fearful of Him either. So, I find it's time to give serious consideration to God and what He says in the Bible. And, I do want to find out what this faith in Christ is all about with you, Leah. I'm just not sure how to go about it."

"I'm unsure, too," Leah acknowledged. "The urge to resist is still there, but I don't want to quit searching and I don't want you to be obligated to change what you believe on my account unless you are convinced yourself. I love you just as you are."

Leah squeezed his hand to guarantee this but he knew it before she spoke.

"We seem to understand each other and are looking for the same answers though we're coming from different thought processes. Thad, you weren't swayed by what others expected of you; but I chose to try to do what others thought I should do to keep up a godly appearance. My attempt was always frustrated by hapless mistakes. I couldn't deliver perfection." Suddenly Leah grinned at the foolishness of it all. "It's all just nonsense, isn't it?" Thad studied her transparent eyes with devotion.

"Both of us need to leave misconceptions behind," Thad conceded. As if putting action to his words, he turned and they began to walk again.

"I guess in one way, your invitation gave me a good reason to find out what God wants of me and what I want to do about Him." Leah surmised.

"So, I'm not the main reason you came to Alaska?" he countered. Leah leaned into Thad.

"Well, your accommodations are very nice and this personal tour of the old homestead will be one of the highlights of the hunting trip, I'm sure," Leah promised. She spoke like a travel agent investigating a resort for clientele.

"What hunting trip?" he laughed.

"My husband hunting one." Leah saw Thad's eyes widen at the candid reply.

The path opened to a flat grassy highland meadow with short trees and dense wilderness brush on three sides. In meandering patches of summer color, red and purple petals clung to the top half of the Fireweed. Upon seeing the tranquil beauty of the place, Leah wondered what this meadow would look like in spring with a myriad of colorful blossoms. At present, fall colors beautifully dressed the earth in preparation for winter's soon arrival. The snow would gradually come down the sides of the mountains and head toward the tree line that marked the beginning of the populated farm valley.

"Have you had good hunting?" he asked shrewdly.

"Yes, Thad, I have," she spoke out clearly. They gazed at each other with unspoken pledges of commitment. However, Thad didn't pop the question, yet. He had a plan.

Splatters of rain touched their faces and interrupted the serene wonderland. Thad immediately pulled Leah's hood up over her head and moved them forward through the meadow at a good pace.

"We're not far from the cabin now." He assured as Leah kept pace with him through the tall grasses. She was watching where she stepped because of the uneven ground and the varmint holes. She had suffered a severe ankle sprain before from such dastardly holes in the ground. The word "pain" could not adequately describe the agony of an ankle sprain. When she glanced up to catch a glimpse of where they were headed, she saw the dark cabin of her dreams nestled in a large expanse of tall thin scrub pine trees. They resembled dirty, chewed-up bottle brushes.

"Rustic," Leah commented and wasn't sure if *rustic* was really the right word for what appeared to be more of a tumble down shack than a cabin. Her first impression didn't inspire laughter either. There was a small covered porch about three feet wide and no longer than sixteen feet across the front of the rickety structure. They stepped onto the porch then Thad turned the key already in the padlock used only to keep the wind from blowing the door open to the elements and foraging wildlife. They walked inside.

The few windows in the cabin offered minimal light until the eyes adjusted to the dim interior. The pungent smells of old wood smoke and longtime mildew greeted Leah first as she stepped onto the rough-cut floorboards. Thad lit a Coleman lantern and Leah was surprised to see a small pot bellied stove in one corner. A hole had been cut in the logs for a pipe to vent the smoke; but the pipe was missing.

Thad set the lantern down on a square table beside what Leah assumed was a rough cut cabinet about thirty-six inches high. Shelves ran along the lower half of a wall. A length of particle board about six feet long and twenty-four inches wide rested on top of the shelving. It resembled a counter top of sorts but was bowed and warped by dampness. There was a plastic wash basin, an old aluminum coffee pot, some skillets and a stew pot neatly hanging on huge nails on the wall. One small window above it offered a view of pine branches thick with wispy needles. When the wind blew, these branches brushed against the window like a puppy scratching to get outside and frolic about.

Thad watched Leah's carful study of each corner of the cabin. It was the first time he couldn't read the expression on her face. And, it was a good thing he couldn't, though he could just about guess the descriptive words she might be thinking...or so he thought.

"I'm guessing this cabin has about one hundred and sixty square feet of floor space?" Leah raddled off and Thad was surprised her evaluation was nearly correct.

"I don't know, Thad," she continued her scan. The third corner sported a single bed frame built out of rough wood. The level of comfort it offered might coax a bedbug, a crocked old man, or both. A window above it faced the front and was one of three windows in the cabin offering natural light, a view to the far mountains, and much needed fresh air. Under an adjacent window there was an old threadbare recliner and an empty bookcase with a rusty kerosene lantern on top. One wood stool and an ancient black rocker occupied the middle of the cabin. Both suggested colonial vintage. These pieces faced the wood stove and seemed to invite company and conversation except that there was mud and grass caked on their seats. Leah's eyes were drawn to the ceiling where a gaping hole provided a view to threatening clouds. Thad noted the hole and made mental calculations for its simple repair while Leah considered the cost of tearing the whole cabin down and rebuilding!

Even though there probably had been no curtains, rugs, pictures, knick-knacks or quilts to add personality and warmth to the place, Leah could not be critical of Thad's efforts to build this first place of refuge and practice the skills that forged his present ability to care for others. This cabin spoke of a simple man whom Leah had come to love and respect. In this place, she understood his ascent to manhood and was glad he'd shown her this part of his life. As for decorating ideas, Leah was beginning to see a woman's touch could provide personality and warmth to any place—be it mansion or shack—if she was given the opportunity to fill it with her own dreams of happiness. She smiled up at the hole above her and knew Thad would allow her the freedom. He was not a selfish man who wanted everything his way nor would he expect her to change to fit his lifestyle. She'd try not to nag him too much!

"I know this place looks like a den of sorts," he offered, "but it was snug when I first started the business. The clients liked it then. Some still use it when they want to spend some time alone."

"A den, Thad?" this produced a ripple of laughter from Leah. Then she considered the fact that, had they met two or three years earlier, this would have been where Thad brought her—without a Taima and Alma. Thoughts of Taima, and Thad's reference to a den sparked a thought.

"You know, Thad? When Taima called you 'Wolfe', I almost bolted for the airport to take the first available flight back to Pittsburgh."

"I figured he did. He never uses that name because he knows I don't like it."

"Well, when I asked for 'Thad Tucker' after just arriving at the Trading Post, he acted like he didn't know your right name." Leah mimicked the gruff Taima. "Thad Tucker! We call him Wolfe, Miss Grant!" Thad roared with laughter and Leah enjoyed hearing his outburst.

"He's always been my guardian angel where women are concerned."

"He's good at it," Leah assured but frowned in discomfort when a slight stomach cramp was followed by nausea.

"He was just checking you for a negative response."

"How did you come by that nickname?"

"Oh, I'll tell you later." Suddenly, Thad was anxious to put his plan into action. It was more important than some old nickname he didn't like.

"Did you ever notice a lot of things are *later* with you?" Leah protested mildly. Thad blinked as if smacked by her uncharacteristic statement. She saw him flinch and quickly retreated wondering why she'd snapped at him. Her stomach rumbled again.

"I'm sorry I said that, Thad. Later is okay," she moaned. It was the first time she'd pointed out a fault and it had come out of nowhere just like the present annoying cramp in her lower side. The pain was beginning to be irksome and it was affecting her good mood. Thad saw her discomfort.

"Are you okay, Leah?" he moved toward her.

"I'm fine, just a little indigestion, that's all," she smiled and reached for him as his arms came around her waist. He studied her for a few moments before proceeding, hoping the stew wasn't the cause of her indigestion.

"Leah," he started seriously as if something important to come was promised, but he didn't get any further. Leah's lovely face turned white with misery. She groaned as a gut wrenching pain stabbed her stomach and a wave of nausea nearly overpowered her effort to squelch the coming sickness.

"Where's the outhouse?" she managed to blurt, but Thad shook his head.

"There isn't an outhouse, Leah. A tree fell on it during a Chinook windstorm last January."

Leah's eyes were large with disbelief! All of a sudden her stomach lurched and it wasn't the kind of lurch that comes when someone is in love either. Another stab of pain hit her and shortly after that subsided, Leah's hand came up to her mouth and she turned and sprinted out the cabin door. Thad started after her, but by the time he reached her, Leah was on hands and knees retching over the edge of the porch. He quickly reached for her shoulders and held them firmly so she wouldn't fall forward.

"Taima's Road Kill Stew strikes again." Thad muttered in annoyance and knelt down beside his beloved pen-pal to offer comfort and aid. So much for his plans!

CHAPTER 21

DRIVING MISS DIZZY!

THAD HELPED LEAH SIT BACK AGAINST the wall of the cabin when she was able to lift her head. He reached for a handkerchief from his jacket pocket and gave it to her. With trembling hands she wiped her blotchy face. He brushed her hair away and spoke gently.

"Leah, are you all right?"

"I feel awful," she moaned in agony and leaned against the rough log wall. All dignity was lost in her honest reply.

"Yah, I know. I had a first time experience with Taima's stew myself, with the same results. Just sit back and rest; the fresh air will help until you," he paused knowing this was not the end of it, "...feel better," he finished lamely. Rain pattered softly on the porch roof above them as Thad and Leah sat quietly side by side until a shiver made Leah's teeth chatter.

"Leah, I have to get you back to the Sub. Can you walk?" he asked. Leah managed a feeble "yes". He hoped they could make it back to the Suburban before she was sick again. It was inevitable. There were blankets and toilet facilities there "when" she needed them and not "if" she needed them.

He helped her up, but saw her knees were wobbly, so he picked her up in his arms and started away from the cabin. Leah was too sick to do anything but rest her head on his shoulder. At this point, Thad could have been a grizzly and Leah wouldn't have cared! She continued to groan as the pain in her side intensified and her stomach gurgled. Thad hurried down the side of the slope, grateful to be descending for the sake of time.

They were about halfway to the Sub when Thad had to stop and put Leah down because she heaved again. He held her forehead up and rubbed her back in efforts to soothe the tense muscles in her back until she was able to lift her head once again. She looked totally exhausted, but managed to assure Thad she was beginning to feel a little better. Though he doubted it, he nodded and was about to ask her if she wanted to sit when it started to rain harder. Lifting her in his arms again, he continued descending to the dark green Suburban. Leah's stomach still rumbled between jabs of pain. She cried softly--wishing for a few moments of idyllic peace.

Thad tried to ease her discomfort and reassure her that the stew was the problem and would wear off eventually. What he didn't tell her was that there were other side effects such as dizziness, chills, and diarrhea that would probably all take their course, too. So far, she was running true to course. Thoughts of his foiled proposal came to mind as he stepped carefully along the rugged path. Right where Leah's shoulder lay against his chest was a half carat diamond engagement ring. He glanced down to check her and saw her eyes were closed. She seemed calmer but strands of hair stuck to a sweaty brow. Her cheeks were red and blotchy. This bothered him because a rash was not one of the side effects of Taima's stew.

They reached the Suburban as it started to rain harder. Thad got Leah in the front seat and buckled her seat belt. She leaned back against the head rest as he started the engine and backed out onto the road.

"Thad, I'm so dizzy," Leah replied as she reached for his hand. He took it and squeezed it quickly.

"That's part of it, too," he replied sympathetically. "Here, lie down and put your head on my leg. Just stare at the dash or something that isn't moving. That will help a little bit." Leah followed his instructions, grateful to lie down. The nausea still came in waves at times but, thankfully, that was all it did.

Thad drove as quickly as the road conditions allowed in the pelting rain. He stroked Leah's hair and cheek occasionally and talked to her about the weather conditions in their area. Leah was soothed as she listened to his voice though she didn't catch much of the meaning of what he was saying. Her head felt disconnected from her body and fuzzy. At times everything seemed to whirl for a few seconds, then it would stop and Leah would try to relax and concentrate on what Thad was saying. Except for the pounding rain and the beat of the wipers pushing the deluge to the sides of the windshield, everything else seemed chaotic and out of balance.

Eventually, the turn signal clicked on and Leah felt the vehicle turn to the right. It made her dizzy for a few moments until the vehicle straightened and began to climb the driveway. She was glad to be back at home. However, this thought puzzled her. How was she back in Pennsylvania? Hadn't she flown to Alaska? What was going on? Nothing was making any sense.

Thad beeped the horn as he drove onto the pavement and parked. Thankfully, Alma and Taima hadn't left for Wasilla, yet. Leah tried to sit up as Thad moved around the front of the Suburban and reached to open her door. Sheltering her, he gently drew her from the vehicle and lifted her in his arms. Taima saw him start up the steps and had the door open for the quick entrance. One look at Leah told Taima his stew had done its job!

"That stew again," he muttered with remorse.

Quickly he found Alma who frowned at his wide-eyed urgency. When he told her Leah was sick, she gave him a scalding look and hurried up the stairs to Leah's room. Thad had just laid her on the bed and was carefully removing her jacket. The fact that she was lethargic worried Thad. This reaction to the stew was more serious than he'd figured. He talked to her but she was dazed and wasn't responding easily.

"Alma, we're going to need help." Thad said while he was thinking he should have taken her on to the hospital in Palmer.

Alma took one look at Leah's red blotchy face and turned from the room at a run. She met Taima at the foot of the stairs and began signing to him to call emergency assistance. Taima was startled but moved to the phone and dialed 9-1-1 to reach the Palmer EMT.

Moving over next to a lethargic Leah, Alma got her attention by quickly slapping Leah's hand to get her attention. Leah looked at her and Alma signed, "What are you allergic to, Leah? Tell me!" she commanded, urgency reflected in her eyes. Thad read Alma's hands to Leah.

"Mushrooms," Leah mumbled almost incoherently.

"Do you have medicine, Leah?" Leah didn't answer so Alma slapped her hand sharply to encourage response.

"Medicine?" Thad spoke louder. Leah managed a faint nod, "yes".

Alma clapped to get Thad's attention.

"The green case on the bathroom sink. Get it!" She signed and Thad moved quickly to retrieve the case. Alma grabbed it and dumped the contents on the bed beside Leah. She rifled through cosmetics until she spotted a small box of pink tablets. She knew these tablets were for allergies. Ripping open the box, Alma pulled a card of the pink tablets out and tore a tablet away. Thad brought a cup of water from the bathroom and Alma motioned for him to lift Leah. Alma put the tablet in Leah's mouth and held the cup to her lips so she could sip enough water to swallow the tablet.

Leah's hand came up to the cup long enough to help Alma with its direction as she swallowed the tablet and water. When her hand dropped limply, Alma reached for Leah's hand and caressed it gently. A calm smile of peace on Alma's face brought encouragement to Thad.

Thad didn't know what to do until Alma looked up at the ceiling as if gazing into Heaven. She began to sign a prayer Thad sat on the bed beside Leah, his arm still around her shoulders. Both Leah and Thad watched as Alma prayed for the first time since accepting Christ as her Savior. Leah had never seen anything so beautiful even though it was all dream-like.

"My Father, Who art in Heaven, I pray to You not knowing how to say the right words to help our Leah. I only know that You can help her and heal her when we have done all we know how to do. Thank you, Jesus. Amen."

Peace settled over the room after Alma prayed. Thad could not take his eyes from Leah's as she blinked them slowly. When she seemed to be dozing off, Alma would pat her hand rapidly to keep her awake. Thad also made efforts to talk to her though his own voice faltered with rising emotion.

Taima was first to hear the siren of the ambulance as it approached the cabin. The sound of its approach unnerved him as he paced the deck anxiously. At times he formed words of requests to any native spirits who would hear him. But he felt it was useless. What could such childhood reflections do for him now? They could not speak, or touch, or hear, or comfort. It was he who had spoken to them, heard their voices in the keening winds, and praised their strength. Where were the spirits of the wild when he needed their help? Who governed them and gave them power to aid mankind?

When the ambulance arrived, two EMTs, Adam and Joel, jumped from the truck, then grabbed medical packs and headed up the steps towards Taima who gave directions and followed them up to the third floor.

When they entered the bedroom, Leah was trembling. Adam quickly came over beside the bed and began taking Leah's vital signs while he asked questions of Thad. Thad spoke of the allergy to mushrooms and mentioned about Taima's stew. Joel nodded understanding as he spoke to the Valley Hospital base in Palmer.

While he transmitted information, another man entered the room in waders and a flannel jacket with fishing lures dangling from a chest pocket.

"How can I help?" asked Dr. Andersen. "I just left the hospital headed for some relaxing fishing and heard your call. Thought I'd just stop in and see what the hullabaloo is all about." Adam gave Andersen Leah's vital signs and other information while Joel notified Valley Hospital that Dr. Andersen was on site. The hospital replied that ER would stand by. Joel came around to assist Dr. Andersen as Thad gently laid Leah back on the pillow and moved off the bed to stand against the wall. He felt so useless. Taima's hand rested on his shoulder.

"Let's wait out in the hallway, Thad. She's in the best hands there are." Thad looked over at Alma and she motioned for him to leave with a small smile of encouragement. He glanced at Leah whose eyes were closed. The sight of Dr. Andersen, Adam, and Joel working over her was more than he could stand. He turned and left the room quickly. Taima followed him out to the hallway and down to Alma's room. Once there, Thad went directly to the glass solarium and sat in a wicker chair with his head in his hands.

Taima could say nothing to him. The possibility of tragedy stunned him profoundly. Strangely, he thought of Sonya and wished she were here. He remembered her stability and steadiness. These qualities had endeared her to him when Sonya was his for a season. He'd ruined that relationship with his wild lifestyle and now he scolded himself for the wild stew!

Thad could not quiet the turmoil in his heart. Love for Leah stirred every nerve in him to save her. His mind and heart worked at a solution to keep her near. Reaching into his shirt pocket, his fingers felt the metal of a circular object. He pulled the engagement ring out of a pocket that had held popped buttons just a few months ago and held it tightly. Like capturing a rose's blooming, his fingers gradually opened to reveal the golden ring marked with diamond flashes in his palm.

Taima came over and stood by Thad as he turned the ring over in his hand. The diamond sparkled brilliantly in its cone setting. Two smaller diamonds glittered on either side of the gem's heart.

"It's beautiful, Thad." Taima offered quietly.

"I was going to give it to her today."

"I'm sorry I ruined this special time for you two. I'll never make that miserable stew again," Taima vowed. He turned and left before Thad could reply.

As time passed, Thad thought about his mother and the many times she had reminded him she was praying for his soul. He hadn't thought much about it then, but right now he was glad to know she still prayed for him. He also knew God answered her prayers and with this thought, Thad stood up and reached for the phone by Alma's nightstand.

"Thad, why are you calling at this hour? You always call around noon." She glanced at the wall clock which ticked past seven o'clock Mountain Time.

"I need you to pray for Leah, Mom," Thad's voice cracked with emotion.

"Leah?"

"Yes, she's the girl I've been writing to for several months and she's here for a visit."

"She is? Oh, yes! I remember you mentioned you were writing someone. So, her name is Leah? What's wrong, Thad?"

"She had some of Taima's stew and is having a bad reaction to it. The EMTs are here and I just needed someone to pray for her, Mom."

"Oh, it's that terrible stew of his, again!" Louise Tucker huffed in disgust. "Of course I'll pray for Leah. Let's pray for her right now." So saying, Louise Tucker began to pray as Thad bowed his head and listened.

"Dearest Heavenly Father, we lift up Leah before you and ask for your hand of healing to touch her body and restore it to good health. We know You are able to do abundantly above all we can ask or think so we praise You for what You will do on her behalf. Bring comfort to Thad's heart and give him peace that You love both him and Leah and are able to work all this for good. May You be glorified. May they realize what a mighty God You are. Please, Lord, be gracious unto us for Jesus sake and restore health to Leah..." Louise continued on unburdening her heart before the Lord on her son's behalf.

For the first time in years, Thad listened to the words his mother spoke in reverent prayer. His concept of a Savior had been all wrong. He'd looked at Jesus as being a crutch instead of a foundation. As a foundation, he was beginning to understand that Jesus could also be a friend; a divine Friend with whom he could fellowship forever. He thought about how his Mom prayed and it was as though she spoke to God intimately as one friend making a request for the other's help. The respect in her voice was not out of fear but love and devotion. She prayed as if God really would hear and help. There was no need to appease God, because his Mom had received the gospel of reconciliation to a Holy

God. And Thad was beginning to understand why his Mom's prayers got answered. She could approach God about anything, anytime. He couldn't because his sin and rebellion prevented any approach to God without receiving faith and forgiveness. Thad thought about Leah and he definitely wanted God to hear his prayers.

"Father, I pray that my son will come to know Jesus Christ as Savior and Lord. I pray he will simply put his trust in you and forsake the rebellion that has kept him from knowing your love to the fullest." As she prayed, Thad grew calmer as peace entered his heart and soul.

"Son, wouldn't you like to trust Christ as your Savior right now?" she asked in the middle of her prayer. "You know the gospel message of Salvation. Ask God to forgive you of your sins, son. Believe on the Lord Jesus Christ and be saved," she quoted as naturally as breathing. "I pray the Holy Spirit will encourage you to respond in faith. Will you believe on Jesus, son?" his mother gently entreated. All was quiet for several moments before Mom Tucker heard the words of her son's prayer.

"Jesus," Thad said simply, "I know I can't ignore You anymore. I've tried to leave You out of my life because I was mad at You for not giving me a dad. I'm sorry for my resentment. I am a sinner and I ask for You to forgive me. I want to make things right with You, my Heavenly Father. I know what You said in Your Word is true and I'm done with trying to live without acknowledging You, God. I ask for faith to believe You and to live like You are Who You say You are." Thad swallowed with difficulty, "Please help Leah to believe, too."

"Amen." Mom Tucker rejoiced as tears streamed down her face.

"Thanks, Mom."

"Praise God, Thad! Call me when you can and put Leah on the line, too. I'd love to talk to your girlfriend and get to know her."

"Sure." Thad paused then, "I love you."

"Love you, too, dear. Bye."

There entered into Thad's heart and mind the joy that comes from Divine forgiveness. Peace and comfort replaced anxiety and fear for Leah along with a calm assurance that God, in His sovereign power, would care for Leah in ways Thad never could. He recognized with perfect clarity the power of Jesus Christ to forgive years of sin and rebellion and replace it with grace to make all things new.

In the guestroom nearby, Leah was resting quietly. Dr. Andersen observed her progress with a pleased expression. Two IVs had been set up. One was a saline solution to replace fluids and minerals. The other was an IV drip of a larger dose of allergy medicine which would enter her blood stream with far more speed to halt the allergy's progress and reverse the reaction. An oxygen mask had been put over her nose and mouth to ensure she was able to breathe sufficiently. Alma held her hand and rubbed it gently as Leah rested.

After another fifteen minutes, Leah opened her eyes and looked around her in wonder. A tall, thin man of sixty stared down at her.

"Hello, there, Leah! I'm Dr. Andersen. How are you feeling?"

"Better," Leah responded awkwardly as she sensed the oxygen mask over her nose and mouth.

"Good," he turned and spoke to Joel giving him some directions for Leah's care. Then he removed the oxygen mask and checked Leah's breathing. All was normal again.

"You gave us something to do this afternoon, Leah. These guys were all just sitting around the fire station twiddling their thumbs. What with the State Fair in town and people all over the place, they needed something else to keep them on their toes." Dr. Andersen teased in a good natured manner. Leah offered a smile. Taking this as a good sign the doctor continued, "I was just going to stand in the middle of a salmon stream and count fish, snag a line, find another leak in my waders, then go home and sulk for the rest of the day." Leah managed a broader smile.

"I hope I'm still in Alaska. The last thing I remember was thinking I was back in Pennsylvania." Leah tried a frown. Dr. Andersen guffawed loudly.

"So, Dorothy went off to see the Wizard, aye?" he joked and Leah gave a weak smile. "You must be feeling better. Nobody smiles at my humor unless they've been to the Land of Oz," he surmised.

"Alma, you can go bring Thad and Taima back in here. Leah will be fine after a good night's sleep. Just give her plenty of liquids, soft foods.

The routine for flu symptoms, you know the drill." Pointing to Leah, he instructed, "No more mushrooms and no more of Taima's stew!"

"I thought the stew was pretty good," Leah replied sincerely.

Dr. Andersen glanced from Alma to Leah and back to Alma with raised eyebrows.

"Alma, don't let this woman in the kitchen!" he enunciated so Alma could read his lips.

"No more stew!" she signed back.

CHAPTER 22

MARY JO TAKES CHARGE

ALMA MET TAIMA IN THE HALL with an encouraging smile. He took a deep breath and was almost to Leah's room when Adam stopped him.

"Leah's in the bathroom, Taima. She'll be out in a few minutes."

Leah felt incredibly weak and shaky as she maneuvered the IVs attached to her arms. Joel had hung the transparent tubes over the top of the bathroom door for her and left the door opened a crack in case his assistance was needed. When she returned to bed, Leah felt a sense of well being returning though strength still waned.

Dr. Andersen gave her instructions similar to what he had given Alma and left to "go count fish." Joel was monitoring her improvement when Adam entered with Taima.

Apprehension registered across Taima's leathery face as he approached the bedside. At his early sixties, Taima was a fine looking man. His thick black hair was neatly kept and though he was shorter than Thad, he had a fine carriage and robust build. Clarity was returning to her thinking processes as details and order came into focus. The troubled frown Taima wore on his face revealed to Leah that he felt awful about the stew's affects on her.

"Well, Taima," Leah spoke lightly to cheer him. "That was one mean stew you made. I hope I'm at least equal to its kick and spunk," she managed light hearted. Taima tried a small grin, but couldn't quite manage it.

"I'm okay now, Taima. You couldn't have known about my allergy to mushrooms. And I guess I'll have to get used to some of the different kinds of meat and seasonings around here, too."

"I'm sorry, Leah. I hope you'll be fine, soon."

"Oh, I'll be right as rain when the sun comes out, really."

"You didn't look so good when Thad brought you in," he stated soberly.

"And I don't smell too good right now, either," Leah wrinkled her nose.

Taima actually chuckled. He seemed more at ease than he had been only moments ago.

"I guess I'll just stick to treating you to rides on the Harley," he suggested with a sly smile.

"You'd better! I'm counting on it."

Thad was still gazing at the sparkling diamond ring as Alma walked into the room. She wasn't sure what condition Thad would be in when she entered. But he had a peaceful grin on his face and when he turned to acknowledge her, Alma could see there was a change in Thad. He looked at her expectantly as he slid the ring into the black velvet sack and placed it back in his shirt pocket. Alma smiled and signed.

"Leah is fine, Thad. You can come and see her now."

Thad stood, eagerness showed both in his eyes and in his quick steps down the hallway.

"Thanks, Alma." He said over his shoulder. Alma smiled and looking up, simply signed, 'Thank you, Lord.'

Thad was almost to Leah's room when a hospice nurse came up the stairs and greeted him.

"Dr. Andersen called me," Mary Jo stated to Thad as she saw him at the top of the stairs. "He sent me over to relieve Joel and Adam so they could go back to the fairgrounds. I'll stay until Miss Grant's IVs are finished."

"Thanks, Mary Jo," Thad replied gratefully and moved aside to allow the nurse to pass first.

Mary Jo was hospice coordinator for the Palmer Hospital. She was an older woman of about fifty or sixty, but nobody knew and nobody wanted to guess out loud either. Facial features revealed her Inuit heritage. Long black hair was kept in a braid that fell to her waist. She was a large woman with a no-nonsense attitude. Those who resisted her instructions soon learned it was well worth the effort to please and appease her. When she smiled, there was an aura of graciousness that promised relief to patients under her care.

Thad knew he would not get anywhere near Leah as long as Mary Jo was observing her recovery. So, he waved briefly to Leah and stood off to the side with arms crossed. Mary Jo greeted Leah cordially enough, checked her vital signs and the IVs as Joel and Adam answered the questions she fired at them. From the moment she entered the room, Mary Jo was in charge! Joel and Adam showed no deference or adversity. They easily accepted her presence and worked smoothly.

"Okay, guys, you're out of here!" She said as they began to collect their equipment quickly. Mary Jo checked Leah over slowly and methodically asking no questions and making no comments.

Leah watched Mary Jo's practiced movements as she took a blood pressure reading. She seemed distant and when she spoke, it felt like the silence of the room was shattered by her brusque manner. Yet she hovered over Leah like a mama bear standing guard over bear cubs feasting on pieces of salmon shredded from her battle with another bear.

Both Joel and Adam nodded to Leah. "Take care, Leah," they encouraged and left with their medical gear.

"I delivered both those boys when they were born," she asserted. Leah attempted a smile of regard for her midwife success. Mary Jo considered Thad for a moment and returned her gaze to Leah.

"I'll probably deliver your babies, too," she said with a calculated confidence.

Leah's eyes grew wide as her face heated with embarrassment. Mary Jo chuckled as Thad uncrossed and crossed his arms while looking down trying to cover the awkward moment. Much to his chagrin, they weren't even engaged, yet!

"It's nice to see that color on your cheeks, Leah. I don't see virtue often enough these days." At that moment Mary Jo smiled broadly at Leah and the whole atmosphere of the room relaxed. The hospice nurse turned from Leah to speak directly to Alma.

"It's nice to see you again, Alma. How about making three strong cups of tea for us ladies?"

Alma nodded understanding and smiled then signed. "We'll do lunch together soon," she mouthed the words slowly to Mary Jo.

"I'd like that, Alma," Mary Jo approved and smiled until she caught sight of Taima. When she scowled at him, he fidgeted and started for the door.

"I'll get a fire started in the fireplace for the evening," he informed, eager to be out of Mary Jo's sights as a target.

Leah smiled after him.

"Don't smile at that man!" Mary Jo barked more for Taima's benefit. "We've had more than a few of Thad's clients over at the hospital after some of Taima's famous Road Kill Stew. There ought to be a law against that brew and a jail sentence for that man," she stressed and shook her head from side to side in condemnation. She added, "Taima doesn't mean *thunder* for nothing."

Leah looked at Mary Jo questioningly.

"Thad, I'll let you tell Leah about 'old thunder', himself." A modest chuckle escaped her lips. "I've got to call the hospital and make a schedule change. I'll be back eventually." So saying, Mary Jo moved leisurely out of the room and down the steps to the phone in the hallway.

At last, Thad and Leah were alone. The room was quiet as Thad regarded Leah thoughtfully. She cocked her head sideways as if waiting for Thad to come over beside her. Her eyes still had dark circles around them testifying a serious ordeal, but she looked to be gaining back her color and spark.

Thad ambled over to the bed and, sitting down beside Leah, took her hand in his.

"You know? You scared me half to death, Leah," he said with raised eyebrows. Leah noted the wave of his dark hair and relished the closeness that prompted her study.

"I've never been that sick in my whole life, at least not that I can remember."

"Well, I'm glad to see you doing better than you were a little while ago, Leah."

"So am I. What's the story on Taima?"

"Are you sure you want to hear a story now?"

"Absolutely, I'd like to know how he got his name. He seems like an interesting person."

"I guess you could say that," Thad nodded and smiled. "Taima was only about twenty-two at the time and pretty wild," Thad reported. "The story is," Thad leaned forward to relay the story carefully, "Taima was working for the Alaska Railroad. He had quite a knack for explosives back then and the railroad needed some tunnels widened. Boulders needed removed or broken apart for removal.

"One time he got a little distracted by this bear that just wouldn't move away from the blasting site. The explosive's team would no sooner get everything set for the blast and that pesky bear would wander back onto the blasting site. Nobody wanted to hurt the bear, but the bear was holding up the work schedule for the afternoon.

"After several attempts were made to 'shoo' the bear away and after still more interruptions from the bear's meanderings, everyone had had enough. That's when Taima had a brainstorm." Thad took a deep breath and expelled it.

"Taima took a couple of dynamite sticks with short fuses and a cigarette lighter and headed for the bear. He had no intentions of hurting the bear, only scaring him away from the blasting site." Thad shook his head at the fantastic idea of anyone scaring a bear away with dynamite!

"Others told him it was a stupid idea and warned him not to do it, but Taima was cocky and daring. Well," Thad sat up and crossed his arms, continuing, "Taima took off towards that bear on a run, yelling at the top of his lungs. Everyone else ran for cover." His eyes met her attentive ones.

"That crazy bear watched Taima coming and just looked at him. He didn't move an inch from where he sat. One observer said Taima actually came within twenty feet of the bear, before he stopped. The two of them just looked at each other in bewilderment. But the bear still didn't budge from its spot by a berry bush.

"Again, Taima waved his arms and hollered at the bear. But the bear remained undaunted and unimpressed by a skinny Indian with a lighter and orange birthday candles of sorts. Then Taima did something that got the bear's undivided attention. He reached for some berries from a nearby bush, grabbed a handful, and ate them. That bear went absolutely nuts! It reared up, growled angrily, and started towards Taima at a territorial charge. Nobody was going to eat that bear's berries!"

Leah enjoyed Thad's animated telling of Taima's story. "When Taima realized he had the bear's full attention, the twenty feet separating the *dynamite man* and a charging beast meant death was imminent…for everyone! Taima was so shocked he did the first thing that came to his mind, he lit the dynamite sticks short fuse and started to walk backwards without any thought to where he was walking.

"When the bear saw the fuse sparking and all the smoke rising, it backed off then turned and loped off into the woods. Just before Taima would have fallen over a twelve-foot ledge, miraculously he stopped… much to his workmates relief. It was then he realized he had lit sticks of dynamite still in hand and he began to dance all around looking for a place to throw them out of harm's way. But everywhere he looked, the side of the mountain was set to blast rock and earth away! So, Taima headed for the woods at a fast sprint.

"The railroad men watched as he sprinted into the trees and disappeared from sight. It is said that a few men swore, a few crossed themselves, and a few fainted." Thad paused for a few moments in deep thought. When he didn't continue, Leah urged him on.

"What happened, Thad?" This prompted a smile on Thad's part. Leah saw a little smirk and nudged him playfully.

"Everyone waited for the inevitable KABOOM, and it surely came. A huge convulsion shook the ground as the thundering boom sounded and reverberated along the mountain range echoing in waves like distant thunder. A billowing cloud of smoke rose skyward as trees and debris fell everywhere. None of the workers dared move from their safe spots for fear of what might fall on them. It was also possible such a blast could set off the other explosives.

"Minutes later, an ALL CLEAR was sounded. Slowly the workmen emerged and moved into the blast site to start removing debris. A group of volunteers was formed to recover Taima's body for burial—if there was anything left of him! They headed towards the direction of the blast to start the recovery and discovered the blast site was wiped clean of all life—plant, animal, and human.

"Those men searched for Taima's body for hours only to find Taima alive and sitting beside a small pond of water cleaning some abrasions and cuts on his arms and legs. The men were astonished to the point they couldn't speak, but Taima did! 'Hey, guys!' he greeted them, 'Look what I got. It's that stupid bear that kept messing up our blasting schedule. I guess the blast must have scared him so much he died right in his tracks!' Taima started laughing. The other guys just couldn't believe Taima was alive and the bear was dead. Indeed, they were shocked when they didn't find a mark on that bear. It was agreed they would drag the bear back to camp on a transit fashioned from fallen tree limbs. When the camp physician took one look at the bear, he promptly declared the bear's death to be the result of heart failure."

"Is Taima's bear skin the one hanging on the wall at the Trading Post?"

"Nope! The bear hide at the Trading Post was one Tyrone got a few years ago. That's another story I'll let him amaze you with sometime. Anyway, because Taima was cited and fined for illegally killing the bear, he couldn't keep the hide. It was unfortunate because there wasn't a bullet hole anywhere or a wound mark made by man's designs. Oh! I will tell you that Taima's birth name is John Green; at least Green is his English name. I don't remember what his Athabascan family's name was before it was changed. Anyway, he was given the name, 'Taima' because he made the sound of thunder in order to conquer a bear."

"But how did he survive the blast?" Leah asked, frowning.

"Don't know. Taima doesn't know either. He said when he regained consciousness he was buried under a pile of lily pads and molting salmon. When the Alaska Department of Fish and Game investigated, Taima ended up paying a huge fine for his part in the bear's untimely death. Of course there were a host of other penalties incurred." Thad grinned. "Taima said the list of violations was so long they handed them to him in a notebook binder."

"They're pretty tough up here," Leah was amazed.

"*Very* tough," Thad emphasized.

"Taima's lucky to be alive."

"Yes, he is."

Conversation halted as each considered Taima's narrow escape with a bear and dynamite followed by the recent excitement on Leah's behalf.

"Thad, there's something I want to tell you, but I'm a little hesitant."

"Go ahead." He urged as his eyes softly regarded hers. Leah cleared her throat to quell the quickening of her heart beat which he stirred again and again.

"Thad," she started and paused, "I think I'm ready to trust Christ as my Savior." A small grin etched the side of Thad's mouth as she continued to speak with some difficulty.

"I knew something was happening to me that wasn't good and I was very frightened. I couldn't even think straight. My thoughts were all jumbled and disconnected. I was afraid if I were dying that I wouldn't have time to ask God's Son to save me from my sin. My mind would not function right to form the thoughts I needed to say." Leah looked down as tears formed in her eyes at the peril. Thad squeezed her hand.

"I remember wanting to call out to Jesus and then I couldn't remember His name or anyone's name for that matter," she stopped and swallowed to clear her throat.

"It's all right, Leah. Take your time," he advised and handed her a tissue. Leah wiped her eyes and nose.

"When Alma began to pray it was as if my mind cleared for that length of time and I understood every word of her prayer." Tears welled to overflowing and Thad put his arm around her shoulders. The peace and joy of his heart seemed to reach Leah's and it brought calm.

"I know what Salvation is now, Thad. It's the love of God sacrificed for my rebellion when Jesus died on the cross. I don't want to ignore the gospel any longer. I want to ask Jesus Christ to be my Savior; but I'm concerned about you."

"You are? That's nice to know," Thad was trying his best not to tease. Leah was so serious she missed the joy Thad quietly displayed.

"Would you like to accept Christ as your Savior, Thad?"

"Nope!" he laughed lighthearted. Leah looked dumbfounded.

"Leah, I've already accepted Christ as my Savior." He beamed. "I was so worried about losing you I called my mother and asked her to pray for you. I knew God would answer her prayers. She helped me to realize I need to trust Christ, too. Everything just seemed to make sense all of a sudden. Maybe it was because I was finally willing to listen and allow God to open my heart in faith."

Leah's eyes were wide with surprise.

"Leah, I'm going to ask you what my Mom asked me just a little while ago. Would you like to trust Christ as your Savior?" His invitation touched Leah, heart and soul.

"Yes!" Tears rolled down her cheeks as she bowed her head. "Father, for Christ's sake please forgive me. I'm trusting you to be my Savior and I willingly give my heart to You in faith." There was a quiet pause then a whispered, "thank you". Peace radiated from Leah's eyes.

"What a day this has been," Leah commented.

"I agree. First, Alma, now you and me."

"Pastor Paytor may have a small revival on his hands," Leah blew her nose.

"And to think it all started with buttons," Thad winked and Leah laughed outright. It was good to hear her laugh.

"Do you realize how chaotic these past two days have been since you came?" he teased.

"I'm worn out," she replied truthfully. Thad gave her a side-glance and laughed.

"So am I. I didn't get any sleep last night. You kept me up all night talking on the phone."

"Right!" Leah shot back with a smirk that made Thad laugh. He stood up, turned toward her and issued a command.

"You need to get some rest and so do I. We have a lot to talk about later." As Thad leaned close to Leah, she lifted her lips to meet his with eagerness. The ardent flame in Thad's eyes told Leah he appreciated her response. Both understood there was nothing more distasteful than a dead fish kiss!

"Thanks for the chaos, Leah. I didn't realized how dull and gloomy my life was before you came along." Leah laughed heartily and Thad relished the sound, thankful to be hearing it. "I would never have admitted any such thing before, but I know God has answered my Mom's prayers by sending you here. It's amazing to see how God works, especially when He's given a chance." Thad commented and watched Leah's head bob happy agreement.

"My Dad had a phrase he often included in his sermons and it comes to mind at this moment; 'The will of God will never take you where the grace of God cannot keep you.' Sometimes he would add by saying, 'if you're willing to let Him take you where His grace can richly keep you." Leah's brow furrowed. Thad wondered what she was thinking.

"I need to call my Dad and Mom, Thad," Leah determined.

Immediately, Thad reached for the phone on the nightstand and dialed the number he'd memorized months ago. For a moment she thought Thad would give her the phone, but he didn't. Leah regarded him with hero-like wonder. She could only guess what kind of greeting he would receive.

"You're a brave man, Thad Tucker!"

CHAPTER 23

DADDY, DO YOU LOVE ME?

"HELLO?" MR. GRANT ANSWERED EXPECTANTLY.

"Hello, Reverend Grant?" Thad ventured.

"Yes," he answered dryly.

"Thad Tucker, here—

"Thad Tucker! Where is Leah? We've been very concerned about her. She hasn't called to let us know she arrived safely." Given the circumstances, Thad could understand her father's anxious advance.

"Leah arrived safely and she's doing much better, Reverend Grant." Again, Grant rushed in.

"Was there something wrong with her? Is she okay?"

"She had a reaction to some mushrooms in a stew we had for lunch," he hastened, "she's fine now, though, and she wanted to talk to you and Mrs. Grant."

"Fine, Mr. Tucker. Thanks." He seemed relieved.

"You're welcome, sir," Thad replied politely and handed the phone to Leah. She smiled and mouthed a "thank you" to him. He winked and waved as he left the room. Leah waved as she greeted both parents and answered a barrage of questions.

"I'm fine, Mom and Dad, really." She urged. "I didn't even think about asking if there were mushrooms in the stew." She confessed and wisely chose not to tell them about the IVs still dripping medication above her pillows.

"How are you getting along up there?" her mother asked stiffly trying to be positive. Leah thought briefly. It was almost a surprise to hear her mother's voice after the silence of the last several days before her departure.

"So far it has been a wonderful experience, Mom. And it's more than just being here to visit Thad. I have something very important to tell you." Both parents braced for the worst. "I want you and Mom to know that both Thad and I accepted Christ as our Savior just a few minutes ago," Leah announced with enthusiasm. "That's why I called."

All was silent on the other end of the phone. Leah waited, confused by their lack of response, and wondered if the phone connection had been lost.

"That's fine, Leah," her mother said dryly. "I thought you already were a Christian." Leah was stung by the sarcasm and fought to hold on to the joy that started to seep like falling sands in an hourglass. The lump in her throat made talking almost impossible. The unexpected lack of encouragement and joy from her Mom and unusually silent Dad wounded her deeply. After struggling with the issue of faith and trust in Christ for many years, salvation had been a hard-won victory. Yet the triumph seemed to come in slow motion.

"What made you think you needed to be saved?" The question came to her. There was doubt evidenced in Mrs. Grant's voice. For the first time, Leah called on God to give strength as she answered steadily. Disappointment with her parents battled for standing ground as an adult. Quietly, she answered what seemed to be an accounting of herself to her parents and this made her feel juvenile. But this wasn't an accounting, this was her testimony!

"For years I've just gone along with the program trying to fit into the church groove and stay out of trouble. I wanted to please you and to do everything right, but it seemed like the harder I tried the more mistakes I made. Then there was Sunset, my horse. I could take care of him and he never complained. No matter what happened, he was there to hear my complaints and problems until the night he…was sick and I couldn't help him get better. I remember asking God to make Sunset well again, but he only got worse. When I needed God the most, it seemed like He ignored me then I decided to ignore Him and just keep going along with the church program. I did what was expected of me until it felt like my life had become one big box filled with expectations and limits. It wasn't because of anything you did or didn't do, Mom and Dad. It was me. I made the choice to rebel and become bitter against God. I realize it, now. I realize the grace of God has placed me where the Spirit of God could break my stubborn heart and bring me to a saving knowledge of Jesus Christ. I understand now why you preach what you preach, Dad. I'm sorry for deceiving you and Mom all these years." Leah finished. Again, all was quiet as she waited.

"I see, Leah." At last her Dad spoke. Doris Grant spoke up. Her voice remained condescending.

"Leah, we're just a little confused by all of this. We still have not reconciled ourselves to your impetuous decision to visit a man who was a total stranger to you only a few months ago. Your father and I have been left to make explanations for your rash behavior." Doris Grant expressed her further irritation as if Leah's testimony had made no difference at all. "Leah, this has caused your father a great deal of pain. Just about the time…"

It was the same old diatribe her mother had used on her sisters and her over the years. Leah well knew its guilty intent and worked to squelch the resentment it provoked. As usual, she said nothing but endured the rant until either her Dad would intervene or the phone conversation would end.

"…but," Doris continued pointedly, "we can see you've made up your mind and—"

"Doris, I'd like to speak to Leah, please," he cut in, a matter-of-fact tone suggesting he had something monumental to say, finally. Leah thought about the way her parents interacted and couldn't help a little grin of acknowledgment that Dad was the epic movie and Mom was all the commercials!

"Well," Doris pricked, "I have to see if Sarah's Angie is home from Kindergarten Camp, yet." Then she added quickly, "At least Rachel and

Clive are doing well at their church in Michigan." There was a pause and for a moment Leah wondered what more her Mom could possibly say. "Good bye, Leah. Take care. I hope things work out for you." Mrs. Grant finished stoicly. Leah frowned on her end. It was the most show of affection from her Mom in a long time. Leah's eyes brimmed with tears as she heard the click of the telephone replaced. One tear rolled down her cheek as she fought for control.

"Leah," Dad Grant's voice was gentle. Leah swallowed and cleared her throat.

"Yes, Dad," she answered thickly.

"I'm glad you asked the Lord Jesus Christ into your heart. If your trip to Alaska to visit Thad Tucker was the means God used to form faith in your heart, then I claim God's grace to accept your statement of faith and I rejoice with you, Sweetheart. God bless you, Leah," his blessing brought relief and release from years of guilt.

"For many years, I've especially wondered about your relationship with Christ, Leah. When I gave you my Bible, it was with hope you would come to know Christ as a result of reading His Word and listening to the Holy Spirit. I'm glad your Mom asked you how you knew you needed to be saved, because I wanted to know if your salvation was based on the truths of the scriptures and not the desperation of a fleeting moment soon forgotten. It was not meant to hurt you, Leah. We love you, daughter, and I am especially relieved to hear of Thad's faith in Christ as well. I trust he means it with all his heart and will love the Christ Who saved him." His soothing words were a balm to her heart and she breathed deeply as she gained control of all the whacky emotions of the moment.

"Thank you, Dad," she said as joy returned in full. "I love you."

Her father corrected her gently, "Love your Mom too, Leah. She has struggles that only the Lord knows about. It's not been easy for her to accept the ministry her husband has been called to either. You two are a lot alike! She has not yet learned to love the will of God for her life. Don't count it against her when she has been a faithful wife and mother all these years. She does care for you, worries about you, and snaps at you like a doting hen keeping her chicks all in a row. Your calling us today will help her come to terms with it in her own way and time. I'm here to go to bat for you and Thad, too!" he chuckled. "I would anyway!" he declared. "When it comes to my girls I'm a marshmallow through and through." He heard the girlish giggle ring over the phone some four thousand miles away and his eyes misted; but he forged on blinking quickly.

"Have your Thad give me a call when he gets a chance. I'd like to get to know him a little better and encourage him in the Lord. Besides, if he's let you stay this long, I'm figuring he's pretty taken with you!" he laughed suddenly, "or, have you kept him so occupied with your shenanigans he hasn't had time to think about a proposal? You haven't mentioned an engagement, yet."

"Well, I think he's been on the verge of proposing several times, but things seem to happen…" her voice drifted off. Dad Grant grinned knowingly.

"You've just got to give him a chance, Honey," so came the fatherly counsel.

"I'm trying, Dad. Thad has been so kind to me after all I've done to him." This contrite confession made Dad Grant roar with laughter.

"You've managed to turn his life up-side down haven't you?" He'd been the recipient of her bungling over the years even sporting some scars with stories he'd love to share with a perspective husband!

"Dad!" Leah scolded but smiled as he teased some more.

"Remember the hose that lay in the scorching sun in the back yard all day?" he began. "I'd just returned home from making a hospital visit as a thunderstorm threatened the area. You were trying to clean up the yard and put things away before the storm hit with a vengeance. You needed help putting the garden hose away and I asked if you'd turned the water off. You faithfully promised the faucet was off and to prove it, you aimed the nozzle at me and squeezed the trigger. A blast of scalding hot water hit me full in the face and chest making me dance a jig trying to get away from you. Then, in your panic to shut the faucet off, you set the lock on the nozzle and continued spraying me. I couldn't seem to get away from that possessed hose! By the time you did get the hose under control, I was drenched from head to foot. One of my good Sunday suits was ruined, so you know!"

"I remember your grabbing the hose from me and chasing me around the yard." Leah chirped. "It's a wonder we weren't both struck with a bolt of lightning!" Father and daughter laughed together.

"I don't know which one of us was shocked the most," he chortled. "Come to think of it, maybe I should send Thad a list of hazards on you!"

"Too late, Dad! He's already half-way down the list as it is," she said tongue-in-cheek. Grant laughed with sheer delight.

"Well, I *almost* feel sorry for him, but not *too* sorry, though. If he decides to keep you, he'll be taking a lot of joy out of my life, Leah. I'll miss you, Sweet Leah, but I'll know you're both believers in our wonderful Lord and you'll be happy together in Him—if you choose to follow His ways." He took a deep breath and released it with a cough to clear the congestion laughter had caused. "We love you. Take care and don't be too rough on Thad. Well, maybe a little for my sake," he said jocularly. "Bye for now, Sweet Leah."

"I love you, Dad. Tell Mom, Sarah, and Angie that I'm sending my love to them, too."

"Sure enough!"

"Bye Dad."

"Bye."

It was amazing how that phone conversation had started out so badly and ended up so well. Leah thanked the Lord for her Dad and prayed for her Mom. This was something she wouldn't have done a week ago. The harbored resentment towards her Mom seemed to fall away as a desire to make amends moved her fervent prayers from selfishness to gratefulness for her Mom's sacrifices. Eventually sleep replaced meditation as the caress of a soft pillow invited rest. Later, Mary Jo removed the spent IVs from the sleeping Leah's arm and hand, checked her vital signs and facial skin for any further rashes or hives and swelling. Finding everything normal, she gave instructions to Alma for Leah's care through the night then left a peaceful Rose Glen.

Thad tried to stay awake in case an opportunity came to talk with Leah, but the drone of TV small talk dulled his senses until he slept—on the couch in the great room. Twilight gently covered the nearby Matanuska Glacier in evening shades of light blue. Patches of clouds moved over Palmer and passed above the farmland cradling potato fields full of goodness.

Before Alma went to bed, she checked on Leah and saw a sleeping princess. After reading the portion of scripture Pastor Paytor had preached from that morning, she offered a prayer of thanksgiving for Leah's recovery. The flowing movements of her hands and the silent whispers of a humble heart ended the first day of eternal life in Alma's faith walk.

A restless Taima sat by the fireplace in his room and mused about the day's hectic activities. When he lay down to sleep, his thoughts were troubled by Alma's confession of faith in Jesus Christ. For some reason he could not understand, he felt cut-off from his sister. It angered him and left him with one question reverberating in his subconscious realm. 'Who is this Jesus Christ who changes people and separates them from their loved ones and traditions?'

Chapter 24

Name Calling

Thad met Leah as she descended the stairs the next morning. He pushed an arm through a jacket sleeve as he greeted her with a smile.

"Hi! Leah! I was hoping to see you before I had to leave. I'm sorry I slept the night away. So much for having a talk with you," regret was evident. 'Foiled again!' he thought.

"I slept the night away, too," Leah smiled. "I feel much better this morning."

"I'm glad to hear it and I can see you are much better," he said with admiration then added, "I have to drive to Anchorage to pick up three lady clients for a fishing excursion. I'll be back sometime around noon. We'll dine out tonight, if you want to?" What started as a statement ended up as a request for a date.

"Sounds good to me," Leah said cheerfully.

"I'll see you later, then," Thad returned. Leah stood at the bottom of the stairway looking like she had just walked out of his dream. Indeed she might just as well have been a dream because he had to leave her.

"Have a safe trip, Thad," Leah said simply and wished she could ride along.

"Thanks." He hesitated, seeming unsure about something. Leah stepped over to Thad and took his face in her hands. He was a little surprised at first but managed to overcome it nicely and, for a few moments, knew she wasn't a dream. This fact carried him out the door in happy reflection

It was around noon when another eligible bachelor decided to pay a visit to Thad Tucker's cabin. Taima and Alma had gone to the trading post for the morning so Leah had the cabin all to herself to relax. She enjoyed catching her journal up to date by recording the events of the last few days. She wondered what her grandkids might think about all of this in the years to come—a forward thought indeed! Especially did she write about her faith in Christ and found that writing about it seemed to plant its wonder deeper in her own heart.

The journal was something she had kept on and off for many years. She only wrote in it when memorable events occurred in her life. Thad's correspondence had encouraged more attention to journaling over past months.

After a while, Leah stood up and pulled a sweater on before walking out onto the deck to sit in the warm noon sunshine. The journal opened to some early entries of her impressions and thought about Thad. How different she viewed many things now that she was actually in Palmer. Her new faith was also changing her view of life because there was a Source of guidance to tap for help. Amazingly, the relationship she and Thad enjoyed now had a focus and a direction resulting from a mutual faith. They weren't floundering anymore. Tomorrow was a secure place because there was Divine guidance for every circumstance of earthly life, for both the good times and the times of trouble.

While reclining on a wooden chaise enjoying the sunshine, Leah heard the distinct sound of a man's heavy footfalls on the deck steps to the front door. They couldn't be Thad's yet, nor were they Taima's. Leah sat up, alert and wary. Moving her legs over the side of the chaise, she prepared to stand and sprint into the cabin. A vivid picture of Kroft and Bachman came to mind and Leah checked the panic that rose in her throat.

"Lord, protect me," she prayed.

"Hello," the masculine voice said friendly enough. Upon seeing the startled look on the lady's face, he hastened to introduce himself.

"I'm Tyrone Johnson, Thad's friend and business partner. We haven't met yet. Thad and I go way back to college days. You must be Leah Grant?" He assumed rather then asked and took a wooden deck chair opposite Leah. She nodded as she took in his smile and tall African American frame.

"Yes, I'm Leah Grant," she managed still trying to place him as Thad's partner.

"Didn't Thad mention me?" He asked somewhat surprised.

"Yes," Leah answered slowly. "He mentioned you in his letters but I've kept him so busy…keeping me alive," she chuckled, "that he hasn't had time to tell me about your experiences as partners in the business." At last she remembered and smiled in welcome friendship. "Yes, he did! I'm pleased to meet you, Mr. Johnson."

"Please call me Tyrone, Miss Grant," he requested as they shook hands.

"And please call me Leah, Tyrone."

Tyrone began to talk to Leah as if they were old friends. At least he thought they were old friends because Thad had read parts of Leah's letters to him.

"I'd hoped to be introduced when Thad picked you up at the Trading Post, but when the motor on the fishing boat burnt, plans changed. You know the rest of the story. Then I had to get Ishioti and O'Brien back to Anchorage so they could catch flights out to Seattle, Sunday afternoon. I just got back last evening from a quick trip to Alyeska. So, here I am. I hope I didn't startle you too much?"

"Only a little, Tyrone. I've already had the privilege of meeting two men by the names of Lance Kroft and Charlie Bachman at the Trading Post." Tyrone's eyes widened.

"Those miserable two!" the disapproval was clear in the baritone quality of his voice.

"Not to worry. They entered like lions, but left like lambs," Leah assured him.

"They're trouble where ever they show up." Tyrone stated and covered his mouth to hide a long tired yawn.

"A little rough around the edges we'd say down my way," Leah added, "but congenial enough when charmed."

Tyrone frowned at the very idea of "charming" such scoundrels. They liked to sabotage trap lines by stealing valuable pelts and replacing them with lesser valued game. They had managed to evade the law so far, but sooner or later they'd get caught.

"So, you're a snake charmer, too?" he teased.

"Only when panic isn't an option."

Tyrone's laughter sounded like music and Leah wondered if he could sing. She liked Thad's partner, Tyrone Johnson. He was a fine looking man, amiable, and had a disposition that put people right at ease. Leah recognized these same characteristics in Thad and wondered if they were typical of Alaskan men in general then remembered Kroft and Bachman and decided to keep a discerning sense of balance. An eagle flew over and Leah shielded her eyes to catch a glimpse of it in the noon sun. The wingspan of the huge bird looked to be four feet in length. No wonder these birds could nab a rabbit and fly off effortlessly. When she looked down, Tyrone was studying her face like a father evaluating his son's new girlfriend.

"You know? I knew from the first time Thad described you that you were a nice girl. I even thought about going to the dating service in Anchorage and signing up, too. But I just haven't gotten to it, yet. Besides, I probably wouldn't be as lucky as Thad anyway. He found the one in a million, I'd say."

"Thanks, Tyrone, but I'm sure there is someone out there that would love to hear from you," Leah encouraged.

"Finding a nice pen pal is a little harder up here. There are more men in Alaska than women. Especially black women," he said candidly. "And some of the ladies up here have a saying about us Alaska men, too." Tyrone paused reflectively. "The odds are good but the goods are odd!" he laughed and saw that Leah didn't see the humor in the statement. Of course, Thad was the exception!

"Denise Cox!" Leah blurted. "My college roommate," she chirped and watched Tyrone's eyebrows rise with surprise. Leah smiled at his reaction.

"You're kidding?" he was skeptical; but interested.

"No kidding! She's single, although she's been engaged about a half dozen times since I've known her. I'm not sure whether she's engaged at the moment or not." Leah considered this with a frown as she regarded the handsome Tyrone thoughtfully.

"Come on, Tyrone. Let's go find out!" Leah said on a whim. "I need to call DeDee anyway and tell her I'm doing just fine."

"Well...I don't know," he hesitated. He'd need some time to consider this idea. No sense rushing into anything.

"Sure you do. I don't like the guy she's been seeing anyway. Never liked him at all and I've told her so, too!" Leah led the way as they entered the cabin. She went directly to the phone by the wing chair and dialed the number. A quick glance in Tyrone's direction showed he had WHOA! all over his face.

"You know Tyrone, Denise deserves a great guy like you." Leah chattered on. "She'd flip for you in a second. I know Denise Cox well. She's put up with a lot from that two-timing skunk she thinks is her fiancé." Leah took her wallet out of her purse to find Denise's recent phone number. The one she had just dialed from memory was a disconnected number. She also took out a photo of Denise and handed it to Tyrone.

"Here, take a look at this." Leah redialed the number and waited for an answer. Tyrone looked at the photo then stared at the image in amazement.

"She's beautiful," he commented as he gazed and blinked. His WHOA! vanished. Denise had lovely ebony skin that glowed softly around high cheekbones. Her shoulder length black hair fell straight and soft around her heart-shaped face. She had a dazzling smile of even white teeth that looked like pearls framed by red twin-sail shaped lips. Large cocoa brown eyes enhanced her photo-perfect features. Denise Cox had made a life-long first impression on Tyrone Johnson!

"Hello? Hello, DeDee?" Leah tried. She pressed the speaker phone button so Tyrone could hear her friend's voice, too. He still held Denise's picture.

"Leah Annette Grant!" Denise declared loudly. "Where are you, girl?" she demanded. "I called your parents Saturday morning to see if you had arrived safely and they told me they hadn't heard a word from you!" Denise sounded a little ticked. Tyrone looked amused and grinned at Leah. Denise Cox wasn't the bashful type!

"Are you married yet, girlfriend?" she charged on.

"No, Denise. Don't be silly! It's only been three days. Besides, Thad's cabin is really beautiful. You wouldn't believe how nice it is. My room is—

"What!" Denise cut in gangbuster style and Leah knew the conversation wouldn't get any better any time soon.

"You're staying at his cabin?" Denise barked in shock.

"Yes."

"Well, are you engaged, then?"

"Well, no, but—

"What! You aren't even engaged yet and you're staying at Thad's cabin? What in the name of heaven do you think you're doing?" she practically yelled. Tyrone cocked his head to the side, crossed his arms over his chest and frowned like a perturbed father. He was surprised Thad hadn't popped the question by now, too!

"Denise, wait!" Leah tried to get a word in, but it was no good. The proverbial train had left the station and Leah couldn't stop it. Tyrone had the biggest grin on his face. He was enjoying this way too much. Leah looked frustrated.

"What happened to those missionaries you were supposed to be staying with?" Denise's voice suddenly became quiet for the first time. "Honey, how is this Thad person treating you?" There was a tinge of ugly directed at Thad. The conversation was so ridiculous Leah unwisely found it funny. Before giving careful consideration to her reply, she uttered the first thing that popped into her head.

"Well, I broke a broom on him already," she joked. Tyrone gasped with laughter and collapsed onto the couch guffawing loudly. Leah realized too late that in exercising her humor she'd lost her mind! There was total silence on the other end of the phone.

"Denise?" Leah searched for a response. "Are you there?"

"Not for long, Leah. I'm on my way!" Denise guaranteed with a huff. "I'll call you from Seattle to let you know what time my plane gets in." Tyrone's loud laughter could be heard in the background.

"Who is that laughing fool?" Denise demanded righteously.

"He's Tyrone Johnson, Denise, Thad's business partner and good friend. Please, Denise, it's not what you think—

Click.

"Denise?" Leah said weakly. "Good-bye." She said to herself.

At that moment, Thad walked into the Great Room. Tyrone was still laughing hilariously and Leah was standing perfectly still a dubious expression frozen on her guilty face.

"Oh, no," she sighed mournfully. Thad could tell right away that some catastrophe was afoot, again. He had an uneasy feeling it wasn't going to be a pleasant experience.

"What can I do for you, Leah?" He was almost afraid to ask as he dropped fishing tackle on a nearby table next to the wall.

"Marry me today, Thad." She sounded desperate. Thad frowned.

"You better marry her, Thad," Tyrone piped up merrily, "Leah's girlfriend is on her way up here to give you a piece of her mind." Thad was not amused. For the first time, Leah saw Thad put his hands on his waist. The "irk" of the present situation was reflected in the no-nonsense expression on his face.

"When is this going to stop?" she asked aloud and exhaled deeply.

"I'm beginning to think it never will," Thad answered mildly. There was mounting evidence of this truth but her genuine remorse tested his efforts to remain irritated with his lovely Leah. "You'd better let me in on the latest fiasco, Leah," he directed and started toward her. However, he was stopped by the whizzing sound of a fishing reel as it released line. Thad began to look all around for the snagged line only to realize that a hook from a fishing pole mounted on the wall above the table had attached itself to his jacket sleeve. Gingerly, he untangled the sharp hook and walked back to the pole. Without a word, he lifted the fishing pole off its mount and reeled the hook and line to the end of the pole. The only way Leah could keep a sober face was the realization that her best friend's arrival meant yet another explanation to an already irritated sweetheart!

Once again, Thad approached Leah. He noticed she was trying to keep a straight face. When he stood directly in front of her, Leah bit her lip to squelch the rising mirth. She was absolutely thrilled to find that Thad might just have a penchant for snafu, too. When he grinned, she burst out laughing. Thankfully, his pleasant grin remained as he took her hand and led her over to the couch where they sat down across from a beaming Tyrone. He regarded them both with raised eyebrows. He knew Thad's own flair for foul ups very well and being witness to both of their little melodramas within a short period of time gave him the satisfaction that joy would have an enduring place in Thad's home as long as everyone could laugh at themselves.

"I haven't laughed so hard since Thad—

"We're not talking about me right now," Thad shot a warning glance at Tyrone. "By the way, when did you get back?" he easily changed the subject.

"Last night. I decided to drop by and introduce myself to Leah since I hadn't had the opportunity to meet her, yet. We had a nice chat. You're a lucky man, Thad. I am a little surprised, though," he shook his head disapprovingly, "for such a lucky man, I'm a little surprised you haven't asked Leah to marry you by this time, Thad." He saw that one looked guilty while the other looked frustrated.

"I'm not so sure Thad thinks he's a lucky man right now," Leah countered. Thad glanced at Leah and smiled. Her hand rested easily within his.

"I'm not sure luck has anything to do when there's a miracle sitting right beside me." Leah felt warmed by the unconditional love she saw in his eyes.

Tyrone rolled his eyes and gave a long sigh. "You two love birds are making me feel like a crowd." He declared then teased, "From a wolf to a love bird! What a change." To Leah he asked, "Has Thad told you how he got his nick-name, Wolfe?"

Leah's eyebrows rose in interest. "No, he hasn't and I'd really like to know."

Thad cocked his head off to the side. "Leah, it's just a nick-name that came with this job when Tyrone and I started the business years ago. Few people call me Wolfe anymore." He was brushing it aside.

"You might as well tell me and get it over with, Thad." She encouraged. It was Tyrone who took up the telling of the saga.

"Shortly after we agreed to start our hunting and fishing excursions, we decided to select specific areas where we would take our prospective clients when they came, if they came. But I'll go back and give you some of our mutual history first.

"I was from Anchorage but passed through Palmer for camping vacations with my family in Denali Park. During those vacations, I'd find a park ranger or two and tag along with them for the whole week if possible. Over the years, I learned a lot about wilderness survival during those vacations. In high school, I took classes about fishing, hunting, and tracking then I studied forestry in college. Thad took some of the same classes with me while he was studying agriculture as his major. When I began to plan a business venture as a guide for hunting and fishing trips, I asked Thad to be my business partner. He changed his major from agriculture to forestry and business management.

"Anyway, we began to check various places for permits and access to good area. Thad had lived here in the Mat-Su Valley on and off most of his life, so I depended on his information and knowledge of the trails completely. He knew ALL the hunting trails and fishing spots."

"Just some of them," Thad corrected nonchalantly. Tyrone laughed. Leah smiled and listened trying to catch their unspoken meanings.

"Right!" Tyrone teased back. "All of a sudden he's modest and only knows SOME of them. Back then he knew ALL of them!"

Thad shrugged. A small roguish grin etched itself across his face. Tyrone shook his head at his partner and continued.

"Somehow, Thad heard about one hunting trail that promised great results for our clients. He had the facts and the map."

"Rumor," Thad cut in. "RUMOR," he emphasized a second time, "had it that there was one trail that was a hunter's bonanza."

Tyrone snickered. "Thad figured he was the man to find it. Nobody else could locate it; but Thad knew he could."

"I THOUGHT I could." Thad smiled and both men laughed. Leah considered Thad curiously. His young adult years must have been very interesting if he knew everything! She wondered if the old adage "older and wiser" had somehow transformed those young-adult years into the man she knew now.

"Thad studied the suggested trail on a map he had procured from—who—knows—where." Tyrone turned to glance at Thad, "You never did tell me where you got it," Tyrone frowned.

"An old Native Alaskan friend gave me that map," Thad informed and crossed his arms in front of his chest. Tyrone's eyes grew large in comprehension. The direction of Tyrone's story changed all of a sudden.

"Taima!" Tyrone pointed at Thad and he nodded positively. Tyrone leaned back in his chair and laughed heartily. Thad looked somewhat abashed then looked straight at Leah to fill in further details about Taima while Tyrone regained his composure and listen to Thad.

"Taima has only ever gone hunting once in his life and he got miserably lost that time, Leah. But I didn't know it when he gave me that ridiculous map of his." Thad said pointedly. Leah's mouth dropped open in astonishment that Thad could have been so gullible. It was a delightful revelation that made her eyes twinkle with merriment.

"So, the map was faulty?" Leah surmised.

"Faulty?" Thad blinked at the word she had used. Some of her words baffled him.

"Yes, faulty. There were problems with the directions," she further clarified. Thad smiled at the use of her teacher's prose.

"It was faulty," he agreed and winked at her.

"It sure was," Tyrone resumed. "Early one morning we left to follow that designated trail and by noon we were lost. The trail WE forged was through thick dense scrub pine, tundra brush, and waist deep streams. It began to dawn on me that this map was nothing but a maze of someone's fun loving imagination. I was upset. Thad, on the other hand, was convinced we should proceed on anyway. My reasoning was lost to him, Leah. He can be pretty stubborn. Anyway, we continued on until we decided to make camp and get some sleep. By this time we had no idea where we were. We had given up on the map hours earlier. Our gear was wet, we were cold and exhausted and no nearer to finding that 'hunter's bonanza'. Tyrone made quotations marks with his fingers to emphasize the illusive paradise.

"We made camp setting up a tent and starting a fire to warm up ourselves and dry out soaked socks after changing to dry ones. All was fine until about midnight when the wind picked up to gale strength and blew the tent down around us. The wind kept whipping the tent so hard we had to get out or be blown around like a beach ball! Of course it started to rain then pour. At this point, we started to look for shelter of any kind," Tyrone snickered. "Thad was mad." He looked at Leah. "At that time, Thad's language was not exactly fit for Sunday School."

Thad was aware of Leah's study. He knew she did not use such language and he hadn't used it since corresponding with her. Subtle changes had occurred in his life as a result of her influence. Somehow it was very important to him that these changes showed. Now that he was Christ's own reflection as a Believer, it was more than an outward effort. Thad was becoming a new creation from within out of honor for the God Who loved him.

"We began to look around us and Thad spotted an opening in some rocks. It resembled the entrance to a cave of sorts. We headed for it cautiously entering the small opening on hands and knees. There was nothing inside the cave which was only big enough for two small munchkins and maybe a couple of Smurfs, but it was dry and out of the wind. We settled in to wait out the storm. Thad decided to take the first watch so I could sleep for a while. We had no idea what animal or animals used this cave, so we figured it was best for someone to be alert.

"I wasn't even asleep an hour before Thad woke me and told me we had company. I was groggy and shaking all over because of the sudden wake-up call. Out of nowhere came a howl that sounded like a wounded wolf. It was very close by. The cave was dark and I couldn't see anything. As I reached in my backpack for a flashlight, I called over to Thad and asked what was going on.

"My only response was that awful howling and several more howls sounding only a short distance away. Once I had the flashlight, I clicked the ON button and started flashing it around the rocky walls of the small cave. Thad was hunched down a few feet away from the entrance. I started forward with the flashlight on Thad's backside until I was beside him and could see the opening in the cave." Tyrone chuckled. "All of a sudden Thad started howling at a pack of wolves standing not thirty feet from the cave's entrance. It was obvious we had taken over their den and they meant to have it back!

"Thad motioned for me to start howling, too. I must have been crazy; but I howled until we were both hoarse. I figured Thad had a plan. It was a standoff. Thad's voice was beginning to crack something awful. I think those wolves were beginning to get wise to us. We needed to do something fast because I was starting to sound like a bullfrog!" Leah could contain herself no longer and laughed out loud. Thad sat tolerantly quiet though there was a slight grin fixed on his face.

"Thad suggested we shoot off the flare gun to scare them away. We had several flares with us, thank goodness. I grabbed the backpacks and retrieved our flares and the guns. After loading both of them, we proceeded to shoot one flare off. We kept the second gun handy in case the wolves were not thwarted by the first shot. However, one shot into the air sent those wolves scattering to the four winds. We both sat there for a long time to make sure they stayed away. But, after a while, we dozed off only to be awakened by the sound of twigs breaking and the approach of a whole bunch of footfalls coming our way. It was almost dawn, but still dark enough to make clear vision impossible for the middle of November. It was also hard to see for any distance.

"We figured the wolf pack was back with reinforcements and we readied ourselves for their return. As the footfalls sounded closer and closer, old Thad let out a howl...like howling was going to do us any good at all." Tyrone assured while Thad shrugged it off and Leah laughed in delight. "I loaded another flare and was about to shoot it off when Thad abruptly stopped his miserable howling and put a hand out to halt me from pushing the trigger. I looked beyond him only to see two pairs of Army boots blocking the narrow cave opening. Knees bent and two camouflage faces peered in at the two of us. 'Hello in there!' A commanding voice bellowed loudly. It happened that the Army National Guard was on maneuvers in that area. They saw our flare in the sky so they came to see if someone was in trouble and needed assistance." Tyrone smiled slyly at Thad.

"Thad asked them if they could howl," Tyrone directed to Leah. Thad smiled and shook his head.

"Those guys fell all over the place laughing at us." Thad put in.

"That's how Thad earned the dubious nickname of Wolfe Tucker, spelled W-O-L-F-E after the old English tale of Little Red Ridinghood and the Big Bad Wolfe that pretended to be something he wasn't!"

"Since several of the Guardsmen and women live here in the Mat-Su Valley, his nickname became famous overnight!" Tyrone finished and stood. "I'd better get out of here. Leah's friend, Denise is on her way up to Alaska even as we speak," he chuckled. "I don't think there's an army anywhere that can stop her either." With that remark, he waved at them and left.

"Denise?" Thad was puzzled.

"Yes. She thinks I'm in trouble or something."

"What?"

"Oh, Thad, I tried to explain why I'm staying at your cabin but DeDee jumped to some conclusions and…" Leah drifted off.

"I see," Thad nodded. "Well, I think we need to go for a walk and talk about this, don't you?"

"Sure, why not? The fresh air might be good for the mind and body. Where are we going to walk?"

"Let's take a walk around the perimeter of the cabin."

"Good," Leah sighed relieved. "I'm not ready for another hike up to the old homestead."

Thad considered her statement and smiled.

"Neither am I." Apparently the old homestead didn't inspire any romantic memories for her either.

CHAPTER 25

BEAUTIFUL FOR SITUATION

LEAH PUT HER JACKET ON AND waited by the closet with Thad's jacket in hand. He'd walked over to the desk to put some receipts away before joining her at the front door. They walked outside and down the deck steps to begin their walk around the property. As they walked, Thad pointed out various details about the construction of the cabin and spoke of his ideas for further landscaping. However, Leah had a nagging thought in the back of her mind. Both Tyrone and Denise had been surprised that Thad hadn't asked her to marry him, yet. Granted, the last few days had been chaos even though there had been moments when Leah had entertained the idea he was going to ask her. But he hadn't, and at the moment, Leah was baffled. Thad continued to showcase his home with glowing pride and enthusiasm. He seemed to be interested in what she thought of his home, too.

Leah checked the sincerity of her voice as she attempted to match his fervor, but couldn't without some effort at it because she felt insecure at the moment. What if he had no plans of asking her to marry anytime soon. Maybe this was just a visit after all, and an engagement would come at another time. She knew he loved her as she loved him and there was good reason to believe they would eventually get married, but she wondered how this was all going to work together.

Thad raised his arm to point to a distant peak behind the cabin. Her attention returned to a mountain zenith on Pioneer Peak and then was turned to a picturesque view of Palmer as they stood behind the cabin on the side of a rising grade. The tranquility of the frontier calmed her and slowed the rapid thoughts that caused anxiety. Learning to trust meant learning to be patient and Leah struggled with these two virtues all the time. As she acknowledged this, the uncertainty of her present situation was committed to prayer right then. In letting God take charge of her life as a loving Guide, Leah relaxed and enjoyed these special moments at Thad's side. Indeed, there was no need to rush ahead and forfeit the present joys by wishing for tomorrow. She watched as he told about the cabin's construction and hoped he would soon make it her home, too. It was a matter of trust on her part. Letting Thad care for her in his way and not as she felt he should was hard to do. Expectations often caused great disappointment.

"This is a gorgeous view, Thad. It reminds me of a verse of scripture that was made into a song. It was sung often when I was in Sunday School.

Great is the Lord,
And greatly to be praised
In the city of our God,
In the mountain of His holiness.
Beautiful for situation,
The joy of the whole Earth,
Is mount Zion on the sides of the north,
The city of the Great King.

"These are beautiful words, Leah. I hope to read the Bible as much as I can, and to learn it as you have done. I have a long way to go to catch up to you," he reckoned as they walked into a naturally shaded arbor above the rear of the cabin. A stone wall rose about two feet in height on one side of the path and ran about thirty feet in length. Wild flowers of all colors spread blossoms over the rock wall in pink, white, and lavender.

Although it was cooler in late August, Forget-me-nots and Bleeding Hearts remained hearty under the protection of the natural arbor. Leah reached to touch them and remarked on their beauty. She paused before speaking earnestly to Thad.

"The truth is, Thad, I have a lot of catching up to do as well. Sometimes I remember bits and pieces of Bible stories and sermons, but nothing connects too much because I purposely chose not to listen. I'm seeing life much differently than I once did."

"We'll learn together then," he amended. Leah smiled and nodded positively.

They had stopped and Leah sat on the stone terrace to look at the golden fall foliage along the tree line. Thad sat next to her and stretched his legs out in front. The fresh air was invigorating.

"The ground over there looks freshly turned," Leah commented.

"Right. Alma and I will be planting the tulip bulbs soon for next Spring. You can help if you'd like to, Leah."

"I'd like to, but I'm not sure I'll be happy while I'm planting them." It was out before Leah could stop it. Recent doubts concerning her future surfaced again.

"Why is that?" he asked puzzled.

"Spring is a long way off, Thad. I'm not sure I'll be able to see them bloom," Leah struggled to finish the sentence. She was starting to dig her own holes and couldn't seem to stop.

"Why not?" Thad inquired further as he stifled a grin of comprehension. Finally, his "plan" was falling neatly into place!

"Well," Leah knew he would finally get it out of her anyway, so she spoke frankly. "I broke the bank just to get here. And when I finally arrived in Anchorage, I cashed in my return ticket so I'd have a little more emergency cash then just thirty-two dollars and some odd change. I'll have to find a job and a place to live. I'm not going back to Pennsylvania."

"I know," he said and took her hand to calm the anxiety that was rising. "When Alma dumped your cosmetic case out on the bed to find the allergy tablets, I couldn't help noticing the empty ticket folder," he admitted and released her hand. Reaching into his flannel shirt pocket, he pulled out a navy blue button.

"Here's another button you can add to the collection. It popped off the cuff on this shirt somehow," he handed it to Leah and she noted it was a two-hole button and not a four-hole button. "I think there's a hole in the cuff, too," he added.

"Let me see your cuff," Leah requested quietly. "After all, I did promise to sew the buttons back on your shirts for you, didn't I?" He smiled at her and extended his arm. Leah unrolled the sleeve until the cuff appeared. When she found the little hole where the button had been, there was a safety pin with something dangling at the tip.

Surprise turned to joy on Leah's face. It was a diamond ring! When she started to laugh, Thad took that as a good sign. Moving from the rocky ledge beside her, he took her hand in his and knelt on one knee.

"Leah Grant. I love you and I want you to know that you are a miracle! You will always be my miracle. Not just because you came all the way to Alaska to sew buttons back on my shirts, but also because you pointed me to God through the goodness of your searching heart. I am honored that you came to me and humbled that you have chosen to love me for who I was and who I am, now. I promise to be faithful to you and faithful to God. Will you marry me?" Time seemed to stop and wait for the maiden's answer.

"Yes!" she cried. Thad removed the safety pin from the cuff and slipped the ring off the pin. After placing the ring on Leah's finger, he stood as Leah reached for him. The wonder of their love filled him with happiness as they embraced under the shaded arbor of flowers and trees. Views of Alaska's rocky summits, broad green valleys, and meandering streams would often beckon the couple to this tranquil betrothal setting at Rose Glen.

"I love you, Thad," Leah welcomed the unconditional love she saw radiated in the eyes of her Alaskan husband-to-be. It matched the wonder she'd experienced at finally realizing God's fervent love for her soul and Thad's. For all of life's incredible hurts, all things could work together for good when surrendered to Christ. Soft breezes stirred the birch and aspen branches around them. Rays of sunlight poured through yellow leaves until one sunbeam bounced off the diamond engagement ring and sparkled Thad and Leah's devotion to the heavens.

Thad Tucker had found someone to ride the other horse. Leah Grant had found honor as someone's miracle!